VANISHING
EDGE

Also available by Claire Kells

Girl Underwater

The National Parks Mysteries:
An Unforgiving Place

VANISHING EDGE

A NOVEL

CLAIRE KELLS

CROOKED
LANE

NEW YORK

Copyright © 2023 by Kathleen Coggshall

Published in the United States by Crooked Lane Books, an imprint of The Quick Brown Fox & Company LLC.

Crooked Lane Books and its logo are trademarks of The Quick Brown Fox & Company LLC.

Library of Congress Catalog-in-Publication data available upon request.

ISBN (hardcover): 978-1-64385-867-8
ISBN (paperback): 978-1-63910-373-7
ISBN (ebook): 978-1-64385-868-5

Cover design by Nicole Lecht

Printed in the United States.

www.crookedlanebooks.com

Crooked Lane Books
34 West 27th St., 10th Floor
New York, NY 10001

First Edition: November 2021
Trade Paperback Edition: March 2023

10 9 8 7 6 5 4 3 2 1

For Teddy

1

I WAS PEERING DOWN at two broken ski poles on Yosemite's Line of Fire when the call came in to my satellite phone. With the gusting winds at my back, I debated even trying to wrestle the thing out of my pocket, but the park rangers flanking me on either side were getting antsy. One grunted, "Do you need to take that, ma'am?"

I nodded. "Should just take a second."

Bracing myself against a tree, I got ahold of my sat phone and immediately recognized the number as the Investigative Services Branch field office. I took a breath, the kind that rattled a bit on the way in. I hoped the caller figured it was altitude, not nerves.

"Felicity Harland," I said.

"Special Agent Harland with the Investigative Services Branch?"

"That's—yes." I was still getting used to my new title. The caller didn't stumble over it, which made me think he was probably a chief ranger. He had a gravelly voice that could only have come from decades spent in the cold, dry air. I'd been warned by seasoned ISB agents that a lot of these older rangers lost their social skills over the years—not that they'd had them in abundance to begin with. Rangering didn't tend to attract social butterflies.

"Hello, ma'am. This is Rick Corrigan with the Park Service," he said. "I'm the chief ranger out of Mineral King Ranger Station in Sequoia. You familiar with it?"

I was, thanks to an extensive orientation to the National Park System in the months prior. There were sixty-two national parks in the United States, and in terms of annual visitors, Sequoia was somewhere in the middle. "Yes, sir," I said.

"I called the ISB switchboard, and they told me you were the one covering my territory this time of year. That right?"

I had my schedule memorized—that is to say, the one that came down from headquarters in Washington D.C. My first official assignment had me working the nine California national parks, but it wasn't a permanent post. In ISB, temporary duty assignments were typical; you could be sent to Alaska one week and Florida the next. For the next six months, though, I was more or less based in California, which was not an easy assignment. Yosemite was essentially Disneyland at this point, with millions of visitors every year.

"Yes, sir," I said again.

"Well, I've got a situation out here."

A *situation*—probably the most dreaded word in my vocabulary. It itched the corner of my brain that liked facts and logic and hard evidence. I could handle a dead body or an accident or even murder, but I didn't like the sound of "a situation."

"What do you mean by that?" I asked.

"I've got an abandoned campsite way up at Precipice Lake," he said. "I called you 'cause the ranger who found it doesn't feel right about it."

I'd been warned about such calls. An abandoned campsite wasn't a crime in and of itself, and to be honest, it wasn't all that unusual for people to ditch their stuff in the woods. The most common explanation was that a group of delinquents with no concern for "leave no trace" had simply moved on out of boredom. Usually the rangers waited a while to see if the campers returned, and if they didn't, then they called ISB.

"What did the ranger say?" I asked.

He took a moment to consider his reply. "Well, he said the tent hasn't been wastin' out there all winter—it looked like somebody'd been there just a day or two ago. Left in a hurry, though. Gear all over the place. Oh, and about the gear—it's nice. Real fancy stuff. Glampist is the outfit. You ever heard of 'em?"

"I think so," I said.

There was a pause.

"Actually, no," I admitted.

"It's a private company that specializes in luxury camping," he said. "In other words, the devil incarnate."

I pictured a demon pitching a diamond-encrusted tent. "I see," I said.

"There's a bunch of 'em in the business," he said. "Somebody takes you out to the trailhead or wherever it is you wanna go, and they set up the camp for you, cook your food, wipe your butt. It's a thing now."

I could picture this grizzled ranger shaking his head the way older folks did when lamenting the habits of the younger generation. My parents did it, too.

"These damn Millennials," he went on. "I don't know why they can't just stay in their fancy apartments and watch a nature show."

As a rule, I rather enjoyed listening to the older generation complain about clueless youth, but I didn't want to be standing on the Line of Fire any longer than I had to. "Mr. Corrigan, I only get involved if you suspect a crime has been committed." I tucked my head against the wind. "Is that what you're telling me?"

He let the silence play out for a bit before asking, "How old are you, ma'am?"

"Pardon?"

"'Cause I'm sixty-eight. I've been a ranger in Sequoia for comin' on forty-five years. I've dealt with hundreds of lost hikers, and lemme tell you, the world's changed. The young folk, now, they come up here with all kind of gadgets. It's real hard to get lost these days."

"I don't know, sir," I said, with gentle skepticism, fully aware that my ranger guides were listening in. "I hear it still happens from time to time."

"Not if you're campin' with the likes of Glampist."

"Is it possible they went off on their own?"

He sucked in a breath. "It's possible, but like I said, these types don't like to do any actual work out here—they don't explore, hike, whatever. Some of 'em hire mules or a private chopper to drop them off at the campsite. God forbid they lift a finger."

"Was there any blood at the campsite? Signs of a struggle?"

"My ranger didn't report that, no."

I wondered how reliable this ranger was. In Yosemite, a lot of the rangers were lifers, in larger part because YOSAR—Yosemite's search-and-rescue team—was world-renowned. But Sequoia was a much smaller and lesser known national park than its neighbor to the north. Corrigan's ranger could very well be a kid fresh out of high school with no investigative experience whatsoever.

"Tell me again when he found the campsite," I said.

"About an hour ago. He was up there conducting a wildlife survey."

Today was Monday, April 8th. I made a note of the date and time of the discovery on my hand because my iPad had died—which was unfortunate for all kinds of reasons. I used the same model that was issued to the military for their missions, but mine, somehow, had decided to crap out on me an hour into the hike up Line of Fire. The only good news was that I had a pen from a LaQuinta Inn in my jeans pocket.

"Any clues to where they might have gone?" I asked him. "Footprints?"

"No. Not up there. It's all rock."

"How about search and rescue? Have you mobilized your local resources?"

He pushed out a breath. "Not yet. I called the glamping company again, and they told me there's no problem on their end."

"Did they give you the names of who was camping there?"

"No, ma'am."

Of course not. My mentors at ISB had told me about these luxury camping services and their obsession with protecting their clientele's privacy, but I had yet to interface with any of them. It made sense that Sequoia or Yosemite—the parks with relatively easy access to Silicon Valley and Hollywood—would be the first to go that way.

Corrigan asked, "You nearby?"

"I'm in Yosemite," I said. "On a mountain, actually."

"Might not be worth your time, then. Got a storm movin' in."

"The weather's irrelevant, Mr. Corrigan. You called me, so I'll be there."

I was already picturing the drive down the 41 to the 99, which I'd done once as part of a training assignment. Aside from the first and last thirty minutes, which took place on mountain roads, the route down to Sequoia was the kind that could crush your soul or lull you to sleep, depending on your mood. The highlight was Fresno at the halfway point, with its abundance of chain restaurants and fast-food joints. I always relished a late-night stop at In-N-Out Burger, even though I'd never admit that to a guy like Corrigan.

I checked my watch. "By the time I get off this mountain, it could be five o'clock. How far is the campsite from your ranger station?"

"Twenty-two miles."

My mouth went dry. "Oh."

I was hoping Rick Corrigan couldn't hear the deep-seated fear in my voice. Seasoned rangers could cover that kind of mileage in a couple days if they had to, but I wasn't seasoned. Worse, I wasn't sure I was physically capable of a twenty-two-mile hike through Sequoia at a ranger's pace. If we had to go out there on foot, I could very well embarrass myself in front of Corrigan and his team long before I had the chance to prove my competence as an investigator.

"Can you get a helicopter to take us up there?" I asked.

"What? Couldn't hear you."

"Are there any choppers available?" I practically shouted in humiliation.

"I could try, but no guarantees. We're low on personnel this time of year."

"I understand." Deep down, though, I was already fixated on those twenty-two miles. I might be able to manage that distance if it was flat, but with thousands of feet of intervening elevation change, no way. Corrigan didn't know about the rods and screws in my back, and I didn't want to have to tell him. All in all, this was not a good start to my second official case.

"So what's the terrain like up there?" I asked.

He barked a laugh. "It's not a stroll down the beach, if that's what you mean. There's about ten thousand feet of elevation change 'tween here and there, and a lot of it's unmarked trails. My best guy can probably get up there in a day, but for the average backpacker, it's a three-day hike. This time of year, maybe even four."

Turning my back on the two rangers listening in, I tilted my head toward the sky in a feeble nod to the weather gods. The skies were clear, at least—that brilliant alpine blue that just didn't exist in the city. I tried to draw some strength from it. It had been three years since my accident—three years, three surgeries, and some three-hundred visits to various physical therapists. Despite all that, I felt like if I couldn't get to Precipice Lake on my own two feet, then I didn't belong out there at all.

Corrigan asked, "What time are you comin' in?"

I did the calculations in my head—an hour to get off this rock, another thirty minutes at my rental cabin to pack up and leave, and a good five hours on the road to Sequoia, assuming Mineral King was centrally located in the park. Seven hours, then—including a stop at In-N-Out. That was a must. I would need that milkshake to help me power through.

I wanted to tell him I'd be there tomorrow, but national parks weren't like the urban grid; evidence tended to disappear within days, even hours. If there was one lesson my instructors at ISB had managed to drill into my head, it was to get to the scene of any potential crime as quickly as possible, even if that meant pulling an all-nighter on the road.

"I can be there by midnight," I said. "If your missing party returns to the campsite before then, call my cell phone. Here's the number." I gave it to him.

"There's no sense in drivin' like a maniac—"

"I'll be there tonight."

"Alrighty," he said. "I'll be waiting for you at the station."

After he hung up, I called my assistant agent in charge, or ASAC, at ISB headquarters—Ray Eskill. A twenty-five-year veteran of ISB, Ray believed in expediency, efficiency, and common sense. He wouldn't be thrilled about my decision to leave Yosemite so soon. For one thing, he wasn't convinced I had the chops to juggle multiple cases. I knew this because he'd told me so on my way out the door last week. The dead skier at the Line of Fire was my first solo investigation, and to be fair, it was a softball; the victim had clearly collided with a tree. An abandoned luxury campsite was a little less clear-cut.

"Ray Eskill," came the greeting. "Who's this?"

"It's Felicity Harland."

"Who?"

"Felicity—"

"I'm just messing with you, Harland. Jesus. What's the problem?"

I tried to smile, but those muscles often failed me during my conversations with Ray. "No problem, it's just—I got a call from the chief ranger out of Mineral King in Sequoia." I told him the rest of it—or at least as much as I thought he'd want to hear. Ray had a habit of cutting me off when he was bored or impatient. I tried to stick to the facts.

"Well," he said, once he'd digested my thirty-second rapid-fire report. "I guess you oughta go down there."

"Are you sure?"

"Are *you*?"

"Yes," I said, projecting my voice with such force that both of the rangers standing nearby turned their heads. "I'll circle back with the chief in Yosemite by the end of this week. I don't think it'll take long—the glampers probably just wandered off for a day hike."

"Could be," he said. "But I wouldn't bet on it."

C H A P T E R

2

THE DESCENT DOWN the Line of Fire took two grueling hours, and from there it was another thirty minutes to the trailhead. I thanked the rangers for their guidance and, once they were safely out of sight, hobbled across the parking lot to my truck. At times like these, I felt three times older than my thirty-two years. It didn't matter how much time I spent at the gym; there was no fixing a broken back. My spine surgeon had said as much: *"This is as good as it's gonna get, Felicity. I'm sorry."* I was sorry, too, but I was also stubborn.

I reached for one of the battery-powered heating pads in the backseat of my truck and wedged it between my tailbone and the seat cushion. Dusk was on the horizon, feathery blues and purples lighting the sky. I couldn't believe how fast the afternoon had waned.

Feeling the time crunch like a physical weight on my shoulders, I raced back to my AirBnB in Yosemite Valley to collect my shepherd-mix, Ollie. He was waiting for me at the kitchen window, his snout pressed up against the glass. At times like these, I wondered if my dog hated me for taking a job that required so much travel. I rubbed the fur behind his ears and whispered yet another apology. "You'll get a burger out of it, though," I said.

We were on the road again at just past eight o'clock, long after darkness had descended. A light snow began to fall, but by the time I picked up the 41 outside Fish Camp in the Yosemite foothills, the snow had turned to rain. The heater hummed in tune with the wipers.

"This could be a long week," I said to Ollie, who liked to stick his head out the window and take in the fresh air. "A long year, maybe."

The rain was making him antsy. At the sound of my voice, he looked back at me with those giant, knowing brown eyes. *"I don't mind,"* they seemed to say. I wondered if he did, though. I wondered if he missed our garden apartment in Lincoln Park, with its rattling radiators and constant street noise. I wondered if he even remembered Kevin, who had disappeared three years ago, when Ollie was only a puppy. *Three years, four months, and seven days.* It felt like a lifetime ago—and yet on other days, it felt like no time at all had passed.

I couldn't remember how long Kevin and I had been together—not exactly, anyway—but my brain refused to let me forget how long we'd been apart. This obsession with time and statistics were a manifestation of an intense interplay of trauma and guilt, one therapist had said. My dad's take: *"For Chrissakes, move on, Felicity. Life's too damn short."*

My departure from the FBI hadn't happened overnight. The Bureau had granted me an extended medical leave after my accident, but as the months passed, my cases in the criminal investigation unit were reassigned to other agents. I was suddenly an afterthought, and worse than that, my superiors questioned my fitness to return to active duty.

Then, one morning six months ago, my dad emailed me a link to a job opening on the U.S. Office of Personnel's website. It was for the Criminal Investigator Series 1811 with ISB, which matched my skillset and experience to a tee. The only thing that gave me pause was the actual job description: *Any physical condition that would cause the applicant to be a hazard to himself/herself or others is disqualifying.* The hiring personnel at ISB would request my medical records, of course. Depending on how they interpreted all the bad stuff in there, they might disqualify me right off the bat. I'd wondered if it was even worth applying.

But I did apply, and a day later, I ended up on the phone with Ray Eskill. He had already reviewed my medical records, and yes, they gave him pause—or rather, to quote him directly, they scared the shit out of him. But he was impressed with my work as a criminal investigator, and he thought I could be an asset at ISB. He was willing to give me a chance.

Two days later, I left packed up my stuff and left Chicago for good.

3

THREE RIVERS WAS the last town off the highway before
Sequoia National Park, and despite its miniscule population, traffic was at a standstill. According to the radio report,
the 198 was blocked due to an overturned tractor trailer. The
rain had eased up a bit, so I rolled down the window for Ollie.
He stuck his head out and sniffed. The air smelled faintly like
raw sewage, which was confirmed by the Highway Patrol's
Twitter account: *A word of warning to travelers on Route 198 near
Three Rivers; the east and westbound directions are blocked due to
an overturned tractor trailer carrying Honey Buckets . . .*

"Port-a-potties," I explained to Ollie.

He just looked at me and sniffed some more.

According to Google maps, the closest motel was on the
other side of the barricade, so I pulled onto the shoulder and told
Ollie we were walking the rest of the way. It wasn't like we were
going to get out to that campsite tonight anyway. I called Rick
Corrigan and gave him the update. He told me to drive safe.

Ollie bounded out of the truck. Steeling ourselves against
the odor of fallen Honey Buckets, we set off on foot toward the
blinking motel lights in the distance.

* * *

Rick Corrigan was standing in front of his ranger station with
his hands on his canvas-clad hips when we arrived a few

minutes before dawn. He looked every bit like a career park ranger—gray collared shirt, green pants, and a wide-brimmed straw hat that tilted just a touch to the left. He was lean, too, built like a marathoner, with reedy limbs and a narrow waist. I could tell just by looking at him that there was no way in hell he was going to let me slow him down.

I climbed out of the trunk with Ollie in tow. My dog always helped break the ice a little bit. He was well behaved, with a Labrador's disposition and a collie's smarts. I couldn't remember the last time he'd barked at someone.

"Mr. Corrigan, it's a pleasure to meet you." I stepped right up to him and shook his hand—hard, maybe a little too hard. "I'm Felicity Harland." His palm was rough, the skin thick with calluses.

"Pleasure's mine," he said.

"Sorry we're late."

"Nothin' you could do about it." He fleeced me with his gaze as he spoke. I was used to being sized up by strangers—in fact, it struck me as odd when it *didn't* happen. I didn't fit the profile of a typical federal agent, in part because I was female, but also because I was so damn petite—five-foot even and a hundred pounds.

"You're, uh, smaller than I pictured you," he said. "And younger."

"Oh—well." I instinctively tried to stand a bit taller, a habit that had taken root in kindergarten when Marina Harwood first introduced me to the word "midget." I'd always been the shortest kid in the class, and not only that, but the shortest in my family. *Felici-tiny* had been my nickname growing up. Thirty years later, I was still living it.

"Is your ranger back yet?" I asked, pushing a strand of hair behind my ear. I always wore my shoulder-length blond hair in a ponytail high on my head—the soccer ponytail, I liked to call it. Girls who wore their hair that way always seemed to score the most goals.

"No," he said. "I told him to camp up there for the night."

"Have you tried the glamping company again?"

"Yes, ma'am. Same thing. Nothin' to report."

"Could they verify that the campsite was theirs?"

"They wouldn't verify a damn thing, but it's their campsite, no doubt. They gave me the coordinates, which matched exactly where my ranger found it. Plus their logo's all over the place—you'll see."

"What time did you call?"

He looked at his watch. "About fifteen minutes ago."

"We need to get someone from that outfit out here."

"Good luck. Their offices are in the Bay Area."

"Who pitched the tent, then?"

"A local crew. No real connection to the company."

"Right." I wondered if he could hear the frustration in my voice. In a park like Sequoia, you could camp anywhere you wanted with the right permit. Dispersed camping was becoming more and more popular. Millennials didn't want to pitch a tent in a noisy campground, where people drank too much beer and let their kids run wild. They wanted to rough it. I understood the urge to escape a world overrun by technology, but for the tourist crowd, that escape was intended to be brief and comfortable. It was odd that no one had yet returned to the Glampist tent.

The weather up there worried me, too, as did the altitude. Mineral King ranger station was at 7,500 feet, which would have had a noticeable effect on someone living at sea level. Even after a few days in Yosemite, I was feeling a little short of breath.

"Let's go inside," I said. "We can talk more there."

Corrigan led the way up the wooden steps to the ranger station, where an American flag proudly flapped in the wind. Looking around, I couldn't help but admire the redwoods with their impressive heft and beauty. As Kevin used to say, every wilderness had its own energy. Some were characterized by wide open spaces and an abundance of light, an infinite expanse of nature that filled your soul. Others, like this one, made you feel impossibly small, crushed by the weight of an encroaching wood and a menacing sky.

The interior of the ranger station was cozy and warm, with a centrally located broad reception desk flanked by glass display cases. Trail maps were everywhere, stacked in neat little piles next to doors, windows, and trash bins. I couldn't help but think that in a few years, maybe they wouldn't be. For now, though, Corrigan seemed committed to the old way.

Once we were seated at a small folding table in the break room, I took out my cell phone to take notes. The iPad had failed me on the mountain, so I was done with it for now— maybe forever. That said, I was comfortable in my decision to ditch notepads; pages fell out, they turned to mush in the rain. In my view, technology wasn't all bad.

"Let's start with the scene up there," I said. "Tell me about Precipice Lake."

Corrigan pointed at the faded topographical map that took up most of the wall. "Well, there's Precipice—right smack in the middle of Sequoia." I followed his finger to the speck of blue on the map that was, as he'd said, at the geographic center of Sequoia's vast acreage.

"Precipice is a tourist trap, that's for sure," he said, "but it's not as bad as it could be 'cause it's so far from the trailhead. Folks usually start with a hike to Monarch Lake, which goes off toward Sawtooth Peak and some other nice canyon routes. In summer, it's busy. This time of year, not so much. Some of the trail is unmaintained, and the snow makes it worse. It can be treacherous: loose rock, ice, real steep in some places. The upside is that there isn't a whole lotta vegetation out there except down by the lake. But for the most part, it's just rock. Hardly any trees at all. Easy to spot someone from above."

"You said it's twenty-two miles from here?"

"Yes, ma'am. It's a three-day hike for most. But like I said, I bet the folks camping there hitched a ride up to the campsite."

"How?"

"Private copter's my guess."

For not the first time, I wondered when Corrigan planned to get search and rescue involved, but I wasn't about to tell him how to do his job. Ray Eskill had made it clear that if you couldn't get along with the rangers, you wouldn't last long in ISB. Corrigan and I were a team for the foreseeable future, like it or not. He was better positioned than anyone to help me find these people, and I didn't want to piss him off.

I glanced down at my notes. Later, I'd pull up the same file on my delinquent iPad, integrating it with photos, maps, witness reports, and other pieces of information gathered during the course of my preliminary investigation. I was hoping this file was going to stay small, which it would, if whoever had gone missing from that campsite at Precipice Lake was on their way back to their tent right now. It wasn't that I shied away from difficult or complex cases; I was just trying to stomach the reality of hiking twenty-two miles in Corrigan's shadow.

"I'd like to see the campsite," I said. "I know we had talked briefly about a chopper—"

"You're in luck," he said. "It's on its way."

"Great." I hid my relief with a smile. "What about your ranger—the one that found the campsite? Will he wait until we get there?" I watched his eyes track to the clock on the wall, with its old-school face and numbers. It made a soft clicking noise with each passing second.

"Who knows. I told him to camp up there for the night, but he said he wanted to come back down to talk to you in case the chopper didn't work out. He'd be nuts to attempt a route like that at night, but that's Hux."

Not ten seconds later, the door blew open, propelled by a gust of wind and a decked-out park ranger in all his gear—hat, ski mask, snow pants, parka, radio. As he peeled the ski mask off his face, his wind-beaten cheeks glowed red in the dimly lit station. He was a good-looking guy, and young too—thirty-ish, with scruff on his face and wild blond hair that poked out of his red beanie. His skin was slick with sweat and snowmelt.

Stomping his boots to shake out the snow, he said to Corrigan, "Sorry, Rick. I ran into a big cat on the way down— had to go off-trail for a bit. Don't worry, we're good." He grinned at the chief before shifting his gaze toward me.

Even Corrigan looked surprised—and maybe even a little impressed—to see his ranger. "This is, ah, Ferdinand Huxley," he said to me, tripping over the guy's first name. "He's the one that found the campsite."

Before I could react to this storybook moniker, the younger man stepped forward and offered his hand. "Hux," he said, saying the word with such gusto that it was almost like he was trying to obliterate his given name. I wondered who had burdened him with it.

"Felicity Harland," I said, with a crisp handshake that was meant to intimidate him, just a little bit—not easy to do when the person shaking my hand towered over me. Ferdinand Huxley was like Mount Everest to my local sledding hill. Unlike Corrigan, though, he wasn't put off by my diminutive stature. He met my gaze head-on with an easy, natural smile.

"Pleasure to meet you, Agent Harland," he said.

"*Special Agent* Harland," Corrigan said, eyeing Huxley like a father silently chastising his son for not saying "sir" at the dinner table.

"Actually, I'm good with just Harland," I said.

"I'm with you there," Huxley said. "I never was a fan of first names."

When I didn't respond, the smile on his face tightened up a bit. I could see that he was struggling to get a read on my sense of humor. For all he knew, I didn't have one. Most ISB agents came from a law enforcement background, and, well, we had a certain reputation.

"Can I trouble you for a cup of coffee?" I asked Corrigan, who looked at me like I'd just asked for filet mignon, medium rare, thank you very much. "Instant's fine, if you have it."

"I might have an old Coke can in the back of the fridge."

"That's fine. Anything with caffeine in it will do. Thank you."

He walked off with a grunt. Huxley pulled out a chair and sat down. He smelled like pine needles and spice, but maybe that was just the lingering scent of his aftershave. I did like it, though. It reminded me of the outdoors.

"So, ISB, eh?" Huxley asked. "Are you thinking we've got a crime on our hands?"

"You tell me," I said. "You've seen the campsite."

"Yep," he said. "I sure did."

"How did you get down here so fast, by the way? I understand the campsite is over twenty miles from here."

"I walked—well, ran. A bit of this and that."

"All night?"

"I've got a dependable flashlight," he said, like that was all there was to it. He wasn't the arrogant type, then. That was a relief.

Corrigan grunted as he walked back to the table. "Hux here is like the Energizer Bunny," he said. "You'll get used to it—or not." He handed me a can of Coca-Cola so ancient that its logo was faded and the edges were tinted with rust. I popped it open and took a whiff. I wasn't sure if soda could go bad or not, but I wasn't about to reject the offering. It would have to do.

I pointed to the outline of Huxley's cell phone poking through his pocket. "I hope you used that to take some photos."

"I did."

"What's the one-liner on what you found up there?"

"Well," he said. "It was a strange scene—real nice gear, top-of-the-line stuff. But it looked like whoever was camping there left in a hurry." He rubbed his hands together and looked at Corrigan. "I couldn't help but think about that crazy situation we had up here last year." There was that word again—except even worse. A *crazy* situation. That didn't sound good.

Corrigan heaved a sigh. It felt to me like they'd been down this road before.

"What crazy situation?" I asked.

"We called him the Woodsman," Huxley said. "We never found the guy. For about a month last summer, he terrorized a number of campsites between here and Kaweah Gap—and, you know, just to mess with us, he marked his territory by carving a symbol in random trees."

"What was the symbol?"

Corrigan huffed. "Looked like an amateur drawing of a decapitated fish if you ask me."

"It was a *djed*," Huxley said.

"Pardon?"

Huxley glanced at Corrigan, a sign of deference that made me respect Huxley a little bit more, if for no other reason than that he had a decently high emotional IQ. "A *djed* is an Egyptian symbol that means eternal life." He plucked a pen from the cupholder behind him and made a sketch on the back of a napkin. "As you can see here, it's like a cross, but with a broader base and four parallel lines at the top."

"Interesting," I said. "How many symbols did you find like this?"

"All told, we spotted eleven of them, spread out all over Sequoia."

"Always at a campsite?"

He nodded. "Yep."

"Did you find one at the Glampist site?"

"No," Huxley admitted. "Looked long and hard, but I didn't see one."

Corrigan grunted again. "I'm so tired of hearin' about this 'Woodsman'. If I see one more of those stupid symbols again, I'm gonna retire on the spot."

"Did he ever hurt anyone?" I asked, directing the question to Huxley, but it was Corrigan who answered.

"No," the older ranger said. "Just a nutjob with too much time on his hands. We get those types out here."

I made a note of it nonetheless. Huxley watched me type the word *Woodsman* into my phone, using my thumbs. Corrigan, muttering under his breath, walked back over to the squat refrigerator, which made more noise than a broken muffler.

Huxley said, "With the Woodsman on a rampage last year, we found a lot of abandoned campsites. People would just high-tail it out of here 'cause they were spooked—heard the stories, I guess. One girl was so traumatized she had to be airlifted to the hospital."

"So it sounds like there *were* injuries."

"Well—"

Corrigan cut in with, "Nobody got hurt—not like what you're thinking anyhow. We had a couple twisted ankles and sprained fingers, but those weren't the Woodsman's fault. I'm not responsible for people scared of their own shadow." He poked his head in the refrigerator and reached for something way in the back.

I looked at Huxley, who said nothing in response to Corrigan's rant. "And you said this Woodsman character was active for, what, a month?"

"Yeah, for most of July and part of August," Huxley said.

"So it's possible he was a tourist that just went home."

"Nah. I always thought he was local. Pitching a tent off-trail in Sequoia isn't like camping in your local state park. It's real rugged terrain up there. We get a lot of falls, like Rick said—broken bones, things like that. A tech nerd from San Fran with too much time on his hands wouldn't last that long out here—not on his own anyway."

Corrigan joined us at the table, with string cheese, hard-boiled eggs, and a single cup of yogurt. "Help yourselves," he said, like he had just served Easter brunch. I could picture his wife at home, cooking up a storm like she'd probably done every day for the last forty years.

Huxley reached for a piece of string cheese and chewed it in silence, waiting for my next question. While he peeled the string cheese, enjoying it the way a third-grader might, I pulled up my notes on my phone. The station had Wi-Fi, thankfully. Not all of them did.

"We'll come back to the Woodsman theory," I said. "For right now, I want to focus on the evidence you've gathered." I looked at Huxley. "What's your email address?"

"Huxhodgeconjecture@gmail.com," he said as he chewed his cheese.

"Huh?"

He spelled it out for me so I could add it to my contacts. "The Hodge conjecture is a famous unsolved math problem," he explained.

Corrigan shook his head. "And you were talkin' about nerds . . ."

To Hux, I said, "Right. Well, I just sent you a link to my Box account. You can upload the photos after we finish up here."

"I took like a thousand."

"Good," I said, trying hard not to flatter him too much. Ray had warned me that most rangers took about three photos and called it a day. "Let's see the highlights."

With Corrigan peering over his shoulder, Huxley produced his older-model iPhone from his snow pants pocket. The photos, which he had saved to a file titled *Glampist*, started with the trailhead. In the snow, it was difficult to make out a defined path through the brush.

Pointing at a gap in the trees in one of the photos, Huxley said, "This here's the trail from the Mineral King campground—which is just up the hill there. You probably saw it when you came in—to Monarch Lake. It's about four miles to Monarch from the trailhead, with twenty-five hundred feet of elevation gain. Kind of a nice, moderate day hike. I know it's hard to tell from the photos, but for the most part, this part of the trail is well maintained and clearly marked."

Corrigan peeled a hard-boiled egg while Huxley went on. "It's a popular route in summer. We don't get the crowds like Yosemite, but the parking lot's usually full in July. The first mile is the hardest because it's a west-facing slope. Lots of sun. Not too much of an issue this time of year, although you've got the snowfields closer to the lake."

"She doesn't need to hear all this," Corrigan said. "We both know those glampers chartered their way up to Precipice."

"I just like to set the scene, Chief." Huxley looked at me. "How long've you been with ISB, Agent Harland?"

"Oh—well." I had been dreading this question. The answer made me look green—which I was, but I wasn't excited about spelling it out for them. Still, honesty was the best policy. "A week, officially."

"*One* week?" He made a soft whistling sound. Even Corrigan cracked a smile.

"That's right. But I was with the FBI for seven years before I transferred."

"You musta been right outta high school when you went in, then," Corrigan said.

"Not quite," I said. "I'm thirty-two."

"Why'd you make the switch?" Huxley asked.

"Um—well. There was an opening." The looks on their faces told me they weren't convinced by this answer, but I left it at that. They didn't need to know the details.

"Hope it works out for you, then," Huxley said. At least he seemed to mean it.

We went back to the photos, which documented the terrain in its awe-inspiring glory. As the redwoods thinned out, steep canyons and alpine lakes took their place above the timber line. The landscape up near Precipice was sheer granite, like plains of gray. When we finally came to photos of the campsite, it almost looked as though Glampist had decided to set their clients up on the face of the moon.

"Okay, so here we are," Huxley said, pointing to a speck of red in the distance—the tent, it looked like. "From this view, we're looking north. We've got about six inches of snow on the ground, fresh from the night before. But you can clearly see the tent here"—he pointed to that red dot, its color like a siren on a gray sky—"and the campfire here and their stockpile of gear over here. And here"—he smiled wryly—"is some kind of portable toilet-shower thing. I went inside, and lemme just say, it's nicer than the Four Seasons. Not that I've stayed there or anything, but I've used the one in the lobby. This thing's got a shiny toilet, a sink, a shower." He scanned through a dozen more photos until he landed on a close-up of a toilet. "See? Swanky."

I had to agree with him. It was swanky, yes, but the red tent and its accoutrements were a human stain on a pristine natural landscape. I didn't like it at all. The plush red towels with the Glampist logo stitched into the fabric irked me, too, along with the battery-powered cappuccino maker and the luxury blankets. In fact, everything in the photos, from the tent to the cookware, to the toilet, was a walking advertisement for Glampist. Their logo was visible everywhere. The "G" was flashy; the "m" was shaped like two tents.

"How about inside the tent?" I asked.

"Here," he said, swiping through photos of the tent's luxe interior. There were no sleeping bags—just a queen-sized bed, which looked plush and new. The sheets, which all but shimmered with silkiness, were bunched at the foot of the bed. One of four pillows lay on the ground, along with an impressive assortment of cookware.

Corrigan cleared his throat. "Look, if there's concern for somebody's well-being, that's one thing, but the photos are crossin' a line—and believe me, people like this know where the line's drawn. The last thing we need is a lawsuit."

"I'll deal with it if there's an issue," I said.

"Are you calling this a crime scene, then?" Huxley asked.

"No, I'm not," I said. "I'm not yet convinced anything untoward happened here."

"We're wastin' your time, then," Corrigan concluded.

"No, you're not. You were right to call."

Corrigan shot a glance at Huxley—not quite scolding, but close to it. Before he could say anything, a call came into the station. With a parting grunt, he went to answer it.

I scanned through Huxley's photos again. Even though I'd seen pictures of Precipice Lake online, Huxley had captured the place in vivid detail, which I took to reflect his reverence for the place—the trees, the sky, the snow. I learned a lot about him just by looking at the photos.

"These photos here," I said, scanning through a series that captured the lake from a vantage point well above its surface. "They were taken where, exactly?"

"From a ledge about a hundred feet up. The campsite itself was about fifteen feet away from where I was standing. There isn't a whole lot of flat ground up on that ridge except right where the campsite was. I'm sure that's why they pitched the tent there."

I used my thumb and forefinger to zoom in on the photo. "It looks like there's a good bit of ice on the lake there."

"That's typical for this time of year. And with the way the light hits it, the water looks almost black next to the cliff. You can't see more than a few feet below the surface." He frowned. "I'm sorry I couldn't get a better picture of the water there."

"It's okay," I said. "You did plenty."

Corrigan had finished with his call. As he sat back down at the table, he was muttering something to himself that made Huxley remark, "Another emergency?"

"Yep," Corrigan said. "A tent infestation."

I was picturing a fire-ant horror show when Corrigan clarified, "Spiders. Two, in fact. The gal wants me to go up there and fumigate."

"Are these venomous spiders?"

Corrigan gave me a weary look. "Don't know, don't care. It's the woods, Agent Harland. Spiders live here. *We're* the invaders."

Huxley said, "He gets these calls a lot."

"Spider infestations?"

"Outlandish requests. Corrigan's right—people are high maintenance these days. The reality's different than what they see on Netflix, and when that fact dawns on them, they call us for help. I got one call a week ago asking for a refund on a permit because it rained."

Corrigan was shaking his head. He looked tired. But then again, maybe he'd been up most of the night waiting for me. I asked him, "How hard is it to search the lake?"

"Hard," he huffed. "I'd have to get a dive team up there."

I knew he was going to say that, but my goal was to plant the seed in case we needed a full-scale search of the lake. "We'll have another look around the campsite first," I said. "Sometimes things turn up on a second pass."

"You saw the tent," Huxley said. "The bed looked slept in. I saw two thermoses and a plate of food—crumbs mostly, since the door was open and the animals had already gotten to it. Like I said, it looked to me like they left in a hurry."

"Or they're just lazy and used to being waited on."

Huxley leaned back in his chair and crossed his ankles. "Hm," he said.

"What about their backpacks?" I asked.

"I looked for a good two hours," Huxley said. "I didn't find anything."

"Hiking boots?"

He shook his head. "Nope."

"So they were probably wearing them when they left the campsite, then. It doesn't sound like a sleepwalking misadventure or an abduction, at least." I was admittedly out of my element here, but I felt it was important to take a position.

"Okay, but to be gone for three nights?" Huxley shook his head. "Nah. These two were from the city, you could just tell. Something spooked 'em. It's the only explanation."

"It's not the *only* explanation."

"You saw the photos, Agent Harland." Huxley kept his voice civil but firm. "Nobody leaves a Glampist campsite for more than fifteen minutes. Hell, even that's a stretch. They've got everything they need right there."

Corrigan wrinkled his brow, perhaps ruffled by his junior ranger's attitude. I liked Huxley's forwardness, though. He reminded me of my grandfather, a career military policeman who never took shit from anybody. I had a feeling he would have liked Huxley.

"How long have you been a ranger?" I asked him.

He didn't answer right away, which told me he was probably pretty green too. "Nine months," he said.

"Feels like nine years," Corrigan muttered.

"The chief here is coming up on forty-five years with the Park Service," Huxley said. "He nixed the big party, though, so we're doing coffee and bagels next week."

"She's not interested in any of that." Corrigan shot Huxley a look as the older ranger got to his feet. "She's got a job to do—same as you. Speakin' of which, we've got those Girl Scouts from Fresno comin' in today, and it's your turn to show 'em how not to burn down the forest."

"Roger that, Chief," Huxley said, but despite the levity in his tone, he sounded a touch disappointed. "If we're all done here, I'll just get on with my day then—"

"Wait a minute," I said. He was halfway out of his chair. "We're not done here."

"Oh." Huxley sat back down.

"The photos are excellent, but I still need to see the campsite," I said. "I'd like you to show me around up there."

With a glance at Corrigan, Huxley said, "It's really up to the boss—"

"I don't think we can spare him," Corrigan said to me. "We're low on manpower."

"Maybe someone else can hang out with the Girl Scouts?" I asked.

Corrigan put his hands on the chair and sighed. "Look, if you're really worried about these folks, then even I'll admit that Huxley's your man. He's a finder."

"Pardon?"

Huxley started saying something along the lines of "never mind," but Corrigan interrupted him. "Sure, he thinks every litterbug is an HVT and every weird-lookin' campsite is a war zone, but you can't blame him for that. He spent three tours looking for terrorists in Afghanistan."

"HVT?"

"High-value target," Corrigan said.

"You're ex-military?" I asked Huxley.

Huxley met my gaze with a curt nod.

"Ferdinand here doesn't like to talk about it," Corrigan said. "But I thought you should know who you're goin' out into the woods with." I didn't tell Corrigan that I planned to run a background check on Huxley long before we hit the trail. For anyone in ISB, it was just good practice; for a woman, it was necessary. I wasn't taking any chances.

"What branch of the service were you in?" I asked him.

"Navy."

"He was Special Forces," Corrigan clarified.

"But you're out now?" I asked Huxley.

Corrigan crossed his arms. "He's out, but he won't talk about *why* he's out."

"I was honorably discharged," Huxley said, more to me than to Corrigan. "I don't see why I need to say any more than that."

"You don't," I said, but in the back of my mind, it made me wonder. Navy SEALs tended to have long careers in the military; after all, they were the elite of the elite. I had a friend in the FBI that had connections in the Navy's personnel office. Maybe he could pull Huxley's file.

I turned back to Corrigan while Huxley worked on uploading the photos. "I think I've got everything I need for now, Mr. Corrigan. Is your pilot ready?"

Corrigan said, "Well, yes and no. She wants to pick us up at a different location—our helipad's in bad shape, 'parently."

"That's fine. Where?"

"A little ways up the trail."

"Am I still invited?" Huxley asked.

There was a pause. Corrigan turned to me and said, "It's your call, Agent Harland."

It wasn't a difficult decision, really. Something told me Huxley's dogged nature could be an asset rather than a liability, and I liked that he was relatively new at rangering. He might take some of the heat off me when I inevitably said something stupid to Corrigan.

"We have to leave now," I said. "Don't you need a nap or something?"

He grinned. "Sleep is for the weak."

Corrigan just rolled his eyes.

"All right," I said. "Meet us out front in ten minutes."

CHAPTER

4

WE SET OFF from the Sawtooth Trailhead at 7:15 AM with a violet dawn on the horizon. Warblers and wrens marked the break of a new day, their birdsongs marking the arrival of spring. I checked my shoelaces and tightened the straps on my new pack, determined to weather this journey right along with the best of them—in this case, Corrigan and Huxley. And of course, Ollie came too. Huxley had assured me that Sheila had no problem with dogs in her helicopter; she had two of her own, including a chihuahua with its own harness.

The plan was to hike out of the woods to Sawtooth Pass, where the chopper would pick us up and transport us to Precipice Lake. Corrigan grumbled about the whole arrangement. "Pilots can be hard to come by this time of year," he explained. "I'm runnin' out of favors."

"I appreciate it," I said, growing weary of thank-yous.

Huxley and I took up the rear, while Corrigan set the pace with his hardy walking stick and plodding steps. Every so often he'd bend over and collect a piece of trash and toss it in his thirty-gallon garbage bag; didn't matter if it was heavy or gross or whatever—he never passed anything by. I couldn't imagine doing that on a hike like this. When I remarked on it to Huxley, he shrugged and said, "That's Corrigan. He loves the land like a father loves his son."

"Does he have kids?"

Huxley shook his head. "No. Sequoia's his passion—you should hear him talk about her. The man is on a mission."

"To do what?"

"To save this park from the destructive forces of humanity."

"That's . . . deep."

Huxley laughed. "Well, that's the title of his talk—the one he gives to Girl Scouts, Boy Scouts, school groups, bus tours, and pretty much anyone who walks into his ranger station. I'm sure he'll make you sit through it at some point, too—don't worry." He smiled.

For an older man, Corrigan displayed the fitness of a college coed as he hoisted the bag over his shoulder and plowed onward. I was glad he wasn't hanging back with us, though. Huxley was a little more approachable than the crusty chief. "Have you run into any Glampist clients before?" I asked him.

He thought for a minute. "Once or twice out on the trail. You know the type—brand new gear, maps always at the ready, everybody walking at a glacial pace while checking their phones for service. The one group I found was in complete freak-out mode when I spotted them a quarter mile off the trail. They thought I was Jesus, not kidding." He chuckled at the memory. "The sad thing is, you could literally *see* the parking lot from where they were. They'd been on the trail for less than ten minutes."

"Nice," I said, hazarding a smile.

"Eh, it's unfortunate. No one respects Mother Nature anymore."

After another hour or so on the trail, we reached the designated rendezvous point on Sawtooth Pass. The helicopter was already there, perched on a flat slab of rock. The pilot introduced herself as Sheila Reyes—good handshake, very professional. But to Huxley she said with a laugh, "Oh Christ, it's you again."

"My thoughts exactly," he said with a grin. They embraced like old friends, and as we climbed into the chopper, I overheard Sheila asking Huxley about his dog, Betta. From the pieces of their conversation, I gathered that Betta had died not along ago.

As for Ollie, she welcomed him aboard with a hearty "come on in" gesture.

I was no big fan of helicopters, but the bird's-eye view was spectacular. After leaving the forest behind, we soared over alpine lakes that dotted the landscape like scraps of blue on a gray carpet. Sequoia's bald, silvery peaks were flecked with snow. Corrigan commented that the water level looked high for this time of year. It had been a long and snowy winter.

"Precipice Lake's on the other side of the pass," Huxley said as we flew directly over it. Sawtooth Pass had earned its name, with a snaggle-toothed peak at one end and a wall of spiked rock in its shadow. I'd done my share of difficult hikes all over the world—with Kevin, not as a federal agent—but this was something else. The terrain was stupefying.

"How high is the pass?"

"Eleven-eight," he said, which meant 11,800 feet in ranger speak.

"How is it that you don't seem at all tired? I can't believe you covered this entire distance in one night."

"What can I say? I'm a gym rat." This comment made Corrigan roll his eyes.

"Is that true?" I asked.

"Yep. Rick's got a state-of-the-art fitness center in the basement back at the station." His green eyes gleamed behind his sunglasses. "Actually, it's two barbells and a pull-up bar."

"You broke the pull-up bar," Corrigan said.

"Nah," Huxley said. "That was Steve."

Before I could ask who Steve was, Sheila motioned to a flat area adjacent to a small alpine lake—*Precipice,* I thought. A peregrine falcon soared over the edge of the cliff, disappearing behind the lake's granite curtain. I couldn't imagine a couple of glampers hiking all the way out here with all their gear. There was just no way.

After we landed, it took me a moment to get my bearings. As the chopper's rotors whirred overhead, kicking up dust and dirt, I grabbed my pack from the hold and headed toward the water's edge. Ollie loped after me. I was struck by Precipice's desolate beauty, like a theater with no players. Its signature rock wall, at least a hundred feet high, rose out of the blue waters at a sheer vertical angle, earning the place its name. We set off toward it.

"I've got a call coming in," Corrigan said when we were halfway up the ridge. He put the satellite phone to his ear, muffling the static that filtered in and out, loud enough for us to hear. "High wind advisory." He paused. "And a high school group's got norovirus."

Huxley said, "Not 'it'!"

"I'll send Steve," Corrigan muttered.

While Corrigan made another call, I battled the lunar terrain, with its uneven rock and patchy vegetation. My hiking boots were new—too new, damn it. I'd tried to break them in with long walks on the treadmill, which obviously hadn't been enough. A baseball bat would have worked better. I was loosening my laces when I realized Huxley was talking to me.

"Sorry, what?" I asked.

"Precipice gets a lot of cliff jumpers in the summer," he said. "Not this time of year, though. Hardly anybody comes through here till May."

"Any injuries or drownings up here recently?"

"Nope," he said. "Not a one."

"That seems surprising."

"Well, it's a long way from the trailhead. It used to be only the true adventure seekers came all the way out here. Things have changed with these glamping services."

He had a point there. Long before we reached the actual campsite, Glampist's flashy red tent announced itself like a billboard on a desolate stretch of granite highway. Its flaps fluttered in the wind, but someone had nailed it down pretty good. Still, Mother Nature was winning this battle. In another week, the tent would be gone, blown into the lake or otherwise dismantled by a storm. The bits of food and trash would be eaten by wild animals. There might be signs that someone had been there once, but few clues as to who or when. I was eager to get up on that ridge and salvage what we could before it was too late.

"I don't see anyone up there," Huxley said, passing me his binoculars. "Not that I really expected to, but still."

"No," I agreed. "It looks abandoned, all right."

Ollie settled on his haunches beside me and unleashed a sonorous howl that echoed through the basin. I wondered if he felt it, too—the remoteness of the place, its total and utter isolation. It was where you went not to enjoy life, but to escape it.

It was the kind of place where you could simply disappear.

CHAPTER

5

THE CAMPSITE WAS a mess, the wheels of chaos already set in motion. In some ways, the tent and its ruined accoutrements had that staged Hollywood feel, like the cast and crew were going to walk on at any moment and reset the pieces for the next shot. Except no one was coming back, clearly. At this point, there wasn't much to come back for.

Ollie poked his nose into the tent and sniffed, turned off by the scented sheets, perhaps. I stepped over canteens, cookware, and other remnants of a campsite that at least purported to be functional. The firepit had signs of recent use, with a good amount of firewood left over. I sorted through the charred remains with a pair of forceps.

"Well?" Corrigan bent down next to me.

"Let's have a look around," I said. "See if you can find anything with a name on it."

"There's enough trash 'round here to fill a goddamn landfill," he mumbled.

Huxley hid a smile while Corrigan walked off toward the tarp that doubled as a storage shed. Now that I'd seen the campsite, I was admittedly more worried about the possibility of a missing person scenario. Huxley was right about Glampist's commitment to top-of-the-line accommodations. I couldn't imagine why someone would want to abandon a setup like this unless they were scared, injured, or impaired. It didn't feel right.

While Huxley and Ollie prowled the campsite and Corrigan inspected the firepit, I went over to the tent and stepped inside. A putrid smell filled my nostrils—spoiled milk maybe, leftover from the cappuccinos brewed some days before. The plates had been licked clean, although it was hard to say what kind of animal had done it.

I rummaged through the corporate sheets, blankets, and other items that had no place in a wilderness setting. The sheets smelled faintly like men's cologne, which gave me more to work with than anything Glampist had offered over the phone. The only other thing of note was a card with the word *Glampist* on the front. On the back it said, *Does your campsite need refreshing?* There was a number at the bottom, with an invitation to call anytime.

My own cell phone didn't have any service whatsoever, but I knew Glampist didn't make its clients rely on their personal technology for their morning refreshment. Per their website, the company provided all client groups with an Iridium 9575, the most expensive satellite phone on the market. It retailed for close to two grand.

I was looking for the Iridium now, which would have provided a great deal of information—calls, text messages, maybe even some identifying information. Deep down, though, I wasn't optimistic. The people camping here must have taken it with them. But if they were lost, why hadn't they used the sat phone to call for help? I kept coming back to Huxley's story about the so-called Woodsman terrorizing campers in Sequoia. Perhaps this Woodsman character had escalated his game this year to kidnapping. It was an elaborate theory, though, and in my experience, the simplest explanation was usually the right one. I decided to let it marinate for a while.

"I've got something!" Huxley called out.

I crawled out of the tent and inhaled a breath of fresh air, grateful for the reprieve from the stuffy interior. Huxley was headed toward me, with Ollie trailing close behind. Corrigan, inspecting a cast-iron pan, lingered by the burnt remnants of the campfire.

"Here," Huxley said, handing me a receipt. "Found this near the latrine."

It was from a bagel cafe in Burbank, dated the previous Friday at six fifteen AM, for two bagels with cream cheese and two coffees. Paid for with a credit card, with the last four digits listed. The customer's name also appeared on the receipt: Tatum.

"This is good," I said. "Very good. Nice work, Huxley."

He grinned. "Thanks."

"Let's call the bagel place when we get back to the station," I said. "Tatum is a unique name. Maybe they'll remember her."

Corrigan trudged over to where we stood, his cheeks red with windburn. He was holding the same bag of trash he'd been carrying from the start, plus a Ziploc bag for evidence collection. Every time the garbage bag seemed to be overflowing, he'd throw it on the ground, stomp on it, and make room for more.

"Find anything?" I asked.

"Plenty," he grunted.

Huxley turned and looked back at the tent. He just stood there for a while, staring at the red canvas as it rippled in the wind, while I sorted through the items Corrigan had recovered from the campsite. I would ask the lab to process them, which might give us a lead on who had been camping here, but those results could take days. When it came to people missing in the wilderness, we didn't have that kind of time.

Huxley muttered something under his breath.

"What is it?" I asked him.

"It's just strange, is all," Huxley said. "You've got coffee makers and high thread-count sheets, but no cell phones, wallets, or cash—you know, the things people tend to hang onto, even when they're away from home. If there's one thing you take with you on a wilderness adventure, it's your cell phone. Gotta keep up with your Instagram account."

"So now you're thinking they went for a day hike."

"I don't know, to be honest. There's something off about it, that's for sure. I guess it's possible they got out on the trail and lost their way or maybe got into some other kind of trouble, and they never made it back."

"What about theft?"

"What do you mean?"

"Could someone have stolen those items?"

Huxley looked around at the decimated remains of the campsite. "I *guess*," he said, emphasizing his skepticism. "But then you've got to carry it all. I'm just saying Sequoia isn't exactly a hotbed for thieves. Too much effort involved."

Corrigan sidled up to us. "So what's your take, Agent Harland? Worth the trip?"

I didn't respond right away because something told me that he'd never let me live down my answer, whatever it was. "It certainly does look abandoned."

"Well, if you want my opinion, I think these two are out on the trail somewhere, wastin' everybody's time. I'm sure they took their sat phone with 'em."

"What about their cell phones?"

Corrigan shrugged. "The company probably told 'em to leave all that at home."

"Could be," I said.

Huxley said, "You don't sound convinced."

"Well, I agree with you that no one leaves their cell phone at home these days. Social media has a powerful hold over people."

I stood and surveyed the site, swiveling my head around to get a sense of the place from a limited perspective. Corrigan liked to call on his experience dealing with campsites and campers, and he certainly had a lot, but my expertise was in crime scenes. I'd convinced myself that it didn't matter if things had gone bad high on a mountain or on a city street; I could tell when something didn't feel right.

"What a mess," Corrigan muttered as he paced the remains of the campsite. Every so often he'd bend down and inspect the dirt for some tiny scrap of litter.

Huxley looked at what we'd collected and said, "Think we'll get anything from all this?"

"We've got a first name," I said. "That's something."

Ollie's sudden barking made us all turn our heads. We looked back at the tent to see his tail sticking out of the latrine. "Ollie," I called out. "Get out of there. Ollie, come on."

I went after him and found him sniffing a soaked T-shirt. Snagging it in his teeth, he placed the shirt on the ground at my

feet and looked up at me. I knew that look; he had the owner's
scent and was ready to follow it to the ends of the Earth. Still,
Ollie wasn't an official search dog. He had no structured training in HRD, or what law enforcement called human remains
detection. I preferred to keep him out of that world.

Huxley poked his head inside the latrine. Scrunching his
nose, he said, "Got a quick update for ya—Corrigan called
Search and Rescue."

"Finally," I muttered.

"I know he's crusty, Harland, but he doesn't want anybody
to get hurt."

"He is indeed crusty," I said.

Huxley ruffled the fur behind Ollie's ears. "What'd your
dog find?"

"A shirt. It was, uh, in the latrine. Like, really in there." I
held up the shirt with a gloved hand. It was wet, but worse than
that, it had a brown tinge—fecal matter.

"I can see that," he said with a laugh. "Looks like your dog
here wants to be a part of your investigation."

"He wants to, but he's not." I inspected the shirt Ollie had
found. It looked lived in, the kind of thing you reached for
before climbing into bed. More interestingly, it was a men's
shirt. Size M. On the front it read "BURT'S BOAT RENT-
ALS," and below that, "Big Bear Lake, California." We already
had the receipt from the bagel place with a Burbank address,
but the T-shirt was additional evidence that we were likely dealing with folks from Southern California.

After bagging the shirt, I walked over to the ledge closest to
the campsite. From there, it was about a hundred-foot drop to
the water—or ice, rather, as it was partially frozen. In fact, the
ice directly below me appeared to have an actual hole in it. It
was a good size, too—big enough to accommodate a person
plummeting through the air.

Huxley was standing next to me, peering over the edge. He
must have seen it, too, because he said, "Well, damn. I knew I
missed something the first time around."

"The light's much better now than when you saw it," I said.
"You didn't miss it."

Huxley called over to Corrigan, who was on his sat phone again. Something about severe dehydration in the norovirus group. He ended the conversation after a brief exchange with the caller about getting MedEvac involved.

"I gotta go deal with this," Corrigan said. "Sheila's gonna take me down. No guarantees she's gonna be able to come back up for you two."

"Hold up a second," I said. "We need a dive team up here."

Corrigan's gaze went from me to Huxley. "What for?"

I pointed at the hole in the ice. "Because I think there may be a body in that lake."

6

SEARCH AND RESCUE was one thing, but getting a dive team up to Precipice Lake was quite another. Corrigan argued that a "big ol ' hole in the ice" wasn't enough of a reason to mobilize a professional cadre of divers. He was right, of course, but I couldn't just wait for a dead body to float to the surface on its own time. That only happened after the body had decomposed enough for its own gases to make it buoyant. In water this cold, that process could take weeks or even months. I needed a dive team to search the lake *today*.

In the end, Corrigan let his junior ranger handle the norovirus situation while he got the dive team together. His reasons for doing so weren't exactly magnanimous; he just didn't want me to involve the FBI. Like most career rangers, he was all about his own turf and his own trusted personnel. I understood the impulse. I was responsible for the handling of the crime scene, but he was responsible for the park. He wasn't going to relinquish all control to a neophyte from ISB, nor did I expect him to.

Sheila offered to pick up the divers down by Three Rivers, and by the time she returned, the afternoon sun was trending toward twilight, casting a golden hue on the gray sheet of rock. The winds blowing in from the north were brisk and brutal. By tomorrow, the Glampist site would be a ruin, and most of the evidence would be gone.

Four divers carrying massive duffel bags climbed out of the helicopter—an older guy about Corrigan's age and his three young apprentices. They all had carrot-red hair and grass-green eyes, which made me think theirs was a family business. The team leader shook my hand and vowed to "get 'er done" before nightfall. He really seemed to mean it, too.

The team's expediency impressed me—in under ten minutes they were all in their wetsuits, thermal caps, fins, and dive masks. I gave them some direction on where to search, starting with the deep water directly beneath the Glampist campsite. They waded in one after the other, moving in perfect sync. And as their heads went down, their fins came up, and with a choreographed precision they disappeared under the still waters.

Fifteen minutes in, I heard a shout.

* * *

The night sky was lit by stars and spotlights, shining their light on Precipice's placid waters. I watched as the four divers coaxed a body to shore, its long blonde hair fanning the surface in ghoulish fashion. Corrigan and Huxley wore somber faces, echoing my own feelings about the situation. I had been hoping for a better outcome.

The divers laid the body out on a shelf of granite, shielded from the wind by Sheila's chopper and the wall of rock. Huxley and I made our way over to the site, careful to avoid any loose rock that might pitch us over the edge. I wasn't dressed for cold water immersion.

The deceased was a young woman, somewhere in her mid- to late-twenties. Her features were small and symmetric, her frame quite slim. She was wearing a pink parka, black ski pants, and nice hiking boots with very little sign of wear. Her beauty had dimmed in death, but it was still there, plastered on her gray skin like a mask. It was impossible to tell how long she'd been in the water; her body was so well-preserved that it could have been hours, or it could have been days. We would need the medical examiner to give us a better estimate.

Huxley crouched down next to me. "Poor lady," he said.

"Yes," I said. "It's not what I was hoping for."

I'd read up on a few water-related ISB investigations and had learned enough to know that alpine lakes had their hidden dangers. For one, they were cold. Precipice Lake was still frozen where the cliff cast its shadow on the water. Cliff jumping at this time of year could kill any number of ways—trauma, thermal shock, hypothermia. It didn't look like our victim had gone over the edge intentionally, not with all her clothes on and with ice at the bottom. I wondered if drugs or alcohol had played a role.

"You seem captivated by the top of that ridge there," Huxley said, remarking on the cliff adjacent to the Glampist site.

I said, "It's quite a drop."

"Sure is," he agreed. "About a hundred feet."

"Survivable, though, in ideal conditions."

"I wouldn't say these are ideal conditions."

"No," I said. "Not with ice on the lake, plus she's got her boots on. I don't think anyone in their right mind would jump off a cliff into a lake that's partially frozen."

"Unless she *wasn't* in her right mind."

"That's a possibility. The toxicology report will tell us for sure."

Corrigan walked over with his satellite phone in one hand and a banana in the other, which he peeled all the way down to the stem before taking a bite. "SAR's goin' up toward Lost Canyon and the Big Five Lakes at first light," he said. "But I'm not sure I see the point in sendin' a team all the way out there if we've got a dead body right here."

"We've got *one* dead body," I said. "And we have reason to believe she wasn't out here alone. We have a men's T-shirt, the receipt for two bagels, a queen-sized bed . . ."

"So she's got a boyfriend," Corrigan said. "No surprise there. She was a pretty gal."

"Maybe it's a boyfriend, or maybe it's somebody else. The point is, we need to find him."

"Could be he's in the lake there." Corrigan folded up his banana peel and put it in his pocket. If he was anything like me, he'd remember the banana peel a week later when his parka started to stink. I'd learned that lesson the hard way.

As for the victim, my search of her pockets hadn't yielded much—two Luna bars and a polished gray rock that she must have been holding onto as a souvenir. There was no cell phone, no driver's license, and no other hints as to her identity. All we had was the receipt with the customer's name: Tatum—which seemed to fit, for some reason, but I couldn't say why.

I stood up and stripped off my gloves, the wind whipping my face as I tucked my head against the assault. Chicago was the Windy City, but this was something else. I hadn't banked on being out here after dark either.

"You two should head back to the ranger station," Corrigan said. "Part of the dive team's taking the chopper down in ten minutes."

Huxley looked at me for direction. I knew he'd follow my lead, and right now my gut was telling me to get back up on that ridge for one more look, especially now that we had a body. I might not get another chance.

"I'll camp out here for the night," I said, knowing full well that I wasn't really equipped for such a venture, but I wasn't about to admit that to these rangers.

"You don't have the gear for that, Agent Harland," Corrigan said. "It's gonna dip into the teens tonight."

"I can handle myself out here, Mr. Corrigan."

"Look, there's stubborn and there's stupid. Don't be stupid." Corrigan stripped off his parka and handed it to Huxley. "Don't let Agent Harland freeze to death up here tonight. It makes us all look bad."

I had a thing about people bigger and stronger than me thinking they knew best. That misplaced paternalism never went down easy. Through gritted teeth, I said, "Mr. Corrigan—"

"Huxley's stayin' up here with you, and that's the end of it."

I looked at Huxley, who had the decency to meet my gaze but said nothing. He was still holding a parka that would have fit two of me.

As Corrigan made his way toward the chopper, I marched off toward the campsite. "I can handle myself, you know," I said over my shoulder to Huxley.

"I hear ya, boss," he said. "But I'm with the chief on this one—it's not a great night to be out here. We can hitch a ride back up with Sheila at first light tomorrow."

A part of me—the sensible part, really—knew that he was right. I wasn't packed for an overnight excursion in subfreezing temperatures—didn't have the right clothes, gear, or food. I silently cursed myself for such an amateur mistake. There had been a time, not all that long ago, when I'd relished the opportunity to pack my gear and hit the trail with confidence. But that was before I'd broken my back, not to mention my mental fortitude.

"We're on a time line," I said. "I want to do a detailed survey of that entire ridge, not to mention where she went in."

Huxley tilted his face toward the sky. "Aside from the cold—which will only get worse, let me tell you—the weather's looking good for tonight. The wind's supposed to die down." Looking me in the eye again, he said, "I'm not telling you what to do, Agent Harland—I'm really not. It's just—it's part of the job, you know. Your safety's my priority."

I wondered, though, if he would have said the same thing to an ISB agent with a decade's worth of experience. Then again, there was stubborn and there was stupid, as Corrigan had said. I wasn't going to become the laughingstock of the Park Service by calling for a rescue at three AM—which was entirely possible, much as I hated to admit it.

"Fine," I said. "But I want to be back up here at first light."

"You got it, boss," Huxley said with a grin.

As we headed off toward the chopper, I tried to convince myself that the lake would still be there tomorrow—and the ridge, too, although the dust and rocks on it would be different.

It would *all* be different, and there was nothing I could do about it.

CHAPTER

7

THERE WERE THREE seats left on the helicopter, which was
good news because it meant I wouldn't have to ask one of
the divers to give up his seat for Ollie. With a little help from
Huxley, I strapped my dog into his seat. I was starting to realize
there were a lot of things my ISB training hadn't covered. Worse,
there was no doubt it showed. Compared to these rangers, I was
greener than the carpet on a miniature golf course.

When we got back to the station, park rangers and volunteers were everywhere, organizing their gear and chatting about
the conditions out on the trail. Some of them feasted on burri-
tos and beers while they planned their route. The mood wasn't
somber, as I'd expected, but hopeful. Everyone was anxious to
get out on the trail and find our missing glamper.

Not me, though—not right then. I'd hoped to catch some
sleep in the ranger station, but that wasn't happening tonight.
My only other option was the truck.

"Sorry, bud," I murmured to Ollie. "It's just for one night."

Huxley materialized behind me with two Cokes in one
hand and a slice of pizza in the other. "What's just for one
night?"

"Oh—well. The motel." I bit my lip, annoyed at myself for
lying to him for no good reason. "Actually, we'll probably just
bed down in my truck for the night."

"That sounds fairly unpleasant."

"It won't be so bad."

"Uh-huh." His Coke can made a *pfft* sound as he opened it. "Look, I've, uh—maybe this isn't kosher, who knows, but I've got a sweet cabin about a mile down the road. Or you can do the truck thing."

"Oh." I scrambled for something to say. Huxley was a nice guy and all, but I wasn't so sure about spending the night at his place. "You know, that's okay. Maybe the couch will open up in Corrigan's office."

"You can't sleep here, Harland. These guys can get rowdy, lemme tell you."

One of the rangers had just blown up the microwave with his burrito wrapped in tinfoil. I watched him attempt to inspect the circuit board. *"Shit damn,"* he yelled, and his buddies laughed. Not a good sign.

"I can make my own arrangements, thanks."

"Look, you can have the bedroom." He offered me the other can of Coke while he gulped his down. "Hell, I can sleep in the shed out back if that'd make you more comfortable. I've got a sleeping bag in there anyway." He picked up a pepperoni that had fallen on the ground and dusted it off on his pants. "Anyway, just wanted to extend the offer."

"Don't make this a thing, Filly," my mother would have said. *"It's just one night."* Huxley wasn't a creeper, in any case. I didn't get that vibe from him at all. The problem, really, was me. I didn't like getting to know the rangers any more than necessary. For the most part, they were young dudes with an attitude, and a lot of them were single. I didn't need that kind of drama.

But at the same time, I didn't want to sleep in my truck. I was tired of being on the road, and so was Ollie. He needed a comfortable place to rest, and I needed a bed to sleep in. There was always the chance we'd have to hike back up to Precipice Lake tomorrow, and I couldn't do that on just a few hours' sleep.

"All right," I said. "What's the address?"

* * *

Huxley's cabin was off the main road, an unfathomably dark, winding ride through dense forest that felt like something out

of a horror movie. It was only a twenty-minute drive to his property, but it may as well have been hours. Ollie poked his head
out the open window, which made the heater irrelevant as the
bitter mountain air filled the cab. I wanted to keep him happy,
though. It wasn't like he had a choice in any of this.

I relaxed a little when Huxley's cabin came into view. Tea
lights hung from the trees out front, giving it a homey, welcom-
ing feel—not at all dark and deadly like the woods that surrounded it. Huxley also apparently had a thing for garden
gnomes and reflecting balls, which lined the narrow path leading from the driveway to the front porch.

He met us out front. "I like those balls," I said.

He laughed. "My mom loved 'em. They're ugly as sin, aren't
they?"

As he showed me the rest of his lawn ornaments, Huxley
struck me as a bit of a contradiction, the sentimental type who
also happened to work a supremely macho job. I wondered what
his story was—and there *was* a story, surely, and not just the one
his background check had spat out. According to my research—
conducted mostly while sitting on the toilet back at the ranger
station—he had indeed left the Navy about a year prior, but
even my contact at the FBI couldn't shed any light on why. His
service record was exemplary. His military personnel file was
mostly classified, but there were no red flags. He could have had
a prestigious career in Special Forces if he'd wanted it, but
instead he'd applied for an entry-level job in the Park Service. It
was quite a change of pace for a decorated Navy SEAL.

I wanted to ask Huxley about all that, but I worried about
him turning the tables back on me. I might feel compelled to
give an honest answer, which would make things awkward
between us for the rest of our time together. So I kept quiet.

"You travel light," he remarked as I grabbed my backpack
out of the trunk. It was the first purchase I'd made as an ISB
agent, and one that had required weeks of online research.
There just weren't that many packs suitable for a very petite
woman with serious back problems. I'd even asked a guy at REI
about packs for people with chronic back injuries, and he'd
looked at me like, *"Lady, TUMI is across the street."*

But here I was, proud of my emerald-green pack and determined to wear it like a natural. Huxley watched me sling it over my shoulder, but it unfortunately slung too far and landed on the ground with a thud. My face felt like it caught fire as he bent down to pick it up.

"Don't worry—I've got it," he said. With a casual glance over his shoulder, he grasped my pack with one hand and hauled it up to the front porch.

Ollie chased after us with his tongue lolling out of his mouth, discharging a day's worth of energy as we climbed the porch steps. Like me, Ollie thrived on the thrill of discovery, even if it was something as mundane as a half-eaten cookie under the couch. He would've made an excellent police dog, but I liked him better as my companion.

"Well, here we are." Huxley turned the key in the lock and pushed open the door. "What do you think?"

Falling in step behind him, I absorbed the coziness of the space—the hardwood floors, the walls made of oak, the tidy living room and functional kitchen. It had a pleasant smell, like spiced chai. The shelves were lined with plenty of dusty paperback books, but there was no television. "It's nice," I said. "I'm jealous."

"I thought you ISB folk all had lakeside cabins in Tahoe or wherever."

"Not me," I said. "I rent a place in Reno."

"Big gambler, eh?" He met my gaze with a sarcastic gleam in his eye.

"It was the pragmatic choice," I said with a shrug. "Temporary duty assignments are the rule in ISB—six months, twelve months. Figured Reno was pretty centrally located for a California assignment."

"Did you request California?"

"No. Alaska, actually."

He put my backpack on the ground and studied me for a moment. "Alaska, eh? Sounds like a vacation compared to this tourist trap."

I couldn't help but smile. "Yup."

He walked into the kitchen—which was only about five paces away from the front door—turned on the tap, and filled two glasses of water. He handed one to me. "Well, *before* Sequoia turned into a tourist trap, it was actually pretty far off the grid," Huxley said. "My grandfather bought this land after his time in the Korean War. He built it himself, lived on his own out here for a couple of years, then leased it to some hunters when he moved East. He came back later in life, though, and enjoyed it for a while before he burned it to the ground."

I wasn't sure I'd heard him right. "He did what?"

"It wasn't intentional. His mind was pretty much gone by then. He nodded off with his pipe in his mouth."

"I'm sorry," I said.

Huxley shrugged. "It's how he wanted to go. Out here all alone, nothing but nature to keep him company. We were just glad it happened in winter. A cabin fire like that in summer can burn millions of acres. I'm sure you've seen your share of forest fires."

"Not up close," I said. "Knock on wood."

"Pun intended?"

"Sure," I said, which made him smile.

"Anyway, I rebuilt it after college. I modernized it a little, as you can see."

"Where did you go to college?"

"Harvard."

"Really?"

"No," he said with a snort. "Hell no. I never cracked a book in high school. The only place that would take me was my local CC. Got my degree from Boise State eventually, though."

"What was your major?" I asked, expecting to hear something far afield of my major, which was political science. He didn't seem like the political type at all, even for a combat veteran. At least, he hadn't made any remarks to that effect.

"Raptor biology."

"Very funny."

He snickered. "Okay, fine. I majored in math. But there really is a raptor biology degree at Boise State. I dated a girl who was so obsessed with birds of prey that she used to mimic their mating calls right as we were—"

"Yeah, yeah," I said. "I got it."

He was still chuckling as he walked into the living room, which was adorned with photographs of the natural world. I didn't have to ask who had taken them. They were all imbued with the same reverence for his subject matter that had colored his iPhone photos.

"So, why math?" I asked him. "From what I hear, that's a pretty tough major."

"You sound skeptical," he said with a laugh.

"Well, no—I, er, I didn't mean—"

"Relax, boss. I'm kidding. Here's the thing. I love numbers—not the application of it so much, but straight-up numbers. I love how you can have this super-complicated equation, and there's only one answer to it. It's all about figuring out how to get there."

"Like the Hodge conjecture."

His eyes lit up. "*Exactly* like the Hodge conjecture. You know it?"

"I mean, I googled it."

"Hey, that's something. I'll get you into it, don't worry."

While we talked, I peered at a framed photo of a desolate landscape—Afghanistan, maybe. There was something distinctly foreign about it, as if the photographer himself were trying to keep his distance from the place. "Are you, um, trying to solve it?" I asked him.

"Always."

I couldn't tell if he was being serious or not. "Well, I guess you could say that solving crimes is a lot like working through a complicated equation."

After a moment's thought, he nodded. I considered the possibility that rangering was just a temporary gig for him, as it was for a lot of guys his age, especially the ones transitioning from military life. The wilderness was a natural sanctuary for people accustomed to war, and to all the horrible things that war entailed. If Huxley had been traumatized by his experiences there he sure didn't show it, but that didn't mean he wasn't working through his own demons. In that way, perhaps, we had something in common.

He showed me to the cabin's lone bedroom, which was small but well appointed. A full-sized bed covered in a homespun quilt served as its main fixture, and there was an antique desk by the window. To my relief, he kept the room nice and warm—no pesky drafts seeping through the panes or the floorboards. I immediately felt at home.

"I've just got to change the sheets and all," he said, even though the bed could have won a competition for tidiness. "I wasn't expecting company."

"Don't go to any trouble—"

"It's no trouble. Oh, and there's beef stew in the fridge—made it last night. Help yourself."

With Ollie at my heels, I took the hint and went to the kitchen to fix myself some stew. My dog waited patiently while I rummaged through the refrigerator and tried to work the microwave. Huxley was humming as he worked in the bedroom—stripping the bed, changing the sheets, even switching out the duvet cover. I had long since given up on trying to figure out duvet covers, but Huxley changed the damn thing in under ten seconds. His domestic sensibility surprised me—and shamed me a little, too, if I was being honest. Kevin used to refer to my cooking skills as abominable, my vacuuming efforts laughable. And folding laundry was more like sorting laundry in our apartment—a pile here, another pile there. *Have you seen my Loyola sweatshirt?* Kevin would ask, and I'd direct him to pile four. It wasn't that I was a slob. I just didn't have the mental bandwidth for housewifery.

Five minutes later, he strode into the kitchen. "There's plenty of that stew to go around," he said. "I hope you gave some to your friend here."

"Are you sure?"

"Of course." He spooned some leftovers out of the pot and set them out for Ollie. "He's a good dog for your line of work," he said. "You take him on the road a lot?"

I nodded, even though we both knew I'd only been on the road a week, technically. "He loves the outdoors."

"Betta did, too."

He had mentioned her twice now. I decided it would be worse to avoid the obvious question than to pose it head-on. "How did she die?"

When he didn't answer right away, I wondered if I'd made the wrong call. He reached for a ladybug-themed salt shaker and seasoned his stew with it. "It was my fault," he said.

Somehow I doubted that, but I wasn't going to say so.

He took a breath, put the salt shaker down. His eyes were a rueful shade of green. "She got shot," he said.

"Out here?"

He nodded. "We were out on the trail for a weekend hike." He set the pot aside and gazed distractedly at its contents. "Some kids were out there with their dads' guns—shooting stuff, having fun. It was a freak accident kind of thing."

"But if those kids weren't supposed to be there—"

"They weren't," he said. "I mean, yeah, I talked to them, and they got the message. What else are you gonna do?"

My stomach clenched as he painted the picture of Betta's violent end. It was hard for me to talk about loss. It wasn't fair, really, since I encountered it all the time in my line of work, but it was always easier when it was someone else. When it came to me and my life, I just couldn't go there—with anyone. A total of six mental health professionals at the FBI had given up on me—or maybe I had given up on them. Their timetable for grief just didn't work for me.

Huxley asked, "Are you going to tell Glampist what we found?"

"I will, but I'm not sure it'll make a difference."

"What do you mean?"

I reached for the other ladybug shaker. "They won't give me anything without a warrant."

"Why not?"

"Discretion is king, Huxley. That's what they're all about."

"But we've got a dead body right under their campsite."

"I know," I said. "But you'd be surprised how uncooperative people can be when it comes to their reputation. A company like Glampist doesn't want to get caught up in an investigation like this, especially given their clientele."

Huxley spooned a second helping of stew into Ollie's bowl because my dog, bless him, had polished off the first. "Sounds like a waste of everyone's time, then," he said. "If it were me, I'd haul 'em into court."

"That's always an option." I snagged a piece of oven-warmed cornbread that Huxley had set out on the table to complete the meal. "At least Corrigan was able to get the name of the guy that set up the campsite," I said.

"Who? I might know him."

Since my phone was in the other room, I had to think for a minute. "Sinclair, I think it was."

"Oh yeah." Huxley layered his cornbread with stew. "I know the Sinclairs—Ian and his brother Ash. They live down in Three Rivers."

"How do you know them?"

Huxley finished off his milk and poured himself another glass. "They're around a lot—you get to know the locals. Ian's ex-Army; he's got a wife, two kids. Works mostly odd jobs. Nice guy, though." He paused. "Ash is different. He's whip-smart, but a total jerk. Last I heard, he was living with Ian and his family in a trailer just outside of town. Ian's wife usually kicks him out after a while, then he comes back. The cycle repeats. It's a weird dynamic there."

"We should talk to them."

"When?"

"As soon as possible."

Huxley nodded. "I'll call Ian right now, see if they're around."

My parents had always forbidden my siblings and me from calling anyone after nine o'clock in the evening because they believed that everyone on the planet went to bed at that hour, but Huxley clearly didn't subscribe to that rule book. He walked over to the kitchen sink and flipped through a tattered notebook, and then he picked up the phone and dialed. It only took a moment for someone to answer.

"Oh hi, Grace, it's Hux," he said. "How are ya?"

I listened to Huxley's side of the brief exchange. His landline didn't have a speaker capability, and cell phone service was scarce out here. It seemed that Ian wasn't home at the moment. There was no mention of Ash.

After he'd hung up, I asked, "Well?"

"Good news is they're both up in Sequoia right now, working on a house not far from here. I bet we can track 'em down tomorrow."

"Great," I said. "Thanks for making that happen."

"What's the plan for tomorrow, by the way?"

"The plan is A, to get back up to Precipice and figure out how exactly our victim ended up in that lake." I spooned the last bit of stew into my mouth and chewed slowly. "And B, track down whoever was wearing a men's medium shirt."

"Do you think he's in the lake, too?"

"It would almost make more sense if he is."

"Yeah," he said with a nod. "A drunken accident."

"That's what I'm thinking—or maybe a rescue gone wrong kind of thing. You know—the girl goes in the water, the guy goes in after her and drowns."

"Yep," Huxley said. "I've seen that happen."

As a ranger, Huxley would have been well acquainted with wilderness rescues. I had heard from my ISB colleagues that SAR could either be an asset or a liability, depending on the national park. In Yosemite, YOSAR was an elite group. But that wasn't the case for most national parks. The volunteers could be hit-or-miss.

"What's SAR like up here?" I asked.

"It's small this time of year," Huxley said. "You've got your year-round operational staff plus volunteers, but it takes some effort to mobilize."

"I hear that's the case anywhere in April."

He shrugged. "Yeah. I guess." He put his fork down and met my eyes. "You must have a theory about all this. It's not every day you find a dead body in an alpine lake, right?"

I said, "No, it's not every day."

"Well?" Huxley pressed.

"We've got to find the friend, boyfriend—whoever was camping with her. He's key. And we need to ID the body we found as soon as possible."

"Will that be hard?" he asked. "With DNA technology and all that, I mean?"

"It won't be if someone reports her missing."

Huxley asked if I was interested in seconds before gathering up the plates and carting them over to the sink. "Maybe the Woodsman killed her and her boyfriend," he said over his shoulder. "Or he killed her and chased the other guy into the woods."

"That's another way to go with it. But it sounds like the Woodsman is a menace, not a killer. Corrigan seemed to feel that way, anyway."

Huxley shrugged. "He's not all that concerned about some nutcase that messes with people—probably even respects 'em, to be honest. He hates tourists."

"I noticed."

"I mean, not *all* tourists, but in his opinion there's been a generational shift. He feels like the younger folk don't care about the land."

"*We're* younger folk."

"Yep, and he's not all that fond of me either," he said with a smirk.

"Can't see why," I said, which made him laugh. Huxley could take a joke, I'd give him that. I was used to being around people in law enforcement who took themselves way too seriously, and those types got old fast.

To fill the lull in the conversation, I buttered up the last piece of cornbread. I had to admit, Huxley had impressed me so far—he was organized, attentive, trusted his gut. I liked that his cabin was clean, because I'd seen field offices that were a complete disaster, and those guys were never fun to work with. I liked that he could cook; it meant he could fend for himself. And I liked that he loved his dog, because any park ranger that hated dogs was probably a sociopath.

Still, the guy had a Wild West feel about him that made me nervous, and his sheer physicality could make a witness nervous if we ever managed to find one. Then there was his military history. While his Navy SEAL background certainly spoke to his competence and abilities, I was worried he might question ISB protocol and my role as his superior. But then again, this was all speculation based on past experience.

"I know it's early," I said, having finished off two bowls of stew and cornbread. "But I want to be rested for tomorrow—gonna call it a night after I do the dishes."

"No problem, boss." He flinched. "Sorry, I don't mean to keep calling you boss."

I studied him for a moment, trying to read the look in his eyes as he glanced down at the table. Huxley was the forthright type, I'd learned, but right then he seemed unsure. "I don't mind, really," I said. "But it does make me wonder."

"Wonder about what?"

I put my hands on the table and considered my next question carefully. "Are you happy as a ranger?"

He looked up, a question in his eyes.

I said, "It just feels to me like you enjoy the investigative side of things."

"I do."

I nodded. "Well. I appreciate your help with this one."

"Not a problem. It's my job."

"Rangers have a lot of jobs. Being involved in a federal investigation isn't necessarily one of them."

"I'm not your typical ranger then, I guess."

The truth was, I wasn't in the position to define a "typical ranger" after one week on the job. All I knew was that Huxley had done solid work from the jump—which was critical, really, because so much of an ISB agent's success depended on the local park rangers. For one thing, they were always the first on the scene, so they had to know how to conduct a preliminary investigation. In some cases, they were called to testify as witnesses in court. On top of all that, they played an essential role in search-and-rescue and recovery missions. All in all, having a ranger like Huxley in my corner felt like a tremendous stroke of luck.

"Let me tackle the dishes," he said.

"No, no, you've done enough. Really."

"Come on, boss." Realizing his mistake, he shook his head. "Ah well. *Boss* it is."

"It's fine, Hux," I said, reddening at my own slip. At this point, I didn't think it was worth the trouble to correct myself. Everyone else called him Hux. It was just his name—not a nickname, not a pet name, not anything of the sort.

After I was done with the dishes, I headed off to bed. *His* bed. In retrospect, of course I should have taken the couch, but my back hurt from the long drive—an old injury wrapped in an old memory, the kind of thing you resigned yourself to after three major surgeries and years of therapy, both physical and psychological. The surgeries had fixed my back, but the therapy hadn't done a damn thing for my psyche.

Maybe that was about to change.

8

T HE CALL CAME at six AM, the landline phone's shallow ring
reverberating throughout the cabin like an alarm. It jarred
me awake, shattering a dream that lingered momentarily before
fading into the same emotional hangover that plagued me most
mornings. A strong cup of coffee always helped to banish the
fog and set me straight again—that, and some fresh air.

Hux called out, "Sorry—that's my landline. I'll get it."

Ollie didn't usually sleep in bed with me, but he shuffled a
little closer and rested his chin on my pillow. I looked into his
wolfish eyes and wondered what he thought about this whole
arrangement. He probably thought it odd.

"Hello?" I heard Hux say.

I opened the bedroom door to listen in. What followed was
easy enough to piece together: Corrigan was calling about some
new information that had come into the station via telephone
that morning. Hux took notes on a pad while I put on a sweatshirt and a pair of leggings. After he'd hung up, I walked out to
the kitchen. "What's up?" I asked him.

His hair was a wild mess, his flannel pajama pants sagging
a bit on his hips. I tried to look elsewhere, but there was no
denying Hux's rugged sex appeal.

"Corrigan got a call from someone in L.A. about a missing
person."

Now *this* was news. "Who called?"

"He wouldn't say. He wants us down at the station right now."

"Great, let's go."

It took me ten minutes to pack my things and prepare some breakfast for me and Ollie. Hux had a more chaotic morning routine—he downed a towering glass of orange juice, popped some bread in the toaster, washed his dishes. We took turns in the bathroom, each of us taking a frigid military shower that was under sixty seconds, since the water heater didn't have time to heat up. While I toweled off, I noticed his preferred brands of soap (Dove), shampoo (something nicer than you'd expect for a guy that lived out in the woods, but not so nice that it made me wonder about a secret hair obsession), and deodorant (a few varieties; no real allegiance there). He had a toothbrush that looked new and toothpaste that made your tongue burn. The toilet paper was ultra-soft. It was the reading materials, though, that told me the most about him. Hux had crime manuals, detective novels, and even a workbook called *Master the Special Agent Exam* stacked knee-high on the floor. That last one had some Post-it notes marking the pages.

It was endearing, in a way. Had Hux simply forgotten to clear them out of here, or had he wanted me to see evidence of his interest in crime scene investigations? Either way, I wasn't going to say anything about it. If he wanted to talk about ISB, I'd wait for him to bring it up.

He came out of the bedroom with his hair soaking wet and his shirt hastily buttoned, looking every bit like he belonged at a *GQ* shoot. Except, maybe, for the park ranger's uniform—but even those dowdy green khakis looked pretty good on him.

"Ready, boss?" he asked.

And with that, we were out the door. The air was crisp and cold, with a light wind that made the hairs on my bare neck stand on end. I'd always prided myself on my ability to dress for the weather in Chicago, but the Sierras were a different story. After a week here, I'd learned that it could be numbingly frigid at dawn and sweltering by midday. My answer to that was layers—many, many layers. I was especially devoted to my long underwear.

Deciding at the last minute to carpool, we piled into my truck and drove down to Mineral King with the early dawn's tepid light guiding our way. Hux was quiet. I kept both hands on the wheel and focused on the road as it snaked through dense forest.

We parked right out front since there were no other cars in the lot. It was early, after all, and the trailhead was a quarter mile up the road. This early in the morning, the small log cabin radiated a homey warmth, with wisps of silver smoke leaching from the chimney into the night sky. Somewhere in the distance, a hawk shrieked its wake-up call. The frost on the ground crunched underfoot as we made our way up the steps.

Corrigan met us out front, smelling like a masculine mix of cologne and shaving cream. It was too much for my taste—nothing subtle about it. He ushered us inside with a gruff "good morning" and a wave of his hand.

We congregated around the folding table in the break room. I took my phone out, prepared to take notes if necessary, but something told me Corrigan didn't have all that much to report. In fact, he seemed a little uncertain—befuddled, even.

"Well?" I said. "Hux said someone called about a missing person."

Corrigan nodded. "A fella in Los Angeles got in touch with me—said he hasn't heard from his wife since Saturday. She was up here on an expedition of some sort."

The silence swelled. "With Glampist?" I asked.

"Her name's Tatum, so I'm thinkin' so." Corrigan pulled a yellowed notepad out of his pocket, which said "Messages" at the top and had space for caller, time, and other notable details. The notepad was straight out of the 1960s—literally—as the old block print had faded to a gray shadow. It looked like it had come off an ancient printing press. "The fella's name is Edwin Delancey. He called a couple minutes after oh-five-thirty this morning. The call was connected from a local precinct in Los Feliz in Los Angeles County."

Corrigan pronounced it "Lost Felix," which was linguistically incorrect in more ways than one, but so was its colloquial pronunciation, "las-FEE-lays." My sister lived in L.A., so I had some knowledge of the local neighborhoods. Los Feliz attracted the rich and famous, I knew that much. Hannah was always driving around its hilly streets, searching for celebrities out walking their dogs. I didn't have the heart to tell her that the mega-rich hired people to do that for them.

"Mr. Delancey said his wife was goin' camping in Sequoia over the weekend, but she was supposed to be back two days ago."

"When did he last see her?" I asked.

He scrutinized his notepad. "Friday morning."

"And he hasn't been able to reach her?"

"That's what I gathered."

Hux shot me a glance that, in my mind at least, echoed my own frustration. I desperately wished someone other than Corrigan had taken Mr. Delancey's call. This, here, was our first break in the case—and he'd compiled barely enough information to fill a Post-it note.

Then something dawned on me: *Delancey.* That name sounded familiar. "Wait a second," I said. "What's the wife's name again?"

Corrigan checked his notes. "Tatum Delancey."

I looked at Hux, who seemed as confused by my reaction as Corrigan was. "Tatum Delancey is an actress," I said. "She's fairly well-known."

"You mean Channing Tatum?" Hux asked. "'Cause, yeah, I've heard of him."

"No, I mean Tatum Delancey. It's a she."

"Oh." His face reddened.

"She stars in an HBO show called *Glenview*," I said. "It's about a third-grade teacher who's tasked with helping her students navigate the AI takeover." I searched for some sign of recognition on the men's faces but found none.

"The *what* takeover?" Corrigan asked.

Ignoring his question—because really, I didn't even know where to begin—I redirected his attention back to the call. "Did you record your conversation, by chance?" I asked.

"No, ma'am. We don't have that capability here."

"Right." I asked Hux, "Can you see what else you can find out about Tatum Delancey? I'm going to call Glampist and see if they can confirm that she was on the reservation. They might talk now that we've got a name."

Hux nodded. "You got it, boss."

I turned back to Corrigan. "What else did Mr. Delancey say?"

Corrigan gave me a stern look. "That's it."

"Can I see your notes?"

He pushed the flimsy piece of paper in my direction. Dust particles littered my fingers as I pried it off the table. His handwriting was meticulous, but the content was sparse. The caller was a man named Edwin Delancey. Under the Notes section, Corrigan had written the following: *Wife Tatum Delancey. Drove to Sequoia on Fri 5 April. Last contact Sat 6 April.* There was a callback number to a 626 area code.

On the bottom of the page, Corrigan had used military time to document the time of the call and its duration— 0515–0518. I wondered why Mr. Delancey had called at such an odd hour. Had he been up all night, worrying about his wife? Or had something else prompted him to call?

"No mention of a boyfriend or friend?" I asked.

"No, ma'am. All's he said was his wife went camping for the weekend."

"Without him?"

"I assume so, but he didn't come right out and say it."

I looked at Hux, who was trying to get my finnicky iPad to work. "What are your thoughts on expanding the search area?" I asked the chief ranger.

"I think it's premature," he said. "We don't even know who we're lookin' for."

He was right, of course, but we knew there was *someone* out there. We just didn't have his name. "I'm going to try Glampist again," I said. "Mind if I use your phone?"

He made a "help yourself" gesture, pointing me toward the landline bolted to the wall. Hux leaned back over his chair, one arm swinging free as he held up the iPad. "Hey, so, the famous Tatum Delancey is in fact married to a guy named Edwin."

Both their faces filled the screen. I recognized the woman immediately—not just from the show, but from yesterday's grim discovery up at the lake. It was definitely her.

"How old was she?" I asked.

"Twenty-eight."

"And him?"

"Forty-nine." He whistled. "I'd say he really went for it."

"Do they have kids?"

"He does. None between them, though. They were only married a year."

"What does he do?" I asked.

"He's a writer—his last project was a movie called *Fred Turk's Uncle Sleeps in My Attic*." He made a face. "It didn't do so hot."

While Hux scanned through Edwin Delancey's writing credits, I waited for someone to pick up at Glampist headquarters. Since it was off-hours, the call eventually went to an automated menu rather than a live person: "Press zero to speak to our twenty-four-hour-support services." Someone picked up as soon as I entered the number.

The voice that answered sounded caffeine powered. "Good morning, this is Jeremy with Glampist Concierge Services. How may I assist you today?"

"Hi Jeremy, this is Special Agent Harland with the Investigative Services Branch. I called yesterday about a campsite in Sequoia National Park—"

"Oh yes," he said, his voice tightening. I could still hear the smile in it, though, plastered on his face like a stiff coat of makeup. "I'm sorry, ma'am, but I'm not at liberty to divulge anything about our clients."

"Uh-huh. So, we received a report up here about a missing woman. I've got her name here and just wanted to see if you wouldn't mind cross-checking it with the clients you put up near Sawtooth Peak last Thursday."

"I'm sorry, ma'am. I really can't—"

"We've called you five times requesting information, so, you know, I'm losing patience. I need your client list, and I need it now."

He sighed. "I have to check with my manager."

"You do that."

The interlude that followed was classical music—modernized, catchy, like something you'd expect to hear coming through the speakers in a Tesla dealership. Too bad I wasn't in the market for a waterbed in the woods.

The music cut off abruptly. "Hello, this is Lucinda Wu, head of operations at Glampist." The woman sounded surprisingly alert for an early-morning call. "Is this Agent Harland?"

I put her on speaker to get Hux's take on her tone as well as her disposition. In my five years with the FBI's criminal investigation unit, I'd always worked my cases solo, but I wasn't opposed to soliciting outside opinions. As a SEAL, Hux had surely received some training on how to read people. I welcomed his input.

"Yes, it is. I'm calling about your campsite up near Precipice Lake."

"On what authority?"

"I'm with the Investigative Services Branch with the National Park Service. We're a federal law enforcement agency that investigates crimes that occur on national park lands, and right now we're investigating an accidental death in Sequoia National Park—specifically near one of your campsites."

There was a pause. "Where?"

"Precipice Lake."

"*In* the lake?"

"Yes."

"It sounds like a drowning, then. These things happen."

Her response took me aback—it was so retaliatory and matter-of-fact, like something you'd hear on a witness stand. There was no sympathy in her voice either.

"I'm not positing any theories at the moment," I said. "Now back to the names—"

"Our clients pay for discretion, Agent Harland," she bristled. "And as I'm sure you're aware, California has very strict privacy laws in place to enable that discretion."

"I understand that, Ms. Wu, but we're simply asking for your voluntary cooperation in this matter. If you're not willing to do that, then I'll get a court order."

There was another pause on the line, as I knew there would be. Maybe Wu didn't know that Tatum Delancey had made a reservation with her company, or maybe she did. But she wouldn't want the baggage that came with a missing celebrity. In some industries, there *was* such a thing as bad press, and Glampist didn't need it. All it took was one high-profile tragedy to scare people off from wilderness adventures for a good long while.

"I can't give you the name on the reservation," she said. "Because it sounds to me like one of our clients associated with it may still be alive, and as I said, we take the state's privacy laws very seriously."

"Ms. Wu, that doesn't change the fact that one of your clients is dead. I'm trying to figure out what happened to her."

"I'm sorry," she said. "If you want access to our records, you'll need a court order."

With that, she hung up. The silence that followed was almost painful. Wu had schooled me on privacy law in front of two rangers, and there was nothing I could do about it—not right then anyway. She was right in that California had some of the strictest privacy laws in the country, especially with regards to the living. I might have gotten somewhere if Tatum Delancey herself had made the reservation, but it was looking like her male partner had done so. If he was still alive, then Wu was right; she didn't have to disclose any information without a court order.

I asked Corrigan, "Is the helicopter available? I need to get back up there ASAP."

"Sheila's takin' a breather," he said. "She's been flyin' back and forth all night."

This was bad news—and judging by the look on Corrigan's face, it was about to get worse. "Is there another pilot that could take us up there?"

Hux looked at Corrigan. "What about Rod?" he asked.

"Rod had his gallbladder out last week," Corrigan said. "He's laid up."

I gazed at the cold pizza and a liter of Mountain Dew sitting on the table, the remnants of a busy night at the ranger station. The party was over, and we had nothing to show for it. I couldn't even get a *glamping* company to cooperate.

Also on the table were scraps of paper that had accumulated over the last twenty-four hours. While Hux and Corrigan discussed alternatives to the chopper, I used my phone to capture photos of all the pertinent ones and saved them to my file—now titled "Sequoia." I'd learned long ago not to rely on discardable materials for critical pieces of information.

"So what's the plan?" I asked.

"Corrigan's going to call Sheila one more time," he said, as Corrigan marched off with his satellite phone. I noticed he didn't like making calls with an audience.

"Great," I said. "While we wait, let's call Mr. Delancey."

"Now?"

"Right now." These notification calls weren't easy, and in fact, I much preferred to deliver bad news in person. But it had to be now. I couldn't risk calling Tatum Delancey's husband on the satellite phone while we were out the trail, only to lose our connection right before I had the chance to tell him what had happened.

"Here we go." I walked back to the phone and dialed the number.

The two of us sat around the table waiting for an answer. It came on the second ring.

"Hello?"

I took a breath, steeling myself for the conversation to come. "Hello, this is Special Agent Harland with the Investigative Services Branch in Sequoia National Park. Am I speaking with Edwin Delancey?"

"Yes, this is Edwin." He sounded wired—on caffeine, emotion. It was hard to tell. "What happened? Did you find her?"

I used to struggle with these calls—the emotions, the blame, the personal responsibility. But I'd learned over time to let all that go, and to allow the facts to speak for themselves. I could be compassionate while maintaining the professional boundaries that felt necessary.

"Are you driving, Mr. Delancey?"

"No. Why? Please just tell me."

"I'm very sorry to tell you that we recovered a body in Sequoia National Park," I said. "We strongly suspect it's your wife, Tatum."

He cleared his throat, a clamorous grunt that caught me off guard. Someone was talking in the background—his son, maybe, or another family member. This person sounded young, maybe in his early twenties. Edwin Delancey relayed the news to him while I stayed on the line. More silence followed, as somber as it was tense.

"Where?" he asked.

"We found her body in Precipice Lake, which is up in the Sequoia wilderness."

"She drowned?"

As soon as he spoke, voices erupted in the background. There was the young male voice from before and at least one other, also male. The argument was punctuated by a defiant "That's crazy, Dad!" which was immediately silenced by Edwin Delancey as he ordered everyone to be quiet so he could talk to the police. I didn't bother to correct him that I wasn't technically police.

"I can't say for certain, sir. We'll know more soon."

"Are you sure it's her?"

"We can't be one-hundred percent certain until you make the identification yourself, but we're confident that it's her, yes." I wasn't sure how to convey the fact that I'd recognized his wife without ever having met her before. "I know this is difficult, sir. I'm sorry."

He cleared his throat again, like he was preparing for a fresh barrage of questions. "I'd like to know who's in charge," he said. His accent was vaguely Kiwi, like maybe he'd been born there and raised in the States. I had no ear for music, but a decent one for accents.

"I am."

"And you're with the police up there?"

"No, I work for the Investigative Services Branch. We investigate crimes that occur within the U.S. National Park system."

"Yes, I understand all that," he said. "You're a glorified park ranger."

Somehow the guy had managed to insult both of us at once, but I reminded myself that this was probably the worst day of his life. As such, he deserved a little leeway. "No sir," I said. "I'm a federal agent. And I want you to know that we've got all our resources on hand. You have my word that I will do my utmost to uncover the truth about what happened to your wife."

The line went dead before I could arrange for another time for us to talk. Hux was looking at me, waiting for me to say something profound. Nothing came to mind. These conversations were always hard to interpret, but this one was stranger than most.

"Well," I said. "We should check on the chopper."

Right then, Corrigan walked back in the room. He saw the question on my face and said, "I'll try dispatch again, but it's lookin' like you may have to take it on foot. I'm sorry." The phone rang in the other room, and he walked back out again.

I didn't get the feeling he *was* sorry, though. These rangers specialized in physical work, and I'd barely covered a mile on easy trails. This was a test of sorts, and I wasn't sure how I felt about it. Corrigan was making me question my own abilities.

I asked Hux, "How fast can you get up there on foot?"

"To Precipice?" He thought for a moment. "It's a lot harder going up than it is coming down, but I could do it in twenty-four hours if the weather holds."

I unscrewed the bottle cap on the Mountain Dew and rolled it back and forth across the table, catching it right before it fell to the floor. Hux crossed his arms and leaned back, balancing on the two rear legs of his chair. I could feel him watching me.

"Here's the thing," I said. "I need to get back up there as soon as possible, but there's no way I can do it in twenty-four hours."

"Well, it just so happens I know a shortcut," Hux said.

"You do?" I asked, realizing before the words were out that he wasn't being serious. I felt my face go red—an intense, prickly heat that he had to have noticed.

"I've done that route a hundred times," Hux said. "I'll be your guide, your cheerleader—whatever you need me to be."

"I don't need a cheerleader. I need a helicopter."

"Look, you're fit, you're capable—you can do this."

I didn't think so, though. The massive map of the Sequoia wilderness behind Hux's head was taunting me. "Maybe you should go up on your own, and I'll wait until Sheila can fly me up there. I'll tell you exactly what you need to do—"

"No."

"No?"

He leaned forward and propped his elbows on the table. "Look, don't let Corrigan get in your head. It's a tough hike, yeah, but doable. Trust me."

His words caught me off guard because they reminded me of Kevin—always my cheerleader, pushing me to my limits. Kevin and I had traveled to some of the remotest places on Earth in search of adventure. Our trip to the Australian outback was supposed to be all of that and more, until suddenly, somehow, it had all gone wrong. That mistake—or rather, a series of mistakes—had leached the life out of me in Chicago. But that was then, and this was now. All I had to do was walk outside and put one foot in front of the other.

Besides, the alternative—staying here like a glorified spectator—was unthinkable. I couldn't stomach the thought of telling Corrigan that Hux was going out on his own while I waited for a personal escort. He'd think me soft, and word would get out. All the rangers in Sequoia would lose respect for me before they'd even met me. It would be hard—no, impossible—to rebuild my reputation.

I rose from the table. "Get your gear. We're heading out."

Hux slapped the table with glee. "Yes, ma'am," he said.

Now that the day had broken, volunteers from search and rescue were starting to filter in. Even though Corrigan spent most of his time sweeping the floors—the volunteers tracked in a lot of dirt—he brightened at the sight of old friends. It was the first time I'd seen the chief laugh; maybe he wasn't such a grinch after all.

Hux and I were getting our own supplies together—backpacks, water bottles, an improvised evidence collection kit—when Hux looked up and said, "Huh."

"What?"

"They're here."

"Who?" I followed his gaze to the reception area out front, which was occupied by three bruisers with barrel chests and scruffy faces. One was a teenager, and the other two looked about forty, although it was hard to tell with their thick beards and bushy eyebrows. Maybe it was their lack of gear, or maybe it was something else, but they didn't look like search and rescue volunteers.

"That's them," Hux said. "The Sinclairs."

CHAPTER

9

H ux walked over to the tall redhead in the middle and
greeted him with a handshake and a man hug. The other
two didn't even say hello; they just stood there with their hands
in their pockets. The oversized teenager stared at the floor while
the other man—with black hair and a square jaw—eyed me
suspiciously from across the room.

We assembled in the break room for a chat. In addition to
Ian, the redhead, there was Ian's older brother Ash, and Ash's
son, Zeke. Zeke's disdain for the law was obvious when he spotted a can of Bud Lite languishing on top of the refrigerator and
helped himself.

Despite the hubbub going on elsewhere in the ranger station, Corrigan barged in, wagging his finger. He growled at
Ash, "You owe me sixty-five bucks for those permits, son.
Don't make me drive down to your shithole trailer and collect
on it."

The big man shrugged. "You'll get your money, Chief."

Ian tried to diffuse the tension with a hearty laugh. "Well,
hey," he said. "Heard ya's found a body up in Precipice Lake."
He leaned back in his chair and propped his feet up on the
table. One sharp look from Corrigan was all it took to get his
boots back down on the floor.

"Where'd you hear that?" Hux asked.

"Oh, ya know—word gets 'round."

Corrigan walked over to the table and stood behind Ash. The older ranger glared at Zeke, who was slouched in his chair like he had no intention of ever getting up. As he sipped the Bud Lite, he used his thumb and forefinger to pop a pimple near his left nostril.

Hux said, "I defer to Agent Harland here."

"Agent, eh?" Ian asked, flashing me that same grin. "You ISB?"

"That's right. You're familiar with the Investigative Services Branch?"

"Oh yeah," he drawled. "I done work all over Cali 'fore I moved to Three Rivers five years ago. I got a wife, two kids. Needed a house and a yard and all that, ya know. But yep— 'fore that, I ran into ISB a few times."

"Not as a suspect, I hope," I said, which was meant as a joke, and to my relief, Ian laughed. Any hesitation there would have made me wonder.

"Nah," he said. "I just always seem to be in the wrong place at the wrong time. Even got called to testify at a trial once."

"What was the case?"

He thought for a moment. "I think a hunting-accident-gone-wrong kinda thing."

"Huh," I said, feeling the heat of Ash's gaze on the side of my head. Zeke let out a belch loud enough to wake any bears still hibernating in the vicinity.

While Corrigan cleared the pizza boxes from the day before, I asked Ian, "So are you familiar with a company called Glampist?"

"Oh yeah," he said. "We set up a camp for 'em last Tuesday."

"Thursday," Ash said, stunning everyone with his sudden participation in the conversation.

Ian looked at his brother. "Yep, that's right. Thursday."

"How long have you been working for them?" I asked.

Ian leaned even further back in his chair, nearly tipping it over. I could tell this was a guy whose brain didn't operate at lightning speed; it took him some time to get his thoughts in order. "I can't remember how I heard about 'em, but we started doin' some work for 'em last year. The pay's pretty good, and it's mostly off the books."

"Mostly?"

"We get a cash bonus on top of the minimum wage they pay me as a contractor."

"How much?"

"For a two-person campsite for a long weekend, which is kinda their standard package, we get a grand for the setup and another grand for the takedown."

"Each?"

"Nope, we split it. I'm the only one on the payroll, but they're fine with me havin' help. We get it done faster."

"And this was a two-person campsite? The one at Precipice Lake?"

He nodded. "Yep. One tent with a queen-sized bed. That's standard."

"What do you mean, 'standard'?"

"I mean they're all about romance, ya know? One tent, one bed—always. It's never a big party or a family or whatever. Couples only."

"I see." I wasn't sure how a company could possibly mandate a couples-only policy, but so far Glampist had surprised me in a number of ways. "So how does it work? You carry all the gear out to some designated location and set it up before the clients arrive?"

"They've got a copter that makes a supply drop near the campsite, and we haul it in from there. We set it up—takes a morning or so. The company gives us a map kinda thing that tells us what goes where—they're real particular."

Zeke tilted his face toward the ceiling to expel a series of burps. When that was done, he took his beer can and smashed it under his foot. Corrigan shuddered with fury.

I asked Zeke, "And how long have you been doing this kind of work, Zeke?"

He looked at me with his dead eyes, no light in them at all. "Dunno."

"Care to wager a guess?"

"He doesn't have to answer you," Ash said. "He's a minor."

A minor who drinks beer like a pro, I thought, but decided not to push it. Zeke put his elbows on the table and glanced at the clock on the wall.

"Fair enough," I said. "Look, we just want to know who the clients were, and the company won't give us any information. Now, I know you're not supposed to go through anyone's personal belongings—"

"No ma'am," Ian said. "That's for damn sure."

"But did you see anything with any names on it?" I wasn't about to reveal Tatum Delancey's name to these three, none of whom struck me as particularly trustworthy. One whiff of her celebrity and they'd be selling out their story to whoever came knocking.

Ian shook his head. "I ain't out there goin' through other people's shit," he said. "Don't wanna know, frankly. Like yeah, I know that gear's real expensive and you could sell it on Craigslist or whatever, but this here's a stable gig., and I ain't gonna mess with that."

"I understand that," I said. "I was just wondering if you happened to catch a name—"

"I did," Ash said.

Everyone at the table turned to look at him. Hux, in particular, glared at Ash with a startling intensity. I wondered if there was some bad blood between them, and decided that, yes, there absolutely was, but it hadn't affected his relationship with Ian, apparently. Maybe Ian was just too dim to pick up on it.

"What was it?" I asked.

"Delancey," he said.

"First name?"

"Delancey's all I saw. There was a tag on her suitcase."

"*Her* suitcase?" I asked. "How do you know it belonged to a woman?"

"'Cause it looked like it did."

I looked at Hux. "We didn't see any suitcases."

"Oh, they were there," Ian said. "We left 'em in the tent right next to the bed."

Which was interesting, if true, because they were gone now. There was no doubt in my mind about that. "Anything else you remember that could give us some insight into who was camping there?" I asked.

"Yeah, I found a box of condoms," Zeke said with a nasally laugh.

I deadpanned, "Pardon?"

He opened his mouth to say more, but Ash shot him a look that silenced him on the spot.

"Where?"

"I dunno," he mumbled.

"Try to think."

Ian said, "Look, Agent Harland, Ash and I been doin' this a long time, and the company stocks all kinda shit for their clients—condoms, lube, booze. It don't necessarily belong to the people that camp there. It's like the soap you get at motels. It comes with the room."

He smiled at me like, *"Sorry we can't be more helpful."* Ash maintained his cold stare. Zeke belched again, as he reached for the closest empty chair and put his feet up. Corrigan looked like he was on the verge of booting the kid out the door—literally. His right foot was about six inches from Zeke's chair.

I felt like I was losing control of this interview, even though it had just begun. "Can you tell me when you arrived at the campsite and when you left?" I asked.

"We got there at like noon," Ian said. "We finished up 'round six, then we camped there for the night—"

"That's not right," Ash said.

"I'm sorry?" I directed my question at Ash.

"We got there around ten, finished at two. Camped in the Big Five Lakes basin that night, and Columbine the next night. Drove back to Three Rivers on Saturday."

Zeke was still staring at the floor. Ian, too, was looking at his shoes, at the walls, at Corrigan's noisy refrigerator— anywhere but at his brother. I got the feeling they'd rehearsed a story on the way in, and Ian had blown it.

"So you were nowhere near Precipice Lake after Thursday?"

"That's right," Ash said.

"You never saw who was camping there?"

"No. We were told they were supposed to arrive on Friday."

Ian forced a laugh. "Trust me, they want us outta there before the payin' customers get there. The best service is supposed to be invisible and all that."

"Uh-huh," I said.

Ash placed his hands on the table and stood up. "Look, we've got another job to get to," he said. "Are we done here?"

"We're done when you pay up," Corrigan said, but Ash just snickered at the older ranger like he was amused by his vane attempts to intimidate him. Corrigan's ears were red. He looked ready to tackle the guy.

"We can wrap this up for now," I said in an effort to diffuse some tension. I distributed my business cards to the two brothers, fully expecting Ian to lose it on his way out and Ash to throw it in the trash. "But let's talk in a couple days."

Ian responded with an enthusiastic "Sure thing!" but Ash was already out the door. Zeke left his crushed, empty beer can on the table, like he expected the maid to come by and clean up after him. Neither one of them bothered with any parting words.

After they'd gone, Hux shook his head. "I just don't get it."

"Don't get what?"

"The loyalty there. I mean, I do get it—blood's thicker than water and all that, but Ash is a criminal. Ian needs to cut him loose."

"What's he done?"

"All kinds of things. Drug possession, armed robbery, assault—some serious crimes. He's smart, though, so he always manages to get out of jail time."

I made a mental note to run a background check on the Sinclairs—Ash first, but Ian too. "What about his brother?"

"What about him?"

"Ian's not a criminal?"

Hux sighed. "Ian's had his scrapes here and there, but he's a good guy. He was wounded in Iraq—traumatic brain injury while riding in a convoy. His wife said he came back a different person. And look, I hate Glampist, but it's the first time he's had a steady job in years."

"I understand that," I said. "It's just that—"

"Look, Harland, I'm telling you—leave Ian alone. He's been through enough." Hux rose from his chair and lifted his pack off the floor. In one swift motion, he got the hulking mass on his shoulders and fastened the straps around his chest and hips. Not once did he meet my gaze.

"Hux, he set up the campsite. I can't just leave him alone."

He blew out a breath, his frustration showing in a way that surprised me. It wasn't like Hux to lose his cool, but then again, it was no surprise that I'd touched a nerve. Ian was a former solider like Hux, and a wounded veteran to boot. Hux was looking out for his friend.

Which was fine, to a point. But it wasn't going to stop me from investigating the whole Sinclair clan. I would just have to tread carefully with Hux when it came to Ian.

"We should go," I said.

Hux nodded. He watched while I went to grab my brand-new, overstuffed backpack, which weighed at least twenty-five pounds. I managed to lift it off the ground without shrieking in pain, but Hux had to hold out a hand to keep me from falling over.

"I've got it," I said. "I don't need help."

"I know you don't," he said. "It's just that, well—your pack is bigger than you are."

"It's the smallest one they had."

"Did you try the kids' section?"

I looked up to see a smile on his face, which was a relief—no hard feelings, then. I couldn't imagine hiking all the way up to Precipice Lake with Hux mad at me. I was relying on his good humor to carry me through.

"All right, let's go," I said. "Before I change my mind."

* * *

Corrigan stopped us on the way out the door. "SAR's coverin' the Lost Canyon and High Sierra trails," he said. "They'll search Columbine first, all the way up to Precipice, and then they'll loop back through Eagle Scout Creek."

"How big is that search area?" I asked.

"Huge," Hux cut in. "Huge, huge, huge."

"Indeed it is," Corrigan muttered. "Good luck to ya's."

We said our goodbyes and headed out. Ollie was on the porch out front, playing fetch with the backpackers and volunteers who had congregated there. I took some comfort in the fact that Ollie loved the outdoors and would relish the chance to tackle a trek like this. It was better than being on the road, at least.

The sky was a robin's-egg blue, and it glimmered in the early morning sunshine. I inhaled deeply, willing the fresh air to work its magic on me. Once we were out the trail, I said to Hux, "Let's try Glampist one more time." I handed him my satellite phone.

"You sure?"

"Yep." It was a gamble, trying Glampist again so soon after my tense and admittedly futile conversation with Lucinda Wu. But I also knew it must have rattled her, maybe enough to get her to reconsider. Even if Tatum Delancey's name wasn't on the reservation, I suspected she knew *exactly* who was out there using her company's services.

"Hi," Hux said into the phone. "This is Ferdinand Huxley with the National Park Service." There was a pause. "Yep, that's the one. It's official—we're harassing you."

I couldn't hear the response, but whatever it was brought a smile to Hux's face. Ten seconds later he had Lucinda Wu on the line.

As it turned out, Hux had more than a few tricks in his toolbox. He took a casual tone with Lucinda Wu—casual, and almost flirty. There was a joke or two here, a bit of laughter there. It irked me a little, sure, but I knew it was mostly an act.

When Hux hung up, he had a smug smile on his face. "Colton Dodger," he said. "That's the name on the reservation."

"Are you sure we're talking about the right reservation?"

"One-hundred percent sure. She confirmed the coordinates."

Well, then. We had a name, at least. Unfortunately, it didn't have Delancey at the end of it, which could complicate things. "And that's the only name?"

"Yup."

"Huh," I said.

"The reservation was made online—Lucinda's gonna email it to me."

With only a hint of snark, I said. "Lucinda, huh?"

"She softened up quite a bit when I complimented her website."

"Uh-huh."

He caught the look on my face and laughed. "Are you jealous, Harland?"

"I mean, yes. I wish you'd compliment me on *my* website." I liked bantering with him. Hux seemed to grasp sarcasm, at least. A lot of guys didn't.

"I'll be sure to check out www.irritableagent.com," he said with a grin. "Now, don't get too excited about the reservation. It's just the guy's name, an email address for the receipt, and a Bitcoin account number for payment."

"He paid in Bitcoin?"

"Seems that way. And the email is just a bunch of random numbers and letters, not a personal account."

Another disappointment. I didn't try to hide it.

"But I did get the dates," Hux said. "The reservation was made for Friday, April fifth, to Monday, April eighth, which matches the time line Edwin Delancey gave us. Our man Dodger made a twelve-hundred-dollar deposit on March twenty-third, which covers the first night's lodging for two people. In fact, there is no single-occupancy option. The Sinclairs were right about that."

I processed this information as we walked, integrating these scattered details into a narrative that made sense. Colton Dodger sounded to me like a fictional name. It was possible that Tatum Delancey had used an alias to make the reservation, but my gut said no. The name was almost too unique. If I were trying to protect my identity, I'd have gone with something like Ann Smith—something that would have flown completely under the radar no matter who was processing my reservation. Colton Dodger struck me as a kind of joke, although for whom that joke was intended, I couldn't guess.

I wondered if Hux was having thoughts along the same lines. "Does that name sound familiar to you at all?" I asked him.

"Colton Dodger? I figured it was a fake name."

"Could it be a famous pen name or something like that?"

"Sorry, boss. I don't read obscure Westerns."

"Me neither."

Hux said, "He sounds like the porn star of all porn stars."

I chuckled at that. "So he *does* sound familiar."

"Nah, I'm not into cowboys," he said, with a gleam in his eye that I was getting to know well. "So assuming Colton Dodger is a real person and not some name Tatum Delancey made up, then who is he? A side piece?"

"Could be."

"The husband?"

"Not unless Edwin Delancey was lying to us about when he last saw his wife."

"So where was he, then?"

"We need to figure that out."

I slowed to a stop, gasping for air that felt woefully thin. It didn't help that Hux set a pace that was somewhere in the realm of otherworldly. Worse, I knew that to *him*, it probably felt slow. Glacial, even.

"You okay, boss?" Hux asked.

I gave him a thumbs-up to save my breath.

"All right," he said. "Just tell me if you need a breather."

I needed an oxygen tank and a mule, but I wasn't about to tell him that. Ollie bounded ahead of us as the forest thinned and the trail dissolved into loose rock. Whenever we hit a downhill portion of the trail, Hux would break into a modified run, only to stop abruptly when he remembered I was behind him. Ollie, for his part, seemed to relish the aggressive pace. He was used to my slow-and-steady mantra.

By the time we'd reached Lower Monarch Lake, my lungs had adjusted to the thinner air, but my lower back was on fire. When Hux wasn't looking, I unzipped the side pocket of my backpack and popped three ibuprofen, plus a Tylenol for good measure. Not wanting to trash my kidneys, I gulped down the water in my canteen while using a pump filter to replenish.

"How's it going back there?" Hux asked.

"Great."

"Want to stop for a snack?"

"No," I said. According to my watch, we'd only been on the trail for two hours. I was determined to push on until it was time to stop for lunch. That had always been my rule with Kevin—hit it hard in the morning when you're fresh so you can cut yourself some slack in the afternoon. It was all part of the mental game.

Hux led the way onto unmarked trails up on the pass. He was sure-footed, having covered this ground many times before. When we stopped for another water break, I asked if he'd had a chance to look into Tatum Delancey's background.

"Oh yeah," he said. "I did a mega search."

"What's a 'mega search'?"

"Eh. Learned a few tricks in college."

"You mean Google? Because if so, wow. Congratulations."

"You wish," he said, breaking into a smile. "Sorry to say it, Harland, but there's a lot more of you out there than what's on Google. And no, I didn't do a mega search on you. In case you were wondering."

"I wasn't." The truth was, I did kind of want to know what Hux had found out about me online, but I wasn't going to ask him. Most of what people needed to know about me was easily searchable. Despite my aversion to social media, my name was unique and therefore identifiable. Every so often I'd plug my name into Google, and to my ongoing dismay, that same article always popped up: *"Woman found in critical condition in Australia's Red Centre; husband still missing."* There was no hiding from it, even though I'd tried to get the link removed. The only real solution was to change my name, but so far, for some reason, I hadn't been able to bring myself to do that.

"So what'd you find?" I asked him.

"Well, Tatum Delancey was born Tatum Fail—you can see why she changed it—in Iowa. Her big break came last year on that HBO show you like so much."

"I didn't say I liked it."

"Look, Harland, I'm not one of these old school, anti-technology rangers. You can admit you like TV. I'm not gonna lose all respect for you."

I was quiet for a beat. "I like TV."

"*Thank* you," he said. "I feel like we're finally getting somewhere." He tackled a vertical portion of rock and extended a hand to help me up, which I accepted. I was past the point of trying to impress him. If we wanted to get to Precipice by tomorrow, we were going to have to do things his way.

"Anything else?" I asked.

"She liked the party scene. Dated a lot of guys, including some pretty high-profile ones."

"Makes sense. She was an attractive woman."

"I guess," he said with a shrug.

I let that one go. Hux was my colleague, and the best way to maintain a professional boundary was to steer clear of conversations like these. Of course a *tiny* part of me wanted to know what his type was, but all I could picture was the girl at Boise State shrieking like a hawk while Hux—*don't go there, Felicity.*

I said, "So we've got an older guy and his much younger wife, and she goes to Sequoia with a guy named Colton Dodger—or someone who simply used the name Colton Dodger to make the reservation, or maybe it was her own alias—to escape the city for a bit, maybe take their affair to the wilderness for a change of pace."

"So you're convinced she was having an affair?" He reached his arm around to grab some string cheese from his backpack. Hux had some manly qualities, but he also had some distinctly juvenile ones. I watched him evaluate two strips and start in on the thicker one.

"I think it's the most likely explanation."

"*Lex parsimoniae,*" he said.

"Pardon?"

"It's Latin for 'Occam's razor.'"

"So you're into math *and* Latin? Are you a real person?"

He grinned. "My mom loved Latin. It was kind of our thing."

"You're very strange."

He offered me an extra packet of string cheese, which I took because my stomach was roaring with hunger. We were still a ways from lunch, but I felt like I hadn't eaten in days. Another perk of the job: intense calorie burn.

When we reached the top of Sawtooth Pass at 11,800 feet, the sun was high in the sky, the daytime warmth tempered by a brisk wind. Sawtooth Peak loomed ahead of us, jagged and foreboding. The trail was dust and dirt and rock, every step a potential landmine. Hux took it in stride, but I had a hard time keeping up. The air was thin, the path treacherous. I was wearing too many layers, and yet somehow not enough. Sweat dripped into my eyes.

In the end, my abundance of caution didn't matter. I was climbing up the ridge, admiring the view of Columbine Lake and its surrounds, when my left foot flew out from under me. It happened fast—no warning at all. As my body tipped sideways, I was transported to that viciously hot day in Australia's Red Centre, the day Kevin and I ventured out to a place that dared to be explored. Not once had it crossed my mind that we might not return. Kevin was a checklist guy—always super prepared, no matter how mundane the task. I was similar. We never went anywhere without a plan. But that day, our plan had given way to that dangerous mix of bad luck and arrogance. *And here it was, happening again.*

But then—a hand, strong and firm, grasping my forearm. My knees never hit the ground. "Harland?" came the voice—Hux's voice. "Are you okay?"

I forced out a breath. "I—yes. I'm fine. Sorry about that."

"Sorry about what?"

Ollie sidled up to me, his body heat warming my leg as I reached down to scratch the soft fur behind his ears. I wondered if he could hear the thunderous beat of my heart.

"Let's rest a while here," Hux said. "I need a break."

"No you don't."

He slung his backpack off his shoulder and sat down on a rock. The look in his eyes was a challenge of sorts, an invitation for me to do the same.

"I didn't do a mega search on you, Harland." He reached for his canteen and took a swig. "But I did do a basic one."

"Good," I said, without missing a beat. "I did the same."

"And?"

"Pretty clean, I'd say. There was that one arrest in high school, though—simple assault, was it? I know the charges were dropped, but it was a bit of a red flag."

"Yep. The asshole hit my sister, so I hit him."

"You broke his jaw, Hux."

He shrugged. "I know this is where I'm supposed to say I'm sorry, but I'm not." He looked at me. "You know where the guy is now?"

"I do, actually." It helped having unrestricted access to the FBI's personnel files; every question about someone's dirty past deeds had an immediate answer. "He's serving a life sentence in Colorado."

"That's right. For beating his wife to death. So yeah, I wish I'd killed him when I had the chance. Hopefully somebody else in there'll do it for me."

"Do you consider yourself a violent person?"

He thought for a moment. "I mean—no, not really. But as a SEAL you're trained to kill people, so I can't say I'm totally opposed to violence. It has its place."

"So does clemency."

"So does justice."

He was right about that, in any case. For me, justice was the endgame that informed my choices as a law enforcement officer. I could have been a prosecutor to that end, maybe, but I relished all the things that went into an investigation: the mystery, the chase, the elements of surprise. And when it all came together at the end—making that arrest, telling the victim's family that we had someone in custody—*that* was what lit my fire. It was the same for my grandfather, this drive to catch the bad guys. He'd convinced me it was hereditary.

"Look, we should keep going," I said.

"You don't want to know what I found out about you?" Hux asked.

"No," I said. "It doesn't matter."

Except it did, of course, and we both knew it. I wasn't going to get into it with him, though; we were hardly more than acquaintances, and once this investigation was complete, I probably wouldn't see him again. It was easier to defer, deflect, decline. He didn't need to hear the details of my life story. Kevin had been missing and presumed dead for three years, and Hux had surely gathered that much from a Google search.

"All right, boss," he said.

And on we went toward Columbine Lake.

10

AFTER SEVEN EXHAUSTING hours on the trail, we stumbled onto the shores of Columbine Lake, the official gateway to the Sequoia backcountry. The lake itself sat in a bowl of granite, with hardly any vegetation at all except a smattering of moss, lichen, and grass on its shores. Sawtooth Peak, at 12,343 feet, cast its reflection on the lake's calm waters, almost as if nature had figured out a way to paint her own portrait. It was breathtaking.

It wasn't hard finding a scenic spot to break for lunch. We decided to make it quick, opting for granola bars and fruit and some kind of trail mix Hux called "Nutzilla." I checked my sat phone for messages. Nothing from Corrigan or ISB headquarters, which was good news. I had my hands full just trying to survive this expedition.

I tried to stay positive. So far, the weather had cooperated, but I couldn't say the same for my ailing body. My hamstrings were shredded from the uphill climb, and the twinges in my lower back were getting louder and angrier. The hand warmers tucked into my waistband weren't going to fix the problem, and ibuprofen only did so much. All I could do was put one foot in front of the other and hope that my mental fortitude was enough to get me through.

"It's still about six miles to Big Five Lakes," Hux said, as he packed up the remains of his lunch. "Do you want to rest a little while longer?"

"No," I said. "We should keep moving."

He scratched his neck. "You've, ah—you know, I can see you popping pills back there."

I looked up at him. "It's just Advil. I've got a bad back."

"How bad?"

As one orthopedist had put it, *catastrophic*—after that first surgery, there was talk that I might never walk again. But here I was, proving him wrong—sort of. After climbing over three thousand feet on rocky terrain, I was well on my way from walking to hobbling. Hux had noticed, clearly. I couldn't lie to him forever.

"I broke my back in a fall a few years ago," I said. "It set me back a bit."

He responded with a soft nod. "That sounds serious."

"It was and it wasn't. I'm not paralyzed, so there's that."

The article online had mentioned my being in critical condition, but thankfully it hadn't gone into detail about my injuries. If it had, I might never have gotten in the door at ISB. Ray, of course, had done his due diligence by requesting my medical records, but if he hadn't heard from my physical therapists about my dogged determination to get back to baseline, he never would have hired me. I knew this because he'd told me so, to my face.

"Are you sure you're up for this?" Hux asked.

"I'm fine. My spine is a bionic structure at this point, so it's not going to break. I just need to get past the mental barrier."

"Pain, you mean."

I nodded. "Pain is mostly psychological, if you believe what you read in most medical journals." I put my hands on the ground and rolled awkwardly to the side, conceding to the reality that I wasn't going to pop right up like a gymnast. I pushed myself up slowly, ignoring the hand Hux held out for me.

"Pain is real," he said, "and I can see that you're in it."

"I used to do this a lot, Hux," I said. "Before my injury—I was out on trails like this all the time. It was my lifeblood. I'm just trying to rewire that muscle memory is all."

"All right," he said. "What can I do to help?"

"Downhills would be nice."

He lifted my backpack off the ground like it weighed nothing at all and handed it to me. "You're in luck. We're about to hit a big one."

He was right, and as we set off on the descent, the views on the Lost Canyon trail proved a worthy distraction with blue sky above, conifers ahead, and mountains as far as the eye could see. A creek swollen with snowmelt nourished the low-lying vegetation that covered the canyon floor, guiding our way down the mountain into another lake basin. My quads were trashed by the time we got there, but I wasn't going to complain about the downhills. I could roll down the mountain tumbleweed-style if I had to.

As daylight waned, we made our final push to the Big Five Lakes. By some miracle, the muscles in my lower back had loosened up a bit—or maybe they were just numb. I was too tired for conversation, so we marched on in silence. Even Ollie seemed drained as he took up the rear. Every few minutes he'd sidle up to me and lick my hand.

"Here'll do," Hux finally announced, and since it was after dark, I couldn't really determine if it was a good spot or not. I didn't have it in me to argue, so we dropped our packs and pitched our tents and ate our dinners in silence. Mine was a mealy turkey sandwich.

We were sharing a bar of dark chocolate when Hux broke the silence. "You did good," he said. His voice was softer than usual.

I peered up at him. His eyes were kind.

"Out there, I mean. You really held your own."

As he went to stand, he put a hand on my shoulder—strictly professional, but warm, too. I didn't want to admit that Hux's approval meant something to me, but it did.

It meant the world.

* * *

After a restless night's sleep marked by the sounds of a remote wilderness, I woke at dawn to the decadent scent of bacon sizzling on the pan. The fumes reminded me of my childhood, when my culinary-challenged father would attempt his one meal of the week: Sunday breakfast. Fortunately he'd never taken me or my sisters camping; he probably would have burned down the forest trying to scramble an egg.

According to my watch, it was 5:58 AM. Outside, a starry darkness resisted the dawn, and a bird of some sort—there were over two hundred species in Sequoia, according to my research—sang its morning song. Hux called out, "I'm making breakfast. Better eat some because we've got nine miles to cover, a lot of it uphill."

As Ollie scrambled out of bed, I pulled on a pair of pants and a sweatshirt. With my hair thrown back in a ponytail and a toothbrush shoved in my mouth, I made my way out of the tent. Hux greeted me with a crooked grin.

"Do you sleep with that thing?" he asked, eyeing my toothbrush. "Jesus, Harland. How nasty is your morning breath?"

"Survivable, unlike yours."

He turned his attention back to the bacon, which was cooked to a crisp and therefore, from I could gather from Hux's expression, nowhere near done. He flipped the eggs without breaking a yolk. There was toast, too, which he plucked from the frying pan and piled onto a plate. It all looked pretty good. I told him so.

"Well, you heard me," he said, as he shoved a piece of toast into his mouth. "We're going for the record."

"What record?"

"My personal record."

"I'm not breaking any records."

"Okay, fine. You can carry my snacks, then." He winked at me. "Don't worry, the hard part is behind us."

I reached for a piece of toast—also burnt, which was starting to feel like Hux's style.

He topped off each egg with a slice of cheese, which he added to the toast to make an open-faced sandwich—two for me and two for him. The plate of bacon sizzled and popped, and as he stretched out his legs, he reached for five greasy strips. The bacon was so charred it broke into bits in his fingers. I liked it that way, though.

As I devoured the hearty breakfast, he poured me a cup of coffee—which was, by contrast, quite bad. Hux offered no explanation for it. He seemed to approach coffee as a necessary dose of caffeine, not something to be enjoyed.

"Any revelations after a good night sleep?" Hux asked.

"About the case, you mean?"

"Or, you know, my orienteering skills."

"You're quite the outdoorsman," I said, fueling the fires of his ego because, well, he deserved it. "But as for any major revelations, no, not really. The only update I got was a text from Corrigan that the dive team called off the search."

"Well, that's disappointing," he said over a mug of black grainy liquid that he insisted on calling coffee.

"How so?"

"Well, it means Colton Dodger is still out there somewhere."

I shrugged. "Or it could mean he's in Mexico by now, living a new life."

Hux shook his head. "Nah. Very few people could pull that off."

He was probably right, but the ISB agents I knew had lots of stories about people gone off the grid, never to be seen again. At least a few of those disappearing acts had to be in Europe or South America, living out their lives under a completely new identity.

"What about the Woodsman?" I asked.

"I guess it's possible he scared or chased them into a bad situation, but I don't think so."

"You were into the Woodsman theory two days ago."

"We didn't have a body two days ago. Now we do. And let's say the Woodsman is still out there—this isn't how he operates. You don't go from painting symbols on trees to killing people over the course of a season."

"So how *does* he operate?"

He thought for a moment. "There was a campsite up in Kaweah Gap last year that looked a lot like this one—gear all over the place, but no people. And no one ever came back for it. The difference was, we found credit cards and a cell phone . . . it was clear they'd all left in a hurry. And the tree was marked with the *djed*."

"So why'd they leave?"

"Corrigan followed up on it—the couple that was there said it was food poisoning, but I dunno. I think they said that just to get their money back from the camping company."

"Was it Glampist?"

"No—a competitor, though. They had the fancy tent and the catered meals and all that."

As Hux described the campsite, I couldn't help but think of the Sinclairs and their little side hustle. A thousand bucks a pop wasn't bad money. "Do you know who set it up?"

He let that question marinate for a while. "I don't."

"Maybe it was the Sinclairs."

"Could be, but I'm not seeing the connection."

"Of course you see the connection, Hux. Come on."

He stared at the bottom of his mug as a hawk tore across the clear blue skies. "Look, I'm not opposed to talking to them again. I just think we should focus on other angles for now."

"Fine. What did Corrigan think about the Kaweah Gap campsite?"

"He was satisfied with the food poisoning explanation, but then again, Corrigan's not a detective. He's a chief ranger. It was high summer, too—he had a lot on his plate."

From what I'd heard during my orientation, it wasn't unusual for novice rangers to misinterpret abandoned campsites for something else, but Hux had military experience, which put him a notch above the average park ranger. Anyone who had to rely on their instincts to survive had damn good instincts in my book. But I also understood the dangers in making a connection that didn't exist.

"Kaweah Gap is, what, a mile from Precipice?" I asked him.

"Yeah. It's close. I know that area pretty well—been up there a number of times. The trails are pretty treacherous once you venture out of the basin, with a lot of narrow switchbacks and steep cliffs. A lot can happen up there, but it's pretty remote, so it's mostly experienced backpackers. That was the other thing that worried me about that campsite. Those folks looked like they knew what they were doing."

"Okay." I tried to process Hux's theorizing while downing the worst cup of coffee on God's green earth. "SAR said they were searching the other lakes up there."

"Not *in* the lakes, though."

"Let's not lose the forest for the trees," I said. "*Lex parsimoniae*, remember?"

Since Hux had prepared the meal, I insisted on washing the dishes. He didn't protest. He kicked his feet up on a rock and nursed his grainy coffee.

While I scrubbed his dishes with a tattered brush, he said, "Look, I hear you on the Sinclairs. And Ash is a bad dude, no doubt about that. But in a weird way, he's protective of his brother. He wouldn't want to ruin a good thing for him."

"And you think Glampist is a good thing for Ian Sinclair?"

"Definitely. It makes him feel useful again."

"What do you make of the missing suitcases?"

He took a bite from his apple. "I don't know yet. I might have a better answer when we find Colton Dodger."

I checked the satellite phone again—still no updates from SAR. It was a disappointment, but not a surprise. "I don't think they're going to find him at this point," I said.

"Agreed," he said. "The search area is too big."

"Do you have a better idea?"

He plucked the seeds and stem from his apple and finished off the rest. "Maybe."

"Corrigan said you were a people finder."

"Well—sure. But it takes a lot of prep and all that. It's a process."

"And what are the chances of you embarking on that process in this case?"

"Depends. Can you afford my fee?"

"Your finder's fee, you mean?"

He answered with a smirk, like he not only got the joke, but admired it a little bit. As I was loading the cookware back into his rucksack, the satellite phone started to ring. Hux passed it to me. I didn't recognize the number, but the area code was local.

"Hello?" I said.

After a brief interruption in service, the caller introduced herself as Carla Bianchi, the local medical examiner in Visalia. Her New York accent was so thick that I briefly wondered if it was put on. I pictured her in knee-high leather boots and an Italian peacoat, her desk adorned with photos of her teenage kids.

"I'll email the final report to you when it's done," Bianchi was saying, "but I wanted to hop on the line with you now since I'm told you had some doubts about this being an accidental death."

"That's true."

"Well, I'm not sure what to tell you. The official cause of death was drowning."

There was a pause, as the words sank in. Hux was listening in, and judging by the look on his face, this didn't surprise him. A woman had been found at the bottom of a lake, and as such, drowning made sense. Still, the fact that she was wearing all that gear—hat, parka, shirt, pants, gloves—raised a lot of questions. Most adult drowning victims in national parks were either skinny-dippers, swimmers, or cliff-jumpers, and Tatum Delancey was clearly none of those.

"There's something else," Bianchi said. "Your victim had a spinal fracture at T11."

I knew T11—knew it better than any bone in my body. T11 was the eleventh vertebrae in the thoracic spine, the geographic center of the back. Mine was mostly metal at this point—screws and implants and the like—thanks to a burst fracture that should have paralyzed me, but it didn't. I'd taken my rehab seriously, no doubt about that, but I was also lucky. "What kind?" I asked, hearing the tremor in my voice. I hoped Hux didn't catch it.

"A burst fracture."

It was hard to talk, suddenly. I had to push the words out. "I see."

Hux gave me a quizzical look.

Bianchi went on, "It was a new injury, too. So new that I didn't see any swelling around the spinal cord. She likely sustained that injury moments before or at the time of death."

Hearing this confirmed my impression of Tatum Delancey's final moments—a fall from height. She may have drowned
in that lake, but she had fallen first. I said to Hux, "T11 is part
of the thoracolumbar spine: the most commonly injured area in
falls from a height."

"You know your fall pathology," Bianchi said, a smile coming through in her voice. "Yes, that's absolutely right. Not all
jumpers or fall victims have a spinal injury, but of those that do,
T10 to T12 is a real hot spot for fracture. It has to do with the
way the impact occurs." Bianchi sipped on something—my
guess was a cappuccino, based on nothing more than how I
pictured her. "Now, it's possible she sustained it some other way,
but this fracture would almost certainly have paralyzed her
from the waist down. If she fell into the lake, she would have
had a hard time swimming to shore."

"Was she intoxicated?" Hux asked.

"That's not something I can officially answer for another
couple weeks. Her BAC was zero, but I can't say for sure she
wasn't drinking before she died. As for other drugs in her system—those tests are gonna take a while."

"Huh," he mused.

I asked Bianchi, "Was there anything else?"

"There was some bruising around the left orbit. It looked
premortem."

"So it could have occurred at the same time as a fall."

"Certainly possible." She cleared her throat. "I'm told the
victim was found in Precipice Lake, is that right?"

"Yes."

"How big a drop is it from the ridge up there? The one that
all the kids like to jump from?"

I looked at Hux, who said, "About a hundred feet."

"Interesting."

"So you're saying her injuries are consistent with a fall from
that height?" I asked.

"I'm saying they *could* be. I didn't note any head trauma, but
that's not necessarily unusual. It all depends on how she landed."

"We think the lake was frozen where she fell," I said. "Or at
least partially frozen. Does that change your calculus?"

"Well, a hundred-foot fall onto rock or solid ice and you're talking multiple fractures, internal injuries, massive head trauma. Not always, but it's a fair bet. If the ice was fairly thin, then it makes more sense. Did you see the impact zone?"

"No," I admitted. "We were under some time pressure."

"Might be worth having another look."

My fear was that the ice up there was already starting to thaw, and in another few days or so, it might be completely gone. The problem was, I couldn't possibly go any faster. I was already at my physical limit.

"You should have my preliminary report by lunchtime," she said.

"Thanks," I said. "You've been a tremendous help."

"It's no problem—I love my job."

She hung up. Hux feigned a shudder. "How could any sane person love that job?" he asked. "Forget the dead bodies. There are never any windows in the morgue. It smells, too. All that processed air coming through the vents . . . it's my worst nightmare."

"Thanks for the vivid picture," I said.

"Anytime." He helped me hoist my backpack onto my shoulders. It felt a lot heavier than it had any right to be, even after Hux had off-loaded a lot of the weight, but that was just the little voice in my head talking again—the pain voice. I tried to ignore it.

"So," he said. "Do you think Tatum Delancey fell . . . or was she pushed?"

"You don't beat around the bush, do you?"

"Nope," he said with a laugh.

The truth was, I didn't want Hux to see the wheels turning in my head. Sometimes those wheels stalled, or squealed, or turned the wrong way. In Tatum Delancey's case, though, the wheels weren't just turning—they were firing on all cylinders. We had a dead young woman who had been camping with someone other than her husband. We had evidence of a fall and other trauma just prior to death. We didn't have motive, but the wheels were turning on that, too.

"Let's see the impact zone first," I said. "Then I'll answer your question."

I called out to Ollie, who scampered out of the frigid water and shook out his salt-and-pepper coat. As Hux and I made a quick pass through our own campsite, eliminating any trace that we'd ever been there, the satellite phone rang again.

This time, Hux answered. "It's Corrigan," he said, holding his hand over the receiver. It was a brief call, an expedient back-and-forth that lasted less than a minute.

"What is it?" I asked.

"SAR found a satellite phone up at Columbine Lake."

CHAPTER

11

T HIS WAS GOOD news for the case, but terrible news for me and my battered body. I knew Hux would have no problem turning right around and going back up that mountain, but for me, the prospect of treading old ground was soul-crushing. That hadn't been easy terrain either. It would take us hours to get back to Columbine—and those hours mattered out here.

"I could go back up myself," Hux said. "You could wait here, or—"

"No," I said. "I'm coming."

"What if we asked someone to bring it down?"

"That won't work. If they found a sat phone, it means a body could be nearby. And SAR doesn't know how to secure a scene."

"All they found was the phone—no mention of a body."

I put up a hand. "We're going back."

"Harland, this is nuts."

"Look," I said, stopping short of pointing a finger at his face, "if I can't do what needs to be done to figure out what happened to this woman, then I don't belong out here. End of story."

Hux shook his head, his own frustrations playing on his face. "There's stubborn, and there's stupid. Corrigan was right about that."

"I'm not being stupid."

"At least let me carry your pack, then."

"No way."

Before he could wrestle my pack out of my hands, I put my arms through the straps and clicked my belt into place around my hips. The wind had gone from steady to ferocious overnight, but it was at our backs, which helped. A refreshed Ollie led the way, darting forward and circling back, as he liked to do on long treks. Every so often I'd take out my binoculars and scan the rocky terrain. There wasn't much going on in terms of vegetation—small conifers making a stand against the elements, a thin carpet of bunchgrass at our feet, and whatever else managed to take hold on the granite landscape. I couldn't help but think that it would be difficult to get lost out here, but easy to die.

The hours passed mostly in silence as we made our way back over familiar terrain. We were just coming up on Sawtooth Pass when I caught a glimpse of color on the fringes of one of the lakes in the basin. "Did you see that?" I asked Hux, who already had his binoculars out.

"Yep," he said. "Looks like a tent."

A lone tree near the shore was blocking our view, so we found another spot to get a better look. Once there, we both took out our binoculars for another look. Indeed, the scrap of teal on the rocky shore was a tent—a two-fer, by the looks of it.

"What do you think, boss?" Hux asked, as he lowered his binoculars.

"We should go down there and check it out."

He nodded, then said, "It's off the trail a ways."

"Is this an unusual place to camp?"

"This time of year, it's a little unusual. You're going to get a lot of wind coming over the pass. It's not where I'd choose to spend the night."

"Let's make this quick, then." It was only nine o'clock in the morning, but it felt like the day was slipping away—along with any evidence that might still be at Precipice Lake, if we ever made it back there.

With Ollie loping alongside us, Hux and I kept the conversation to a minimum so as not to startle the tent's inhabitants.

When we were about a hundred yards from their campsite, Hux stopped. "I don't like these loner types," he said. "Are you carrying?"

"Carrying what?"

"A weapon."

"Oh." My cheeks flushed, which Hux surely noticed but didn't comment on. "I have some bear spray."

"Maybe keep it handy. I've got my Glock."

I tried not to appear too surprised that he had a gun, even though it was an oversight on my part not to have asked him about it sooner. He had every right to carry one, of course; Sequoia was black bear country, and this was mating season. I just felt that as the law enforcement officer between us, I probably should have inquired about any weapons before we set off. More than that, I probably should have *brought* my weapon like any respectable federal agent would have done. In Chicago, I'd always sworn by my routine. I needed a new one.

"Is that a bear gun?" I asked.

He nodded. "I had a little encounter with a black bear last summer," he said. "The crazy bastard charged for no reason— annoyed by my singing maybe, who knows. We wrestled for a bit. I almost pissed myself, not gonna lie."

"So what happened?"

"I got him in a chokehold."

"A bear?" I said, with a smirk that made his cheeks redden. "How big was he?"

"Well," he said, flicking at something that landed on his shoulder, "he was on the smaller side."

"Are you sure this was a bear?" I asked. "Or somebody's dog, maybe?"

"It was a bear," he huffed. "Look, I hope I never have to use this thing. But I'm not messing around with that spray any-more. I'm telling you, Harland, the bear *liked* it."

"If you say so," I said with a laugh.

We put our packs down and fixed our attention on the teal tent holding its own against the wind. Ollie ambled over and ate some beef jerky out of my hand.

Hux asked, "What's the plan, then?"

"We go over there and have a chat."

"How confrontational is this chat?"

"Not very."

He considered this. "You want to lead, or me?"

I saw the earnestness on Hux's face and decided that his time had come. "You take this one," I said.

"All right, boss."

Leaving our packs under a small tree, we set off toward the tent in tandem. Hux holstered his Glock 20 under his jacket. He was wearing his ranger's uniform, so the fact that he was armed should not have come as a surprise to whoever was in that tent. Still, I wasn't about to take any chances. Ray had told me about the shooting of a park ranger just two months into his career with ISB. It was an accident, as it turned out; two women camping alone off-trail had gotten spooked, and one had used her rifle to dispatch the threat. What they'd thought was a bear turned out to be a forty-three-year-old father of three. I resolved not to make the same mistake.

The two-person tent looked neat and orderly, unlike the Glampist disaster at Precipice Lake. It was a compact Marmot, not new but in good condition, which told me these folks knew what they were doing. The firepit nearby also showed a knowledge of the craft, with the kindling charred black and larger pieces of wood arranged at the base. The Bear Vault canisters that protected their food from scavengers appeared to be well secured.

"Hello, hello," Hux called out to no one in particular. A gust of wind blew through the trees, raining pine needles on our shoulders. The tent's canvas flaps fluttered in the breeze, but the door, zipped shut, remained closed. It was quiet, almost too quiet. When the wind died down, there was no sound at all.

"We're with the Park Service," Hux said in a loud, clear voice. "We've got a few questions for you if you've got a minute."

Still no movement from inside the tent. Hux grabbed his walking stick and marched over to it. The look he threw back at me told me to stay put, but Ollie was harder to convince. He pawed the dirt, whimpering as he pranced in place. I grasped his collar and told him to sit down.

"Come on out," Hux said to the tent's inhabitants. "You need a permit to camp here."

After a tense few seconds, the tent shuddered a bit, as someone inside lumbered about, trying to reach the zipper. Then came a cough, a few hushed words. A young male with a scratchy voice told Hux to wait a minute because he had to put on his pants.

The guy—early-twenties, with a surfer's haircut and a climber's build—emerged from the tent. He'd located his pants, but his shirt wasn't a priority, apparently. He scratched the fuzz between his nipples and released a belch that echoed through the canyon. "Uh, hey," he said. "Is there a problem, officer—er, ranger?" He waved at Ollie. "Nice dog."

"Do you have a wilderness permit?" Hux asked.

"Sure do," the guy said, producing it from his pocket. He handed the piece of paper to Hux, who looked it over.

"Thanks," Hux said. "You a climber?"

"Yep. Me and my girlfriend."

"She in there?"

"Yeah, but, ah—it was her birthday yesterday." He tried to wink at Hux, his one eye crinkling awkwardly, but his meaning was clear. He looked pretty hungover himself. At least he was awake. At that point, I wasn't sure we could say the same about the girlfriend.

Hux said, "Look, here's the thing—we're looking for someone that might've come through here. Hard to say when—maybe a day or two ago. Have you seen anyone?"

"A hiker?"

"Anyone, really. Have you seen anyone else at all up here in the last few days?"

"Well, yeah—there was that search-and-rescue team."

My heart sank. If SAR had come through here, then they must have already talked to these two. Since Corrigan hadn't mentioned it, I could only assume that our hungover duo hadn't been able to provide any useful information.

Still, I didn't like to assume. Maybe SAR hadn't asked them the right questions. Maybe this guy was even more hungover then than he was now, and his memory had cleared a bit since.

I was tempted to butt in, but this was Hux's show. It was important that he learn to navigate this interview on his own.

"Did you talk to them?" Hux asked.

"Yeah."

"What did they want to know?"

"Just if we'd seen anyone hiking alone out here. Same as
you."

"What did you tell them?"

"That nobody came through here," he said, staring at the dirt
as he answered. The guy was a lousy liar, that much was clear.

It was hard to tell what Hux thought about him, though.
Before he could ask this hungover climber another question, the
tent suddenly shifted, and the entryway zipper came undone
with a violent thrust. As we all watched, another person crawled
out, this one small, wiry, and olive-toned. She was a young
woman with a pretty face, despite the bloodshot eyes and dis-
gruntled frown. Her faded T-shirt said "Mama's Pasta."

She settled her gaze on me. "Who are you?" she asked.

"Felicity Harland," I said. "I'm a federal agent with the
Investigative Services Branch." Gesturing to Hux, I added,
"And this is my partner, Ferdinand Huxley."

"I know about ISB," she said.

"You do?"

"My dad's a detective in San Bernardino. He's worked with
you guys a few times."

"I hope it was a good experience."

She nodded, then looked at her boyfriend, who was mas-
saging his head with the pads of his fingers. He squinted at the
sun.

"What's your name?" I asked her.

"Delia."

"And you?" Hux asked the shirtless guy.

"Jeb," he grunted.

"Nice to meet you both," I said, with about as much warmth
as a high school disciplinarian. "Can you tell us about your run-
in with the search-and-rescue team?"

Delia answered. "Well, they asked us if we'd seen anybody
out here, and then they showed us that same stupid sketch of

the Woodsman." She rolled her eyes. "I dunno who your sketch artist is, but he sucks."

I looked at Hux. *SAR was circulating a sketch of the Woodsman?* I hadn't seen the sketch myself; hell, I hadn't been aware one even existed.

Turning to Hux, I said, "Did you know about this?"

"No, I didn't," he said. "But could be a SAR volunteer brought it along."

"Why would they do that?"

Hux shrugged. "Because everybody who lives up here knows the whole Woodsman debacle was never solved. At one point there was some reward money on the table—don't think that's the case anymore, though."

The girl's eyes stayed on us as we spoke. If her father was a detective, then she knew the drill better than most, and I didn't want her thinking that I didn't trust my partner. Hux, for his part, had no reason to lie. I regretted implying otherwise.

"That makes sense," I said to Hux, conveying an apology that I didn't want to voice aloud, not in front of two potential witnesses. Hux hesitated, like he wasn't sure the interview still belonged to him. I offered a slight nod to urge him on.

Hux said to Delia, "So you know about the Woodsman?"

"Yeah, of course. Heard about him from our friends who were up here last year."

"What did you hear?"

"That he liked to mess with people—he was real into scary animal noises, cheap scares like that. He'd smear animal blood on their tents, scatter it around the campsite. Our one friend was real freaked out about it."

"Did your friend report it?"

"Yeah."

"Where was this?"

"Near Empire Mountain."

I looked at Hux for clarification. He explained, "Empire's northwest of Sawtooth Peak—different trail, different area."

"I see." I turned back to Delia. "You mentioned animal blood—did your friends say where it came from?" I directed the question to both her and Hux, since he was the one who had briefed me on the Woodsman. I hadn't yet gotten the chance to look through the file that Corrigan kept in his office.

"Uh, I dunno. Deer, maybe? It wasn't human, if that's what you're asking."

I looked at Hux. "No?"

Hux said, "According to the complaint that was filed, the blood was never tested because no one was ever reported missing. I mean, yeah, Corrigan should have kicked it up to ISB, but he didn't. I read his reports. He thought it was just a hunter with a few screws lose."

"Did he keep any samples?"

"Corrigan? Not a chance."

"Witnesses?"

"I'd have to pull up the file. You saw his little message pad—he's old-school."

I was really starting to tire of this excuse for Corrigan's poor record keeping. I resolved to sit down with the chief ranger and go deep on this Woodsman situation, even though everyone—except maybe Hux, although even he was waffling—seemed to think it was a waste of time. Blood of unknown origin, though? Smeared all over a tent, used in a deliberate way to scare someone? That warranted a second look at the very least.

"So why are you two out here?" I asked. "That encounter didn't scare you off?"

"Not really," she said. "I mean—he never hurt anyone, from what we heard."

"Are you sure about that?"

Delia looked over her shoulder at her shirtless companion, and for a brief moment, their eyes met. Something transpired between them, but I couldn't get a read on what it was.

Jeb walked toward us, dragging his feet as he shuffled across the campsite. His toes were callused and his nails chipped, a testament to his outdoor existence, walking on hard earth and scaling granite. He didn't strike me as the type who wore shoes very often.

Delia sighed. It was clear this was ground they had trod before, although maybe not in this exact capacity. She looked back at me and said, "So if it's not the Woodsman, then who is SAR looking for?"

I could see Hux wasn't comfortable answering her question—after all, we hadn't discussed how much to share with these two—but I decided it was best to be straightforward with them. They had a right to know about the dead woman and her missing companion.

"A woman's body was found in Precipice Lake over the weekend," I said. "We have reason to believe she was camping with another person—male, average build. Probably in his thirties or forties, but can't say for sure. His whereabouts are unknown."

Delia looked at Jeb. "Maybe Spark's involved in this," she said.

"Who?" I asked.

"A guy we know—er, knew," Jeb said. "He went missin' last year."

"What's his full name?"

"Spark McAllister," Jeb mumbled, with a furtive glance in Hux's direction.

Hux shrugged. "Never heard of him."

I added the name to my notes. "We'll look into it," I said. When I looked up again, Delia was giving Jeb the side-eye. He stared at the ground, curling his toes in the dirt. There it was again—the dodginess, the distrust. The whole story sounded a little off.

Delia puffed out a breath. "Jeb, just tell them," she sighed. "It's better if you do it now."

Jeb looked from me to Hux and back again. "I don't like cops."

"But your girlfriend's dad is a cop," Hux pointed out.

"Yeah, well, him and me don't get along."

Delia cracked a smile.

"I'm not that kind of cop." I used a gentler tone that was meant to put him at ease. "My agency investigates crimes that occur on national park lands. We have no jurisdiction elsewhere. And like I said, we don't care what you're into. We're just trying to find out what happened to the woman in Precipice Lake, and also find the person she was with."

Jeb whispered something in Delia's ear. Hux looked frustrated. Folding his arms over his chest, he muttered under his breath, "Gonna be here all day at this rate."

After a few minutes of hushed conversation, Jeb snorted and walked off toward the tent. With a parting glance in our direction, he went inside and zipped the door shut.

Delia stood there for a moment, seemingly torn between loyalty to her boyfriend and duty to a federal agent. I wondered if she was thinking about her father. It was one thing to hear your dad's voice in your ear, telling you to do the right thing; it was quite another if your dad happened to be a cop. In that case, the instinct to cooperate probably ran deep.

"Delia?" I pressed.

She turned slowly toward me, as the wind kicked up and blew her long brown hair into oblivion. She tilted her face toward the sun.

"Well?" Hux asked.

It was a moment before she spoke. "Jeb lied to SAR," she said.

"About what?" Hux asked.

She glanced over her shoulder at the tent, almost like she was checking to make sure that Jeb wasn't standing outside. "About not seeing anyone out here." When Jeb didn't emerge, she added, "We *did* see someone—and he looked scared."

12

DELIA GRABBED A blanket from around the firepit and wrapped it around her sinewy shoulders. Clouds were moving in, and the air had grown cold. Hux kept an eye on the tent while Ollie sat on his haunches between us.

"So Jeb lied to SAR," I said, settling into an improvised folding chair—Jeb's, from the looks of it. It was adorned with ketchup and beer stains. "But where were you?"

"I was there," she admitted. "They just didn't ask me."

"Why not volunteer it?" Hux asked with a little more bite than usual.

"It was stupid, okay? I should've."

I didn't want Delia to clam up on us, so rather than hammer her for being evasive, I said, "Look, it's fine. It isn't SAR's job to investigate—it's ours. So tell us what happened."

Delia planted her boots on the ground and seemed to study them for a moment. The silence worried me a bit. I couldn't help but wonder if she was rehearsing her story, or at least preparing to filter some details. Either way, it put me on my guard.

"On Sunday night," Delia said, "we crashed pretty early because it'd been a long day of climbing. We grilled some sausages and had a few beers and passed out—not from the booze, though. We were just beat. A few hours later, I heard somebody messing around outside our tent. I knew it wasn't an animal."

"What time was this?" Hux asked.

"It was 9:07. I checked my watch."

"You've got a good memory," I remarked.

"My dad always complains about unreliable witnesses," she said. "Anyway, I armed myself and went out there." She looked at Hux. "What are you carrying, by the way? A Glock 20?"

"That's right," he said, trying not to show his surprise, because the thing was barely visible on his hip. Even *I* had missed it.

"That's a good one. I keep mine handy 'cause there are a lot of weirdos out here. And believe me, I'm not afraid to use it."

"Noted," I said.

"Yeah. So anyway, I slipped out of the tent while the guy's back was turned. I told him to put his hands up or I'd shoot him through his spine."

"Jesus," Hux said. "What happened next?"

"He turned around real slow, seemed scared out of his mind. Put his hands up and everything. He said he was lost."

"What did he look like?"

"It was dark, but—I dunno. He looked about twenty-five. I'd say he was five ten, one hundred and ninety. He had a tweaker look about him except for his clothes—Patagonia, head to toe. That doesn't mean anything, though. The Woodsman stole from a lot of campsites."

Ash Sinclair's ugly mug drifted to the forefront of my consciousness again. "Do you know if the Woodsman ever stole suitcases?"

"Suitcases? Who brings suitcases on a camping trip?"

"It's just a question."

She shook her head. "I dunno. All I can say is that we heard the Woodsman went after people with flashy shit, which is probably why he never bothered us."

I looked at Hux, who was scrutinizing Delia's expression; it didn't seem like he totally trusted her account either.

"Back to the guy in your campsite," I said. "You said he had a tweaker look. Was he on something?"

"Um, yeah." She said this like it was abundantly obvious.

"Did he say anything?"

"He asked me for a map, which I thought was weird."

"Where was Jeb during all this?"

"Passed out."

I glanced at Hux to see if he'd registered the same hiccup in her story. "So he *wasn't* lying to SAR."

"Huh?"

"If he was passed out, then he didn't actually see anyone."

"Well, no—I mean, he came out later to see what the hell was going on, but by then the guy had taken off. All he saw was the back of his head."

While I took notes, Hux said, "Sounds like a strange encounter."

"It was, yeah. I mean, it's after dark and he's going through our shit looking for supplies? He's lucky he didn't get shot. He was either really desperate or really stupid."

"Which way did he go?" Hux asked.

"That way." She pointed west, toward Sawtooth Pass. "Anyway, I figured he'd be fine in daylight. Is he still missing?"

"*Someone's* missing," I said.

Delia put her hands on her thighs and stood up. Looking us both in the eye, she said, "Look, it's everybody for 'emselves out here. If he froze to death or whatever, well, that's too bad. But I'd check the trail going back to Sawtooth Trailhead."

"We came up that way," I said. "We didn't see anyone."

"Well that sucks. I hope he's okay."

Delia's constant flip-flopping was another concern, but despite the half-truths and vague details, she didn't strike me as a flake. I wondered if she was trying to protect someone—Jeb, maybe. He hadn't contributed a single piece of useful information, and now he was hiding in his tent doing who knows what.

"Thank you for your help, Delia," I said, and held out my hand for her to shake. The strength of her grip did not surprise me. Climbers had more power in their fingers than most people had in their biceps.

"Yup," she said, but as she started back toward the tent, Ollie started barking. It was the first time he'd made a sound all day. *Good instincts, boy,* I thought. Something was definitely off here, and he was letting her know it.

I called out, "Delia, there's one more thing."

"What's that?"

"Jeb's friend—Spark McAllister."

"Yeah." Her expression tightened, as she looked at Ollie with a wariness in her eyes. The feeling was mutual. Ollie stood still as a statue—his muscles tense, almost coiled.

Hux said, "No one by that name was ever reported missing in the park."

"Yeah, well—I don't know what to make of that. He was Jeb's friend, not mine."

"You never met him?"

"No."

She gathered the blanket a little tighter around her shoulders. "Look, Jeb's not a bad guy," she said. "Yeah, he's had his problems, but he's clean now. We both love to climb and that's good enough for me."

I caught her looking at the tent again, and this time there was some movement from within. Jeb's silhouette was shifting and amorphous, an alien thing. I wondered what he was doing in there, when suddenly he unzipped the flap and stepped out. This time, though, he had one hand behind his back, like he was hiding something. He stood there a while—still shirtless, with his pants sagging a good four inches below his navel. And that's when I saw the tattoo on his lower abdomen, reaching toward his nether regions—a *djed*.

Ollie started barking again—louder now, the echoes rumbling through the basin. The sounds of his frenzy were amplified a hundred times by the walls of granite. I couldn't decide which was more ominous—Ollie's barking or Jeb's silence.

Hux was feeling it, too. He said, "I think we're done here."

We backed away slowly, never breaking eye contact with Jeb and arranged so that Hux could reach for his Glock at a moment's notice. His other hand brushed my elbow, and I could feel the tension in it—the strength, the intentionality.

As soon as we were over the ridge, we grabbed our packs and started to run.

CHAPTER

13

WE WERE OUT of view of the tent when my back spasmed and every last muscle fiber in the vicinity of my thoracic spine seized up like a vise. My vision dimmed with the pain, a blinding jolt to the system. It took everything I had to stay upright. I gritted my teeth to keep myself from crying out, but I couldn't stop the pitiful whimper that made it into the world.

I didn't dare look at Hux because I didn't want him to see my face locked in a grimace, didn't want him to know that my body was failing me. Ollie put a paw on each of my knees, his version of a hug. He looked into my eyes as if to say, *"I'm here."*

Shrugging my backpack off my shoulders, I bent over and sucked in air until the agony subsided. At some point, Hux walked over. Saying nothing, he placed his hand in the groove between my shoulder blades. It was almost like he was giving me permission to breathe again. I started to feel better.

"You all right?" he asked.

"Yep," I managed.

"I shouldn't have let you carry your pack."

"Yeah, but it's mine. I've got to pull my own weight out here." Deep down, though, I was starting to think that our adventure was over—or at least my role in it was. Hux must have sensed it, too. While he looked on helplessly, I kneaded the muscles in my back until my fingers ached. That was the thing about surgery; afterward, you were never as good as new.

"Maybe we should take a breather," he suggested.

"I don't need a breather."

"Harland, this is insanity."

"No."

He looked almost wounded. "Let me carry your pack the rest of the way then."

Having Hux carry my load was a serious transgression in the backpacking world, and one I'd never live down if another park ranger saw it happening. But at this point, I had no choice. There was no way I could haul twenty pounds over that pass. "Okay," I mumbled.

After the worst of the spasm had passed, we plodded onward at a pace that would have satisfied my grandmother. Hux insisted that I lead because he didn't want to push me past my comfort level, and he didn't trust me to tell him to slow down.

Determined to ride this out, I asked him, "What did you make of Jeb's tattoo?"

"Well, it's suspicious as hell."

"Do you think he's the Woodsman?"

"He's at the top of my list now, that's for sure."

He was at the top of mine, too, but I was struggling to connect him to the Glampist site. We hadn't found a *djed* symbol there, and Hux had searched for at least an hour. "What are your thoughts on the Spark McAllister story?" I asked.

"It sounded fishy."

"How so?"

"Well, if Jeb's the Woodsman, then it could be he's trying to pin it on Spark—or maybe they were in it together. Some of the campsites were so wrecked it looked like a two-person job."

"Interesting theory."

"Here's the thing. I've read every single missing person's report ever filed in this park. Anybody that went missing in the last fifty years, I know about 'em." He gripped his belt strap as he walked, hoisting both of our packs a little higher on his broad shoulders. "No one reported him missing, and that makes me wonder."

One thing that had come up on Hux's background check regarding his time in the Park Service was the Vasser case. A married couple had gone missing on a day hike fifteen years earlier—just vanished without a trace. Last fall, on a solo recovery mission, Hux had found their bodies. The local news had picked up the story and run an article on him. It certainly supported his reputation as a "finder."

"So what do we do about Jeb?" Hux asked.

"Nothing at the moment."

"He's gonna take off the first chance he gets."

"I know," I said. "But I'm sure you'll find him."

* * *

It had turned out to be a glorious spring day—a stark blue sky overhead, no clouds in sight. Most of the peaks were capped with snow, but that would change with the arrival of summer. As we walked, I thought about Kevin, who used to relish springtime adventures—the wildflower and wildlife, the rivers and creeks overflowing with snowmelt. I recalled one Easter weekend we spent together, a last-minute trip to Isle Royale in Michigan. It was opening weekend—the campgrounds weren't open yet, and the weather was terrible. I cracked a tooth from shivering. But it had been an adventure, all right, the kind of thing you did when you were young and stupid and invincible. We had been all of those things once.

"Harland?"

I looked up. "Yeah?" My voice had a thickness to it—those damn emotions. I wished time would do its job and just let me think about a memory without drowning in it.

"You okay?"

I nodded.

Hux took my non-answer for what it was and confirmed the good news—we'd reached Columbine Lake. *Again.* I was feeling pretty good, all things considered. Hux wasn't the least bit out of breath. He said, "Well done, Harland. We're even ahead of schedule."

"Must be that shortcut you were talking about."

"More likely your badassery."

"Okay, fine," I said, brightening up a bit. "I'll take it."

We found the SAR volunteer who had made the call to Corrigan, sitting on a small boulder. Her name was Cathy, a stout but hardy woman who looked to be in her fifties. She shook our hands with the strength and gusto of a lifelong outdoorswoman.

"Howdy," she said. "You made good time. Musta really hoofed it up here."

"We gave it our best," Hux said. "Thanks for waiting for us."

"Not a problem at all. You want to see where I found it?"

"Please," I said.

She rose from the boulder with a jovial smile, and together we walked down to the water's edge, which was marked by pieces of red duct tape affixed to pebbles and dirt. From her pocket she pulled out a plastic bag with a satellite phone inside—an Iridium 9575. And to seal the deal, right there at the bottom was Glampist's logo.

"Found it right over there," she said, pointing to a spot about five feet into the lake.

"You found it *in* the lake?" I asked her. "How?"

"Well, somebody found a hat in the water yesterday. That person didn't think much of it, but for me, it was a clue." She pushed her hands into the pockets of her jeans. "I figured maybe somebody was trying to get rid of evidence."

"Well, we're not sure yet how things went down." I kept my tone neutral. "But your instincts were right on—this is a very important find."

She looked back at the phone. "I didn't try to turn it on," she said, "but I'm familiar with the model—the Iridiums are indestructible. You could throw that thing in a wood chipper and it wouldn't make a lick of difference."

I liked Cathy. She struck me as someone who spent her evenings reading true crime novels and cozy mysteries, trying to work out the murderer before the author showed her cards. I wondered if she listened to podcasts. Technology was slow to make its inroads around here.

I put on my gloves and fished the device out of the plastic baggie, which had probably been used to store a sandwich not all that long ago. Cathy admitted to handling the satellite phone with her bare hands, but it didn't matter. The prints of its owner were long gone anyway since the Iridium had been found underwater. This wasn't a total loss. I was far more interested in the sat phone's call log than any physical evidence.

As Cathy had said, the Iridium was an impressive piece of technology, and Glampist had gone all out by investing in the Iridium Extreme 9575, the newest model on the market. In addition to its standard features, which included text, email, and a Wi-Fi connection, it was GPS enabled, with a military-grade durability. On top of all that, the Iridium was idiot-proof when it came to emergency assistance. You pressed a button and waited for somebody to show up. In fact, some seasoned rangers argued that it was *too* easy to call for help from the Iridium. No helicopter pilot wanted to risk his life because of a pocket dial.

This Iridium hadn't been used for that purpose, apparently. I searched the call log first. No emergency calls had been placed recently, and in fact the only call recorded was one made the previous Saturday—the day of Tatum's last reported contact to her husband—to a 408 area code. The number felt familiar for some reason, and then it dawned on me.

"That looks like Glampist's customer support line," I said to Hux.

"But Wu said there were no calls from this group—I asked her."

"Mm-hm."

A pause. "What?"

"Hux," I said, in as serious a tone as I could manage without laughing, "I know you consider yourself a real ladies' man, but—well, she lied to you."

"Huh." His eyes shone with a smile. "Well, *I'm* annoyed."

I pulled up all the text messages and emails on the Iridium, surprised to find three text messages from the previous weekend, all sent from this phone and delivered to the same number. One was from Friday, the other two on Saturday. The last message had been sent at 9:34 PM on Saturday night.

"Six-two-six area code," I said, remembering that Edwin Delancey had left a callback number to that area code. I was willing to bet the number was his.

"Pasadena," Cathy said. "My son goes to Cal Tech."

"He must be a smart one," I said.

She blushed with pride. "Timmy always had a knack for math."

While Hux talked to Cathy about his experience as a math major, I checked my Sequoia file to confirm that the number did indeed belong to Edwin Delancey. I scrolled through the messages on the Iridium, my confusion deepening with each pass. The first one, sent on Friday afternoon at 4:50 PM, was rather generic: *Miss you bb. Got here safe. Weather is great and the scenery is spectacular. Feeling refreshed already.*

And the next, Saturday at 9:02 AM: *Love it here so much bb. Wish you were here. No smog! Hope all's well on set.*

The last one deviated from the pattern in that it wasn't generic at all. It was emotional; desperate, even. And it made me question everything I thought I knew about this case so far.

Oh bb. I love you so much. Being here reminds me of our wedding on the cliffs in Big Sur. Remember? Best day of my life. You are the man I always dreamed of. I hate that you had to work this weekend. I hate the grind. I want to go away with you and never come back.

I want to disappear.

14

READING THESE TEXT messages, I felt like I had entered
Tatum Delancey's consciousness—or was it was my own,
six years earlier, when I was newly married to Kevin Delham?
Ours had been a whirlwind romance and nothing at all like what
I'd envisioned for myself at twenty-six. I'd gone through high
school and college with my sights set on one objective: a career in
federal law enforcement. Sure, there were some distractions
along the way—bad boyfriends and abysmal online dates and all
the rest—but for the most part, I wasn't in the market for a life
partner until Kevin came along. And then I just knew.

What we shared were big dreams and big plans for the
future. I was the female FBI agent; he was the underwater
welder who could never seem to take enough risks. It was Kevin
who had stirred in me an undeniable wanderlust. Every penny
of our savings went toward trips to far-flung places that always
required a passport and at least one charter flight. Australia, in
fact, had struck Kevin as too tame a destination. I was the one
who convinced him that the Red Centre was anything but
tame. It would be the trip of a lifetime.

Maybe Tatum Delancey had had the same aspirations with
her own husband, which certainly came through in that last text
message. But he was back home in the city, while she was out
here with another man. Where, then, had their marriage gone so
wrong?

Then again, maybe it hadn't. Human beings were complicated. They were liars and polygamists and misanthropes. No
matter what Tatum Delancey felt or *thought* she felt for her husband, she had been out in this wilderness with someone else.
And now she was dead.

"Hey," Hux said. I looked up and saw him coming down
the slope from the ridge that overlooked the lake. "I looked
around—didn't find anything else except this." He held up an
empty bag of Swedish fish and a rusted Dr. Pepper can.

"I wish we had more time," I said. "But we should get moving if we want to be at Precipice by tomorrow afternoon."

"Let's give Corrigan a call." He looked toward the sky and
seemed to see, like I did, that we were running out of daylight.
"Maybe the copter's available."

"Okay," I said. "You do it."

As he took my satellite phone and walked off to escape the
wind, I wasn't sure what I was hoping for—a respite from more
difficult mileage, or a chance to finish what we'd started. While I
was resting on a boulder with Ollie at my feet, Hux returned with
the bad news.

"No copter today," he said. "Or tomorrow either,
probably."

It was a disappointment, but not a crushing blow like
before. After several days without reliable air transport, I'd
learned to adjust my expectations.

"We should get going then," I said. "I'll carry my own
pack."

"You sure?"

"It's a lot lighter now. You took a bunch of stuff out."

"Nah, I just downsized a bit for you." He adjusted his baseball cap to keep the sun out of his eyes. "So, what do you make
of the text messages?"

"Hard to say." I didn't like lying to Hux—and it wasn't a
lie, really, so much as a distortion of the truth. I couldn't say for
sure what Tatum Delancey was thinking when she sent those
texts to her husband hours before she died. I had an idea,
though.

"It sounds like she loved the guy," he said.

"She probably did."

"So what was she doing out here with Colton Dodger?"

I tried to wrestle my pack back on without grimacing. "Love's complicated, Hux. You learn that day one on the job."

"You learn that day one, period," he said.

I cracked a smile. "True."

"Well, I hope our man is still alive and well out there somewhere. It'd be nice to hear his side of things."

I got to my feet, ignoring the flash of pain in my back as I stretched my limbs. Hux caught me wincing but didn't comment on it, nor did he offer to take my pack again. He must have known the answer would be a resounding no.

We thanked Cathy for her help. She wished us well as we hit the trail—or rather, what Hux *said* was the trail, since it lacked any real markings on this side of Sawtooth. He put the Iridium in his backpack and zipped it up, checking it three times to make sure it was secure.

"Only sixteen miles to go," he said.

"You're complaining about it already, eh?"

With Hux's laughter echoing through the basin, we set off back the way we'd come, with Ollie darting ahead to lead us. Every stride threatened to break my weary bones, but the truth was, I'd been through worse. I'd survived eight days at the bottom of a ravine with a broken back—eight days until someone finally found me. I closed my eyes and thought of Kevin, of the look in his eyes when he'd made the decision to go get help. *"See you soon,"* he'd said. *"Love you."*

I fixed my sights on the trail in front of us. I wasn't searching for salvation this time; just the truth.

Or maybe, if I was being honest with myself—a little bit of both.

CHAPTER

15

THAT NIGHT, WE camped on the shore of "Lake One" in the Big Five Lakes basin, which had its own campsites and a bear locker. On Hux's recommendation, we settled on a campsite right on the lake's northeastern shore, with a spectacular view of its serene waters. The conifers surrounding the lake offered ample shade and shelter, and for the first time in days, I didn't feel quite so exposed. This part of Sequoia was more like Earth and less like some alien place.

Hux made dinner—pasta with beans, cheese, and some leafy greens. He produced two bottled beers from his backpack and handed one to me.

"You carried these all the way up here?"

"Abso-fuckin'-lutely. It's worth the extra weight."

I laughed. Hux certainly had his quirks. He was also a damn good cook, with improvisational skills to boot. He had proven that he didn't need fancy equipment or a meat thermometer to whip up a restaurant-quality meal.

I put my hand to my brow and looked out over the expanse of the lake, which went from blue to navy, to black as the sun went down. Hux was munching on a generous piece of dark chocolate when he said, "There's something about this case for you, isn't there?"

"What do you mean?" I asked, even though I knew exactly what he meant.

"It's personal."

"You can't let this job get personal. You'd never last."

"I don't know that I believe that. Your heart's in it because you're dealing with people's lives." He washed down his chocolate with some beer.

"That's true for a lot of jobs."

"I guess."

He offered me another helping of pasta, which he spooned onto my plate before I could even say yes. "What do your folks do?" he asked.

"Dad's a contract lawyer nearing his retirement, and Mom was an ethics professor who gave up her career to take care of the kids." I looked at the ground as I spoke, well aware of my privilege and how it would sound to him. I was always apologizing for it in some way or another, always trying to downplay my background like it hadn't informed my choices later in life.

"Sounds like you had it pretty good," he said.

"I did." I chewed slowly.

"So why the somber look?"

I shrugged. "It's not somber. I had a good childhood."

"I don't respect you any less for having educated parents, Harland. I know you worked hard to get here."

"Thanks," I said. "How about you? Your mom's a teacher— what does your dad do?"

"Construction."

"Another outdoorsman, then."

He smiled. "Just livin' the American dream."

We ate in silence for a while, which was starting to feel natural, almost familiar. I was grateful for it. Kevin had always been a talker—chatting constantly, always battling the quiet because it seemed to unsettle him. Hux was different. He could hold a conversation, but he could also lapse into long silences that somehow enriched the time we spent together.

"Are you happy?" he asked.

I looked up at the sky, at the trees; inhaled a breath of air so crisp it was almost like ingesting a fine meal. Sequoia was nothing like Chicago; it was nothing like the Red Centre either. For a moment, I felt like the past was truly behind me—like I'd been reinvented.

"Yes," I said, which for the first time in years was the truth.

*   *   *

The next morning dawned clear and cold. Ollie greeted the day with his usual enthusiasm, but I lingered in my sleeping bag for a few minutes, savoring its warmth. The truth was, I'd never much liked the cold. The guys in the Chicago office used to get on my case endlessly because my winter gear swallowed me whole. "Harland the arctic bag lady," they used to call me. I'd had my thyroid checked a hundred times. No problem there—it was just me. *"Wear more layers,"* was my doctor's advice.

After putting on woolen long johns and thick socks, I ventured out into the morning mist. Hux had a pot of black coffee at the ready—terrible, as usual, but at least it was hot, the steam leeching off it in a white haze. To my surprise, he'd already taken down his tent and packed up his things. The guy was efficient, I'd give him that. I thanked him for the coffee.

From where we were camped, it was an eight-mile hike to Precipice. I knew we'd be lucky to get there by late afternoon, especially with all the elevation gain between here and there, but I was determined to give it my all. I finished my coffee, swallowed some ibuprofen, and did some stretches to work out the kinks in my back.

"What're you doing there?" Hux asked, as I reached my hands to the sky—it wasn't an impressive reach, all told. I'd never made it very far in youth basketball.

"Yoga."

He laughed. "Uh, no. That's not yoga."

"It's pretty similar."

"It's not similar at all."

I was smiling now, too, because he was right—my yoga had nothing in common with the things people were doing at reputable yoga studios in Chicago. I'd lifted these stretches off a YouTube video called *Yoga for Kids*.

We set off in good spirits. I tried to enjoy the scenery—the blue-green lakes on a background of granite, the forested terrain of the Big Arroyo Area. The last stretch of the hike took us over Kaweah Gap, where we encountered three hikers traveling together, none of whom had seen anyone else on the trail in days. They wished us luck and continued on their way.

At two o'clock in the afternoon, with many hard miles under our belt and a dangerous quantity of ibuprofen working its way through my kidneys, we stepped foot on the rocky shores of Precipice Lake. I almost wept with relief.

It was no less of a stunner than it had been the first time, with its saw-toothed cliff face that featured a dead drop into the water below. I could see why it attracted daredevils in summer. From my perspective, though, one small miscalculation could mean paralysis or worse.

I said to Hux, "It looks like some parts of the lake are still frozen."

"Indeed," he said.

"Hopefully we'll find that impact zone."

We picked up our pace on our way to the ridge that over-looked the lake, even though Hux seemed reluctant to push me too hard. I told him for the tenth time that I was fine, but I knew he'd ask me again, just to be sure.

As we hiked toward the remains of the Glampist campsite, my heart sank. It was clear even from a distance that nature had reasserted herself—there was no tent, no gear, no remnants of it whatsoever. But as we drew closer, and I saw how thoroughly the campsite had been cleared, my next impulse was to blame Corrigan. I'd asked him to hold off on touching anything until I had a chance to finish my investigation at Precipice.

"Do you know if Corrigan was planning to send some rangers up here to clear the scene?" I asked Hux. "Because I explicitly asked him not to."

"I don't think it was him, boss," Hux said. "There's some-body up there."

I took out my binoculars for a better look. He was right; there *was* someone on the ridge. I couldn't make out his face, but something about him looked familiar.

Hux said, "I think I know who that is."

"Who?"

"It looks like Ash Sinclair."

As we made our way up the ridge, I could see that Hux was right. But it wasn't just Ash; his son Zeke was there, and Ian too. When Ian caught sight of us coming up the ridge, he looked startled—and maybe a little alarmed. He held up a hand to acknowledge our presence.

Once we were up on the ridge some twenty minutes later, Ian greeted us with a wave and a muffled "Howdy," while Ash and Zeke said nothing at all. I wondered if they were responding to the fury bubbling up inside of me. These renegades had singlehandedly destroyed my crime scene.

Looking around, I could see that they'd packed everything with a Glampist logo on it into sacks. Those sacks were now sitting on a mule that was taking a dump upwind from where we were standing. Ash looked at Hux and said, "Can we help you?"

"Yeah," Hux said. "This campsite is under investigation."

Ash shrugged. "Nobody told us."

"We told you," I said. "Just the other day."

"Don't remember hearin' those words," Ash said.

Hux glanced at me with a weary expression that told me he was used to dealing with this kind of attitude. I watched Zeke wander over to the pack mule and stand next to it, almost like he was guarding the animal and its cargo. Ian kept on smiling like that was somehow going to ease the tension and solve all our problems.

"Look, I'm real sorry if we screwed up here," Ian said. "We got a call from the company to clean it up ASAP. And, well—you know, the paychecks come from them, so we gotta do what we're told." He attempted a chuckle.

"When did you get the call from them?" I asked.

"Uh . . ." Ian looked at his brother.

"Yesterday," Ash said. "They told us to get it done by today."

"Who did you talk to there?"

"It's always somebody different," Ash said. "Can't remember the name."

"The phone number, then?"

He shrugged. "Sorry. Don't have it on me."

No surprise there—the Sinclairs seemed determined to fluster me. Mission accomplished. I decided to change tact, if for no other reason than to calm myself down. "How'd you get up here so fast?" I asked.

"Huh?" Ian looked confused, but I couldn't tell if it was genuine or not.

"If Glampist called you yesterday, how'd you make it out here so quickly? We're twenty-two miles from the trailhead."

"We were already close by," Ash said.

"Doing what?"

He gave me a sideways smile. "This is startin' to feel like an interrogation."

"It's just a conversation."

The mule let out a sudden snort, and I looked over to see Zeke wrestling with a sack on the animal's rump. He shoved his hand in his pocket.

"What's he doing over there?" I asked Ash.

"Nothin'."

"Looks to me like he's looking for something."

"Zeke!" Ash called out over his shoulder. "Whatever the fuck you're doing, stop."

Zeke spat on the ground and walked off down the ridge, disappearing from sight. I was tempted to go after him.

"What's he got there?" I asked.

"I didn't see nothin'," Ash said.

"I'd like to ask him about it."

"He's a minor. You talk to me."

Ash Sinclair had me beat, and he knew it. Zeke Sinclair wasn't going to say a word to us, and the other two weren't exactly chatty. My best chance at getting something useful out of them was Hux, who at last had a connection with Ian. So far, though, I hadn't seen any indication that he was willing to ask his friend the tough questions.

Which was a problem, because the Sinclairs had the upper hand here. They'd cleared my crime scene, and I couldn't just go and put it back together. I couldn't prove malicious intent either. Still, it made me wonder—were they murderers? Thieves? Ian Sinclair claimed he didn't want to risk his job by stealing from the company that employed him, but Glampist's amenities were top of the line. The tent itself was worth a couple grand. And where were the suitcases? The divers hadn't found them in the lake.

"Fine," I said. "We'll call Glampist right now to confirm you're supposed to be here."

"Go ahead," Ash said. "We're right on schedule."

"And I'm going to have to ask you to unpack everything."

Ash snorted. "No can do."

"Of course you 'can do,'" I said, seething. "I'm making the calls here."

"You're not the one writin' the checks, though, are ya?"

Hux used my satellite phone to make the call. I could overhear most of the conversation, which started with a no-name employee but almost immediately went to Wu, who confirmed that yes, the takedown team was supposed to be at Precipice Lake. It was Glampist's property, after all, and she had received word that our investigation was complete. I watched Ash's lips curl up in a snide smile.

"Uh-huh," I heard Hux say. "Well, look, you heard wrong."

Hux was doing his best, keeping things civil. I knew I wouldn't have possessed the same restraint. Crime scene fiascos were a common occurrence, and not just here, but everywhere. Hopefully Hux's photos would be enough to fill in the gaps, but I couldn't help but think that the Sinclairs' actions were going to make or break this case. I also couldn't force them to unload all this gear, especially with Wu claiming it was her property.

Hux hung up the phone with a defeated look in his eyes.

"How's the rangerin' going?" Ash asked him.

"It's going fine."

"Hassling folks ain't quite like wipin' out the Taliban, is it?"

"The only hassle around here is you, Ash. We're just looking for a little cooperation."

"Sure you are. That and our civil liberties."

I told Hux with a subtle jab to the ribs that we were done here. I'd have to work this out with Wu and Glampist on the back end. There was no point in negotiating with Ash; he wasn't about to take orders from me, that was for sure.

"We gotta go," I said to Hux when he didn't move.

"Give me a minute."

With a menacing look at Ash, Hux dug his hands in his pockets and started walking over to the mule. I hadn't noticed that Zeke was back from wherever the hell he'd wandered off to. He was hovering out of sight behind the mule's rear.

So far Hux had struck me as an easygoing guy, always on the cusp of a joke, but in that moment I saw someone else—a no-nonsense ex–Navy SEAL with ice in his veins and purpose in his stride. His withering stare made the kid flinch.

"What the hell," Zeke said, backing up.

Ignoring him, Hux reached past the kid's massive arms and stuck his hand in Zeke's pocket. Hux's sleight of hand was incredible, like something you'd see in a magic show. Zeke never had a chance.

Ash marched over to see what all the fuss was about, while Ian hung back like he wasn't sure what to do. Ash barked at Hux, "Don't you fuckin' touch him—"

"This doesn't look like yours," Hux said, turning over a silvery-red pocketknife in his hands. "It's got the Glampist logo right there on the handle."

Ash shot his son a look. I decided to let things play out.

"This knife is evidence in a federal investigation," Hux said. "So I'm gonna have to confiscate it."

Zeke muttered something under his breath, and I couldn't say if it was because he'd been caught stealing or for some other reason. Ash, too, seemed to react to a deeper threat in Hux's words. To my surprise, he took a literal step back and softened his tone. He looked at his son and said, "Apologize to the ranger."

Zeke mumbled something like "Sorry."

Satisfied, Ash slapped the mule on the rear. "We'll be outta your hair now," he said, as the mule plodded down the ridge and hauled our evidence away. I kicked the dirt, disgusted by the way things had gone down. I vowed never to let this kind of thing happen again.

Ian Sinclair started after his brother and nephew, but Hux called out to him to hold up a second. I stood back, thinking for a second that Hux was about to stir up a fight with the burly outdoorsman. Ian hesitated before pivoting in our direction. He gave a sheepish smile that didn't ring quite true to me.

Ian said, "Sorry, man, we're really on a schedule—"

"What's going on here?" Hux asked. "Are you in some kind of trouble with Ash?"

"No, no trouble."

"Are you stealing from these campsites?"

"No!" Ian said. "Heck, no."

"Your nephew is."

He made circles in the dirt with his boot. "I'll talk to him."

I knew he wouldn't, though. Ian made a point of avoiding my gaze, staring at the ground as he talked. He shoved his hands in his pockets and shifted his weight from side to side.

"What's going on?" Hux asked. "Is it Grace? The kids?"

"No, it's—it's nothing, man." He was mumbling.

Hux softened his voice a bit. "You can tell me."

Ian glanced at me, a silent question on his face: *"Can you leave us alone?"* And maybe I should have; maybe he deserved that much as someone who'd sacrificed so much for his country. But I also felt that we'd given Ian Sinclair ample opportunity to come clean about his role in all this, and yet he was still holding out on us. It was time for him to pick a side.

Ian let out a sigh. "There's been some money trouble at home," he said.

"What kind of money trouble?" Hux asked.

"Just—medical bills. Evan's got some kinda blood disease."

"He does?" Hux looked taken aback. "Why didn't you tell me?"

"Because it's my business, my problem. I ain't lookin' for sympathy."

"Yeah, but there are other ways to get money, man."

He barked out a laugh that sounded pitiful and sad. "For you, maybe. Forget workin' for the man—these days I can barely remember my kids' names."

As he spoke, I caught a glimpse of Ash Sinclair coming back up the ridge. He was alone. The meanness in his gaze gave me pause.

"Let's take a look around," I said to Hux. "We can finish this conversation later."

Ian said, "Am I—shit, are you gonna do somethin' about this—"

"No," I said. "But we're going to talk again soon—just you, me, and Hux."

"Yes, ma'am."

Bowing his head in a gesture of thanks, Ian hurried off in Ash's direction. The two brothers exchanged a few words, some of them heated, but none of them intelligible with the wind roaring in my ears. After another minute or so, Ash tossed an inscrutable look in my direction, while Ian kept his back turned.

Then they disappeared down the hill.

* * *

With the Sinclairs gone, Hux and I canvassed the remains of the campsite one final time. Ignoring my bad mood, Ollie sat on a rock with his paws crossed and watched us work. No one spoke. I could tell Hux was feeling conflicted about Ian Sinclair's "money troubles." For me, though, I cared more about the loss of evidence than the theft. A part of me relished the fact that Glampist was getting ripped off.

But I didn't tell Hux that. He had to figure out how far he was willing to stick his neck out for his friend.

"We've only got a few hours of daylight left," I said. "Let's make the most of it."

We walked over to a flat spot on the ridge that jutted out a few inches. I looked over the edge at the vertical sheet of granite that disappeared into dark blue water. It was a dizzying drop, but technically survivable.

"You said a hundred feet, right?"

He nodded. "That's my guess."

I pulled out my altimeter and checked the gauge. "We're at 10,480 right here, and the lake's 10,384, so it's technically ninety-six feet. Let's say you got lucky and entered the water safely—if you weren't prepared for the impact, chances are you'd still break some bones. Especially if you hit ice."

"I don't think the ice was all that thick, though," he said.

"Well, she did go right through it."

I looked out at the vast expanse of the Sequoia wilderness from our perch on the ridge. With the wind at my back, I nudged a round pebble over the edge and into the void. It took some time to hit the ice—an eternity, really. For Tatum Delancey, it sure would have felt that way.

Hux said, "You know . . . I may have a tool that could help us figure this out."

"A tool?"

"Yeah." He scratched the back of his neck. "It's a thing I've been working on."

"Does it involve neoprene?"

Hux was a quick study; his eyes widened as it dawned on him what I meant. "That water's *cold*, Harland. Even for me."

"I know it's cold, but we've got to see the ice up close and take some measurements. It will matter if this case ever goes to trial."

"Okay, but if this affects my fertility down the road . . ."

"Then the world has me to thank."

He chuckled as we started down the ridge. "Well, at least I know what you really think about me, Harland."

He didn't know, though—not even close.

And maybe that was for the best.

16

A S IT TURNED out, Hux relished the chance to get in the water, even though he hadn't come prepared for it. He stripped down to his T-shirt and shorts and waded into the shallows while I stood on the shore, debating whether to follow him in. I was worried about my back seizing up in the cold, but I didn't want to play spectator either. This could very well be my first criminal case in ISB, after all. How I performed here could set the tone for the rest of my career.

"What am I looking for exactly?" he asked, turning back to look at me. Ollie was in the water, too, his tongue lolling out of his mouth as he splashed in Hux's shadow.

"Hold up a sec," I said. "I'm coming in."

"Are you sure? 'Cause it's about fifty degrees in here. My testicles are the size of hamster pellets right now."

"Well, I don't have testicles so we're good there."

He turned back around while I took off my shoes and socks, keeping my T-shirt and pants on because it was important to maintain some professional boundaries. I knew that our wet clothes would dry quickly in the sun, and we both had reserves since we'd packed for a three-day trip. Over the years, I'd gotten used to unsolicited comments about my body and being a female agent and the like. Hux just didn't go there. *"He was raised right,"* as my mother would have said.

Hux wasn't kidding about the water temperature. The diving reflex hit me hard—a sudden, gulping inhale that racked my whole body. The water was so cold it felt like a burn, an icy fire that tore through my skin. It took mere seconds for my feet to turn pink, then a siren red. These were all ominous signs. The countdown to hypothermia was on.

The divers had marked the discovery site with yellow flags and a buoy, which was floating next to the ice shelf about six feet from the cliff face. But even without the buoy, it was obvious where Tatum Delancey had entered the water. Her momentum from the long fall had carried her body straight through the ice, leaving behind a jagged six-by-three-foot hole that was framed by ice on three sides. On the side farthest from the cliff face, though, the ice had melted, giving the illusion of a natural defect rather than a human-made one.

Careful to keep my head above water to preserve body heat, I swam over to the ice shelf. Attached to my ankle was a small orange floatation device, which had a waterproof compartment for my phone and other devices. Using the one attached to my altimeter, I determined the depth of the lake in this location to be eighteen feet, which made it unlikely that Tatum Delancey would have hit bottom. The dimensions of the defect in the ice also suggested that she'd fallen onto her stomach or back, not feetfirst or headfirst. These findings were consistent with the injuries Dr. Bianchi had noted in her report.

Hux climbed up onto the ice shelf, testing its strength. "You better get outta there, Harland," he called out. "Your face looks like an eggplant."

"Thanks," I said, but it sounded like *tanks* because my lips were frozen.

"Swim over here." He gestured to a rock ledge a few feet to his left. "There's no wind at least. You'll warm up a bit."

I decided not to argue with him. My orientation at ISB had covered hypothermia in great detail, both to mitigate risk on the job and to augment our skills as investigators. I recalled from those classes that in water this cold, the average person could survive for about an hour. Hux, of course, was not an average person; he could probably go three or four. But I wasn't about to test my physiological threshold. I scrambled onto the ledge and assumed the Heat Escape Lessening Posture, which was essentially a cross between a bear hug and the fetal position. Hux laughed.

"Feeling better?" he asked.

"I'll survive. What's your take on the ice?"

"Well, it's about two centimeters thick next to the wall," Hux said, showing me the ice pick he'd used to drill down and get a measurement. "But only a few millimeters thick where she went through. It's hard to say what the conditions were like in the days since she fell, but I'm gonna say there hasn't been a whole lot of melt. There's a lot of shade over here."

After taking some photos and making a series of measurements with my altimeter, we shook out our muscles and mentally prepared ourselves for the swim back to shore. Hux beat me by a mile, but he didn't gloat, which made me feel a little better. I pulled my microfiber towel out of my pack and rubbed my skin raw with it. I offered it to Hux, but he said he liked to air dry.

"So," Hux said. "Do you think Tatum Delancey was murdered?"

"Whoa," I said with a laugh. "You got right to it there."

"Well?" He stuck his face in my line of sight, which made me laugh again. I swatted him away with my microfiber towel.

"Still waiting for an answer over here . . ." he said.

"I think it's possible she was pushed," I said, emphasizing the word *possible* to dampen his excitement. I wasn't sure it had the intended effect.

"Which implies murder."

"Not necessarily. It could have been accidental."

"Not according to Newtonian physics."

"Uh-oh. Here we go with the math stuff."

"It's all math, Harland. You saw the ice—assuming she landed where we think she landed, Tatum Delancey hit the water almost twenty feet from the cliff face. That's a long way from the takeoff point—too far for someone with her athletic ability to generate that kind of speed. Horizontal launch speed, that is. Plus you saw the terrain up there—not a whole lot of

run-up space to get yourself going. Now, if you were *really* moti-
vated, you could put all that objective data together—you know,
her weight, center of mass, vertical height, air resistance, wind,
horizontal distance—and plug it into a fairly simple equation
based on Newton's laws, and you could prove right then and
there whether she was pushed or not."

I made a point of folding my towel as slowly as possible,
which seemed to make Hux nervous. He took a swig from his
canteen, nearly choking on it as it went down. The truth was, I
was impressed. I'd run into a few fall-from-height investigations
during my time with the FBI, and none of them had gotten this
technical. In most cases, the lead investigator simply decided if
the death was "suspicious" or not. The former got a second look;
the latter were filed away as suicides or accidental.

"What equation?" I asked.

"Well," he said, breaking into a grin, "I'm thrilled you
asked."

"Is this the 'tool' you were talking about?"

With a nod, he pulled out his cell phone and showed me an
app called Fall Zone. The graphics weren't great—the app itself
looked homegrown rather than venture capital funded—but it
was easy to follow. There were inputs for all kinds of variables,
including depth of the water, body weight of the victim, clothing worn by the victim, injuries, air temperature, toxicology
reports, and impact zone measurements.

"Wow," I said. "You came up with this?"

"I had a buddy help me with the software side of things—
the logo needs work and the font isn't quite right—but yeah, I
developed it."

"When?"

"A few months ago. We see a lot of falls out here, and I
thought, well—I'm a math guy, as you know. And I had some
extra time on my hands."

"It's—just, wow," I said again, enamored by the scope of
the thing. "It's a cool concept. Does it work?"

"Well, I mean—I haven't used it in an open investigation or
anything. But I built it using a test set of closed cases with
known outcomes. I'm onto the dev set now—"

"The what?"

"Oh, sorry. The development set. You build a machine learning tool based on an algorithm, right? That's the app. But you need to teach the app to make adjustments based on specific variables that can be helpful in predicting outcomes—or, you know, the target. The only way to do that is with good data sets. I've been trying to get my hands on as many fall-from-height cases as I can, but I've only got so many connections as a junior park ranger . . ."

He handed me the phone. Down at the bottom of the app's main screen was a big red button that was rather presumptuously labeled, "Solve." I liked Hux's boldness.

"I could help you with that part," I said. "I've got access to thousands of FBI case files."

"That would be awesome."

"But on one condition."

He lifted an eyebrow.

"You let me use this thing. I like it a lot."

His face brightened. "Well, sure. No problem at all. But it's a work in progress—"

"I realize that." I scrolled back to the top of the page. "You want to go ahead and plug our numbers in?"

With an unabashed smile on his face, Hux went to work putting the numbers in—fourteen in all. We were missing a few inputs, but for the most part every field had a number in it. Hux let me do the honors with regards to the "Solve" button. As soon as I pushed it, a disclaimer popped up:

This application was developed to predict the most likely scenario based on a series of objective variables. Fall Zone's algorithm is by no means definitive, and its findings are inadmissible in a court of law.

I looked at Hux with a wry smile. "Way to cover your butt there," I said.

"Yup."

I went back to the app and hit a green button labeled "Yes, I understand." Once that was done, a block of text filled the screen.

Based on the data provided, it is highly likely *the subject fell from a height.*

Based on the data provided, it is highly likely *the subject landed on their back because of (a) the dimensions of the impact zone and (b) injuries sustained. Note that for (b), there were no injuries reported to the forearms or hands, which supports a fall onto the back. There were no injuries to the feet or ankles, which makes a feetfirst entry* unlikely.

Based on the data provided, it is somewhat likely *the subject was pushed because of (a) the conclusions rendered above and(b) the calculated flight distance, which would require a horizontal launch speed of 42 km/hr if the subject jumped unassisted.*

"What does 'somewhat likely' mean?"

"It means it's, you know, somewhere between unlikely and probable."

"Gotta put your nickel down, Hux."

"Yeah, I know. But hey, if you can get me access to those case files, consider the problem solved. I bet I could even go to a numeric system—like, Fall Zone is seventy-two percent certain that the victim was pushed or whatever."

"Let's not go too crazy," I said, which made him laugh.

I read the report again, this time focusing on the calculated horizontal launch speed. "I'm not much of a metric system person," I admitted.

"You can change the settings—"

"What I mean is, how fast is that, approximately?"

"Oh." He scratched his ear. "Well, let's see . . . it's about twenty-six miles per hour—which, you know, is very fast for a human. Usain Bolt's top recorded speed is twenty-seven miles per hour. So unless Tatum Delancey is actually Usain Bolt, then she didn't go flying off that cliff on her own. An external force was applied."

"So in other words, she was pushed."

He nodded at the phone. "Fall Zone thinks so."

Yes, but Fall Zone's conclusions wouldn't hold up in court. The old guard in the FBI and ISB talked about themselves as gods, superior to technology and all its tricks. *"There's no substitute for good old-fashioned police work,"* they liked to say, but I knew better. Machine learning absolutely had a place in law enforcement, and I'd decided long ago to embrace rather than reject it. I felt the same way about forensic genealogy. If these tools helped me to solve a case, then they deserved a place in my repertoire.

I said to Hux, "Look, even discounting the app, it looks to me like Tatum Delancey landed on her back—and yes, she was farther from the cliff face than I would've thought if she had simply jumped or fallen over. Much farther."

"So you agree with the app."

"Here's the thing. It's hard to prove someone was pushed based on evidence that's always changing. A good lawyer could argue that something else fell onto the ice and made that hole there, or that the ice was naturally weaker in that area, or that she had walked out onto the ice and fallen through. I can put all the circumstantial evidence together into a narrative that makes sense, but at the end of the day, it's not definitive."

Even under the brim of his baseball cap, the shadow of Hux's disappointment played on his face. He closed the app and put his cell phone back in his pocket. I thought for a moment he was going to say something else, but he didn't.

"But in my opinion," I said, "*I* think she was pushed, and I believe we can make the case for it. Who knows? Maybe we can legitimize Fall Zone somehow."

He looked at me, squinting into the sunlight. "So . . . you think this was murder?"

"I do."

He thought for a moment. "So who pushed her?"

"Wait, you don't have an app for that?"

When he finally noticed the smirk on my face, he chuckled. "I'm working on it, Harland—it's called *Whodunit.*"

"Good." I pulled my knees into my chest, ignoring the electric hum in my back. At least I was used to it by now. Sequoia had won a few battles, but not the war.

"So what now?" he asked.

Ollie, having dried his fur with a robust shake-out, settled in the space between us. He smelled like the mountains, like freedom.

I looked at Hux. "We figure this out the old-fashioned way."

CHAPTER

17

Now that Precipice Lake was an official crime scene, there was work to be done. Witness interviews, cell phone records, crime scene analysis—all of this was going to take time, and Ray had made it clear to me from the outset that ISB agents didn't have that luxury. When it came to murder, our best hope was to coax a confession out of someone.

The obvious place to start was Edwin Delancey. He had motive, after all, and statistics weren't on his side. His much-younger wife had gone off into the wilderness with some other guy, which couldn't have been easy on his ego. He had called to report her missing days after her death. Then there was the shifty phone interview. He was definitely a person of interest, but there were others, too. I had a long list of people to talk to.

With Ollie trotting happily by his side, Hux set the pace on our way back down the trail. Sheila had called to let us know that she was going to pick us up near Hamilton Lake, but as we were waiting for the copter to arrive, another call came in.

"What's up?" Hux asked.

"Sheila can't make it. She's off on another search-and-rescue mission near Big Arroyo. Earliest she can get here is tomorrow morning." I tried to sound upbeat, but mentally I'd hit a wall. The one-step-at-a-time mantra had given way to *just get to the copter,* and now that she wasn't coming, my feet refused to carry on.

"Let's camp here, then," Hux said.

"No," I said.

"No? Why not?"

"We're wasting time up here, Hux. We've got so much to do."

"We don't have a choice, boss. I'm sorry."

In the end, Hux convinced me that twelve more hours in Sequoia wasn't going to make or break this case. Maybe he was right.

For better or for worse, I was learning to trust him.

*   *   *

As it turned out, Sheila couldn't come the next day either, so Hux proposed that we set off toward Bear Paw Meadow. He figured it was worth a look since SAR hadn't spent much time searching for Colton Dodger there, and in any case, it was mostly downhill.

As it turned out, it was a staggering three-thousand-foot descent over three short miles to the Hamilton Lakes basin, on a trail that was mostly rock and loose stone. From there it was three more miles to the Bear Paw Meadow High Sierra Camp, which at least had running water and sturdy tents. Hux didn't think the camp was open for the season yet, but it gave me something to work toward. I was starting to wish we'd just stayed up at Precipice.

Hux called out over his shoulder, "How's it going back there, Harland?"

"My quads are in full rebellion, but aside from that I'm good."

"Yup. Feel the burn." He put his hand on a fat redwood and leaned against it as he waited for me to catch up. I wasn't about to object to a little breather. A part of me was desperately hoping that my sat phone would ring with a call from Sheila: *"I'm coming to getcha!"* But so far, the damn thing had stayed silent.

"Are you really feeling the burn?" I asked him.

He quirked an eyebrow. "Of course. This is tough terrain."

"It's all downhill."

"This is tough terrain, Harland. I don't know what you're trying to prove."

I tried to will the emotion out of my voice. "I'm not trying to prove anything. I'm just trying to complete the task."

"Uh-huh."

We rested for sixteen minutes, which was my call. Next time, Hux would get to decide how long we rested, and so on all the way to Bear Paw. Hux's breaks varied in duration, but mine were always sixteen minutes. I had decided that it was better to be consistent. As for Hux, the guy clearly didn't require any rest at all, but he put on a good show. I'd never met anyone like him in all my years in law enforcement, but then again, stamina wasn't the name of the game in the FBI. If you could walk from your car to the crime scene, you were good to go.

As we descended into the lake basin, the trail flattened out again, which was great news for my quads. The blisters on my heels refused to heal, but I could cope with open wounds. It was my joints that gave me the most trouble. At least my back was holding up; maybe the bundle of nerves back there had finally gotten the message.

Hux stopped on the last stretch of trail before the mountainous terrain turned to forest, and I was glad, really, because it felt important to mark the transition. It was a strange borderland—a stark mountainscape behind us and dense woods ahead. I leaned on the ragged remains of a tree that had probably been there for a thousand years until lightning took it down.

As Ollie sprinted off into the woods to deal with an errant squirrel, I asked Hux, "So what's your beef with Ash Sinclair?"

He didn't look up from the orange he was peeling. "Ash? I dunno. He treats the rangers like shit, which pisses me off."

"Does he treat *you* like shit?"

"No, because I'm ex-military, but that's no excuse. I'm no better than the other rangers."

I peered up at him. "What about Ian Sinclair?"

"What about him?"

"Is he close to his brother?"

"He is, but only because he's got no one else. I don't know if you've been to Three Rivers, but there's not much going on there."

"I drove through it." I crinkled my nose at the memory. "It might be worth asking Ian's wife if he was home last weekend."

He said nothing, but I could tell this line of inquiry was getting under his skin. He peeled the last bit of his orange and stared at the juicy fruit underneath. Then he tilted his face toward the cloudless sky. "*Lex parsimoniae*, Harland. It's not them."

"That's not very helpful in this case."

"Maybe it should be, though. What's the simplest explanation?"

"There isn't one. If Edwin Delancey was home all weekend, then he couldn't have pushed his wife off a cliff in Sequoia."

"Maybe he hired someone to do it—like Colton Dodger."

"Well, we need to establish his whereabouts, that's for sure."

"But it's usually the husband, right?"

"It is, but if he *was* home, then we're still left with a murder-for-hire scenario, which really doesn't compute for me. Most contract killers choose easier methods."

Hux considered this. "True."

After Hux had finished his orange, we continued on. The camp at Bear Paw had signs posted that it was still closed for the season—another disappointment among too many to count—so we pushed on through dense forest. As the sun set, it began to rain. I took my brand-spankin' new poncho out of my pack and put it on.

Hux said, "We're almost to the Redwood Meadow horse camp—might be worth it to catch a few Z's there and then set out again when the sun comes up."

I knew that we were somewhere in the proximity of Timber Gap, but this deep in the forest, it was impossible to get my bearings. All we had were my GPS and Hux's old-fashioned compass, which he liked to take out now and then and jiggle around.

"What's a horse camp?" I asked.

"It's mostly a pile of rubble now, but the Redwood Meadow horse camp used to be a real business back in the forties and fifties. I've been thinking about it on the way down. Let's say

Colton Dodger took this trail back to the parking lot—it'd be a natural stopping point if he was desperate or lost, especially since Bear Paw was closed."

"I thought Corrigan said SAR searched down here."

"Maybe they missed the camp."

Before Hux could expand on this theory, I called Corrigan to see if his team had explored the area he was talking about. Corrigan's gravelly voice came through in a blast of static. "The what?" he barked.

"The horse camp."

"The Redwood Meadow horse camp," Hux clarified. I handed him the sat phone. Hux said into the phone, "Rick, we're out here on the High Sierra Trail, coming up on Timber Gap. I thought we might have a look around the horse camp."

"Why? SAR searched it already."

Hux looked at me. "You sure?"

"It was in their report if that's what you're askin'."

I could see the disappointment on Hux's face, like he'd expected a different answer. "Look, Hux," Corrigan said, "the place is condemned—suffered some serious damage in a fire last year. Plus there's a storm coming. You two should bunk down where you are."

Hux replied, "Nah, we're all good here."

"You're good, sure, but Agent Harland's not used to these conditions."

Corrigan's assessment hit me like a punch to the gut, but Hux said, "She's an animal, Chief." You might need to send the SAR guys out to get me after this is all said and done, but Harland can take care of herself."

I couldn't help but smile. Hux didn't patronize me with a smile of his own, which made the compliment all the more meaningful.

"Noted," Corrigan said with his usual gruffness. "Look, SAR covered a lot of the High Sierra Trail and didn't find anything."

With a quick glance in my direction, almost as if he were seeking my permission to speak, Hux said to Corrigan, "We might've found something."

The chief grunted. "And what's that, son?"

"I think we found the Woodsman."

"You and everybody else out there," he muttered. "SAR is circulating that damn sketch all over the place. Wasn't my idea."

"Yeah, well, we talked to one couple—"

"You know my opinion, Hux. You oughta move on from the whole Woodsman business."

"I hear you there, but he looks just like the sketch, plus he's got this tattoo—"

"What sketch? That dumb cartoon Ismelda drew last year 'cause you asked her to?" He made a sound like a snort. "I sure as hell didn't pass that around."

"Well, you should talk to your guys, then."

"My guys are done. It's time to send 'em home."

"Rick, we think that whoever Tatum Delancey was camping with is still out there. And with this weather coming—"

"Let's debrief when you get back, Ranger. I've got my hands full here."

Hux ran his hand over his skull. I wondered if he was reacting to the stress in Corrigan's voice, which was meant, surely, to make Hux feel a little guilty for being out here with me. "What's going on there, Chief?" he asked Corrigan.

"Some idiot got himself stuck in a ditch out front. For Chrissakes, if one more imbecile drives up here with a rear-wheel vehicle . . ."

Hux gave me a desperate look. It was clear that Corrigan wanted this whole thing behind him, even if that meant giving up on the missing Colton Dodger. The SAR volunteers had overtaken Mineral King with their gear, food, and noisy energy, none of which jived with Corrigan's solitary disposition.

I couldn't entirely blame him. With summer right around the corner, he was looking at three brutal months of dealing with tourists. There'd be kids having sex in the woods, hikers setting out without food or water, campers leaving their chips and beer out all night for the bears to feast on. There was always the fear of forest fires, too, which was usually the utility company's fault, but not always. Every ranger had a story about dealing with chain smokers and pyromaniacs in the woods.

"Tell him we need a little more time," I said to Hux.

"Harland thinks we need more time," he relayed to Corrigan, but he did it with a pained expression on his face.

"Time is money and resources," Corrigan said. "These guys aren't all local. Summer's a month away, and they know it's gonna kick their asses. They want to go home."

I did, too, at the moment. The rain was just a light drizzle, but once it picked up, we'd be pitching our tents in a soaking downpour, and sleeping in it, too.

"I'm calling off the search tonight," Corrigan said. "I suggest you take cover."

"We'll be back tomorrow afternoon," Hux said. "If we find anything, we'll send word."

"You won't find anything."

I was starting to believe him.

18

I COULD TELL HUX was feeling defeated by his conversation with Corrigan. As we set off down the trail, he mumbled something about budget cuts.

"Look, Hux," I said. "I'm game to search the horse camp. We don't need Corrigan's permission to do that."

"But I know you don't want to waste any more time out here. *I* don't want to waste your time out here."

"If you don't think it's a waste of time, then it's not a waste of time."

"It could be, though."

"I know you don't believe that."

He sighed. Like me, he had his poncho on, but every so often he'd pull his hood off and shake out his hair. He was doing it now.

"Who's Ismelda, by the way?" I asked.

"She's an old coot that lives in Three Rivers."

"And she made the sketch?"

"It's a strange scene up here, boss," he said. "Sequoia is like a small town in some ways. You've got your busybodies, your crazy grandmas, your incestuous ranger relationships. Ismelda got involved in the Woodsman thing because she thinks she's an artist and wanted to help. I can't tell you how many sketches she made. Most of 'em looked like alien blobs."

"So what did Ismelda base her sketch on?"

"Her powers," he said with utmost seriousness before breaking out in a grin. "You should see the look on your face."

"Is that really true?"

"Absolutely, one hundred percent true. She's a psychic of some sort. Don't bring it up with Corrigan, though—it's a sore subject."

"I bet."

He laughed. "ISB doesn't use psychics?"

"*I* don't. I don't use God or Buddha or my lucky pendant either."

"Whatever works for you," he said. "I don't judge."

I wondered, though, if I'd offended him. Some of these ex-military guys relied on religion to make sense of all they'd seen and endured. I respected that choice; it just didn't figure into my worldview. Maybe it had once, but not anymore.

Ollie let loose a resonant howl, which stopped me in my tracks. "Did you hear something?" I asked.

"No," he said. "But I saw something."

I swept my flashlight's beam across the trees, illuminating all its empty spaces in an eerie yellow light. The daytime's natural shadows were giving way to twilight ones, which had an ominous quality. The only sound was the rain, coming down harder now, a constant patter on my poncho and the tops of my boots.

"Not out there," Hux said, as I squinted at the murky scene in front of us. "Down here."

He flashed his light at his feet.

Footprints.

* * *

The prints looked like they belonged to a man with average-sized feet, and they were less than a day old, as per Hux's estimation. In another few hours, the rain would wash them away, and we'd have to rely on Ollie's nose to track them. For now, though, we could both clearly see where the footprints led—straight into the horse camp.

A dilapidated piece of mossy wood hung suspended between two redwood trees, marking the entrance to the camp. I couldn't recall seeing a single hoofprint since embarking on the High Sierra Trail, which told me the place either didn't operate at this time of year or didn't operate at all. Corrigan had mentioned a fire. Perhaps that had been the nail in the coffin for an attraction that couldn't compete with the likes of Glampist.

Hux started after Ollie, who had taken off toward the rusted sign. I looked up at it, with its chipped wood and peeling paint, like it belonged in some prop department at a defunct movie studio. In the distance, a burned-out structure languished in the woods, its blackened edges marking its decay, contrasting with the lush red-brown of the trees that surrounded it. A pervading sense of abandonment was everywhere.

"Well?" Hux turned around. "You coming?"

"I'm not thrilled about it, but sure."

While Hux surreptitiously reached for his Glock, we passed under the sign and onto the grounds of the camp. The trail morphed from dirt to gravel, mostly overgrown with weeds and high grass. Straight ahead was the camp's first attraction: a horse pen. The fence was a ruin in most places, either crushed by falling branches or weathered by time.

"Let's check out the barn," Hux said.

The barn was hardly recognizable as such, with its roof caved in and three of its four walls burned to a charred crisp. The lone wall remaining supported a portion of a thatched roof, which cast a long shadow on a darkened interior.

The footprints, though, were unmistakable, even without the benefit of daylight. They ran the length of the fence, right up to where the last piling met the barn. Hux gripped his Glock with both hands while keeping the gun at his hip. He was a natural and a pro, clearly.

Turning to me, he said, "Just so we're clear, I've only fired this particular weapon once, and that was at a bear. I'd like to keep it that way." He tested the integrity of the fence with his hand. "You want to go first?"

"No, you go ahead. Whoever's in there will be less alarmed by a ranger than a cop."

Hux approached the barn with sure and silent strides, and when he was fifteen feet from the barn's intact fourth wall, he called out in a loud voice, "Hello in there. My name's Huxley, and I'm a ranger with the National Park Service. My partner and I saw your footprints and wanted to check in on you. This barn here's condemned."

We waited for a response, but none came. Hux again identified himself, and this time he explained why we were out here in the dead of night, sifting through a condemned structure. There were signs all over the place—"DANGER: DO NOT ENTER"—with one notice posted on the barn itself, its black ink faded but still legible. Hux glanced over his shoulder at me.

"All right, then," Hux said to the darkness, his voice rising above the resonant din of the pouring rain. "We're concerned about your safety, so we're coming in."

Still no sound from the barn—or maybe there was, and we just couldn't hear it. Hux approached the structure with slow, deliberate strides while I followed on his right flank. Our boots made loud sucking sounds in the mud. Overhead, a falcon shrieked as it soared across the night sky, almost like a warning call. Wind rattled the eaves that clung to the barn's skeleton.

The door to the barn was long gone, destroyed in the fire. The lone window in the wall was just a ragged hole, with no sign of any glass. A tattered blue sheet hung from the interior.

"Hux," I whispered, and pointed to the corner of the barn where the fourth wall ended and a gaping nothingness began. It felt like a safer approach than the window. As Hux changed course, I checked my radio to make sure it was off. I didn't want to spook whoever was inside.

"We're coming in!" Hux yelled.

With one hand gripping his weapon and the other his flashlight, Hux rounded the corner like he'd navigated this situation a hundred times before—total confidence, no fear. He was a big guy, and his imposing figure blocked my view. I couldn't see who or what was in front of us, until Hux suddenly dropped his arms and swept his flashlight over the rubble.

There was someone in there.

CHAPTER

19

A T FIRST GLANCE, it looked as though this unfortunate person had sought shelter in an unstable structure, as one particularly large beam was resting right on top of his thighs. Undeterred, Hux cleared the rubble like he was tossing sticks out of a sandbox. I stayed out of his way, deciding that my interference would do more harm than good. Somehow, he managed to clear the heavy pilings and fallen beams on his own, and he did it in under ten seconds.

I thought for sure we'd found a dead body, in part because of the rubble resting on top of it, but mostly because people who sought refuge in shelters like this didn't last long. But then Hux felt for a pulse, and his eyes went wide. "He's alive," he said.

"He's breathing?" A dumb question, but it was the first one that came to mind.

He nodded before turning back to the man—and it *was* a man, from the looks of him. I could tell by the size of his hiking boots. His face and hair were matted with dirt. He wasn't conscious, or at least didn't appear to be.

"Hey." Hux shook the man's arm. "Hey, you okay? Can you hear me?" There was no response. "He's barely got a pulse," Hux said. "I'd call MedEvac."

While I rushed to unpack the first-aid kit, Hux performed an expedient but thorough initial assessment—known in the field as a primary survey. Once he'd ruled out a neck injury, he maneuvered the man onto his back to make it easier for him to breathe. His breaths were ragged and uneven, and I worried about them suddenly stopping altogether. But Hux, for his part, stayed calm and collected.

With Hux doing everything he could to keep the man alive, I used the sat phone to call Northern California's Geographic Area Coordination Center, which dispatched MedEvac helicopters. From that point on, all we could do was wait. It was a long thirty minutes.

The deafening roar of a chopper's rotors alerted us to their arrival. The paramedics met us out in the abandoned horse pen, and not long after that, Corrigan showed up, having taken to the trail on foot. The older ranger looked tired—weary from the nonstop activity, maybe. With a glance at Hux, who was updating the paramedics, he started walking toward me. I was knee-deep in charred rubble, searching for clues in the debris. The main thing I was after was a form of identification.

"Well," Corrigan said by way of greeting, "this was unexpected."

"Yes," I agreed. "Hux found him. He saw some footprints on the trail."

Corrigan shook his head. "SAR told me they checked this area—checked it more than once, in fact. This poor sod couldn't have been here long." He tugged his hood over his forehead, shielding his face from the wind and rain. In the darkness, I couldn't see much more than the whites of his eyes.

"Is this your guy, then?" Corrigan asked.

"We'll see."

"It's gotta be him. It's not like we get folks goin' missing all the time out here. For the most part, people aren't that dumb."

As much as I wanted to believe this was the man missing from Tatum Delancey's campsite, the time line raised some questions for me. If Dodger had left Precipice Lake the night Tatum Delancey died, and followed the trail without any wrong turns, he should have passed the horse camp days ago. Unfortunately, the only person who could shed some light on the situation was lying on a gurney right now.

Our search of his pockets had yielded some clues, though—
one was a map of the Sequoia wilderness, which meant Delia had
been telling the truth about something, at least. But her description of the man she'd encountered didn't quite fit; the guy in the
horse camp was rail thin, more like one forty than one ninety. It
was possible he'd lost some weight over the last few days, but not
fifty pounds. Maybe she'd miscalculated or misremembered, but
I didn't think so. Her recollection was too precise.

Hux and I watched as the chopper lifted off the ground and
disappeared over the treetops. When it was gone, the silence
invaded with menacing swiftness. A chill coursed through me
that had nothing to do with the plummeting temperatures.

Corrigan walked up to us and said, "Bet the guy lost his
inhaler."

I turned toward him. "What?"

"I've seen it before. See it all the time, actually. People over-
estimating their abilities—teaches 'em a tough lesson."

Hux continued to watch the night sky. "Could be."

Corrigan walked off again. I wondered if he blamed SAR
for not doing a thorough enough search of the area, or if he was
simply dreading the prospect of a more in-depth investigation.
He didn't seem to relish my company, that was for sure.

As Corrigan stepped out into the open, he plucked his
ranger's hat off his head and beat it gently against his thigh,
shaking the dust and dandruff out of it. I caught a whiff of Sel-
sun blue.

"Well," he said, speaking more to the trees than to us, "this
whole damn situation's way above my pay grade. I hope you two
can figure it out." He put his hat back on his head. "As for me,
I'm heading back—got enough on my plate."

According to Hux, it was about a mile and a half back to
the ranger station from the horse camp, which raised another
question about our guy in the barn. He had given up—or been
forced to give up—just an hour's walk to the parking lot. *Why?*
Fatigue was one explanation; disorientation was another. But
what if he had used the barn as a place to hide?

After Corrigan had gone, I said to Hux, "I want to be there
when this guy wakes up."

"Fresno?" Hux asked.

I nodded. "Are you game?"

"Absolutely." He pulled his hood over his head. "I'd sure like to see his face when we ask him if he's Colton Dodger."

"Me, too." I jutted an elbow toward the fence around the horse pen. "Want to see what I found in the rubble?"

"Sure."

The small pile of evidence I'd collected didn't amount to much. Since the fire, the barn's ruins had seen some signs of life—beer cans, empty bags of chips, candy wrappers, and various drug paraphernalia. It was all old, though, thoroughly weathered by the elements. There was nothing that stood out to me as particularly helpful or informative.

"Did you notice what he was wearing?" Hux asked.

"Yeah. Nice stuff."

"Super nice. It just—I dunno."

"What?"

"It didn't jive with the person wearing it. He didn't *look* like a glamper."

I knew what Hux was getting at. The guy in the barn had a pock-marked face, shaggy hair, an unkempt beard, and finger-nails caked with dirt. If first impressions counted for anything, he seemed to fit a certain lifestyle, but I was willing to give him the benefit of the doubt.

Still, no matter who he was or his circumstances in life, he should have had a cell phone. I supposed he could have dropped it on the trail—maybe in his mad dash to escape the Woodsman—but I didn't like that theory either. Most people were unreasonably protective of their phones, even more so than fresh water. One of those things could save your life in the wilderness; the other was useless, except for passing the time while you froze to death.

"Well," Hux said, "I'm not seeing the smoking gun here."

"Me neither. The map was a good find, but I was expecting more."

"Yeah, it doesn't add up," Hux said. "Most people hold onto things out here. The 'leave no trace' mantra means they fill their pockets with things they want to throw away but can't."

"So maybe he emptied them."

Hux considered this for a moment. "Why, though?"

"I don't know. The obvious answer is he was carrying drug paraphernalia and didn't want to get caught with it. Could be he was delirious or a litterbug. Or maybe he's the rare outdoor enthusiast that travels light."

"Or he ran off in a hurry."

"From the campsite, you mean?"

"From somewhere. Could be he came in here to hide."

"Hm," I said. "I thought about that, but we only saw one set of footprints—plus there's the fact that they were spaced pretty close together. Correct me if I'm wrong, but it looked like he was walking, not running."

Hux nodded. "That's a good point. But it doesn't prove anything. He could've been tired, sick, whatever. Maybe he really was having an asthma attack."

Hux knew more about tracking people than I did, so I didn't question his logic. The good news was, we didn't have to speculate. Assuming our horse camp victim recovered, we could drive down to the hospital in Fresno and ask him.

While Hux held a flashlight over my head to facilitate my work, I bagged all the evidence and mentally prepared myself for the last mile back to civilization. My biggest motivator was the promise of a hot shower—that, and a heating pad.

"Are you sure you want to come with me to Fresno?" I asked.

"Hell yeah," he said, and went to fist-bump me.

"Just to warn you, it might turn into a trip to L.A."

"Even better."

I wasn't so sure, though, about taking this investigation into the urban jungle of Los Angeles. By then, the media would be all over the case. I'd dealt with high-profile cases before, but that was years ago, before my accident. I worried about my ability to deal with the limelight, especially with Ray watching my every move.

When I was satisfied with our search of the camp, we hit the trail for the final stretch of our journey. I picked up the pace a little bit—testing myself in the darkness, determined to reach the finish line after so many moments of self-doubt and despair. It was exhilarating to know that I had come this far, even though it felt at times like I was trying to outrun my past.

It felt right to be out here, though. I wasn't stranded in an unforgiving wilderness, crippled from a fall and unable to do anything but sit and wait and hope for rescue. In the shadows of these ancient redwoods, I could think about Kevin without suffocating under the onerous weight of his memory. After all, it was in woods like these that we'd shared each other's hopes and dreams, that we'd talked about the future. And it was here that I felt closest to him, even though our travels had never taken us to Sequoia.

Ollie looked up at me with his big brown eyes as we navigated the final stretch of the trail. He sensed it, too:

We were going to be okay.

20

AFTER A WHIRLWIND seventy-four hours in the Sequoia wilderness, I walked past the sign for the Mineral King Ranger Station. It was just after five AM. Hux checked his watch, told me we'd made excellent time, and recruited me into an enthusiastic high five. For a brief moment, I forgot about the debilitating pain in my lower back and the shredded skin on my heels. Only once in my life had I been happier to see signs of civilization, and that was when my life had been on the line. I took comfort in the fact that at least this time, I wasn't facing years of recovery.

The parking lot outside the ranger station was at capacity. Spilling out onto the mountain road were big white vans with massive satellite dishes on top and garish numbers and letters painted on the paneling. Somewhere in the neighborhood of twenty reporters were camped on the small front deck outside the ranger station. It was clear that news of Tatum Delancey's death had gotten out.

There was one vehicle, though, that looked a little out of place: a black Mercedes SUV, parked right next to the American flag out front. It had California plates and no tire rack.

"This should be fun," Hux remarked.

I slowed my pace as we approached the lot. "Not for me."

"Not a fan of the media?"

"Nope."

He gnawed on the piece of grass in his mouth. "Me neither."

We walked up the steps as a united front, but that was as far as we got before a gaggle of reporters swallowed us like an encroaching tide. We learned from one particularly outspoken journalist that Corrigan had denied everyone entry to the ranger station. "That old man in there is nuts," a guy in a flimsy windbreaker complained as we attempted to make our way to the front door. "We're gonna freeze our asses off out here."

"No you won't," Hux said. "You can always just get in your car and drive home."

He snorted. "The public has a right to know what happened to Tatum Delancey, and that hard-ass won't tell us anything."

I smiled thinly at the reporter. "He's not telling you anything because he doesn't really know anything. He's not in charge."

"So who is?"

"I am."

He looked me up and down with a look that was somewhere between disparaging and bemused. "You don't look like the police."

"I'm not the police. I'm a federal agent."

I should've known better. Those words were like catnip for every person not named Hux standing on the deck of that ranger station, and within a few seconds, I was fending off microphones and cameras. The questions came rapid-fire: *"Is it true that Tatum Delancey was found at the bottom of a lake? Was she alone in the woods? Was there any evidence of foul play? Was she on drugs? Do you have any suspects?"*

"No comment," I said in response to the assault. Hux, with his six-foot-three frame and massive backpack, barreled through the crowd and knocked on the door to the ranger station hard enough to shake the structure's foundation. When it finally opened, Hux pushed me over the threshold—apologetically, of course—and slammed the door behind him.

We found Corrigan pacing the reception area. "This here's a goddamn circus," he said when he saw us. "I feel like I'm in Times Square." He looked tired, the lines in his face cutting deeper than I remembered. I couldn't help but feel a little sorry for him.

"I'll talk to the reporters," I said. "I just need to prepare a statement."

"The sooner, the better," he said. "I can't go home till you deal with 'em." He went to the window and looked out, which only seemed to agitate him. "By the way, Tatum Delancey's husband is in the break room. He's askin' all kinds of questions that I'm ill-equipped to answer."

So the Mercedes out front belonged to him, then. He must have driven all night to get here, which surprised me. He hadn't seemed that interested in the investigation up until now.

"Thanks," I said to Corrigan.

The chief ranger grunted and walked off. Hux said, "He seems cheery."

"Very," I said, as we headed toward the break room. After three days of tackling Sequoia's ragged landscape, my joints were in full revolt. I really just wanted to crawl into bed and sleep for days. But Edwin Delancey's arrival at Mineral King trumped all that; I needed to be on my game when we entered that room. The case could turn on what he said in there.

Delancey was sitting on an old folding chair with rusted edges, the kind my grandparents used to set out for holiday dinners to accommodate my many aunts, uncles, and cousins. He looked up when we walked in, his glasses sliding down his nose as he met my gaze. For not the first time, I was struck by the stark differences between the bookish Edwin and the person who had once been his glamorous wife, Tatum.

"Mr. Delancey?" I asked.

He stood.

"I'm Felicity Harland, and this is my colleague, Ferdinand Huxley."

"I'm just Hux," came the immediate clarification from my partner, which almost made me smile. If there was one thing Hux hated, it was his own first name.

"We spoke over the phone," I said to Delancey.

"Yes, I remember." As we shook hands, I noted that his was clammy and cold, with a weak grip. He was taller than he

appeared in photos, almost Hux's height. He lacked Hux's ath-
leticism, though, and the best word I could come up with to
describe the way he carried himself was *awkward*. His limbs
were too long for his build, like he'd outgrown them as a teenager and had never quite adapted. He was a fidgeter, too—hands
moving, knuckles popping. Every few seconds he'd comb his
fingers through his greasy brown hair.

"Thank you for coming out here," I said. "I just want to say
that I'm very sorry for your loss, Mr. Delancey."

He nodded. "I went down to the morgue yesterday."

"I'm sorry. That must have been difficult."

"It was." He stared at his hands. "It wasn't far from here,
so I decided to come the rest of the way to talk with you in
person."

Hux looked at me, saying a lot with one glance that I tried
to acknowledge without Edwin Delancey noticing. For all his
physical deficiencies, Tatum's widower seemed keenly aware of
his surroundings. I wondered if this had anything to do with his
chosen profession.

"I think that's a good idea," I said just as the door behind
me swung open. It was Corrigan. He had his coat on.

"I'm goin' home," he said. "I can't take it anymore."

Hux rose from his chair. "I'll deal with them, Rick," he
said, and to my surprise, Corrigan didn't argue. The two men
left together.

I wasn't happy to see Hux go, but it was important to keep
the peace with the chief ranger. The door closed behind them
with a soft click. Delancey reached for the pot of coffee.

He didn't bother with cream or sugar—just drank it black
and drank it quickly.

"Mr. Delancey," I said, easing my way into the conversation, still not quite sure how to play it. "I know you must have
questions for us."

"I do. That's why I'm here."

"Let's start there, then. I will tell you everything I know."

For the next few minutes, I filled him in on the entire investigation up to that point, starting with my first interaction with
Rick Corrigan, over satellite phone, to our discovery of an

unidentified male in the horse camp the night before. I also tried to summarize Tatum's injuries, which strongly suggested a fall from height, but I stopped short of implying that she'd been pushed. I worried it might color his answers to my questions.

He laced his fingers together and stared at his now-empty Styrofoam cup sitting on the table. For a while, neither of us spoke. To break the ice a bit, but also to elicit some information, I asked, "Have you ever been camping?"

"No, never. I don't see the appeal."

I smiled sympathetically. "The bugs can be terrible."

"The bugs, the weather, the logistical nightmare of setting up a tent and putting your belongings in bags and hanging your food from a clothesline. It's entertainment for masochists."

"I see your point there."

He shrugged.

I asked, "Did your wife come up here often?"

"No. She didn't much like the outdoors."

"Did she talk to you about the trip before she left?"

Delancey glanced up from his lap and met my gaze, but there was a flicker of hesitation in it. "All she said was that she was going camping with a friend."

"Do you know the name of this friend?"

"No."

"You didn't ask?"

"I trusted my wife," he said in a lashing tone. "We trusted each other. In any case, I didn't care to know how Tatum spent her free time. She had a million friends, although a great number of them were just using her, if you ask me. That said, I respected her wishes to have a normal life, and this trip was an attempt at that. She missed what it felt like *not* to be famous."

I supposed what he said made sense, but then again, Tatum Delancey wasn't here to tell us otherwise. The time had come for me to push him a little bit.

"It would be helpful to know if this friend had any outdoor experience," I said. "Precipice Lake, where her body was found, is quite a ways off the beaten path."

"Tatum told me she was using a luxury camping outfit—said it was safer, everything was provided, all that. I got the feeling it didn't matter how much experience you had—all you needed were ample funds."

"Which, presumably, Tatum had."

Delancey looked at me for a long moment. His eyes were the palest blue, almost translucent. "I'm not sure what you're trying to say, Agent Harland."

"I'm just trying to get some insight into her financial situation."

Another pause. "Perhaps I should call my attorney."

"That's entirely within your rights," I said, "but we're just having a conversation."

"You're talking about our finances, which seems relevant only if you suspect that this wasn't an accident. Is that what you're saying?"

"I'm not necessarily saying that." I held his gaze until he looked away. "Where were you last weekend?"

"I was at home."

"Alone?"

"Yes. I was setting up a surprise party for Tatum's birthday."

"Can anyone vouch for you?"

After the slightest hesitation, he shook his head. "No, I'm afraid not." He looked at me with an intensity that dredged up a lot of old insecurities from my FBI days. I'd always been good at interviews, but being the only woman in the room with a bunch of tough, old-school men, it was easy to feel inferior. I'd learned a trick or two to combat those gender dynamics—wardrobe, for instance. I was always very intentional about my clothing choices. At the moment, though, I was wearing muddy pants and a wrinkled shirt. My hair was a windblown mess. These were things I would have to improve on for the next time.

"How was your marriage?" I asked him.

"Strong. We got along very well."

"You were a good bit older than her."

"Yes." He stared at the gold band on his finger.

"I'm just trying to figure out what happened to your wife, Mr. Delancey." I folded my hands on the table and looked at him. Whereas some interview subjects tended to withdraw under pressure, Edwin Delancey had the opposite reaction. It was almost like he came to life with direct confrontation.

"Yes," he said. "I would very much like to know what happened because, frankly, your suggestion that she was pushed off a cliff makes no sense to me at all. Tatum had no enemies; she was beloved by many. And she was very careful about her own personal safety—*too* careful, at times. She had a full-time bodyguard."

"She did? Who?"

There it was again, that whiff of hesitation as he picked at the Styrofoam on the brim of his cup. I thought he was going to call his attorney then and there, but instead he lifted his gaze and looked at me.

"His name is Colton Dodger," he said.

21

H UX WALKED IN as I was trying to process Edwin Delancey's answer. He paused a moment, his gaze shifting from me to Delancey and back again. I could tell by the look in his eyes that he knew something important had come out. "How's it going in here?" he asked.

"Mr. Delancey just informed me that his wife had a bodyguard who goes by the name Colton Dodger."

Hux's eyebrows just about touched his hairline as he took the empty chair at the table. "Can you tell us what he looks like?" he asked.

"He's a Black man in his thirties, a few inches shorter than you but probably thirty pounds heavier." He assembled the bits of Styrofoam into a pile as he talked. "He has several tattoos on his forearms and one on his neck."

I added these details to my notes, questioning Delancey's description even as he gave it. The guy in the horse camp was white. If Delancey was telling the truth, then it was starting to look like we'd found someone who had nothing to do with the Glampist campsite, and *that* was a tough pill to swallow. It was one more loose end I'd have to tie up before this was over.

"Look, I only met him a few times," Delancey said, while twisting his wedding band on his finger. Hux and I exchanged glances.

"How long had he been working for Tatum?"

"A year, maybe a little less." He slid his ring back on his finger. "I know what you're getting at, Agent Harland. There was nothing going on between my wife and her bodyguard. It was a strictly professional relationship."

"When's the last time you talked to him?"

"Months ago. I hardly interacted with him at all."

"Why not?" Hux asked.

"Because he wasn't my employee. He was Tatum's."

"But he's spending an inordinate amount of time with your wife," I said. "You didn't feel compelled to look into his background? Even just for safety reasons?"

"I wanted to," Delancey said. "I just didn't insist."

"Why not?"

"Because Tatum was fully capable of making her own decisions."

Hux poured himself a cup of coffee from the pot, which had already gone cold thanks to the chill in the room. These ranger stations didn't have the best HVAC systems—or maybe it was just Corrigan, skimping on the heating bill. I put my gloves on and stuffed a hand warmer inside each of them. I was down to my last two.

"Mr. Delancey, I'm sorry for this question, but is there any chance your wife was having an affair?"

"No," he said. "Absolutely not."

Hux raised an eyebrow. "You sure about that?"

"I know—*knew* my own wife, Mr. Huxley." His tone was acidic, not that Hux deserved any less. I'd have to talk to him later about taking a gentler approach.

"She was out in the woods with someone that wasn't you," I said. "We have to ask."

Delancey looked at me unblinkingly. "Tatum hired Mr. Dodger after *Glenview* took off. She came from a small town, and to be frank, all the attention made her nervous. She was worried about stalkers."

"Why? Did she have a stalker?"

"No, but Tatum was the anxious type."

I was trying to decipher what exactly he meant by that when the door swung open. Chad, one of the junior rangers, poked his head in. One of his front teeth was rather conspicuously chipped. "Uh, sorry to interrupt—but one of those reporters just broke a window . . ."

Hux stood, looking every bit like he wanted to shake somebody down. "I'm sorry, Harland," he said. "I'm in charge while Corrigan's gone, and this won't fly."

"It's fine," I said. "Go deal with it."

As Hux walked out, Delancey stood up in a hurry, tripping over his own chair in the process. He smelled faintly like clove cigarettes and a little bit like the air freshener he had used to cover it up. He wiped his hands on his pants, the sweat cloying at his skin.

I stood up, too. "Mr. Delancey—"

"I don't feel that it's in my best interest to continue talking with you without my attorney present," he said. For the first time since our conversation started, he sounded rattled.

"That's certainly within your rights."

"I know it is," he said.

I gave him my card, which he put in his pocket before grabbing his coat on the way out the door. There was no promise to talk again, no reassurances from my side or his. From the window, I watched him make a beeline to his Mercedes, which was covered in a light dusting of snow. He never looked back at the ranger station, even as he pulled away.

I went out to the reception area and found Hux sitting with a short balding man who kept wiping his nose with his fist. I couldn't tell if he had bad allergies or was trying to recover from a crying spell. His hairless head reflected the dim light of the table lamp.

"Hux—"

"I just talked to him," Hux said. "But it was a stern talking-to."

The man blubbered, "Look, man, I wasn't trying to—"

"Don't wanna hear it, don't care," Hux said. "This here is Special Agent Felicity Harland. She'll decide whether to prosecute you for any number of crimes."

The man looked up. "Special Agent? Oh shit—"

"Don't break any more windows," I said. "Now get out of here."

He scrambled out of his chair so fast he knocked it over, and for a moment it looked like he wasn't going to bother to pick it up. But then he glimpsed Hux out of the corner of his eye, lifted the chair off the floor, and pushed it back in under the table in its rightful place. He muttered another apology— this one with *sir* at the end—and headed for the door.

I said, "I hope you didn't scar him for life."

"Nah," he said. "But maybe he'll play by the rules next time." Hux nudged the chair a centimeter to the left before seeming to decide that, yes, everything was in its proper place again. "So what happened to Delancey? Ran to get his lawyer?"

"Could be," I said. "Let's go to Fresno."

* * *

We stopped at Hux's cabin to pack some clothes and feed Ollie before the trip to Fresno in California's Central Valley, a three-hour drive. After Hux had locked up, we all headed out to the truck. He offered to drive, even though we were both sorely in need of sleep.

"You're not too tired?" I asked him.

"Nah, I'm good as new. Feel free to take a snoozer if you need one."

I tossed him the keys. "I might take you up on that."

"It's two and a half hours to Fresno. That's practically a full night's sleep."

"I thought it was closer to three."

"Sure, if you drive like my grandma." He winked at me. "You *do* drive like my grandma, Harland. Just so you know."

"You mean safely and responsibly?"

"I wouldn't say that. She's legally blind."

"And she's still on the road?"

He gave a little shrug that made me wonder if any of what he'd just said was true. Ollie, thrilled to be on another adventure, bounded after Hux, into the driver's seat, before settling into the space between us. I didn't mind being the navigator. Not having to concentrate on the road would increase my mental bandwidth for the case, with all its loose ends and unanswered questions. As for our horse camp victim, it always helped to know what you were getting into when you went to question someone, but I didn't even have this person's name. Based on Edwin Delancey's description, the guy currently recuperating in a Fresno hospital wasn't Colton Dodger, but that didn't mean there wasn't a connection. And it was for that reason that we were on the road again and not sound asleep in a motel somewhere.

I did manage to doze off in the truck, and when I woke up, Hux had the radio set to some country music station. I could tell by the signage that we were just outside the city of Visalia, which was about an hour's drive from Fresno.

"I thought you were a podcast guy," I said.

"I am," he said, "but I'm picky. I stay away from anything that has to do with politics, pro sports, and food. And sometimes I'm just more in the mood for music." He adjusted his grip on the wheel as the drab oranges and reds of Visalia's fast-food corridor came into view. "Ooh, there's a McDonald's up ahead."

"I'm not eating McDonald's."

"Okay, boss. There's a Wendy's across the street, which I'm told is better for you."

"Why, because they have salad?"

"Something like that."

My stomach groaned with the impending doom of a processed burger. I'd done too many drive-thrus as a teenager and a broke college student, and now my colon was in full revolt. At least it was morning, which meant no bacon cheeseburgers on the menu. I supposed I could make do with a yogurt or something.

But as soon as Hux said the words *bacon, egg, and cheese biscuit* to the voice in the drive-thru, the whole yogurt idea went out the window. We ordered biscuits, hash browns, coffees, juice, cookies, and some new promotional item that Hux was intrigued by. Ollie devoured two sausage patties slathered in ketchup. I reminded myself that we'd covered forty-some miles on foot in the last three days and that this wasn't the time to count calories. Hell, it was never a good time.

As we were pulling out of the lot, Hux started in on his second bacon, egg, and cheese biscuit. He said, "I asked a buddy of mine to take up the mega search on the Delanceys."

"What buddy?"

"A college buddy. Don't worry—he's a harmless IT guy that happens to love *CSI*. He's good with computers, though."

"What did you ask him to do?"

"Just asked him to give me whatever he found on our victim and her husband. I mean—we were a little behind the curve on Colton Dodger." He avoided my gaze because, well, the implication was clear. "Thought it might help."

He was right, of course. In retrospect, I should have tried harder to establish Colton Dodger's connection to the Delancey family right off the bat. But I'd been either on the road or out on the trail pretty much since the moment I'd arrived in Sequoia, which hadn't left much time for investigative work. It was something I'd have to figure out going forward.

"Did you explain why?"

"Look, Harland, he didn't leak anything to the media, if that's what you're wondering."

"I wasn't saying he did."

He dunked the remains of his biscuit in a container of ketchup. "Sounds like you have a theory," he said, before washing it down with some coffee.

"Maybe." I reached for the last hash brown before Hux could claim it. "I think Edwin Delancey enjoyed the attention that his wife supposedly hated."

"You think Delancey tipped off the media?"

"It makes the most sense."

"I dunno, Harland," he said. "He doesn't dress the part, that's for sure."

I knew what he was talking about. Edwin Delancey's look could best be described as "schlumpy," which could have been an act. For all we knew, the guy slept like a baby at night, but it sure helped to look the part of a sleep-deprived widower when you were giving an interview to law enforcement.

I inhaled my cup of coffee—the first decent one I'd had in days. The nap in the car and the greasy food had helped my mood. I was feeling almost human again.

"Let's hear what your man found on his mega Google search."

Hux downed a supersized orange juice in a few swift gulps. "Forget it," he said. "You clearly don't respect my man."

"I haven't even heard what 'your man' found."

"You won't take it seriously."

"Don't assume, Hux. And also, since when were you the sensitive type?"

His defensive mumbling made me smile. Now that the highway had straightened out and there was hardly any traffic at all, he put one hand on Ollie's sleeping head. My dog mewed with pleasure. Hux relaxed a little bit, too, as he loosened his grip on the wheel.

We cruised along the 99 for miles as it coursed through the heart of the Central Valley. I'd traveled this road before—lots of farmland and orchards flanking the highway, interspersed with nothing at all. Every ten miles or so the highway would bypass a forgotten town, marked by little more than a gas station and a few fast-food chains. Big rig trucks mostly stuck to their territory in the right lane, but every once in a while, a car or truck would roar past. Hux drove a notch above the speed limit, but nothing crazy. I wondered if he was keeping a lid on his need for speed because I was sitting next to him.

"I'm about ready to talk to you now," he said.

"That's great news."

He smiled. "You're a real piece of work, Harland."

"Just tell me what your *CSI*-obsessed buddy found on the interwebs."

"Well, Delancey's a screenwriter, as we know, but he isn't very good at it. His last writing credit was four years ago."

"What's he been doing since then?"

"Nothing? Apparently he tweets a lot of writing tips and talks about his current projects, but only in vague terms."

"Maybe he writes under a pseudonym."

Hux said, "My buddy didn't get that feeling, mainly because Delancey's always promoting the one movie he wrote that did get made—like, seven years ago."

"Hmm."

"Plus he filed for bankruptcy four years ago."

I looked at Hux. "Seriously?"

"Yup. The guy was broke when he met Tatum."

This new information didn't go down easy. One of the first things you learned in the murder business was that people were capable of anything when it came to money—even people you thought you knew, people who donated to charity and trained service dogs and helped sick kids. Money turned cute little grandmothers into monsters.

"I knew I didn't like him," I said.

"*I* knew you didn't like him," Hux said.

"Was it that obvious?"

"Yeah, but I wasn't a fan either. He had that air about him, you know?"

"What air?"

"Like he was better than us forest dwellers."

"Well, to be fair, you *are* a forest dweller."

He finished off his coffee with a satisfied grin. I sipped mine, pondering all the changes in my life that had come to pass in the last few months. Even Ray had questioned my ability to transition from the gritty streets of Chicago to some of our nation's most desolate places; there was one national park in Alaska, for instance, that didn't even have hiking trails. But in that moment, at least, I didn't miss the city at all.

"Harland?"

"Yeah?"

"You okay?"

Hux had a beat on my emotional temperature, that was for sure. But then, we both knew loss and grief and regret. I could see it in his eyes.

"Hux?"

"Yeah?"

"Just a question—you don't have to answer." It was as if my voice had floated into the ether, completely separate from my own consciousness. "Why did you leave the Navy?"

He put both hands on the wheel, tightening his grip in the ten-two position. I thought he was going to dodge the question—or, worse, give me a bogus answer—but he exhaled, put one hand back on the console, and glanced over at me.

"It's not your typical story," he said.

"But there is a story?"

"Of course there's a story, Harland. I loved the Navy—loved being a SEAL. I was damn proud to serve my country. No regrets."

I waited for the "but," but it never came. "I joined up with my best friend growing up," Hux said. "We went through BUD/S training together—that's Basic Underwater Demolition/SEAL tactical training—all of it. We deployed at the same time, saw all the same horrible shit over there. When we were on leave, he got married. It was a great wedding—guys from home, guys from our platoon, random people from high school I hadn't seen in years. It was just fucking awesome. And his wife, Kerry—just a phenomenal woman. That's all I can really say. The guy had it all."

I felt like I knew where this was going—Hux and his friend were deployed again; his buddy died; Hux couldn't cope and decided he wanted out. It was a familiar story, and I could certainly relate to aspects of it.

"Anyway," Hux said, "the day before we were supposed to go back over there, he called to tell me he had cancer."

Huh, I thought—so not a familiar story, then. I wasn't sure what to say.

"Mesothelioma," Hux went on. "It was a bad, bad cancer. The doctors had no explanation for it—just the world's worst luck, I guess. It was advanced, too—the cancer was everywhere. They pumped him with so many drugs, his legs puffed up and his skin sloughed off and he wasn't there mentally either—not really, not all the time. One day near the end I went in there so fucking pissed at the world—seriously, the guy's twenty-eight-years-old, survived a war, had a beautiful wife, all that—and he's dying. Badly, too. His room smelled like pus and shit. I went in there and said, 'What the hell, man? Aren't you angry? Aren't you just so fucking pissed at the world?'"

"He must have been," I said.

"No." Hux shook his head. "He just looked at me and said, 'It's all good, man.'" And he meant it—I can't tell you how I know he meant it, but the look on his face was so serene, you know? Like he was at peace with his fate."

I could picture their conversation—Hux all bluster and rage while his childhood friend withered away in a hospital bed. Some people died with dignity and grace that defied all logic. Most didn't. But to witness that kind of calm acceptance in the face of such a dismal outlook had clearly changed Hux. Even now, his eyes glistened with tears. One escaped down his cheek before he could wipe it away. He turned his head so I wouldn't see it.

"I left the Navy because I wasn't at that place in my life— and I needed to be," Hux said. "Maybe someday I'll re-enlist. I dunno. I just don't think you can go to war without a healthy outlook on death. I'm trying to get there."

"I wish I could help you with that, Hux, but I'm not there myself."

"You don't have to," he said. "It's just good having you around."

"Why?"

He put both hands back on the wheel and looked over at me, then back at the road. "'Cause you're not angry," he said. "You're just stubborn as hell. That's a better way to be."

"I get angry sometimes."

"I know," he said. "Like when I ordered you a Coke instead of a Diet Coke."

"I was not *angry*," I said with a laugh.

"The veins in your neck were throbbing."

I decided to let him take this one. The truth was, I didn't really care about the calories in a Coke; it was that distinct sweetness that turned me off. But I didn't explain all that to Hux because that wasn't the point.

Even though we had our differences, I liked having him around, too.

CHAPTER

22

FRESNO WAS A city of chain restaurants and highways, and its beating heart—or its liver, at least, where all the bad stuff went before being processed back out into the community—was its medical center. The massive network of hospital buildings, outpatient clinics, parking garages, and a gargantuan emergency department could have been seen from space. We parked in a nearby surface lot and headed for the revolving doors. A woman leaving the ER crossed herself against the backdrop of blinking lights.

We checked in at the front desk easily enough, but what followed was a logistical and bureaucratic nightmare, trying to find our patient. Hux had to call the MedEvac team to track him down, and after that, it was quite a long wait in a windowless room downstairs that smelled faintly like bleach and strongly like urine. An elderly man played a tune on the piano. By the time the doctor showed up, Hux and I were both asleep.

The intensivist introduced herself as Dr. Sara Salazar, although the last name was a surprise. She was a petite blonde and looked Nordic. Maybe Salazar was her married name. "I didn't get much of a story from the MedEvac team." She spoke in a voice that made me sit up and listen. "Can you tell me more about what happened?"

Hux looked at me, eyebrows raised in question. I responded with a nod.

"We're trying to piece that together," Hux said. "We found him in an abandoned horse camp about a mile from the trailhead. It was hard to say how long he'd been there—maybe a day, tops." He added hopefully, "He hasn't said anything yet?"

"He's still sedated." She looked from Hux to me. "Is he under arrest?"

"No," I said, a bit taken aback by the question. "Why do you ask?"

"His tox screen was positive for opioids and cannabis—not that that's a crime, but MedEvac told me he was found under somewhat suspicious circumstances."

"That's true," I said. "He had nothing on him—no backpack, phone, or ID."

"Well, there were no traumatic injuries," Salazar said. "He seems to have suffered a severe asthma attack—almost died. We had to intubate him."

So Corrigan was right about this one. It was a good lesson for me; despite the unpleasantness of working with these grizzled rangers, there was no substitute for experience. Guys like Corrigan had it in spades.

Hux said, "So he was lucky."

"Very."

Salazar's cell phone beeped. She glanced at it and frowned. "I have to go. Come up to the ICU. It will probably be an hour or two before we start weaning him off sedation, but the waiting room up there is a lot nicer than the one down here." Without waiting for our response, she made a call and started walking off in the opposite direction.

"Well," Hux said, "the mystery deepens." He leaned back in his chair, extending his arms to either side. I was two chairs down, a little bit beyond his reach. He had quite the wingspan, I realized. In fact, Hux's physical presence was almost larger than life out here in the real world, like it couldn't quite contain him.

He looked over at me. "You're awfully quiet."

"I'm thinking."

"About what?"

"About how this all fits together."

He tossed the *People* magazine he'd been reading back onto the table. The thing had been flipped through so many times that it nearly disintegrated on impact.

"You must think our asthmatic horse camper is connected to Tatum Delancey somehow," Hux said. "Otherwise, we wouldn't have come all this way to talk to him."

He had me there. I *did* think there was a connection, but only because of what Delia had told us about the encounter. The truth was, we didn't have any real witnesses in this case, and I *wanted* this guy to have seen something—something that scared him, maybe. Investigations built on theories and conjecture never amounted to much.

As for the asthma attack, there was something off about that, too. Most backpackers at this time of year were experienced outdoorsmen, and I couldn't imagine someone with even a reasonable measure of common sense leaving home without their inhaler. But if the attack had come on for some other reason—a sudden burst of exertion, maybe—then that scenario raised another whole set of questions. Had he been trying to get away from someone—and if so, who?

My cell phone rang. It was Corrigan, calling to ask me about some license plates.

"Sorry?" I said.

"Did you ask somebody about the cars in the Sawtooth trailhead lot?"

"Oh," I said. "Yes, I did. I asked Chad to take down the license plates."

"Well, I've got 'em here."

I sat up a little straighter. Corrigan was talking fast, like he had a week's worth of tasks to accomplish before lunchtime and no chance in hell of getting them all done.

"Can you email me the list?" I asked.

"Email?" He scoffed. "Grab a pen, Agent Harland."

I did so, figuring this was one battle not worth fighting. Hux seemed to be enjoying the back-and-forth between me and his boss.

Corrigan informed me that there were six vehicles in the lot—two with Nevada plates, one North Dakota, the rest

California. I took down all the numbers, although Corrigan kept grumbling that he had better things to do than recite plate numbers over the phone.

"I appreciate this," I said. "We're still trying to figure out who Tatum was camping with, and this information will go a long way."

"I thought you found the guy she was campin' with."

"No. It's someone else."

"How the hell did you figure that?"

"The physical description doesn't match."

"Uh-huh." He cleared his throat. "Look, I don't think the plates are gonna tell you anything. Could be she took an Uber cab up here. That's what they all do these days. Folks are too lazy to drive anywhere anymore."

"What's an Uber cab?" Hux mouthed to me, stifling a laugh.

I thanked Corrigan for the list and hung up. Hux glanced at it and said, "So what next? You run the California plates through some database?"

"We run all of them."

"Even North Dakota?"

"Yup. You never know."

I called a buddy at the FBI and relayed the information to him. Jim had been at the Bureau since I was in diapers, and he had a weird fascination with the DMV. He liked to go there and observe human behavior; his theory was that people reverted to base instincts at the DMV.

"Can't believe you're in ISB now," Jim said, while we waited for him to run the plates. He was eating something crunchy. "You like it?"

"I do," I said, feeling Hux's eyes on me. He mouthed that he was going to run to the bathroom. I acknowledged him with a nod.

"It's a good gig for ya, Felicity." Before I could ask him why he thought so—because deep down, I really wanted to know—he had the plate information. None of the vehicles in the lot were registered to an Edwin or Tatum Delancey, nor a Colton Dodger for that matter.

"Not what ya'll were lookin' for?" he asked in his Southern drawl.

"Not quite."

"Well, I'll send you the full report anyway. Oh, and there's one other thing. The Range Rover with the North Dakota plates is actually a rental."

It wasn't a slam dunk, but news of a rental opened some doors and created some opportunities. "Any way to find out who rented it last and where?"

"Yes, ma'am," he said. "Give me half an hour."

"Thanks."

The report arrived in my inbox minutes later. None of the names of the registered owners rang a bell. It would come down to the rental, then. If nothing panned out there, then it was looking increasingly likely that Colton Dodger had made his way out of the wilderness undetected. At that point it would be a matter of going through tollbooth footage.

While I was probing the report for any clues, Dr. Salazar came through the waiting room doors with Hux. Both of them looked mightily refreshed—two perfect specimens immune to the ravages of sleep deprivation. Hux was a few years younger than me, so there was that, but what was Dr. Salazar's excuse? Good genes, maybe.

"He's awake," she said. "I can take you to him now."

"Thank you," I said, scrambling to my feet. With Dr. Salazar striding down the hallway in her two-inch heels, Hux offered me a mint from his tin of Altoids. I was grateful. My attention to personal hygiene would have to wait, along with Ollie, who was passing the time in my truck. I never liked to leave him out there alone for too long.

We found our man in a heavy-duty hospital bed, flanked by tubes, wires, and machines. As Salazar had promised, the tube down his throat was gone, and his eyes were open. Everything about him looked depleted—his face was sunken, his skin sallow. Both his hands were veiny and pale, except for the bruises from his IVs.

The bright lights of his hospital room did him no favors. Like Delia had said about the man in her campsite, he had a "tweaker" look about him, with mussed hair and ravaged skin. His dark eyes darted around the room like a spooked animal's. His gown was too big for him, and he seemed self-conscious about it as he pushed the sleeves up his arms.

"Hello, sir, I'm Special Agent Felicity Harland," I said, extending my hand to shake his. He raised it two inches off the bed and shook my hand with a feeble grip.

Hux introduced himself as "Hux Huxley," which brought a wry smile to the guy's face. Not missing a beat, Hux went on to say, "I'm with the Park Service. We're the ones that found you in that barn."

"Yeah," he said. "Great job."

"Pardon?" I was expecting a thank-you, not a sarcastic jab. He was looking at Hux like he wanted to spit on his shoes.

"I'm just sayin' it took you long enough," he said. "I was out there for days." His voice was raspy on account of the plastic tube that had been living in his throat for hours. It was hard to feel sympathy for him, but having been through several surgeries that required some recovery time in the neuro ICU, I knew what being intubated felt like—the pain, the fiery dryness, the gunk. Being intubated and conscious wasn't something I'd wish on anyone.

"Here's the thing," I said. "I know you're exhausted, but we were hoping to ask you a few questions while your memory's still fresh."

"Now? I'm kinda tired."

"We'll make it quick."

He muttered something like "Okay."

"Great. Thank you. First off, what's your name?"

Hux and I waited for his reply for what felt like an eternity. The squirrely look in the guy's eyes reminded me of Jeb. "Ramsey," he said.

"Ramsey what?"

"Ramsey Smith." He tapped the button on his pain pump with his thumb, but the machine had locked out. "Can you get my nurse?" he asked me. "I'm in a lot of pain here. My throat's on fire." His eyes flicked to Hux, then back to me. "Who are you again?"

"I'm Special Agent Harland with the Investigative Services Branch. We're like the FBI for the National Park Service. And this is Hux, my partner on this case."

Smith's eyes widened a little bit. "The FBI? Shit."

"We're investigating a drowning near Precipice Lake."

"You investigate accidents now? Must be lookin' for work."

"We don't think it was accidental."

He responded with a blank stare, which morphed into jittery anticipation when he saw the nurse walk in. She offered him two white pills in a Dixie cup. Smith swallowed them dry before noticing the pitcher of water at his bedside. With something between a shudder and a shrug, he closed his eyes and waited for the analgesic euphoria to wash over him. Judging by the look on his face, it didn't come fast enough.

"I told 'em Dilaudid was the only thing that was gonna touch this pain," he said. "I mean, Christ, I had a tube down my throat. They're really stingy here."

I wasn't interested in hearing his thoughts on pain management. "Were you up that way recently, by chance?" I asked.

"Precipice?" He tried to pour himself some water from the pitcher, but his hands were shaking, so I stepped in and did it for him. "Nope. Not in months, anyway."

I glanced at Hux, who seemed to be processing this story with the same cautious skepticism I felt. He wandered toward the window and looked out, a tactic that was surely intended to relax Ramsey Smith a little bit, or at least get him talking.

"So what were you doing at the horse camp?" I asked.

"I dunno. Just hanging out."

"You almost died."

Smith gave another limp shrug. Hux was over by the window, peering over the chair's armrest at a clear plastic bag containing the man's clothes. Smith's muddy hiking boots were sitting on top. The brand was top of the line, which didn't mesh with his "look." He didn't have the best teeth either.

Hux was inspecting the boots when Smith said, "Hey, that's my shit."

Hux turned around. "Is it?"

"Yeah, man. You can't just go through my personal property—"

"I'm not going through it. I'm looking at it. And just so you know, this boot is about four sizes too big for you."

"What are you, a shoe salesman?"

"Nope. Just observant." He tossed a nod at Smith's tiny feet, which were poking out of the sheet at the bottom of the bed. Smith's face reddened.

"Foot size don't mean nothin' you know."

"I didn't say it did," Hux said.

"Look, I bought those shoes used."

"Where?"

As I walked over to inspect the boots for myself, Smith proceeded to spout angry threats about privacy laws. "Size twelve," I said to Hux while making sure Smith heard me. "I wonder what size Colton Dodger wears."

"I'm sure we could find out," Hux said.

Smith seemed to shrink into his hospital bed. Having given up on the vitriol directed at my interpretation of his Constitutional rights, he fell silent. He reached for the nurse call button and pushed it hard, and pushed it repeatedly. When no one came, he cussed loudly and slammed the little piece of plastic against the bedrail.

After his tantrum had ended, I went back to the bedside. It was a hostile place, and I didn't intend to stay there long. "We're looking for someone named Colton Dodger, who disappeared four days ago from Precipice Lake," I told him. "If you had anything to do with that, and it sure seems like you did—"

Smith called out for his nurse in a voice that was loud enough to rouse the guy in a coma next door. "I need my rest," he spat at me. "It's time for you to leave."

"We can leave," I said. "But we'll be back tomorrow. And the next day and the next, until you're well enough to go to jail for obstruction."

"I didn't break no laws."

"These boots don't belong to you."

"Like I said, I bought 'em used."

"Sorry, buddy," Hux said. "That story doesn't check out."

"I don't know what the hell you're talking about," he said, slouching down further. He looked like an angry elf, his skin flushed red.

I sat at the very foot of the bed, a maneuver that was meant to put him at ease a little bit, but he tensed up and started yelling for the doctor. Hux strode over and told him to shut up, flat-out. To my surprise, Smith went quiet.

"Look, man," Hux said, "just tell us where you found the clothes and the boots. We don't care if you stole them, okay? Nobody here cares about petty theft. This could turn into a murder investigation, and believe me, you don't want to get tied up in that, especially if you've got a record." Hux loomed over the much smaller man with his arms crossed, exploiting the power dynamic. Intimidation tactics worked in some scenarios, but not all. I wondered if this was Hux's only play. If so, he had a lot to learn; Smith was an easy target because he was already in a vulnerable position. I didn't enjoy interrogating people in hospitals.

"Shit," Smith muttered as he chanced a look at Hux's face. "This ain't fair."

"Life ain't fair," Hux told him.

Smith shifted in his bed, wincing as his eyes darted past Hux in search of his nurse. When he saw her, he started waving his arms, calling out to her like she was his waitress at Applebee's. She disappeared—or rather, hid—behind the triage desk.

Smith resorted to banging on the bedrails with his plastic pitcher. A minute later, the nurse finally came in. "I'm sorry," she said, but her tone suggested she wasn't sorry at all. "It's locked out for the next fifteen minutes. You'll have to talk to the doctor if you feel that your pain isn't adequately controlled."

"Can you go get him, then?"

"It's a she. Dr. Salazar."

"Yeah. Whoever."

With a loud sigh, she left the room again.

Hux turned back to Smith. "I don't think she's that into you, buddy."

"Shut up."

"Look, we can hang out here with you all day," he said. "Or you can tell us the truth. Your choice."

Smith said something under his breath that sounded like an insult, but to my relief, Hux let it go. Careful to avoid Hux's gaze, Smith said to me, "I live out in those woods, okay? Or at least I was livin' there until I ran out of my meds. I thought I could get by without my inhaler as long as I didn't push it too hard."

"The boots," Hux said. "We want to know about the boots."

"Yeah, I'm gettin' there. I was camping up around Nine Lakes for a while when my allergies started rampin' up, and I thought I should prob'ly go to a doctor and get some refills on my meds. So I took the trail down to Bear Paw and, uh—yeah." He picked a scab off his knuckles. "Look, this is gonna sound bad."

"Doesn't matter how it sounds," Hux said. "We just want the truth."

Smith stared at his palms as he spoke. "Yeah, so—I was doin' my business a little ways off the trail and I saw somethin' in the woods there."

"You saw what, exactly?"

"It was that coat over there." He pointed at the bright red parka in the plastic bag. "I thought I could use it 'cause my coat's a piece of shit." He looked down again. The breath he sucked in rattled his whole body. "Shit, man. Maybe I need a lawyer."

"We'll call one for you if you want," I said. "We can finish this at the FBI headquarters with your attorney present. In the meantime, though, we'll have to arrest you."

Smith made a sound like a grunt. "Fuck that," he said, as he wiped his mouth with the sleeve of his hospital gown. "Look, I was just mindin' my own business, swear to God. I didn't know there was a body back in there."

Hux and I looked at each other at the same time, trying to process what Smith had just said. A *body*? If true, this made me think that Colton Dodger hadn't gotten out of those woods alive after all—unless, of course, the body had been there a while.

Smith said, "I took the coat and the boots and that was it. I just left. I ain't got a sat phone or nothin' like that, so there was nobody to call. That's just how it is out there." He tried to clear his throat, but the effort made a horrid gurgling sound. "You know how it is out there, yeah."

He was rambling. Before he could remember that he was still waiting on his pain meds, I cut in with, "You said you found a body. Are you sure the person was dead?"

"Oh yeah. Long dead."

"How long?"

"Well he wasn't bones or nothin' like that, but his skin was cold."

"Days?"

He twisted the bedsheet in his fist. "Prob'ly not that long."

"Hours?"

"Could be. I ain't no coroner."

No, he certainly wasn't. He was a scavenger and a thief, and there was no telling which parts of his story were true and which parts were complete bullshit. There was also the possibility that the "dead body" was in fact an unconscious or otherwise incapacitated person. Ramsey Smith didn't strike me as the type to check for a pulse.

I looked over at Hux, who was staring down at Smith with such intensity that it made the guy squirm. Smith pressed the button again, the one that refused to give him what he wanted. His nurse failed to appear. "This is bullshit," he muttered.

"What else do you remember about the body?" I asked.

"I—uh—not a whole lot."

"Can you give me a physical description, at least? What race was he? How old—"

"Look, I really didn't get a good look. Sorry."

Hux folded his arms and leaned over the bed. "Think a little bit."

"I *am* thinkin'. I'm thinkin' about how much goddamn pain I'm in." He swatted a paper cup and sent it flying across the room. "These assholes think I'm an addict."

I said, "Was he Black?"

"I don't know," Ramsey growled. "He was lyin' on his front, and I really couldn't tell."

He plucked a hair from his brow, and then another. I knew that whatever came next wasn't going to be the truth, but he seemed anxious to be rid of us—and the only way to do that was to answer our questions.

"Where's the body?" I asked.

"Don't know."

"Think," Hux commanded him.

Smith made a clicking sound with his tongue. "Near Bear Paw," he finally said. "But it wasn't just off the trail like I said. It was *all* the way in there." He turned and looked out the window, which offered a depressing view of the parking garage. "Good luck findin' him, 'cause you're gonna need it."

23

WE PASSED SMITH'S beleaguered nurse on the way out as she was signing out to the next nurse coming on. For the first time since our arrival in the ICU, she had a smile on her face and a spring in her step. "Sorry," I heard her say to the young male nurse taking over. "Bed four's a real pain in the ass." She lowered her voice as we walked by, but hey, I couldn't blame her. There were certainly some parallels in my line of work. You took the good with the bad, always, even when the bad sucked the life out of you—bad criminals, bad witnesses, bad cops. I was going to have to add bad weather and bad terrain to the mix.

Once we were in the elevator, Hux said, "Well, that was not how I expected that to go."

"Which part?" I asked.

"All of it, really. Except the dead body in the woods. I did expect that."

I caught the smirk on his face as the elevator doors opened, ushering in a throng of people desperate to see their loved ones. My hatred of hospitals had only intensified since my stint in an Australian intensive care unit, where the surgeons were called "Mister" as a sign of respect. *"Mr. Greene,"* I recalled gasping after waking from my first surgery—an emergent one, meant to relieve the swelling on my spinal cord. *"What happened to my husband?"* The look on his face still haunted me—a memory that refused to fade, even after all this time.

"Are you gonna call Corrigan?" Hux asked.

"I will as soon as we have a plan."

We walked outside into bright but feeble sunshine. The parking lot was already mostly full, and I was glad to get out of there. As we made our way toward the truck, Hux said, "We could get cadaver dogs out there."

"Out where? It'd be a huge search area."

"I bet I could narrow it down a bit—not much, but a little."

"You think Corrigan will go for that?"

"No, probably not," he admitted.

We walked fast, braced against a gusting wind. Ollie was in the passenger seat, sniffing the air through the crack in the window. He started barking when he saw us.

"You think Smith was telling the truth?" I asked Hux.

"Yes and no. I can't see why he'd lie about a body being out there."

"Well, he didn't strike me as an Honest Abe."

"No, ma'am," Hux agreed.

He waited while I fumbled with my keys and unlocked the door. Ollie bounded out of the cab, eager to stretch his legs and do his business. We ambled over to a small patch of grass that separated one massive parking lot from another.

"Would it help if you took him out there with you?" I asked.

"Nope," he said.

"Hux—"

"I'm not going anywhere with that guy, Harland. No way, no how, no thanks."

"He rubbed you the wrong way, eh?" I remarked.

"They all do. These guys think they're living off the land or whatever, but they're really just a menace. I can't tell you how many times I've been called to deal with losers like him. He reminded me of Jeb."

He reminded me of Jeb, too, was the thing—so much so that I was starting to question Delia's story. "So do you think the body is where he said it was?"

Hux crossed his arms and watched a long line of vehicles pull into the lot. "Doubtful."

"We should still ask Corrigan to send a team out there, though."

He nodded. "I will."

As Ollie marked his territory on a patch of grass, Hux placed a call to Corrigan and handed the phone to me before it started to ring. No one answered at the ranger station, so I tried Corrigan on his sat phone. He picked up after three attempts.

"You want my guys to search *where?*" he asked, fighting to be heard over violent gusts of wind in the background. He was practically yelling into the phone.

"Around Bear Paw."

"You gotta be more specific."

"That's all I know." I looked to Hux for guidance—he was the search expert, after all. He took out his phone and navigated to a map of the Sequoia wilderness. "Maybe start in the High Sierra camp and work your way down to the meadow," I said, following his finger on the screen. "But search off-trail."

"How far off-trail?"

Hux said, "I'd say a hundred feet, at least."

"A hundred feet," I said.

"A hundred feet might as well be a hundred miles, Agent Harland. That up there is rough terrain—lots of elevation change, thick brush—you name it."

"Tell them to be careful, then."

He gave one of his loud, this-is-a-pain-in-the-rear-end sighs. "I can spare two guys," he said. "That's it."

"That'll do for now. Thanks."

After Ollie had finished his business, we started walking back to the car. The rumbling sounds coming from Hux's stomach filled the silence. Neither of us had eaten in hours.

"You hungry?" I asked him.

"A little."

"Let's stop for lunch and make a game plan."

Despite the allure of tracking down Colton Dodger on our own—whether alive or dead, I knew our time was better spent investigating the leads we already had. And since we were already halfway to Los Angeles, I figured we might as well drive

the rest of the way to do a little background work. I also wanted
to talk to Edwin Delancey on his own turf.

Hux leaned back in his seat, jutting one hand out the window while using the other to rub Ollie's head. He looked
relaxed—at ease, even. I envied him that. As a ranger, your days
were different but somewhat predictable. As an ISB agent, you
never knew when that next call was going to come in, catapult-
ing you to some other national park hundreds of miles away. I
wasn't sure when I'd get back to Yosemite to wrap up the Line
of Fire case. It could be next week; it could be never. It all
depended on what came down the pipeline next.

Until then, my priority was catching Tatum Delancey's
killer. Failing that, I was determined to prove that she *had* been
killed, because I knew the prosecutor wouldn't relish the chance
to try this case. Fall Zone wasn't going to light her world on fire,
that was for sure.

"Well, I assume I'm headed back to Sequoia," Hux said, as he
tuned the radio. "I could help with the search up there, at least."

"Do you *want* to help with the search?"

He hedged a bit. "I mean . . ."

"Let's go to L.A.," I said, taking the opening he'd given me,
because the truth was, I needed him. "We're halfway there
anyway."

"You sure, boss?" he said, breaking into a grin.

"I'm sure." I looked over at him. "But we need to have a
chat about your interview style."

* * *

We stopped at a place called the Fresno Country Diner simply
because it sounded like the kind of establishment that served
breakfast all day, and for Hux, this was essential. It didn't matter that he'd already had bacon and eggs early that morning; he
ordered the standard American breakfast from this establishment, too: eggs, pancakes, meat, hash browns, and the Diner
Special, which was some kind of French toast casserole topped
with cream cheese.

"You're a breakfast guy?" I asked him.

"Oh yeah. Best meal of the day."

"How're the pancakes?"

"Good. I like 'em a little crispy around the edges."

"No syrup, though," I said, remarking on the fact that he hadn't touched it.

"Nah. Don't like sugar."

"Ever?"

"Not really."

I leaned in, feigning an intense look. "You're not a crazy health nut, are you?"

He laughed, and with a fork in one hand and a knife in the other, gestured to the massive plate of food in front of him. "Does this strike you as a healthy meal?"

Before I could answer, Jim called from the FBI field office in Sacramento. He had more news about the license plates.

"Hold on a sec, Jim," I said. "You're on speaker."

I wanted Hux to hear what he had to say, which meant the elderly gentleman behind us was going to hear it, too, but I was okay with that. The restaurant was otherwise empty, which wasn't a surprise for two PM on a Thursday. I hadn't seen a single new customer in over an hour.

"So here's the interesting thing," Jim said. "The Nissan with North Dakota plates was reported stolen yesterday."

Hux and I exchanged looks. "By who?" Hux asked.

"By Hertz, the rental car company. It was due back three days ago, and they weren't able to reach the person who rented it."

"Do you have a name?"

"They wouldn't give me that. Sorry, Harland. I tried to grease the wheels a bit, but no dice. The guy I talked to wasn't having it."

"It's fine, Jim. I can get a subpoena if we need to."

"This looking like a homicide to you?"

I rubbed my temples while Hux looked at me. "That's my hunch," I said.

"Sounds like you got your hands full, then." He bit down hard on something crunchy, and the sound reverberated over the line. "The Hertz rental office is in San Bernardino. From tollbooth footage, it looks like the vehicle left the city limits on Friday and headed east."

"San Bernardino," I said. "That's outside L.A."

"Yup."

"Thanks, Jim." I hung up.

Hux looked pleased, and maybe a little bit surprised. "I'm not sure I would've bothered with the North Dakota plates," he said.

I slurped down the remains of my Diet Coke. "That's why they pay me the big bucks."

"Do they?"

"No," I said. "Keep that in mind if you're thinking about a career change."

"I'm not about the Benjamins, Harland."

"Didn't think you were."

Jim had helped us out quite a bit with the information about the rental, but our hands were tied without a subpoena. I wasn't going to get one of those by snapping my fingers. It might be worth pursuing later, but for now we had other, more promising leads.

"You think Colton Dodger rented that vehicle?" Hux asked me as he noshed on toast.

"Could be."

"Why not just take his car if she wanted to be discreet?"

"I don't know," I said. "Maybe that wasn't discreet enough for her."

Hux chewed slowly. He had a pensiveness about him, which was an admirable trait. Most men I knew in this line of work spouted off whatever popped into their heads to make sure no one thought they had nothing to say. It was an ego thing.

After a while he said, "I don't think SAR is gonna find that body."

"You never know," I said.

"I do know. Smith was lying about where he found it, which means SAR's looking in the wrong place."

"So then take him out there with you."

He folded his napkin into a neat little square. "I really don't want to do that, Harland."

"But you would."

"I don't think it's necessary. If it's out there, I'll find it on my own." He put his fork down and placed his hands flat on the table. I studied them for a beat—two muscular hands with a smattering of scars on his knuckles and one black, mangled fingernail.

"Look, this is what my platoon did—located high-value targets in hostile territory. I can't talk about the specifics—it's all classified—but I spent the better part of my military career looking for terrorists in caves or bunkers or some other godforsaken hellish place." He ran a finger over one of his scars. "I won't lie—I liked the hunt. It was an adrenaline rush."

"Is that what drew you to rangering?"

"There was some overlap with my skill sets in the Navy, yeah—search and rescue in particular. I was already trained in rope rescues, water rescues—things like that. And I wanted to be outside, on the move, in a place that isn't quite lawless but feels like it sometimes." He looked out the window at the empty parking lot. "I'm not quite ready for a studio apartment and a daily commute, if you know what I mean."

I did, but I wasn't sure Hux would ever be ready for the kind of life I had in Chicago. I just couldn't picture him there.

"Well, rangering seems like a good fit for you, then," I said.

"It is and it isn't."

I decided to take the opening he gave me. "Look, if you're at all interested in ISB, I'd be happy to talk about my career path. It's just not a super conventional one."

"Thanks," he said. "I'd appreciate that."

I nodded. "I'm curious, though—if you have all this experience tracking people down, then where do *you* think Colton Dodger is?"

"Well, let's back up a bit." He leaned back in his seat and draped his arms over the back of the booth. "Our only real lead is what Smith told us, and that's not much of one. I guess it's possible he stole the boots from the Glampist campsite and not a corpse, but if that were the case, he would've just said so." Hux started in on a second order of bacon as he talked.

"Still hungry?" I asked.

"Gotta eat when you can," he said. "Old habits die hard, I guess." He offered me a piece, but I'd finished my grilled cheese over an hour ago.

"So where's the body, then?"

He broke the burnt bits of bacon into even smaller bits.

"Come on, Hux."

He grinned. "Okay, okay. Delia said the guy in her camp-site went toward Sawtooth Peak, but we know Ramsey Smith went the other way. Somebody in a panic like that—they'd head downhill. They always do. It's human nature, really."

"So you're saying Delia was lying?"

"Yes—which raises a few questions for me—but more important, it establishes Smith's location for a moment in time. And if we toss out everything he said, which I'm thinking we should, then I'm betting he found the body near Nine Lakes, not Bear Paw like he said."

"Why?"

"Because Nine Lakes is a lot closer to Precipice, and I don't think Colton Dodger got that far, sorry to say. He just didn't have the gear or the experience."

I lacked Hux's knowledge of the land, but I tried to imagine a guy like Colton Dodger—a city dweller, no outdoor experi-ence whatsoever—trying to find his way back to civilization on a cold, unforgiving night. It would not have been easy. "And he died there? How?"

"I don't know—for now I'm just telling you what I think about *where* he went, not why or how. Nine Lakes is pretty exposed terrain, and Smith mentioned it in his account. I think he mentioned it because subconsciously he knew it was significant."

"All right," I said. "So we ask SAR to search Nine Lakes again."

He shook his head. "I'll go up there myself." In a softer voice, he added, "Just wish I had Betta with me. She was the secret sauce."

"You can borrow Ollie if you want." I looked out the win-dow to see my dog with his snout against the glass, studying the intersection in front of the diner. Ollie was like me in that way; he harbored a real interest in human behavior.

Hux's eyes brightened. "Really?"

"Sure."

The conversation paused there as our server came by to offer us a little dessert, which tempted me, but Hux declined. He did ask for a mint, though.

"How 'bout you?" Hux asked. "How do you deal with loss?"

"Pardon?"

"You wear it like a shadow that you can't shake."

Hux was right. Kevin was my shadow, even now. I didn't want to talk about my dead husband, but it felt like the time had come to open up to Hux a little bit. After all, he had done as much for me. I wanted this to feel like a balanced partnership.

"I'm sure you read all about it in your 'mega search,'" I said.

"I'd like to hear it from you."

I stared at a carving on the table in front of me—the letters were faded now, but still legible: SOS. Were those initials or a call for help? For some reason, I pictured an old man sitting alone in this booth with a half-eaten flank steak on his plate, a cup of coffee in his hand. Maybe he'd taken the knife and used it to send a message that he knew only a stranger would read.

"Kevin was a survivor," I said. "Not war, like you—but when he was eight, he was almost killed by a drunk driver. He lost both his parents and a little sister."

"Damn," he muttered. "That's a tough break."

"Yeah. But Kevin was lucky. He got through all the anger and the bitterness and emerged a stronger person. He could be exhausting, honestly—never wanted to just lie around and watch TV like normal people do. He was determined to make the most out of every day." I felt myself smiling at the memory. "He was good for me, though—taught me to take risks, to dream big. He always supported my career in the FBI."

"How'd you meet?"

"In a courtroom."

"Really?"

"Yeah," I said. "We were both there for jury duty."

"Sparks flew."

I nodded. "Sparks flew."

He was quiet. "So what happened?"

"The trip was my idea," I said. "I convinced myself we could navigate the remotest part of Australia on our own because we were capable people, you know. I mean, Kevin could fix anything from a car to a garbage disposal, and I was good with maps and technology and all that. We both dismissed the idea of a tour group. We were cocky, no way around it."

I remembered proposing the trip to Kevin, selling him on the promise of a once-in-a-lifetime experience. I'd gotten no pushback from him—he was always up for it, no matter the risks. Looking back, I wondered if some part of me was trying to impress him. As his wife, I couldn't help but admit that there were times I felt like the imposter in our marriage—like I wasn't as tough as him, or as adventurous, or even as interesting.

"And you fell?" Hux asked.

I nodded. "We were hiking along a gorge, and I slipped— fell about a hundred feet. Ironic, I know," I said, referring to the length of the drop to Precipice Lake. "I don't remember the impact. I just remembering coming to and thinking I was paralyzed."

I didn't tell Hux that the worst part was seeing the terrified look in Kevin's eyes when he found me. In that moment, he was almost unrecognizable. He screamed, he cried; he talked about dying in the outback even while trying to reassure me that he wasn't worried. In the days that followed, he seemed to lapse into a weaker, more vulnerable version of himself. And *that* version of Kevin, the one that I was in some ways responsible for, had never made it back to civilization. He had simply disappeared.

I met Hux's gaze and said, "The mistake wasn't falling, though. It was skimping on the sat phone. It broke when I landed on it." I breathed out, hearing the shakiness in it. "For three days, we fought about what to do. Kevin eventually went off on his own to find help, and that was the last time I ever saw him."

"But you survived."

I nodded, but it was hard even to do that much—even with Hux. The fact that I had survived was a cruel reminder that if we had only stayed together, Kevin would probably still be alive. For five days after he left, I languished in a ditch that, by some miracle, offered decent protection from the elements. I had a little food and water that I rationed well, and luck was on my side. When a local boy found me at the edge of daylight on the eighth day, I thought he was a hallucination. But no, he was real—and two days later I woke up in a hospital bed.

Hux waited for me to say more, but I couldn't bring myself to talk about what came after my dramatic rescue—the dashed hopes, the guilt, the blame. Kevin's brother never even came to see me in the hospital. He left a message on my voicemail: *He's the only family I had left, Felicity. This is on you.* I still had it on my phone. In my darkest moments, I still listened to it.

"So why ISB?" Hux asked.

"Because we both loved being out in the wilderness—it reminds me of him, of us. But it's a good reminder. Being in the city, in our old apartment—that was a bad reminder. I couldn't move on. Most days, I could barely get out of bed."

"It sounds like you really loved the guy."

"Yeah," I said. "I did."

Our waitress came by again to drop the check, and she lingered there a moment—intrigued, maybe, by the tone of our conversation or the looks on our faces, or possibly both.

When my cell phone rang, I was grateful for the reprieve—at least until I saw the number on the display. ISB headquarters. A call from them could only mean one thing: a new case on the docket. While Hux pretended to scrutinize the placemat, I answered the phone.

"Harland here," I said.

"Agent Harland," the dispatcher said, both a greeting and a confirmation. "We've got a situation down in Joshua Tree—double murder, looks like. It's all hands on deck."

Shit. The only thing worse than a murder case was a double murder. Now I was looking at *three* open investigations, and I'd barely been on the job a week.

"I'm still working on this case—"

"They're expecting you on-site at oh-six-hundred tomorrow."

It was hard to get a word in edgewise with the dispatcher, whose name I hadn't caught—or maybe he hadn't given it. I recognized his voice, though.

"I'm not done here," I said firmly.

"I'm sorry, Agent Harland. You'll have to talk to your supervisor if you've got concerns about your ability to take on another case—"

"I'm not concerned about my abilities—"

"Oh-six-hundred tomorrow."

With an aggrieved sigh, I said, "Yes, sir," and hung up the phone.

Hux was giving me a look that told me he knew exactly what that call was about. "Pressure from the brass, eh?" he asked.

"It's how it always is. There just aren't that many of us."

"You'll get 'er done," he said, in his casual, good-natured way. Hux's reliable good mood relaxed me a little. I didn't share his optimism, but he was right that I had to go to Joshua Tree. The old rules still held true; it was important to see the scene as soon as possible.

"I'm sorry," I said. "The timing isn't great."

"It's not your fault."

No, but it still felt like my fault. I was the one leaving, after all. "Look, if you want to go back and help Corrigan with the search—"

"I'm on it," he said.

"Don't you want to hear the other option?"

"Nope. I want to find that body."

I couldn't help but smile at his enthusiasm. "Let's hope you do, because we need more than your math skills to clinch this case for us." I was shuffling out of the booth when I suddenly remembered Ollie. "Hux, about my dog—"

"Don't worry," he said. "Ollie's safe with me."

"What's your plan? Please don't say hitchhiking."

"Nah. I might just Uber-cab it."

"Hux—"

"I'm kidding. Look, I've got a SEAL buddy that lives in Fresno. He'll give us a ride."

"Are you sure?"

He nodded. "One hundred percent."

I didn't like abandoning them here—Ollie, for one, was still adjusting to life on the road—but Hux insisted they'd be fine, and I trusted him. After some debate, he let me pay the bill, plus a little extra for his buddy's gas money.

It was with an uneasy feeling that I set off for Joshua Tree.

24

B ECAUSE JOSHUA TREE was desert country, April was peak sea-son at the park—the weather was mild, the wildflowers in full bloom. Indian Grove Campground in particular was a magnet for weekend campers, partly for its accessibility, but also because of its aesthetics. I'd seen online pictures of its stark landscape and steep rock formations, which sheltered the campsites from gusting winds and relentless sunshine. I mentally prepared myself for heavy crowds, and sure enough, that was what I got when I pulled up to the entrance gates.

Word of a grisly crime in a tourist hotspot had preceded my arrival—there was no doubt about that. Rangers were shouting at people, in cars and on foot, to steer clear of the crime scene, where yellow tape billowed in a gentle breeze. Between two giant boulders was a body, wedged in there like squished hot dog in a stale bun. Despite the rangers' best efforts to corral the crowds, people were jockeying for position behind the tape, determined to take advantage of the photo op.

I parked the car on the side of the road and tracked down the ranger in charge—a man wearing a big straw hat and a too-tight uniform. He let out a big sigh the moment I produced my badge. I wasn't sure if this was a good sign or a bad one.

"Hi," I said, extending a hand. "I'm Felicity Harland with ISB."

"Neal Grimes," he said, as he tossed another traffic cone onto the road in a vain attempt to control the traffic. "Get back in your vehicle, sir," he shouted. "Now, sir. Do it now." He glanced over his shoulder at me. "This here's a goddamn mess."

"You need to get these people out of here." I gestured to the ones leaning over the crime scene tape. "I can't run a scene like this."

"I know, ma'am, but these folks are camping here—"

"Doesn't matter. Move them out before someone takes a selfie with the victim."

I wasn't sure the message landed. Ranger Grimes had a skittishness to him, turning at every voice, every shout, every fart in the wind. This was going to be a painful investigation indeed if he was my point person. I almost missed Corrigan.

"You ISB?" came a voice from behind me—right behind me, way too close. I whirled around to see a man in his fifties, wearing his cologne like he bathed in it. He was also FBI, with his badge hanging on a gold chain around his neck.

"Yes," I said. "Felicity Harland."

"Charlie McCafferty," he said, sizing me up with a smirk that made me feel even smaller than my sixty inches. "Look, I'm sorry to waste your time, Felicity—this one's no mystery, lemme tell ya." He said my name with an air of condescension, like he was the expert and I was the cute little intern. In that moment I was sorely tempted to correct him—*It's Special Agent Harland, asshole.* But that wasn't going to accomplish anything, so I kept quiet.

"How so?"

"Well, it's murder—that's for sure. It's all on video."

I followed his gaze to the throng of rubbernecks. "Someone recorded it?"

"Yup. There's a bunch of amateur videos out there on social media. It's a sensation." His lips twisted into a smile of sorts. "You're not into that shit, I take it?"

"I only heard about this case six hours ago, and I've been on the road for the last five—so no, I didn't have a chance to look."

He didn't seem to hear me. "So we've got the one vic in the rocks there, and the other one died an hour ago at the hospital.

Our buddy over there," he said, as he jutted his thumb over his shoulder, "died from a stab wound to the neck. Bled out quickly and theatrically. You really should check out the footage—"

"I thought this was a double murder case."

"It is." He smiled at me.

"I'm not following." I knew *he* knew I wasn't following; it was part of his schtick. He was drawing out the story for dramatic effect—pointlessly, in my opinion. During my time with the Bureau, I used to avoid guys like this like the plague.

"Yeah, so, the woman in the hospital was the vic's wife. She died from a gunshot wound—the bullet tore up her liver and the big vessel next to it, and she bled out like her man there. Slower, but still. There's some poetry in that, don't you think?"

I didn't much care about poetry; in my book, death was ugly and brutal and fairly straightforward. "So what happened?" I asked. "I know you keep talking about these iPhone videos, but if you wouldn't mind telling me how this wasn't self-defense—"

"Look, I know this is technically your jurisdiction 'cause we're on National Park lands, but this guy was an informant for us—drugs, worked for a big cartel—so we're already involved. You should just go home, Felicity." He made like he was going to massage my shoulder. As was the case with ninety-nine percent of the male population, he towered over me. I backed up a step.

"At least tell me how this went down, Agent McCafferty," I said—a scolding, and he knew it. His big bushy eyebrows knitted together.

But before he could answer, his cell phone rang—at full volume, the offensive sound echoing through the valley. "I need to take this, Special Agent Harland," he said with Shakespearean emphasis on my title. I rolled my eyes as he walked away.

My cell phone beeped with an incoming text. It was Hux:

Have you seen this?

Below his message was a link and one of those exploding emojis that always made me laugh because, well, they were ridiculous and weird. Hux knew I got a kick out of them.

I clicked on it. The article he'd linked to wasn't ridiculous and weird, though. It was inevitable and deflating: *"Tatum Delancey Found Dead in Sequoia National Park."* I skimmed through the article. Corrigan had given a quote that should never have come from him, but it was his ranger station under attack from the media. At some point he'd gone out onto that deck out front and told the masses that Tatum Delancey's death was an accident and that they were all wasting their time asking questions about it. *"Case closed,"* he'd said, which made my blood boil.

In most jurisdictions, a random quote by someone tangentially involved in an investigation wouldn't have moved the needle very much, but when crimes occurred in the wilderness, a quote from the chief ranger was worth its weight in gold. Few reporters were willing to hike twenty-some miles on rough terrain to an alpine lake that looked like every other alpine lake in a hundred square miles. And even if someone *was* feeling inspired to hike all the way up to Precipice, it wasn't like we'd marked the crime scene with yellow tape. No, most journalists were content to get a quote from a guy in a ranger's uniform and call it a day.

I was pacing the perimeter of my new crime scene when McCafferty bombarded my personal space again. "Tough news there, Fel—"

"You know what? You're right. I'm not needed here."

"Whoa." He put his hands up. "Now, I wasn't trying to offend your delicate sensibilities."

"I'm not delicate, and I'm not sensitive. I offered my assistance, and you declined." I clenched my jaw and worked my muscles into a smile. "It was a pleasure meeting you, Agent McCafferty. Best of luck with the case."

"Don't you want to see the video—"

"Nope. Thanks."

I walked into the throng of onlookers and right on past the chief ranger, who didn't seem to recognize me when I told him ISB was off the case. Short memory, that one.

A few minutes later I was on the I-10, driving north toward Palm Springs. I rolled down the windows, sucked in some hot dry air that made my throat itch, and called Hux.

"Hey," he said. "Sorry, didn't mean to bother you with that text—"

"It was a welcome interruption," I said. "Trust me."

"Uh-oh." I could hear the amusement in his voice. "What happened?"

"Nothing. It's the FBI's problem now—they wanted it." I took a swig from the fountain soda sitting in my cupholder, realizing too late that it had been marinating in the desert heat for hours. "Any updates on your end?" I asked, choking on the liquid, knowing that my rash decision in Joshua Tree would come back to haunt me. Until then, though, I'd put the whole thing out of my mind. There was still hope of solving the Tatum Delancey case.

"On the body in the woods, no. I convinced a few buddies of mine to search in the basin, but we came up empty. Thanks for letting me borrow Ollie, by the way. He was great out there."

"No problem," I said, relieved and proud to hear that my dog had done well.

"Also, I made some calls like you asked—and, well, it's a bit of a mess."

"How so?"

"I managed to track down Colton Dodger's mom."

"And?"

"Dodger told her he was going out of town for a week."

Huh. My first thought was that the time line didn't quite fit, and this troubled me. "When was he supposed to be gone, exactly?"

"The day before Tatum Delancey went missing. Friday April fifth to Friday the twelfth."

"But the Glampist reservation was only made for a long weekend. Are you sure she was right about the dates?"

"She was absolutely sure."

A small discrepancy, but an important one. I didn't like when little details like this didn't quite add up. "Interesting. Did he tell her *where* he was going?"

"Hawaii. He told her it was a spiritual retreat and that he wouldn't have cell service."

"So he lied to her," I said, deflated by this development. Colton Dodger's mother was in for some bad news. "What did you tell her?"

"I told her we think he may have been up in Sequoia and that we're trying to locate him."

"How'd she take it?"

"She was confused. She didn't even know he was working for Tatum Delancey."

I wasn't all that surprised. When it came to clandestine affairs, people sometimes told their closest friends, but never their parents. And for the most part, they told no one at all.

"What else did you find out about him?"

"Well, he's a bodyguard, as we know—used to play in the NFL under a different name. He legally changed it a few years back; mom said he did it because he wanted a name people could pronounce. He was actually a very talented college running back, but he got injured in his rookie season with the Raiders and never got that huge payday. That's how he got into the security detail."

"Relationship status?"

"Never married, no kids."

"Any references?"

"Two former bosses in the security field. I talked to both of them. They liked him."

I waited for Hux to say more, but he didn't. I was impressed with his follow-up. He had talked to the right people.

"That's it?"

"They said he was very professional and polite. He did good work."

"Okay," I said, rubbing my temples to ward off an impending headache. This was California at its worst, where congestion reigned supreme. Seeing signs for the I-10 filled me with dread, especially with rush hour on the horizon.

"In other news, I did find something in the horse camp," Hux said.

I could tell he was enjoying this. "Go on."

"An inhaler."

"Well," I said, "I'm sure Corrigan was happy to hear that."

"He gloated, sure, but that wasn't the main thing. The alb-uterol canister had a label on it."

"What kind of label?"

"Like the kind you see on pill bottles."

There it was—a tiny spot of luck. "Whose name was on the label?"

"Jeremy McAllister."

"Jeremy McAllister." I thought for a moment, registering the familiarity in that name before it hit me. "McAllister . . . could it be Spark McAllister?"

"That's what I was thinking," Hux said. It sounded like he was grinning. I couldn't help but smile, too, sharing the small victory that Hux must have felt.

"So you *are* good at finding people."

"I found an inhaler, boss."

"No, you found Spark McAllister aka Ramsey Smith aka Jeb's friend."

"I looked into that part of it, too," Hux said. "McAllister's from a small town in Iowa. He went missing last year, like Jeb said. His girlfriend turned up in Oregon not long after that, but apparently Jeb never got the memo."

"Where is the girlfriend now?"

"Still in Oregon. I talked to her."

"You talked to her?" I asked, impressed by his ability not just to follow up on leads, but to follow through. It wasn't always easy tracking people down, especially people who asso-ciated with the likes of McAllister and Jeb. Hux was proving to be a man of his word when it came to locating people of inter-est. I just wondered if he was asking them all the right questions.

"How'd you find her?"

"Social media, boss. It wasn't hard."

"Smith—er, McAllister—is on social media?"

"Oh yeah. Instagram mostly. He's a decent nature pho-tographer. And it's definitely him, by the way." He waited for the staticky connection to come back in. "Anyway, she told me Spark and Jeb liked to live off the grid, which she thought was cool for a while, until she didn't. Spark had a few misdemeanors—shoplifting was his gig—but nothing major. He did a few short stints in the county jail, but no hard time."

"Did you ask her about the Woodsman?"

"Yeah. She said she had her suspicions."

"She said that?"

"Yep."

It was aggravating, of course, to hear that the girlfriend hadn't bothered to alert the local authorities about her "suspicions," but I was used to uncooperative witnesses. When your lifestyle skirted on the edge of the criminal, you tended to keep quiet.

"I won't have time to formally investigate and arrest Jeb," I said, "but that shouldn't be a problem for you. I'm sure you'll track him down when this is all over."

"Oh, I will. Corrigan will be happy to hear that he doesn't have to round up another search party." Hux was interrupted by someone on his end, and when he came back on the line, he said, "Sorry. That was the chief."

"What did he want?"

"He said he's had three guys searching Bear Paw around the clock, with nothing to show for it. He wants to call off the search."

"Do *you* want to call off the search?"

"Not particularly, but it's supposed to rain all weekend. Conditions aren't ideal." He let out a sigh. "I'm sorry, Harland."

"Don't be sorry. We both knew Spark was probably lying."

"You know," he said, then added in a painfully reluctant tone, "I could take him out with me—see if something'll jog his memory." He sounded about as enthusiastic as a highway patrolman on New Year's Eve.

As I pulled onto the I-10 with its monotonous stretch of asphalt and concrete barriers, I considered my options. Hux was an asset in the wilderness, no doubt about that, but he was good in a room, too. He could intimidate and charm, and for the most part, he knew when to push and when to pull back. We had complementary styles in some ways. I was almost reluctant to admit it, but Hux made me better at my job. I knew we'd make more headway with Edwin Delancey if Hux was there with me.

"How about you drive down to L.A. and meet me there, instead?" I asked.

He was quiet for a moment. "You serious?"

"I am. Can you drive down tonight?" It was an unorthodox request, really, to have a park ranger leave his post to join a federal agent for witness interviews. But I trusted my gut, and my gut said this was the right call.

"Well, sure. Of course I can." His excitement came through in his voice. "I might need you to talk to Corrigan, though—he's gonna be pissed when I ask for more time off."

"It's not time off, Hux. I'll make sure you're paid for your time."

"I don't think Corrigan'll see it that way."

"I'll make sure he does," I said. "See you when you get here."

CHAPTER

25

M Y FIRST STOP was the Delancey home in Los Feliz, an
L.A. neighborhood known for its serpentine streets and
gated mansions. The homes were all set back from the road,
shrouded in California oaks and hidden behind ten-foot-high
fences so that you couldn't see the front door, much less the
houses' inhabitants. The only person I saw out on the street was
a gardener, hauling bags of sticks and shrubbery from a driveway to the curb.

I parked out on the street, alone on a steep hill. I had no
intention of ringing the bell at Delancey's address until Hux
arrived, but I wasn't going to pass up the chance to do some
recon. Seeing where the Delanceys lived told me a lot about them.
Judging by the twelve-foot-high gate and lush oak trees, they
clearly valued privacy, but image played a role, too. Los Feliz was
flush with celebrities. It was an exclusive neighborhood with
multimillion-dollar homes—a hipper alternative to Beverly Hills.

The famed Griffith Park was only a mile up the road, so I
made my way there to wander around a bit before Hux arrived.
It was a hot day, the sun beating down on the dirt-packed hills
and canyons. The Hollywood sign gleamed in the distance.
Even though Griffith Park was nothing like the forested mountains of Sequoia or Yosemite, it was an oasis nonetheless. I liked
being alone in the outdoors. It gave me a chance to reset.

By the time I got back to my car, drenched in sweat despite having walked less than half a mile, my phone was blowing up with new text messages. I read the five texts from Ray—the general theme was *Call me ASAP*—and decided that I might not have a job tomorrow if I didn't call him. So I hit the callback button and waited for him to pick up.

But the gods were smiling on me then, because no one answered. I sent him a text:

In L.A. working the Delancey case. Sorry I missed you.

Hopefully he wouldn't call me back until after we talked to Edwin Delancey, at which point I might have some good news to report.

There was a text from Hux, too; he was at the Trails Café near the entrance to the park. I'd passed it on my way in and had suggested it to Hux as a good meeting place, figuring he'd prefer it over some random Starbucks on the urban grid. I headed down the main road at a pace that was somewhere between leisurely and pathetic.

When I got to the cafe, Hux was sitting on a bench with his legs outstretched, an iced coffee in one hand and an Italian soda in the other. Ollie was stretched out at his feet, and as soon as he caught sight of me, he darted across the grass and leapt into my arms. Not for the first time, Ollie knocked me over as he slathered my face in a big wet kiss.

"Hiya, boss," Hux said as he walked over. He appraised my sunburned face and dusty trail shoes. "Were you out for a hike?"

"I considered it, but no—it was more of a leisurely stroll."

He held out the Italian soda. "Enjoy."

I took a sip—sweet, icy-cold, delicious—and sat down on a nearby bench to rest my legs and indulge in some shade. "How did you know I liked these?"

"I didn't. But I know you don't like coffee or tea, so that leaves soda."

"I don't mind coffee."

"You didn't seem too fond of *my* coffee."

Sitting next to him, I was aware of my sweaty state, but not at all concerned about it. Hux was a Navy SEAL turned park ranger; he understood basic human physiology and wasn't about to judge me for a natural response to heat. He'd probably be horrified to know just how many men *did* judge me for that kind of thing.

"Your coffee is terrible, Hux."

To my surprise, he smiled. "Yeah. I know."

We sat there for a few minutes, catching up on the events of days past. I told him about the case in Joshua Tree, with its unique but critical cache of evidence.

"Have you watched the footage?" Hux asked.

"Yep."

"And?"

"Sad to say it was like a WWE match, except she brought a knife to the gunfight. Literally. It's honestly impossible to tell who the aggressor was."

"Any witnesses?"

"A lot, but the family was divided on this one—her family said he was an abusive husband; his said she was a crazy 'bi-atch'— that's a direct quote, by the way." I patted Ollie's head. "It's an unfortunate situation, but honestly, I was glad to get out of there."

Hux crossed his ankles and leaned back, letting the sunshine wash over him. "Well, I wish I had better news on the search for Colton Dodger."

"It is what it is," I said. "You gave it your best shot."

"I'm not so sure about that, boss. It was a rush job."

"Well, that's on me—I asked you to come down here."

He shrugged. "Corrigan's short-handed. He was fine with me helping you out for a day or two, but it's back to the grind when we're done here. I could use some vacation time to pick up the search again, but it'll be a while—"

"Don't worry about it, Hux. I'm just glad you're here— we've got a lot of work to do." I plucked some ice cubes from my cup and dropped them down my shirt, savoring the instant chill. I tipped my head back, resisting the urge to moan as the ice trickled over my sweat-slicked skin. The next thing I heard was Hux clearing his throat.

I caught him looking at me, but as soon as our eyes met, he reached for his iced coffee. "So," he said, swirling the ice in his cup. "What's on the agenda?"

The silence that followed felt different than the others somehow—different, and a little precarious. I liked working with Hux. Maybe at some point down the line, we'd work another case together—or if not together, then at least in a collaborative manner. The point was, I couldn't afford even a twinge of awkwardness in our dynamic, and the only way to banish it was to pretend Hux hadn't seen me as someone other than a professional colleague right then.

It was hard, though—harder than I liked to admit. Hux was a good-looking guy, and yes, I was probably a *little* bit attracted to him. Maybe more than a little bit. The thing was, I hadn't even entertained the thought of being with someone else since Kevin. To do so felt like a transgression, a betrayal. Maybe some small part of me believed he was still alive, as crazy as that sounded. Then again, it had been three years. The rational part of me knew he wasn't coming back, but the sentimental part was having a hard time letting go.

"First," I said, in a tone so neutral it sounded almost robotic, "we're going to stop by the set of *Glenview*. We're meeting the showrunner there at ten."

He glanced at his watch. "That's an hour from now."

"I know."

Hux shifted a bit in his seat, like he was suddenly overcome with nerves. "Huh. I just—maybe I should've worn something else." He looked down at his green trousers, which were part of the standard park service uniform. He had shed his jacket, though, reducing his getup to a crisp white T-shirt. It looked a little snug, but only in the way it was supposed to be.

"Look, Hux, wardrobe is important when you're talking to a suspect—it's all a part of the game. But in this case we're just gathering information, so it doesn't matter what you wear. I mean, it *matters* in that you should always look like a professional, but you do."

"I should really press my pants."

"I've got an iron in the truck."

"Oh, Harland," he said with a grin, "you'd have made a fine sailor."

*   *   *

Hux had finagled yet another ride down to L.A. with a ranger who lived in the area, so he joined me in my truck for our journey over to the HBO studio lot. We arrived expecting a buzz of activity—dragons and explosions and such—but *Glenview*'s soundstage had a funereal quality to it. There were only five cars in the parking lot, and the craft services tent was deserted except for a lone banana rotting on an end table, its yellow mush extruding from the peel. Right around the corner, crew members and assistants motored from one end of the lot to the other, all of them in a hurry to get somewhere. The better-dressed ones were carrying iced lattes.

"I've never been on a studio lot before," Hux said.

"Me neither."

"I like the snack tents they have everywhere."

"You mean craft services?"

He looked around. "They have crafts, too?"

I cracked a smile. Hollywood was miles outside Hux's wheelhouse, about as far from the sequoia forests as you could get. The role reversal felt good. L.A. wasn't Chicago, but it had a similar vibe—the density of people, the pace, the adherence to schedules. And of course there was traffic and pollution and overpriced restaurants, none of which I missed very much at all.

I checked my messages for the location—Suite 4B, in the building right in front of us. This was where the writers concocted all their stories, apparently.

"Who're we meeting with again?" Hux asked. "Sorry—I know you told me. I'm nervous, gotta admit."

"Why?"

"I dunno—these Hollywood types. It's not my scene."

"They're just people, Hux."

"Yeah, yeah."

"Her name's Liv Harrison. She's the showrunner."

"The director?" He went to open the door for me, but it was locked. A security guard had to buzz us in. I supposed there was always the risk of a deranged *Game of Thrones* fan storming into the writers' room with a sword or something.

"No," I said. "She's the creator, and from what I understand, she also runs the writers room. I read in an interview that she was the one who took a chance on Tatum Delancey—plucked her out of a pile of audition tapes. I guess she saw something special."

We were ushered into a lobby characterized by its abundance of green plants and framed movie posters, and the elevators displayed more of the same. Liv Harrison's office was up on the fourth floor—not a corner office, but close enough. Her door was open.

"Ms. Harrison?" I rapped on the door with my knuckles.

She looked up from her desk, which was bare except for her laptop and a bottled water. My first thought was that she was bone-tired but determined to hide it. She had dark irises and a sculpted chin, and she dressed well, sporting a white blouse that accentuated her tanned skin. She looked about forty-five to my trained eye, but she could have passed for forty.

"Yes, hello," she said. "You must be Agent Harland—thanks for coming over. She looked at Hux. "And this is?"

"Hux Huxley, my partner on this case."

She rose briefly to shake our hands. For a moment we just looked at each other, and in that moment I saw how the weight of Tatum Delancey's death must have settled on her, and was settling still. The *Glenview* production probably employed a hundred people, and I wondered if the majority of them still had jobs.

Harrison said, "Well, we're all devastated, as I'm sure you can imagine. Tatum was the heart and soul of this show." She folded her hands over her laptop, which she'd powered down to give us her full attention. "I honestly can't believe this happened. It's terrible."

"Yes, it is," I said.

She nodded. "So what happened, then? She drowned?" She looked from me to Hux and back to me again. "That's what I read online."

"Her body was found in a lake," I said, "but we have reason to believe her death may not have been accidental."

Harrison's eyes widened as she leaned back in her chair. "Is that really true? Jesus."

"We were wondering if you could tell us a little bit about Tatum."

"What do you want to know?"

"Anything at all, really."

She looked out the window, which offered an unappealing view of the parking lot and the actors' trailers. "I liked her from the start," Harrison said. "She was the real deal, you know; Hollywood hadn't gotten to her head. And she wasn't a total newbie—before *Glenview*, she'd done a few TV shows, a movie or two. She had that wholesome, earnest look, which was perfect for a third-grade teacher." She scratched at the label on her bottled water. "The studio wasn't so sure about Tatum, thought maybe she didn't have the right experience, but I went to bat for her. It paid off in a big way. She was talented, eager to learn, respectful to the crew. She was always the first on set and the last to leave."

"So she was a hard worker," I said.

"Yes, absolutely. Not only that, she just seemed to relish the experience. I got the feeling she never expected her dreams to come true, but when they did, she savored the opportunity."

It was hard to reconcile Tatum's devotion to her job with her infidelity, but I reminded myself that most people inhabited completely separate spheres in life, or at least tried to. Some were better at it than others. I didn't doubt that Tatum had worked her butt off like Harrison said, but it made me wonder what had been lacking in her personal life.

"Do you know her husband?" I asked.

"Edwin? Yes, but not well. He came by the set a few times."

I looked at Hux, who must've been working on his poker face because he hardly reacted at all. "What was he like?"

"Well, he seemed like a gentleman—he sent Tatum flowers, took her to lunch. I knew he was a struggling writer, so I even offered him an assistant job, but he said no. He didn't want to use Tatum's connections to get ahead, which struck me as both sweet and a little dumb. This whole town is built on who you know. But for him, his wife always came first."

"I'm told they were only married a year."

"Has it been that long?" She thought for a moment. "I guess it has. Wow, time really flies. I went to their wedding."

"How was it?" Hux asked.

"It was small, nothing too fancy. Maybe eighty people."

"Did you meet any of her family? Or his?"

"I met her parents, nice folks who told me they'd been together since high school. And Edwin—well, I'm trying to remember . . ." She tapped her fingernails on the table. "I'm pretty sure his parents are both dead, now that I think about it. His oldest son was his best man."

I asked, "Did they seem happy?"

"They did to me. Their wedding was such a refreshing change from the Hollywood bonanzas you see around here. Even though he was a good bit older than her, I could tell it was a good match."

Hux glanced at me, maybe expecting me to probe a little deeper into Harrison's assessment of the Delancey clan, but I didn't feel the need. Liv Harrison had formed an impression of the couple that I wasn't going to shake with rumors and insinuation. If we did our jobs right, the truth would come out eventually.

"Did you ever meet Colton Dodger?" I asked.

"Who?"

"Her bodyguard."

"Oh." She put her hands on the table. "Sorry, I never even caught his name. But no. He kept to himself."

"Were they . . ." I paused to find the right words. "What was their relationship like?"

She gave me a look that was difficult to interpret. "It was as you'd expect—he was just there, trying his best to be invisible. Tatum was from a small town, and her parents insisted that she hire someone to look after her."

"Her parents insisted?"

"That's what she told me."

"I see."

Harrison's phone vibrated with an incoming call. She looked up and said, "Sorry, I have to take this." Before we could step out, she walked out the door and closed it behind her.

Hux looked at me and said, "Interesting."

"Which part?"

"There don't seem to be any villains in this case. Colton's a professional, Tatum was a hard worker, her parents sound like lovely people—"

"I'm not looking for a villain, Hux."

"It'd be kind of nice to find one though."

Harrison walked back in. "I'm so sorry," she said with a look of genuine remorse. "The casting director is here to talk about Tatum's replacement—it's been a crazy week. Do you mind if we set up another time to talk?"

"There's no need," I said. "I'll follow up by phone if necessary. Thank you again."

"Absolutely." She shook our hands again, this time wearing an expression that struck me as equal parts sad and tired. "I hope you find out what happened to Tatum. Her poor family— I can't stop thinking about them."

"We're doing everything we can, Ms. Harrison," I said.

She nodded, then after a brief hesitation said, "You should talk to Edwin's youngest son, Cade. He and Tatum were very close."

Hux and I had already made plans to talk to Cade Delancey, but we needed to talk to his father first simply because we couldn't find any contact info for him. Hux had determined from his background research that Edwin Delancey had three sons—one was a lawyer, the others worked odd jobs in the L.A. area. At least, that was his best guess.

To Liv Harrison, I said, "We'll talk to him. Thank you."

Harrison showed us out, or at least partly out, as we nearly collided with the casting director on our way out the door. She was tall and willowy and platinum blond, with golden bracelets that dangled from her elbows to her wrists. Her gaze skimmed right over me to Hux, where it settled for an intense moment that made us both squirm.

"Yes," the woman said. *"Yes."* She looked at Harrison. "He is *perfect* for Ryan. Just completely, absolutely, one hundred percent perfect. Forget the audition—please tell me you hired him on the spot." She looked like she wanted to squeeze Hux's biceps—which were admittedly rather nice—to make sure they were real.

Liv Harrison cleared her throat. "He's, ah—this is Mr. Huxley. He works for the Park Service." Her phone rang again, and she stepped out.

"Of *course* he does. Well, it's time to quit your job, honey, 'cause I've got a whole new career for you." She glanced at me. "Is this your agent?"

"No," Hux said. "This is my partner."

"How sweet," she cooed. "How long have you been together?"

Hux's cheeks flamed red. He looked to me for help, but after days of trying to figure out what rattled him and coming up empty, I was enjoying his discomfort a little bit. "Oh, not long," I said. "We're still figuring it all out."

"Well, I'd love to help," the casting director gushed. "Ryan is the new math teacher—a very deep, complex character. He's smart and charming but sexy as all hell, but he's also a woman-izer. I mean, a *woke* womanizer—very respectful, of course, but he's not marriage material, if you know what I mean." She winked at me.

"Hm. It does sound right for Hux."

Hux stepped between me and the blonde. "I'm, uh—we're late," he muttered. He looked back at me. "We've got that, uh, interview."

"Oh right," I said. "We do."

Hux squeezed out the door, but not before the woman managed to wedge her business card in his back pocket—or maybe she was just trying to cop a feel of Hux's butt. Hard to tell.

As we were walking across the parking lot, Hux pulled the card out of his pocket. It was white with a black font and smelled faintly like lavender.

"Considering her offer, eh?" I asked, holding back a laugh.

"Nah," he said. "I'm camera-shy."

With a smile that rivaled the one belonging to the mega movie star who walked right by us, Hux tossed the card in the trash.

26

IN THE AFTERMATH of Hux's broken dreams, we drove back to Los Feliz to talk to Edwin Delancey. Like the rest of the sequestered houses on the street, with gates out front, there was no obvious way to announce our presence. We argued for a while about how best to proceed. Hux thought we should just climb the fence and ring the front doorbell; I was more in favor of calling Delancey's cell phone. In the end, neither was necessary. As we were standing on the curb, peering into the security camera that was hidden in a tree, a voice came through on the intercom.

"Please leave," it said—a female voice, likely belonging to a native Spanish speaker. "I call the police."

I leaned into the speaker. "Ma'am? Hello? We're not reporters—"

"Please. Get back in your car and go home. I call the police."

"We *are* the police."

There was silence as she considered this. "Why you no call first?"

"We did call—three times. Mr. Delancey isn't answering."

More silence. "Wait, please."

A few seconds later, the gate opened. A heavyset Latino woman in black stretch pants and a pink sweater was coming down the driveway. Her dark eyes darted every which way as she made her approach.

When she was about fifteen feet away, she stopped and asked, "Who are you?"

"I'm Felicity Harland," I said. "I'm a federal agent with the Investigative Service Branch." I turned to Hux. "And this is my partner, Ferdinand Huxley, who's with the Park Service. We're investigating Mrs. Delancey's death."

The woman crossed herself and bowed her head. She sniffled. "I loved Mrs. Delancey. She was like a daughter to me."

"I'm very sorry for your loss," I said.

"She planted all these flowers." She gestured to the lilies and petunias lining the fence, which looked out of place in this neighborhood, but charmingly so. "She loved nature—the trees, the flowers, the birds. I told her not to go into the woods. Anything can happen there."

"Are you . . ." I started. "How do you know the Delanceys?"

"I'm their housekeeper. My name is Norma."

Norma told us she was from Guatemala. Her English was pretty good, but she spoke softly, as if she were embarrassed by her accent. A small crucifix hung from around her neck.

"How long have you worked for the Delanceys?" Hux asked.

"Nine months. I start when they move in here." She sighed. "They wanted a baby. It is so sad." She dabbed at her eyes. "I worry about Mr. Delancey. He was so excited about her party." She choked back a sob. "He did all the decorations and *pastel* and *todo*. Everything."

"When was this?"

"Last weekend when she was away. I was here. I helped him."

Edwin Delancey had mentioned a party, but in the moment, it had sounded a little rehearsed. Now I wondered if he had been telling the truth—either that, or he had told Norma what to say. After all, in our initial interview, Delancey had said he was home alone.

"But Tatum Delancey was on a camping trip last weekend," I pointed out. "When was the party supposed to be?"

"It was surprise. Monday night when she come home."

I wondered if the decorations were still up—or if they'd ever been there to begin with. Even with the gate open, I couldn't see much of the house.

"Can we come in?" I asked.

"The house?" She looked over her shoulder. "No, no. Not good time." She reached for the crucifix around her neck. Her nails were short, her cuticles ragged.

"And you're saying Mr. Delancey was here the whole weekend?"

"Yes. *Viernes, sabado, domingo.*" She was breathing fast, almost gasping. "Yes. The weekend. He was here whole time."

I looked at Hux, who was playing his cards close to the vest for once. He smiled at Norma—a soft, kind smile. To my surprise, she managed the tiniest of smiles back. The tension in her features softened a bit.

"Do you know when Mr. Delancey will be home?" I asked her.

"No se," she said. "He is busy with the funeral."

"How about his sons?" I asked. "Do you know where we can find them?"

"John is a lawyer." She folded her hands in front of her waist. "Larchmont, I think. I don't know the address."

"We'll talk to him," Hux said. The truth was, we'd already found John Delancey. His law firm had a nice website.

"What about the other brothers?"

She shook her head. "I don't know." Her voice cracked as she peered up at Hux. "Tatum was so beautiful," she said. "So young." Then the sobbing started.

As Hux fumbled around in his pockets for a tissue, a black Mercedes came up the hill. It slowed down for a second look, then continued on. I saw the driver—an older white male wearing sunglasses. Not Edwin Delancey. I made sure my badge was featured prominently on my shirt and met his gaze head-on. Having Norma break down in front of two people in uniform wasn't a good look for the neighborhood. The folks living here were probably well acquainted with the local police, if for no other reason than to report suspicious cars parked on the street.

Not wanting to traumatize Norma with any more questions, we thanked her for her time and got back in the truck.
Hux was shaking his head while he combed the fur between
Ollie's ears with his fingers. So far, my dog seemed to be enjoying this ride-along.

"What?" I asked him.

"I just felt sorry for her."

"Me, too. Tatum Delancey was well liked, it seemed."

"Does that change things for you?" he asked, as I started
the engine. It was a valid question in some ways, an irrelevant
one in others. For me, the answer was always the same: *no*. At
this point in the investigation, I was more interested in the
facts of the case than a subjective impression of it. That could
change later on, but for now I was just after some basic information, like Edwin Delancey's alibi and Colton Dodger's
whereabouts. Those were big missing pieces in a case that had
a lot of them.

"Not really," I said.

Hux nodded, glancing at the GPS as we turned onto Mel-
rose. "What do you think about Edwin Delancey's alibi?"

"I have a feeling it'll check out."

"Why didn't he mention it right off?"

I shrugged. "Probably didn't want to rely on his housekeeper to vouch for him. It could be that she's not in the country legally, doesn't want to get involved—who knows."

It was deflating to know that Edwin had, in all likelihood,
been telling the truth about his whereabouts the weekend
Tatum was killed. We would follow up on the party planning—
gift receipts, invitations, decorations, etc.—but something told
me we wouldn't have to dig deep. Maybe the guy *was* completely innocent. Yes, there were plenty of reasons for him to be
jealous—the affair, money, fame—but so far, we had nothing
substantive to tie him to Tatum's death. Our next step was to
get his cell phone records, which would be a job and a half, no
doubt about it. I wanted to crawl into a hole just thinking
about it.

Hux asked, "So what's the play with John Delancey, the
fancy-pants lawyer?"

"Don't have one, to be honest. I say we find his office and knock on the door."

                                    *   *   *

A half hour later, we found a parking spot outside John Delancey's law office in Larchmont. Hux gulped down water from his trusty Nalgene bottle as we walked up to the converted bungalow, with its blue shutters and quaint landscaping. After ringing the doorbell, we were greeted by a young woman with perfect hair and abundant cleavage. She flashed us a winning smile—well, it was clearly more for Hux than for me. She flipped her hair over her shoulder and batted her eyelashes at him.

"Hi," I said. "Is Mr. Delancey in today?" I showed her my badge, which diminished her enthusiasm somewhat. Still, she kept the smile going and escorted us to the waiting room.

"The ladies seem to have a certain fondness for you," I remarked to Hux.

"Do they? I hadn't noticed."

"Uh-huh," I said, with an eye roll that made him laugh.

The door at the end of the short hallway swung open. A tall, dark-haired man in an impeccable suit that hugged his glutes stepped out and said, "I've got ten minutes, max."

I noticed the resemblance to Edwin Delancey immediately; he was his father's younger, more successful counterpart. He was what Edwin could have been with a healthy dose of swagger. I wondered if this interview would bear that out.

We followed him inside. His office looked like it used to be a bedroom, with an en suite bath and a walk-in closet. There was even a little wet bar in the corner, which appeared well stocked with high-end liquors. All in all, the place was tastefully furnished, perhaps even a little overdone. I figured this was an attempt to make up for its humble curb appeal.

"It's tragic," he said, before we'd even had a chance to sit down. "It's a fucking waste is what it is."

Delancey's brash demeanor took me back a bit, maybe because he looked so young. From what I'd heard about Hollywood, this industry wasn't exactly kind to newcomers and neophytes. But Delancey didn't strike me as either. He carried himself like someone who'd been swimming with the sharks for twenty years.

Hux must have been thinking along the same lines, because he said, "How long have you been a lawyer?"

"Eighteen months," he said. "I skipped two grades, graduated from USC when I was twenty. Burned through law school at UCLA, and here I am." He spread his hands wide, as if to reiterate the breadth of his physical and professional domain. "I never intended to work for the man. I've got my own clients, some really big names. Entertainment law is where it's at."

"That's good to know," I said. Hux looked skeptical. He propped his ankle on his knee and casually surveyed the room. The artwork was tasteful, the diplomas prominently featured. The crystal paperweight on Delancey's desk looked expensive, but it was clearly a decorative piece. The guy didn't even have a filing cabinet.

"How well did you know Tatum?" I asked him.

If my sudden shift in tone surprised him, he didn't show it. "Not all that well. She was busy with the show and I'm busy here."

I glanced at his left hand—no wedding ring. Not a surprise for a twenty-something in L.A., but even if he were a dozen years older, I wouldn't have expected one. He just didn't seem to be the type to wear his ring around the office—or around town, for that matter. He was the only lawyer in a practice that bore his name, which told me either he didn't play well with others, or he didn't want to. I was willing to bet John Delancey had one hell of a bachelor pad.

"How did your dad meet her?" I asked.

"On set. She had a small part on a pilot he wrote that never got picked up."

"It sounds like your dad has had some career struggles," I remarked.

His tone hardened. "It's a tough business."

"Were he and Tatum happy?"

"Very." There was no hesitation. I was starting to feel a little defensiveness coming from his side of the room; maybe he was wary of where this conversation was going. He had a right to be. Tatum Delancey's social circle was getting smaller by the minute.

Hux sensed it, too. "We were hoping to talk to your brothers, too, but we can't find them. Their landlord at their last-known address told us they don't live there anymore."

"Yeah, they were roommates for a while, but they got evicted." His lip curled in a withering smile. "Can you believe that? Evicted in L.A.? That's not easy to do."

"So where are they now?" I asked.

Delancey shrugged. "Last I heard, Max lives on the beach, and Cade sleeps on a different couch every week." He put his hands behind his head and leaned way back in his leather chair. "Look, I'll be honest with you—they're a couple of deadbeats. Max is a failure and Cade is a flake. Sorry to be blunt, but I'm only telling it like it is."

Blunt was an understatement. Based on John Delancey's tone, there was no love lost between the brothers. Max Delancey hadn't even surfaced on Hux's Google search—no photos, no social media profiles, no evidence that he existed at all. It was a peculiar omission. Cade had a slightly larger online footprint, but his social media accounts were all set to private.

"I'm hearing some resentment there," I said.

"It's not resentment. It's frustration. They're lazy sacks of shit."

"Unlike you," Hux said tonelessly.

Delancey eyed him for a moment before responding with another shrug. "I don't respect their lifestyles, that's all."

"Are they into drugs?" I asked. "Or something else?"

"I dunno."

This was a lie. I could see it on his face, in his eyes. So there was a limit, then—Delancey wasn't going to spill *all* the gory details about his dysfunctional family. He'd give us just enough to let off some steam.

"It would help us a great deal if you could point us in their direction," I said.

"I just did." He glanced down at his phone, which told me time was running short on this interview.

"Tatum was a lot younger than your father," I said.

"Yup." He put both hands on the table. "What's the question?"

Hux said, "Can you think of any reason she'd go on a wilderness trip with somebody other than your dad?"

He didn't flinch. "Look, I know how it looks—my dad was a lot older than Tatum, and yeah, she was out of his league. But I'm telling you, they were happy. My parents got married young and had kids they couldn't afford and all the rest. Dad deserved someone like Tatum. It's a tragedy that she died and tragic for my dad. He's gutted."

"Is your dad the jealous type?" I asked.

"Tatum wasn't cheating on him if that's what you're asking."

"It's a valid question, though, don't you think?" Hux posed the question in a tone that was somewhere between conversational and skeptical. "We know she was out there with another guy."

"How do you know that for sure?"

"We've got a lot of evidence to suggest it."

I shot a glance at Hux; one misstep and we could be in trouble. "You said Max lives on a beach," I said to Delancey. "Which one?"

"He's a surfer. Try Santa Monica. He hangs out with a crew of asshats and losers by the pier." He rose from his chair and ambled toward the window. The view from his office wasn't exactly spectacular—a nice little backyard bordered by a neighbor who was letting his house rot. The small muscles in Delancey's jaw twitched. It probably irritated him on a daily basis to see that eyesore and know there wasn't a damn thing he could do about it.

"All right, then," I said. "Thanks for your time."

Hux took my cue and got up. As we were walking out the door, Delancey said, "Feels like you're really doing your due diligence on an accidental death."

I turned. Delancey's gaze settled on me with an almost predatorial stare. He was a lawyer, after all—a bullish one, too, was my guess. He probably would've made a decent prosecutor if he weren't so obsessed with his own image.

"We're exploring a number of different possibilities," I said.

"Such as?"

I wasn't worried about John Delancey going to the media. This was his family, after all, and his family's dirty laundry was his dirty laundry. A lover's spat turned murderous wouldn't exactly attract a windfall of new clients in an industry built on appearances.

"The evidence collected from the scene suggests that she may have been pushed," I said.

He walked back over to his desk with his hands in his pockets, but I could see the tension in his stride. Something was bothering him, something more than the burden of bad news. He picked up his phone and checked the display. I was waiting for him to say that he had to go—time was money, after all—but he didn't. He looked back at me with a question on his lips. A debate, even. He wanted to tell me something.

But then a dog—the neighbor's, sounded like—started barking with an almost deranged ferocity. Delancey cussed under his breath as he went back to the window. He lifted the sill, poked his head out, and screamed, "I swear to fucking god I'm gonna shoot your worthless piece of shit dog and use it as a doormat, you worthless fuck."

When that was done, he slammed the window shut so hard the panes rattled in the frame. I thought he was going to remember we were here—apologize, make nice, do something to deflect attention from his temper tantrum—but he just shrugged and said, "Neighbors."

Hux was halfway out the door at that point, but I couldn't forget about the words John Delancey hadn't spoken. As he walked back to his desk, I asked, "What is it?"

He looked up from his phone. "Excuse me?"

"You were going to say something just then."

He ran his hands over his handsome mahogany desk and sat down. His eyes matched the wood—dark, unreadable. Then he met my gaze and said, "When you were implying that Tatum's death might not have been accidental—I just didn't want you wasting your time."

"Pardon?"

"Well, my stepmother had some issues."

"Issues? Like what?"

"Mental health stuff."

"Can you be more specific?"

He put his hands behind his head and looked out the window. "Not really. I wasn't her psychiatrist."

"Was she suicidal?"

He met my gaze again. "I didn't think she was, but when you hear she fell off a cliff—I mean, look, she was fragile. That's all I'm saying."

I looked him in the eye, searching for something that he wasn't going to give me in this room, and probably never would. It was hard to get a read on a lawyer as slick as John Delancey, but unlike everyone else we'd talked to about his stepmother, he wasn't exactly singing her praises. In his words, she was *fragile*— and therefore breakable. Is that what had happened up on that ridge at Precipice Lake? Had Tatum Delancey broken under the pressure of newfound stardom?

Or was John Delancey just trying to convince us that she had?

27

I THOUGHT IT WOULD take days to track down Max Delancey in a city as sprawling as Los Angeles, but Hux had a more optimistic outlook. "It'll require a few awkward conversations," he said as we cruised the streets of Santa Monica, looking for a parking spot. "But we'll find him."

The Santa Monica pier was Sequoia's antithesis, packed to the gills with tourists, skateboarders, surfers, and other folks not easily categorized. The pace of the place was medium speed, not quite California cool but certainly slower than the urban grid. Because there was no distinct "type," we blended in better than I could have hoped for. Hux got a few compliments on his ranger uniform, including the shirtless beachgoer who quite earnestly said, "Nice costume."

"So how do you do this?" I asked him. "Find people, I mean?"

"Depends on the situation," he said. "Here, you start with what you know—or at least, what John Delancey told us—and go from there. It's easier when you know the place—and lemme just say, this is all new to me. I've seen *Baywatch*, but that's about it."

"You're a real *Baywatch* fan, eh?"

"My mom loved it," he said. "Go ahead, get your jabs in now."

"I think the show has its merits."

He lifted his sunglasses to look me in the eye. "You bet your ass it does."

We were walking past a place called Calibunga Surf Lessons when Hux stopped and turned around. "Hold on a minute," he said, and went inside. I stood by the railing and peered out at the sea, a vast blue-black that stretched to the horizon. The Pacific smelled different from Lake Michigan—saltier, sure, but there was something else about it. A softness, maybe. The winds gusting off Lake Michigan on a gray January day used to make my hair stand on end.

Hux returned with a sureness in his stride.

"Well?" I asked him.

"He doesn't know Max Delancey, but he told me where to look for him—the best surfing's over there." He pointed to the beach on the other side of the pier. "Told me this is actually a good time to be out there, so we'll have plenty of surfers to talk to. I bet we find the guy by . . ." He checked his watch. "Two o'clock." It was already quarter after one.

"No chance," I said.

"Wanna bet?"

I balked. "Nah."

He grinned. With Hux in the lead, we set off toward the beach that Calibunga had talked about. The surf looked a little rough, but there was no wind, which made for nice, clean waves. I'd taken a surfing lesson once. It hadn't gone well, even with the mammoth surfboard the instructor gave me to ensure a false sense of accomplishment. Apparently the surf instructors called their biggest surfboards "yachts" when the customers weren't around. If you couldn't stand up on a yacht, well, you were either deeply uncoordinated or dangerously vertiginous.

Hux passed two guys—didn't bother to give me a reason—and settled on a third, who was sanding down his board. The first thing I noticed was that his stuff was old—old wetsuit, old surfboard, old bar of wax. He looked kind of old for a surfer, too, maybe in his fifties.

"Oh yeah, I know Max," the guy said, when Hux asked him. "He's around."

"He's around *today*?" I asked.

"He's around every day." He cupped his fingers over his eyes and scanned the water. Everyone looked the same to me— white surfboards, black wetsuits—but then again, I wasn't a surfer. This guy seemed to have a beat on the whole scene.

"Yeah," he said. "He's there."

"Where?" Hux asked.

"Right there." He pointed at a pack of surfers numbering about ten.

"Got it," Hux said. "Thanks."

We thanked the seasoned surfer and walked toward the water's edge. Hux offered to go right in and get Max Delancey himself, but I told him no, it could wait. I wasn't even sure which one was Max, but Hux had him pinpointed with his bloodhound-like instincts.

We stood there a while, watching the surfers swim out in search of that perfect wave, only to miscalculate or decide on another. One guy in particular seemed especially choosy, going in and out and in again, only to sit on his surfboard for a while and watch the other surfers manhandle the ocean right in front of him. By the time he settled on a wave, he didn't even manage to stand up on his board—just kind of kneeled on it for a few seconds and tumbled over the side before the wave had fully broken.

"That's him," Hux said.

I couldn't yet make out the guy's face, but I knew Hux was right. There was something about him—the way he'd fumbled the wave, the hunch in his shoulders. John Delancey had called his brother a "failure." His choice of words stuck with me, especially now as I watched his younger brother make his way to shore.

I realized then that he must have noticed us, because he changed his trajectory a bit and walked in our direction. Hux held up a hand in greeting. I offered a courteous smile.

"Max Delancey?" Hux asked.

He nodded. Edwin Delancey's son had brown hair streaked blonde from the sun, tanned skin, and a week's worth of stubble on his chin. He looked a little like Hux, in fact, except Max had a skinny build compared to Hux's broad one, and by my estimation I doubted he'd last a week in the mountains. There was something about him that felt soft, which I suspected had more to do with his upbringing than his surfer lifestyle.

After a brief introduction that seemed to worry Max Delancey a bit, we bought him a cold beverage and sat outside a small café just steps from the beach. It was a glorious day—blue skies, bright sunshine, the smell of summer in the air. The shallows were flush with surfers and bathers. Sun worshippers occupied every inch of sandy real estate.

Max kept pushing his hair out of his eyes as he stared into the depths of his Arnold Palmer, which he'd made a point of ordering without alcohol. He bounced his legs to a frenetic rhythm that made the table shake.

"Can't beat the beach on a day like this," Hux said. "You been surfing long?"

Max nodded. "Since forever. Well—I started out body-boarding 'cause that's all you can really do in New Jersey. We moved here when I was six."

"What brought your family out here?" I asked.

"My dad. After my mom died, he felt like he needed a change."

In stark contrast to his older brother, Max had the look of a lost child. A part of him had clearly withered with the loss, and while the sea was probably an escape for him, it wasn't a cure. I felt a pang of sympathy for him. Here he was, searching for something in nature that I wasn't sure he'd ever find. I could relate to that, at least.

When we asked him about Tatum, he echoed his brother's sentiments that the thought of her cheating on his father had never really occurred to him. "I really liked her," Max said. "She cared about Dad."

"Did she care about you?" I asked.

He took a long sip from his drink. "Yeah. She offered to rent me an apartment, help me get on my feet. I prob'ly shoulda done it."

"Why didn't you?" I asked.

"Just didn't feel right."

Hux said, "When's the last time you saw Tatum?"

He thought for a moment. "About a month ago—Sunday dinner. Tatum and my dad cooked for us every Sunday, which was nice I guess, but kinda sad."

"Sad why?"

"'Cause most of the time, nobody went."

"Who did they invite?"

"Just me and my brothers. I think Tatum felt bad that we didn't have a mom—that, or she was just homesick. She was really close to her parents."

"Were either of your brothers there the last time you saw her?"

He nodded. "Yeah, I mean, Cade was there a lot, but John never went. He's always busy or whatever." He pinched his straw with his fingers. "Truth is, he just doesn't like hanging out with us. John's kind of an asshole."

I looked at Hux before turning back to Max. "We met him, actually."

Max stared at the table. "Well, then you know."

I wondered about Max Delancey's childhood—about his relationship with his brothers, with his parents. According to Hux's background work, Max's mother had died in a car accident when he was only five. That was a lot of years to be without a parent. Had Tatum filled that hole for him? Had he *wanted* her to fill it for him?

"He told us where to find you," I said.

"What else did he say about me?" The twinge of hopefulness in Max's voice made my heart ache. God, life could be cruel.

Hux filled the pause with, "Not much. He said Tatum and your dad had a good thing going." He gave Max the space to answer, but it was a long time coming.

"Yeah," he said. "They did."

I said, "You mentioned Cade, your other brother. Does he live in L.A.?"

Max was quiet. He had downed every last drop of his Arnold Palmer, and now he stared at the bottom of his glass like it held the secrets to the universe.

"Max?" I pressed.

"I don't . . ." he trailed off.

"You don't what?"

"Nothin'."

"Look, we're not the LAPD," I said. "We're just trying to find out as much as we can about Tatum."

"Why? I thought she drowned." He searched our faces with renewed interest. It occurred to me that maybe Max Delancey didn't read the news—hell, maybe he didn't even have a phone. He didn't have any social media accounts, at least according to our research.

"She fell from a cliff," I said. "We're not sure if it was accidental."

Max's soft features tightened, especially around his eyes. His mouth dropped open a little bit. "Are you *serious*?" he asked. "Nobody told me that."

"It's all over the news, man," Hux said.

"I don't read the news. It's toxic."

Hux said, "Look, your brother isn't in trouble. We just want to talk to him."

Max tore a thread off the paper-thin placemat. His skin looked pretty good—clean, no track marks. I wasn't sure if I was more surprised or relieved to see that Max had avoided that lifestyle, at least. Maybe he just needed a little direction in life.

He said, "The truth is, I don't know where he is."

"Is he homeless?" I asked.

"Not really. He stays with my dad a lot. It's just—I can't reach him."

"What do you mean?"

"He's not answering my texts or calls. I was gonna call the police, but John told me not to 'cause Cade's had issues in the past."

"Issues with what?"

"Addiction."

"I see," I said, exchanging a look with Hux. "When's the last time you talked to him?"

Max went back to work on the placemat. Another ten minutes of this and it would be a pile of tattered bits. "I can't remember," he mumbled.

"Try," I said.

Hux called the waiter over to refill Max's Arnold Palmer. "Do you want anything to eat, man?" he asked. "'Cause I'm gonna order something."

Max nodded. "Uh—yeah. A cheeseburger would be good. And fries, maybe."

"You got it."

I said gently, "Max, our jurisdiction is limited to national parks. We don't have any authority to prosecute Cade for drug-related charges, even if we wanted to. And we don't want to; frankly, we've got too much on our plate as it is. This is about Tatum."

He sighed—a soft, quiet sound. It felt like there was a life-time's worth of resignation in it, or maybe something deeper, like sadness. He looked out at the Pacific where the waves cycled and crashed and receded, a predictable rhythm that seemed to calm him. His eyes glistened.

"Tatum was always trying to help everyone," he said. "That was just who she was." He wiped a tear away before hastily returning his hand to his lap. "Cade, especially. She thought she could turn his life around."

"How?"

"With the drug stuff." He shook his head. "Oxy, mostly. It wasn't even his fault. He tore his ACL playing basketball senior year and the stupid ortho gave him, like, sixty pills." He made a sound like a snort, which struck me as a flash of anger—but only a flash. And then it was gone. "Anyway, she thought she could help him get clean."

"By doing what?" I pressed. "Sending him to rehab?"

"Well, yeah, there was that—a lot of rehab. He went like six times. It never took." He reached for his Arnold Palmer as soon as his waitress finished refilling it. This time, though, he grasped it with his left hand, and I noticed the large bruise encompassing three of his knuckles. It was more yellow-purple than black-and-blue, which meant it had been there for at least a week.

"How did that happen?" I asked, flicking my gaze to his hand.

"Oh—uh, surfing." He stuck his hand back in his lap.

Hux and I exchanged glances. I didn't know enough about the sport to know if this type of injury was consistent with surfing or not, but Max's reaction to my question made me wonder. I decided not to lean on him just then, though. So far, he'd been more helpful than anyone else connected to Tatum Delancey.

"So back to Tatum," I said. "What did she do to help him?"

He thought for a moment. "She started throwing out ideas, things that she thought he might actually like. That's how she came up with the camping trip."

Hux sucked in a breath, while I held mine. Max's attention had drifted to the ocean again, like he was scared to continue the conversation. Even when the waiter arrived to take our order, he pretended not to notice.

"Max," I said. "What camping trip?"

He sipped his drink. I knew he didn't have it in him to lie to us—not now, not after going so far down this road. This was how it always went with witnesses. Once the walls came down, there was no stopping the deluge.

"Sequoia," he said.

28

ORRIGAN CALLED AS we were leaving the pier. "We've got
nothin' up here," he said, regarding the search for Colton
Dodger's body. "Not even a hint of nothin'." He muttered something about a waste of resources and a wild goose chase.

With Edwin Delancey all but off the table as our prime
suspect, coupled with John Delancey's impression of his stepmother's potential suicidality, I was starting to feel like we had
nothin' too. Rather than argue with Corrigan about the merits
of a search, I sighed and said, "All right. Probably time to move
on."

I saw the look on Hux's face—the disappointment, the
frustration. He walked it off, shaking out his baseball cap as he
paced the pier.

"That it, then?" Corrigan asked. "You closin' the case?"

"We're still trying to track down one family member."

"How long's that gonna take?"

"Hopefully not long. But I'll have to open another official
inquiry, which means I'll still be in your hair for a while. We
think the victim's stepson may have been the one who was up
there camping with her."

"Stepson? I thought you were lookin' for a full-grown adult
named Colton Dodger."

His tone fueled the blush in my cheeks, the humiliation so
intense it made my face sweat. I didn't know what to tell him.

He was right—now we had *two* missing people, with no significant leads into the whereabouts of either one. Had the three of
them all gone camping up there together? Were Cade Delancey
and Colton Dodger in on some murderous conspiracy? No matter whom we talked to, I couldn't make the pieces fit together.

"We are," I said. "And now we're looking for someone
named Cade Delancey, too."

"Well, whoever it is you're tryin' to find, we already searched
up there."

"I know." I watched Hux pick up an empty soda can and
make his way toward a recycling bin. "And I know the search
was adequate. I'm just letting you know that I have to do my
due diligence on this."

Corrigan responded with a not-so-subtle snort. "If you say
so."

He hung up. I found Hux scouring the pier for more trash.
His hands were full of food wrappers, straws, napkins, and
other crap that their users had just tossed aside for no good reason. After some careful deliberation, he parsed them out into a
series of bins that were labeled trash, recycling, and compost.

"Hux—"

"It's okay," he said. "I get it." He walked past me as he went
back out on the hunt for more litter. I followed him down the
pier.

"Look, I know it's not the outcome we were hoping for," I
said, talking to his back. "Hux, look at me."

He inspected an old vaping pen before tossing it into the
bin labeled "Trash." He sighed. "Sorry," he said. "I'm working
through some frustration."

"I understand. I'm frustrated, too." I stared at my sneakers,
which were in much better condition than my hiking boots. "It
might be time to take a step back and reassess."

"What?" he asked, his tone demanding that I look him in
the eye.

"We can't prove this was a homicide, and we've got no witnesses," I said. "Edwin Delancey's alibi is going to check out,
but even if it doesn't, we don't really have motive. Was he jealous? Maybe, but no one thinks Tatum was cheating on him.

And as for the money, well—it doesn't seem like he cared all that much about her money. At least not enough to kill her."

"Not unless she was thinking about leaving him."

"But we don't have any evidence of that."

"What about Cade Delancey?"

"What about him?"

Hux put his elbows on the railing and leaned over it. "He was probably sleeping with his dad's wife. That's something, isn't it?"

I shook my head. "That's a stretch given everything we heard about the Delanceys' marriage. No one thought she was having an affair."

"Oh, come on. I thought you'd be more cynical than that, Harland."

I shrugged. "I'm plenty cynical, believe me."

Hux stood upright and looked out at the sea, which was mobbed with people despite the cool water temperatures. Only the surfers wore wetsuits.

"Let's talk it out, then," Hux said.

"Okay," I said. "What are you thinking happened?"

"I think Cade's into drugs, but he's also into Tatum. They had a thing going. Maybe Tatum wanted to end it because she's married to the guy's dad and Cade pushed her off a cliff in a fit of rage—you know, a crime of passion type thing."

In my experience, crimes of passion usually played out in the privacy of one's home, not in a remote wilderness. The way Hux was telling it, the story didn't fit.

I said, "But if Cade and Tatum were together, it doesn't seem like anybody knew about it—including Cade's own brother."

"Nah. Max is protecting his brother. It feels like it's those two against their big bad bro."

I didn't buy it. Max was a weak, forlorn figure with serious parental abandonment issues. He didn't have the chutzpah to lie to a federal agent. He had been telling the truth about Cade.

"You look skeptical," Hux said, making no effort to mask his disappointment.

"I'm not getting a manipulative read on this family, if you know what I mean."

"You think they're all straight shooters?"

"Something like that."

"You think Cade, the couch-surfing drug addict with a very wealthy and somewhat naive stepmom, is a straight shooter?"

I wasn't about to paint all addicts with a broad brush, but Hux had a point. What if the camping trip wasn't Tatum's idea, but Cade's? What if *Cade* was the one after her money, and he'd gone up there to rob her? I'd seen people die for less.

"Look, we don't even know where Cade is, and since we don't have a body or a witness, or anything in between, we can't prove it went down the way you're saying it did. And that's all that matters to the prosecutor."

"I thought the truth was what mattered."

I blew out a sigh that did nothing to temper my own frustration. Truthfully, I was tired. Our epic trek through Sequoia had taken its toll. What I really needed was a comfortable bed to sleep on and a quiet room to think in, but there was no time for either of those. I already had three active cases on the docket, and not much to show for any of them.

"Here's the thing, Hux. We've got two people missing in the wilderness and no sign of either one. I can't mobilize another search team to scour millions of acres, even *with* Corrigan's support, which we're not going to get."

"What about cell phone records? Can't you ping his location?"

"I'm working on a warrant for the cell phone carriers, but it takes time. Tatum Delancey and Colton Dodger had different service providers. With our luck, Cade had yet another one."

"You need a warrant for that?"

"The Supreme Court says we do, yes."

He rocked back a bit on his heels. "Huh."

"Look, I'll work the cell phone angle. But it could take me a while."

He glanced at my phone, which was lighting up with a new incoming call. "Is that your boss there?" he asked, seeing Ray's name on the display. I fought the urge to answer and apologize and beg for forgiveness. The truth was, we finally had some momentum going here, and I didn't want to ruin it by hearing

Ray shut it down. I just needed a little time to put my thoughts together—and to make my case that this was murder.

I nodded. "He wasn't happy with my walk-off at Joshua Tree."

As we were making our way back to the truck, Hux said, "I'll find them."

"Find who?"

"Colton. Cade. And anybody else that's out there." The directness of Hux's gaze told me he was serious—this wasn't a wager or a bet. He was going to get 'er done, as Corrigan would have said. I knew he wasn't going to rest until he found them.

Hux and Ollie ran up ahead, giving me some space to contemplate our next move. I liked that they got along so well. Ollie had been Kevin's replacement, in a way—a companion during my darkest days of recovery. It made me feel good to expand his social circle a bit.

When I got back to the parking lot, Ollie was sitting in the bed of the truck, his tongue lolling out of his mouth. Hux, for his part, was leaning against the passenger-side door like a modern James Dean, with his white T-shirt and aviator sunglasses. It was almost too much. When a tween and her mom stopped and asked him for his autograph, it suddenly *was* too much. I heard the girl swoon, "You were so good on *Olympiad*." Hux took the misidentification in stride.

"Are you always so California cool?" I asked him.

"Huh?"

"Don't play dumb." I yanked on the driver's-side door and climbed in. "You enjoyed that." Hux was chuckling as he sidled into the passenger side.

"Sorry, boss," he said. "I'll try to tone it down."

"Thanks."

He rolled down his window and let his arm hang out. With a not-so-casual glance back at me, he said, "I may need to borrow your dog again."

"Hux—"

He held up a hand.

"What?" I said, frowning.

"I'm not trying to be difficult," he said. "It's just that you don't get participation trophies where I come from. You either succeed or you fail. And sometimes when you fail, people die, so nobody ever wants to fail."

He waited for me to start the engine and get us going on our way again, but I couldn't do it—not right then anyway. It was almost like he needed me to listen.

"Harland, I can't go back to being a ranger, knowing that we've got two people unaccounted for in my own backyard."

I wanted to fight him on it—to say no, it's over, this whole damn case is a mess with a rapidly diminishing chance of resolution. But he had me with that look.

"What's your plan?" I asked.

"Well, I'll explain my methods to you on our way back up to Sequoia, but it's mostly gut instinct and a capable hound."

"I don't have time to go back up to Sequoia," I said, knowing it would take us the rest of the day to drive back up to Sequoia, another two days to hike up to Precipice Lake, and who-knows-how-long to search an area based on Hux's "gut instinct." And that was assuming I even made it up there in one piece.

"I mean this in the nicest way possible, Hux, but it sounds like a gamble."

"Five days, then we quit."

I pulled up the call log on my phone. McCafferty had gotten my cell phone number somehow, and his most recent text message damn near made my head explode. *My apologies, Felicity. We could really use your assistance on this one.*

Which was bullshit, of course, but I couldn't ignore him or Ray forever. I was still debating how best to respond when Hux grabbed the phone out of my hands.

"Hux! For Chrissakes—"

"Call your boss back," he said. "Tell him you need five days."

"Hux—"

But before I could argue, he scrolled down to Ray's last call and pressed the callback button. I tried to grab the phone back, but Hux wasn't having it. He held onto it with his monster grip

until Ray picked up, at which point Hux handed it back to me.
He mouthed, "Five days."

As much as Hux's antics pissed me off, there was something
to be admired about his tenacious nature. He wanted this case
solved as badly as I did—maybe even more so. Ray had warned
me that most park rangers were more of a hindrance than an
asset, not because they weren't capable, but because they often
put too much stock into the investigations they conducted prior
to our arrival. Hux, on the other hand, had been collaborative
from the start.

Meanwhile, Ray had picked up, and he was talking—no,
shouting—into the phone. I let him vent for a minute while I
figured out what to say to him.

"Are you hearing me, Harland?" he said. "We work *with* the
FBI, not against them. I need you back in Joshua Tree."

"Ray, the agent down there said—"

"I don't care what he said. Joshua Tree is *our* jurisdiction.
You go down there and remind him of that."

I took a breath. "Here's the thing, Ray. I have reason to
believe that Tatum Delancey was murdered, but I need a little
more time—"

"Murdered? Harland, she *fell*."

"She was pushed."

"And how the hell do you figure that?"

Looking at Hux, I said, "Well, there's Fall Zone." Hux
broke into a grin.

"Fall *what*?"

After a thorough explanation of the physics involved in
Tatum Delancey's death, as well as a promise to follow up with
the chief ranger in Yosemite and McCafferty in Joshua Tree, I
somehow managed to wear him down.

We were going back to Sequoia.

*   *   *

After an uneventful drive north, we stopped off at Hux's cabin
to plan our itinerary. He had reliable internet, which was key,
plus a collection of maps that rivaled those of even the most
seasoned topologist. He kept them in an old wooden chest, the

maps organized into distinct piles that were labeled with Post-it notes.

"So here's the general area we're looking at," he said, opening a two-by-two-foot topo map of the Sequoia wilderness. He spread it out on the kitchen table and pinned it down with bits of tape at the corners. It was a standard topographic map with a detailed rendering of the natural landscape, including its mountains, rivers, and forests, but also with color-coded symbols for trails, ranger stations, and roads. Topo maps varied widely with regard to detail, and ISB used the ones produced by the National Geospace Program of the United States Geological Survey, which were freely available on their website. The USGS maps also included aerial photos and shaded relief images, as well as other fancy features that weren't necessarily going to help us out on the trail, but might give us some insight on which areas to avoid.

"I'm impressed by your map collection," I said.

"Gotta love the wizards at USGS." Hux reached into the depths of his wooden chest and pulled out a laminated black-and-white topo map. "Check this one out—printed in 1883. This is from the David Rumsey map collection."

"Yosemite Valley," I said, noting some familiar features on the hand-drawn map—Yosemite Falls, El Capitan, Half Dome. They were all spectacular in their own right.

"Yep," Hux said. "As you may or may not know, USGS started putting together a topo map collection of the United States back in 1878," he said. "I know we've come a long way since then, but this here's still a damn good map."

After admiring his map collection like two nerds in geography class, we shifted our focus back to Sequoia. Hux pulled up the USGS's topographic map of the park on their website, which had been updated the year before. All of their topo maps were downloadable. Hux didn't have a printer, so he used the online USGS map to take some notes onto the one we did have. Meanwhile, I took a look at Hux's collection of trail maps. Among them was a version of the same one we'd discovered in Spark McAllister's pocket. It was a map of the Sawtooth Trailhead and its various routes through the wilderness.

Hux took a highlighter and marked a massive loop starting at the Sawtooth Trailhead, which went all the way to Columbine Lake, Big Five Lakes, Precipice Lake, Nine Lakes Basin, Eagle Scout Creek, Timber Gap, and back to the trailhead. Seeing it highlighted like that made me realize what a monster loop we'd covered—twenty-two miles out to Precipice Lake, and about twenty miles on the High Sierra Trail back to the trailhead, with thousands of feet of elevation change in-between. According to my math, the interior of the loop encompassed a search area of about 160 square miles, which was over a hundred thousand acres—and that was assuming our missing persons had stayed *within* the loop, rather than venturing outside of it, which was a big assumption to make. Even with a hundred SAR volunteers out there searching day and night, it would take months to cover that kind of ground.

"I know what you're thinking," Hux said.

"And what's that?"

"That we can't possibly search this entire area—and you're right. But we're not totally in the dark here. I never thought Bear Paw sounded right, mainly because it's kind of hard to find the trail if you're not familiar with the terrain."

"So if not Bear Paw, then where?"

"Well, it depends a little bit on who we're looking for and what we think happened. For instance, Colton Dodger sounds fairly capable—a professional athlete, bodyguard, all that. I could imagine he made it out alive."

"Then why haven't we heard from him?" I asked. "I can't imagine why a bodyguard for a Hollywood actress would suddenly decide to disappear off the grid." I'd considered the possibility that Tatum had taken Colton Dodger into the woods for protection while she had her tryst with Cade Delancey, but it didn't explain why Dodger had lied to his own mother about where he was. If he was up in Sequoia for his employer's protection, then why not just tell her he had to work?

"Could be he did a bad thing," Hux said. "Or witnessed a bad thing."

"We have no evidence of that."

"We don't have evidence saying otherwise, though."

"True," I admitted.

"In any case, let's forget about our man Colton for now. Spark's description of the body sounds like it could be Cade Delancey, so I'm going on the assumption that he's out there somewhere—specifically, here." He pointed to the Nine Lakes basin region on the map, specifically the area between Kaweah Gap and Lake WT 10725T, which was about a mile and a half northwest of Precipice Lake. The other, smaller lakes were unnamed except for WL 11682T, which was farther east and less accessible. I had to agree with Hux that if Cade Delancey had gone for help, he would have followed a trail, and one of those trails went north.

"This assumes he was lost, then," I said. "Nine Lakes is out of the way if you're trying to get back to civilization as quickly as possible."

"Agreed. But it's easy to take a wrong turn up in that basin. The elevation change there is brutal. It's not like you can just hike from lake to lake and take in some views—you've got to go up a mountain to get to one lake, and down another to get out. It's a chore to see two lakes in one day—next to impossible to see three." He pointed to an area where the trail divided at Kaweah Gap—to the north was Lake WT10725T, west was Precipice, and south was the route back to Columbine Lake. "He made a wrong turn here. I've seen it happen before—people are always getting lost up in there."

"What about the satellite phone?" I asked. "How did it end up all the way over in Columbine Lake if he was in Nine Lakes Basin?"

"Glad you asked. That's where Colton Dodger comes in. Unlike Cade, he was going the right way. And *he* had the phone—but it broke, he couldn't get a signal, whatever—so he threw it in the lake."

"The Iridium is bomb-proof."

"He didn't know that, though."

Still, I couldn't quite picture the sequence of events that Hux was describing: Tatum Delancey goes over a cliff into the lake below, Cade panics and takes off in one direction to get help, and Colton goes in the other? I supposed it made a little more sense if the stepson and the bodyguard were both under the influence, but Tatum Delancey's tox screen had come back clean. Given that, their Glampist weekend didn't strike me as a rager in the woods.

"What about the Sinclairs?" I asked. "What if *they* stole the sat phone?"

He shook his head. "Nah."

"Nah? Come on, Hux. We *watched* Zeke steal from that campsite—he did it right in front of us. Maybe he figured the sat phone wasn't worth the trouble."

Hux went quiet as he looked over the map. "I guess it's possible," he finally said.

"We need to talk to them again—"

"I'll talk to Ian," Hux said. "He'll be straight with me."

I wasn't so sure about that, but in my mind, it was better to let Hux have a crack at him first. If he could find a way to talk to Ian without his brother around, he might actually get the truth from him. It was worth a shot.

Looking back at the map, I felt that familiar doubt creeping in. Hux was right about one thing: the elevation change between Precipice and Nine Lakes was a game changer, and not in a good way. We might have time to explore two lakes, *maybe* three—and that was after a two-day hike just to get there. I wasn't sure I had it in me to go up there again.

"It's too big an area to search in a day," I said. "I'm not sure it's an efficient use of time."

He used a purple pen to mark the two biggest lakes in the basin, which also happened to be the two closest to Precipice. "Here," he said. "I just made it a lot smaller."

"Smaller, sure, but it still feels random."

Hux stepped away from the map and looked at me. "Try to think like Cade Delancey—he's scared, maybe he's drunk or high. He runs off to get help, except this isn't the Santa Monica pier; you're really on your own out there. The problem is, he's not thinking about that. He takes the trail map and decides to go to Bear Paw because there's a ranger station there. He doesn't know it's closed for the season, but it doesn't matter, because he goes the wrong way. And because he's tired and cold and he's just climbed a mountain to get nowhere, he panics. It was ten degrees below freezing that night. I bet he didn't even make it till morning."

I looked at the map again. The smaller lake Hux had marked—the one closest to Kaweah Gap and Precipice Lake—didn't even have a name.

"Well?" Hux said. "Are you game to go up and have a look?"

It was almost nine o'clock, which meant we'd have to be up and at 'em in six hours to make this expedition happen. That strange mix of adrenaline and exhaustion was humming in my veins, opposing forces that made me question what, really, was the best way forward. I couldn't afford to waste days out on the trail, especially in my condition. If I trashed my back, I might not be up for another assignment any time soon.

But then again, I couldn't stomach the thought of calling up Max Delancey to tell him that we'd given up. There was an innocence about him—a boyish optimism, dimmed but not dead—and he deserved to have someone on his side. As for the hike back up to Precipice, I'd be smarter about it this time—a lighter load, more ibuprofen, better socks. And what if we *did* find Cade Delancey? What if he was the missing piece we needed to crack this case?

"I'm game," I said to Hux. "But I'm making the coffee this time."

29

WE SET OFF from the Sawtooth Trailhead at the ungodly
hour of four AM. It was cold but clear, with a light wind
that blew through the trees. Ollie and Hux led the way while I
took up the rear, using the early morning stillness to think
through the case and all its unanswered questions. I thought
about Kevin, too, and how he'd always been an early riser.

"Harland," Hux said, after an hour on the trail, "you still
back there?"

"Yup."

"Hungry?"

"Nope."

"Tired?"

"No."

"Annoyed that I crop-dusted you a little while back?"

"Very," I said. He laughed.

We were almost through the forested part of the trail, but I
was trying not to calculate the mileage in my head. The goal
was one step at a time; keep it simple. Knowing that I'd done it
before gave me the confidence that I could do it again.

"Let's play ask-me-a-question," Hux said.

"I've been asking you questions for about a week now."

"Nah. I want you to ask me anything—can be personal,
embarrassing. Whatever. It just can't have anything to do with
the case."

I was wary of where this could go, but at the same time, I was curious about Hux's past, particularly his time in the military. His entire career with the Navy was a black box—strictly confidential, no way for me to know the details without hearing it directly from him. At the same time, though, I didn't feel like I needed to know the details. He was good at tracking people down, could capably handle a firearm, and knew his way around an interrogation room.

"Okay," I said. "What's your favorite food?"

"Wow," he said with a laugh. "That's a real doozy."

"Sorry."

"Scrapple," he said.

"Huh?"

"That's not my real answer. But I do like a good scrap of scrapple in the summer."

"What is it?"

"It's pork, kind of. Anything else you want to ask me?"

I almost asked him about his favorite color, but this wasn't the first day of kindergarten, and I wasn't going to insult him with meaningless questions. If we were going to be out on the trail together for days at a time, he had a right to know a little more about me.

"Who decorated your cabin?" I asked.

"Now that's a better question." He grinned at me. "I did, actually. Why?"

"It has a woman's touch."

"If you're trying to ask if I've got a woman in my life—"

"I'm not," I said, a little too quickly.

"Well, the answer's no, not at the moment. I've had a few girls up here, though. Some of them tried to change the decor, which was a real deal breaker."

"Really?"

He still had that smile in his eyes. "No, not really. I'm always open to suggestions."

"I'd get a TV."

"I had a feeling you'd say that."

"Well, you know. For your *Baywatch* marathons."

We talked like that for a while—about nothing and everything all at once—until Hux suggested we stop for water. Ollie sat at my feet and looked up at me with those big brown eyes, devoted and faithful. He didn't doubt me like I doubted myself. And Hux didn't seem to doubt me either, which made me wonder if it was time to put all that self-flagellation behind me.

Hux was checking the map against the GPS when a sharp *crack* rolled through the woods. We heard it at the same time, both of us swiveling our heads to see where the sound had come from. Ollie barked twice. I reached for my service weapon, which I hadn't forgotten this time.

As we were standing there with our hands on our holsters, a shadowy figure materialized on the trail in front of us. It was still dark out, the predawn sky streaked with violet. As the figure made its way toward us, Hux yelled out, "Good mornin'," while in the same breath tightening his grip on his Glock. I did the same.

The figure stopped. I didn't want to be rude, but since whoever it was had made no effort to identify themselves, I did the honors by shining my flashlight in their face.

Zeke. In the darkness, he looked massive, more like a bear than a teenage boy. His oily skin glistened in the beam of light. In his hands he was holding something dark and boxy—a suitcase, looked like. It was about the size of one, anyway.

"Zeke?" I called out.

He didn't move.

"Put your hands in the air!" I shouted.

He dropped the thing in his arms and bolted. We all three took off after him, but Hux and Ollie had the jump on me, and they were gone within seconds. My left toe caught a root, and I went down hard—face-first in the cold mud. I scrambled back up again, ignoring the flash of pain in my spine and the warm blood dripping down my chin.

Before I had the chance to go very far, Ollie came tearing out of the woods. Hux was close behind, with his Glock in one hand and a handful of Zeke's parka in the other. The kid walked with his shoulders slouched, his gaze fixed on the ground. He was shuffling rather than walking. Hux gave him a nudge.

"Zeke," I said—or rather, sighed—"what the hell are you doing out here?"

"Nothin'," Zeke said.

"Somethin'," Hux corrected him. "That's for sure." Hux aimed his flashlight at the discarded suitcase. The Glampist tag was right there on the handle—along with a name: *Cade Delancey*. I sucked in a breath.

"That ain't mine," Zeke said.

"Oh no?" Hux said. "Then why were you holding it?"

"I was movin' it to a new campsite."

"In the dead of night?"

"Yeah," he muttered. "It goes that way sometimes."

"Zeke," I said, exhaling loudly so he could hear my frustration. "Look, don't lie to us. We've caught you red-handed twice now. You could go to federal prison for this."

His eyes bugged out a little. "Is that worse than regular prison?"

"It's pretty bad, yes."

"Shit," he muttered.

"Where's your dad?" Hux asked.

"He's, uh . . ." Zeke twisted a strand of his greasy hair around one of his long fingers. "He's back at the house. It's just me and Ian on this one."

"Ian's out here?" He released his grip on Zeke's coat.

"Yeah—well."

"Well, what?" I pressed.

Zeke made a guttural snorting sound. He stared at the ground like it held the secrets to the universe. Hux, sensing an opening, rolled the suitcase directly into Zeke's line of sight. In response, Zeke spat on the ground next to it.

"Where did you get this?" Hux asked.

"I dunno," he mumbled.

"Look, it's got the guy's name right on it—there's no talking yourself out of this one. So when did you steal it? Was it before the glampers showed up? Or after?"

More mumbling.

"Zeke," I said, peering up at him. He was still a kid, after all—a big kid, about three times my mass, but still with that adolescent disposition. "You really don't want to get mixed up in this, Zeke. Just tell us about the suitcase."

He was softening. I could see it in his eyes.

"Zeke," I said again.

"It don't make sense to steal shit before they get there." He spoke in a tone that reminded me of his father, Ash. "'Cause then they know it's you."

I stood up straight. "I see."

"It was Ian's idea."

"To do what?"

"To wait 'em out. I was the lookout."

Hux and I exchanged glances. As far as witnesses went, Zeke had suddenly established himself as one. "So you watched them?" I asked. "Who was there?"

"The hot girl and her boyfriend."

I tried to keep my expression neutral, but it was hard to contain my surprise. Maybe Zeke had seen everything, and now that we had him cornered, he was going to spill the whole story. "What did you see?" I asked.

"A whole lotta nothin'. They argued a lot. I kept hopin' they'd have make-up sex or somethin', but nah—"

"They argued?" I asked. "About what?"

"I couldn't really hear. It was just a lot of yelling." Zeke zipped his parka up to his chin and tugged his hat down over his ears. "I'm cold, lady. Can I go?"

"Not a chance," Hux said. "What else did you see?"

"Nothin'! I swear to God."

It sounded like the truth, so I decided not to push him. "When did you leave?" I asked.

"Uh . . . I dunno. The day after they got there, I guess. I mean, I didn't really leave—I camped out up there 'cause we had another job Sunday. Honestly, I was kinda pissed 'cause they just stayed there the whole time—makes it hard to steal shit when they don't go anywhere. But when I woke up Sunday, they were gone."

"They were both gone?"

"Yeah."

"Did you hear anything during the night at all?"

"No," he said. "Well, I mean—Ian got up to take a piss at some point. I heard that. He pisses like a racehorse that's got dia-beet-is." He added, "My grandpa's got dia-beet-is."

Hux couldn't have been happy to hear Ian's name in this context, but he didn't say anything. "So Ian was up there camping with you?" I asked.

"Yeah." He swallowed.

"And he left his tent to pee?"

"Yeah."

"Did he come back?"

Zeke shrugged. "I dunno. He's got his tent and I got mine." He looked up at the sky, which was turning pink with the rising sun. I could see his face clearly now—the constant sneer, the vacant eyes. "Are you gonna handcuff me?" he asked. "'Cause if not, I'm gonna go."

I didn't even have handcuffs on my person, but there was no way for him to know that. He did, however, seem to sense that we weren't in a position to hold him here.

I grabbed the suitcase by the handle. "We're going to confiscate this."

"Whatever," he said with a shrug. He turned to go but tripped over Hux's foot—intentionally placed, judging by the half smile on Hux's face. Zeke cussed under his breath as he loped out of sight, empty-handed.

As soon as Zeke was gone, Hux walked over to me and said, "Close your eyes."

"What?"

"Your face is a bloody mess, Harland. I'm about to shine my flashlight right in your eyes here, so you better close 'em."

I put up a hand, blocking the glare. "I'm fine."

"Just let me have a quick look."

He waited for me to put my hand down, which I did, eventually. The beam from his flashlight warmed my face, which felt raw and wet. After a brief inspection that had me standing on my toes, Hux said, "Can I touch your face?"

"Oh—um." I wasn't prepared for the question, but Hux had been right to ask. Maybe he sensed that no one aside from a medical professional had touched my face in a very long time. "Okay. Go ahead."

He used a towel to wipe the mud off my chin so he could inspect the wound there. It was a strange feeling, Hux's hands on my face. My instinct was to back away and create some distance between us. But in less than sixty seconds, he'd cleaned the wound and glued the skin back together again. "There," he said. "You might need to cancel that appointment you had for headshots next week, but it's decent."

I opened my eyes to see him grinning at me. "Oh, right, that reminds me," I said. "The casting agent from *Glenview* called. You lost out to someone with actual acting ability."

With my face intact and our usual dynamic restored, Hux and I unzipped the suitcase and plowed through it. The first words that came to mind about its owner were "woefully unprepared." Aside from a small toiletry kit, Cade Delancey had packed exactly one pair of jeans, four T-shirts, one sweatshirt, and some loose cotton socks. The concept of layering had clearly not occurred to him—a fatal mistake in the varied and brutal landscape of Sequoia. There was always the possibility that he'd been *wearing* those layers on the night his stepmother died, but I didn't think so. These weren't the belongings of an experienced outdoorsman, but rather the thoughtless purchases of an online shopper.

"Yikes," Hux said. "This is just sad."

"And scary."

"Seriously scary. He never would have lasted a night out here on his own."

Cade Delancey's toiletry kit didn't yield much either: a toothbrush and toothpaste, a razor, some hair gel. There was an unopened bottle of ibuprofen and a prescription for Xanax. No condoms and no illegal drugs. All in all, it was a little disappointing.

With our time running short, we decided to hide the suitcase and come back for it later. Hux helped me with my pack, which seemed to fit a little better than the last time. It didn't hurt as much, in any case. I actually got the straps on without wincing.

"You ready for this?" Hux asked.

"Do I have a choice?"

"Nope." He waited for me to fall in step behind him,

setting a pace that felt aggressive but doable. It wasn't all that conducive to conversation, though. I was breathing hard by the time we stopped for a water break about a mile in.

I wasn't sure what Hux thought about our encounter with Zeke, but it must have raised some questions for him. It turned out Ian Sinclair was at Precipice Lake the night Tatum Delancey died; his own nephew had blown his alibi. Things weren't looking so good for Ian.

I said to Hux, "Maybe Ian's the key to all this."

"How so?"

"Maybe he caught Tatum Delancey unawares—spooked her somehow. I could see it—threats were made, tempers flared. Who knows."

Hux shook his head. "No chance."

"A momentary lapse in judgment, I mean."

"Again, no chance. Ian's not Jeb or Spark McAllister, and he's definitely not his brother. He respects Sequoia, and he respects the people who come here. He would've kept his distance."

"But why was he out there at all?"

"I *know* this guy, Harland." He stuffed his canteen in his pack and zipped it up again. I could see his frustration in the way he yanked on the zipper, but I wasn't sure if it was directed at me or the situation. It couldn't have been easy for him to realize that he might have been wrong about a fellow combat veteran. He had every right to be angry.

The truth was, even the best of us got it wrong sometimes. When it came to the complex psychology of human beings, there was always the chance of a misfire or a miscalculation. It's what kept us law enforcement officers in business.

"Why don't you call him?" I meant for it to be a gentle suggestion. "Clear it all up."

"Right now?"

"Right now."

Hux gave me a questioning look, like he wasn't sure I was serious. When I held out the sat phone, he took it and dialed a number that he had clearly memorized. It rang endlessly until at last the voicemail picked up. Hux's message was brief:

"Hey man, it's Hux. Call me on the sat phone if you get a chance—here's the number." He gave the number and repeated it once. "It's, uh—it's pretty important. Thanks."

He gave the phone back to me without a word. I knew he wasn't happy, but a few hours on the trail might give him some perspective, at least.

With Ollie in the lead, we set off toward Columbine Lake.

30

Hux's silence out on the trail spoke volumes. I figured it was one of two things: either he thought he had completely misjudged Ian's character, or he was trying to figure out a way to explain his friend's behavior. Whatever it was, we hardly exchanged a word on the six-mile trek. I didn't mind. The sights and sounds of nature put me in a reflective mood.

By nightfall, we were too exhausted to do anything other than meet our basic needs. Hux prepared a pesto pasta dinner, which we ate over the fire. He nursed a beer; I had decaf coffee. Ollie gnawed on a bone he'd found in the woods.

I said, "You're awfully quiet tonight."

Hux allowed a small smile. "I'm usually pretty quiet, believe it or not."

"I'm not sure I do, actually."

He made a face that told me he got the joke. "That's fair. It's just—eh . . ." He poked his stick at the embers. "I've been thinking about the Sinclairs."

"And?"

"I realize I came into this biased, and that's not a good way to be."

"Biased how, exactly?"

He put his plate aside and rubbed his hands together. "Ian's the one who really got me acquainted with Sequoia—the guy knows this park like the back of his hand." He bit off some beef jerky and offered the rest to Ollie. "It just got me thinking that if he's stealing from these campsites, then he's probably got a bunker somewhere."

"For storage?"

"Yeah," he said. "And who knows what else."

It was a dark thought, as unsettling as the distant howl of coyotes somewhere beyond the ridge. But I couldn't entirely dismiss it either. The Sinclairs might have made a couple grand selling high-end gear on eBay, but what if one of them had recognized Tatum Delancey as a bona fide movie star? Would that have changed their plans? For a few days at least, Zeke had been in possession of Cade Delancey's suitcase. Was this an abduction scenario gone wrong? What if Colton Dodger wasn't living his double life in Mexico, but in the Sinclairs' bunker?

Hux met my eyes for a brief moment and shook his head. He must have seen the wheels turning in my head, and for once I wasn't embarrassed by my own transparency.

"Could you find the bunker?" I asked.

"It wouldn't be easy."

"What! I thought everything was easy for you."

He broke into a smile. "Well, *that's* true." He pulled out his map and pointed to a speck of blue, which looked a lot like the other specks of blue in the vicinity except it had more of a tadpole shape. "Speaking of easy, this is where we're going. The rangers call it Sperm Lake."

"Nice."

"Or Tadpole Lake if you prefer." With a bit of a smirk, he tucked his map back into his pack and rummaged around a bit for a bar of dark chocolate. I took the piece he offered me, indulging in the unique sweetness that followed a savory meal in the woods. Chocolate had never tasted this good in Chicago.

"Any more calls on the sat phone?" he asked.

"Not yet."

"Well, good. I don't want you flying off to Gates of the Arctic in Alaska." He zipped his parka up to his chin, a rare concession to the cold. I was already wearing four layers under

my heavy winter coat, and I'd add one more before the night
was over. I was getting used to it, though—the wind, the altitude, the vast expanse of stars and sky and the universe. It was
hard even to imagine life in the city.

"I should hit the hay," I said.

Hux nodded. "Need any help with your tent?"

"Nah, I've got it," I said. "Thanks, though."

"How's your back?"

To my surprise, I found myself resisting my usual impulse
to lie. Hux was a better man than most. He wasn't out to exploit
my weaknesses, to make me question my own abilities. He was
a partner, not a competitor, and I respected him for that.

"Not bad," I said. "As long as I keep shredding my kidneys
with ibuprofen, I should be good."

"Pissing brown, Harland?"

"Not yet, but I'll keep you posted."

He smiled at me.

I smiled back.

*   *   *

I woke in the night to the sound of a scuffle—footsteps in the
dirt, voices, a shout. I grabbed my Glock and scrambled out of
the tent. It was like emerging into a dream—a colorless, sound-
less dream. I shined my light in the direction of Hux's tent and
saw the door flapping in the wind. Ollie bolted out of my tent
and disappeared into the mist.

My first thought was that Zeke Sinclair had gone running
to his father and was now back with reinforcements, namely, his
dad and uncle. This was their domain, after all. I knew Hux
could handle himself out there, but I felt like a sitting duck.
And Ollie was gone, too.

I went back to the tent for my satellite phone, debating
what to do, whom to call. This wasn't Chicago with deputies
on patrol; this was Sequoia, with the closest backup hours
away. It was the middle of the night. Corrigan was probably
asleep.

I had my finger on the button for emergency dispatch when
Ollie, barking like mad, came tearing out of the woods. Hux

was close behind, running without shoes on terrain that wasn't at all conducive to such a thing. He was wearing his pajama bottoms and a flannel shirt.

With my heart in my throat, I lowered my weapon. "What the hell was that?" I asked.

"I don't know exactly," he said. "I heard something."

"An animal?"

"Could've been."

I didn't believe him. Hux wasn't the type to get spooked by a wild animal. I waited for him to admit as much, but he just stood there with his hands on his hips, breathing hard from his sprint through the woods.

"Maybe the Sinclairs?" I asked.

"I can't say." He rubbed his bare hands together. "I really can't say."

"Are we being watched?"

Hux shook his head. "Look, whatever it was, it's gone now. Get a little more sleep—we've got ninety minutes until dawn."

"I can't sleep. Not after that."

He sighed. I knew that guys like him possessed the uncanny ability to fall asleep anywhere, but I wasn't built that way. It was hard to turn my brain off.

"All right," he said. "You owe me an hour of sleep, though."

"You can go back to sleep if you want. I'll make breakfast."

"Not stale Cheerios again," he said, and snickered.

"I could attempt an egg."

"I dunno, Harland. That feels like a stretch for you."

He was right—scrambling an egg even in the best of conditions posed a challenge for me. But before I could defend my culinary pursuits, he went back inside his tent to change. I did the same, determined to layer up before the adrenaline wore off and a chill settled in my bones. It would be with me for days if that happened.

As I was searching for a pair of socks, the satellite phone rang. I didn't recognize the number, but my first thought was that it was Ray, calling me from someone else's phone. He was probably wondering where the hell I was.

"Hello," I said. "This is Felicity Harland."

"Who?" The man who spoke had a deep voice that reverberated over the line. Being that it was 4:54 AM, I was surprised to hear that the caller sounded wide-awake. Maybe he was calling from the East Coast.

"This is Agent Felicity Harland with the Investigative Services Branch."

"Oh. Good. This is Colton Dodger."

I sat up straight, startling Ollie in the process. He flipped from his side onto his front and stood up on all fours. Suddenly we were both on high alert.

"Are you—where are you?" I asked him.

"I'm at, uh, Kinema Fitness in Las Vegas." He was a loud breather, but I couldn't tell if he was working out or just recovering from one. "Listen, I—my buddy here told me about Tatum. I didn't know."

Were you in a coma? I almost asked him, but instead said, "We've been looking for you."

"I know. My mom told me. I just got off a plane this morning—came straight to the gym. My phone was dead, couldn't check my messages . . . I'm sorry."

"For what?"

"For not calling you earlier."

Someone in the background started shouting out reps. I heard a door open, then close again. There was the distinct echo of someone urinating into a toilet.

I unzipped my sleeping bag and clamored out of the tent. Hux's light came on the moment I stepped outside. He poked his head out of his own tent with a question on his face, and I waved him over, wanting him to hear this conversation as it happened. He put his shoes on and ran over with long, loping strides.

"Where have you been, Mr. Dodger? We've been looking for you for over a week now."

Hux and I exchanged looks while we waited for his answer.

"Yeah, uh—I can explain that." He sounded apologetic—ashamed, even. Not scared, though. My first impression was that he was genuinely remorseful, that Tatum Delancey's death had taken him by surprise. He was calling me from a men's room, for godssakes.

"Your name was used to rent a vehicle that was abandoned in a parking lot in Sequoia, not far from where Tatum Delancey's body was found. Can you explain that, too?"

"Yes, ma'am, I can. I told Mrs. Delancey she could use my name anytime. She felt safer that way."

"So you weren't in Sequoia?"

"No, ma'am."

"I see," I said, noting the way he referred to his employer. It certainly sounded like they had a professional relationship rather than a personal one. "So where were you, then?"

In the background, doors opened and closed and banged against the walls. People came and went; some of them had loud conversations while they peed. The acoustics weren't very good. If Colton Dodger was feeling self-conscious about talking to me from a bathroom stall, he didn't act like it.

"I don't get much time off, Agent Harland. Mrs. Delancey always needed me—at work, at home, on vacation. So when she said she was going away and didn't need my services, I, uh—I decided to take a trip."

Hux and I exchanged glances. It was a while before Dodger spoke again, and when he did, it was drowned out by the sound of the hand-dryer going full blast.

"What?" I asked.

He lowered his voice. "I was filming a reality show."

Hux raised his eyebrows while at the same time trying to muffle laughter. I put my head in my hands. Colton Dodger had gone from victim to suspect, to man-on-the-run, but it turned out he was just a reality show star. Corrigan would've had an aneurysm at this news.

"And you didn't tell anyone about it?" I asked.

"I couldn't. The producers took our cell phones and everything."

"I see."

Hux rubbed the back of his neck, while Ollie licked my hand the way he always did when he wanted food. I gave him my last stick of beef jerky and watched him swallow it whole.

"So you didn't know anything about the Sequoia trip?" I asked him.

"No, sorry."

"Anything at all?"

"No, ma'am."

I didn't want to end the call, not after all the time and effort we'd invested in trying to find him. But despite his weird story, I believed him.

"Your mom said you were going to be gone for a week, and it's been ten days," I said. "And Tatum Delancey only made reservations for a long weekend. Can you explain those discrepancies?"

"She told me to take some time off," he said. "I asked for a week 'cause that's how long the production was supposed to last, but—well. I did a little better than expected. I had to stick around for the winner's circle."

"Good for you."

"Thanks."

"All right, Mr. Dodger. Let's talk again soon."

I was about to hang up when he cut in with "Wait a minute."

"Yes?"

"Did somebody kill Mrs. Delancey?"

"Pardon?"

"I was paid to protect her, ma'am. I have to know."

"We're looking into that possibility, Mr. Dodger," I said.

Another toilet flushed, but even the forceful swirl of water couldn't mask Colton Dodger's soft, pitiful sobs. "Thank you, ma'am," he said, and hung up.

Hux sighed. "Poor guy. Do you believe him?"

"I do." I cinched my hood around my face to fend off the wind. Hux pulled his beanie down over his ears and rubbed his gloved hands together.

"So we're only looking for one guy, then," Hux said.

"At the moment, anyway."

"Good. That simplifies things a bit." He tilted his head toward the sky. "I bet we can be at Nine Lakes by noon if this weather holds."

We set out in opposing moods, Hux's optimism playing against my deepening anxiety about the plan to search an area known for its inhospitable terrain. But by the time we were a mile in, Hux had managed to boost my spirits a bit. "Colton Dodger's got the name for a reality show star, at least," he said, as we rehashed that morning's conversation.

"He texted me the production info, Hux. He's not gonna be a star, trust me."

"Why not?"

"Because it was a show about competitive bodyguards."

"Huh."

"Yeah."

"Well, I'm rooting for him."

I wasn't sure if I felt the same, not after all the time we'd wasted pursuing the ghost of Colton Dodger in Sequoia. We reached Kaweah Gap right before noon, with clouds on the horizon and a smattering of backpackers on the trail. Instead of continuing on toward Precipice, we took the turnoff toward Nine Lakes Basin. I cracked open my last hand warmer and tucked it in the waistband of my pants. Overall, I was feeling pretty good—no muscle spasms, no crippling joint aches, no spiraling feelings of self-doubt.

For the last stretch, we walked in tandem on mostly flat terrain. The views were spectacular, with fields of granite stretching in every direction until they either dived into an alpine lake or sprouted into a rocky peak. The vegetation up at this altitude was sparse. We put our packs down and looked out at the lake that was supposedly reminiscent of sperm or a tadpole or something to that effect. I wasn't seeing it.

"Well," I said. "I'm not seeing a dead body."

He caught the smile on my face and said, "Well, if you do, give a shout." He slung his pack off his shoulder and reached into a side pocket. I supposed he thought I didn't pay attention to things like his obsessive approach to packing a bag. Things weren't just stuffed inside for retrieval later—oh no. Hux had a system—or rather, a religion. He clearly didn't want me to see what he was about to pull out of there.

"Don't you have something to do?" he asked.

"Nope."

I grinned at him, as if to say, *"I'm on to you."* His cheeks were red—with shame, not exertion—by the time he pulled out a gallon-sized Ziploc bag with all kinds of knickknacks inside: evidence bags, a Sharpie, forceps, a notepad, and a number of other tools he must've gleaned from one of those dusty textbooks back at his cabin.

"Oh boy," I said.

"Shut up," he muttered.

"Did you buy this off Amazon? I hear they make detective kits now."

"Yeah. It came in the same shipment as your Glock."

Smiling in spite of myself, I sat down to eat my lunch while Hux and Ollie set off to search the lake. Sperm Lake was, like its namesake, quite small, and Hux had assured me that he could cover the perimeter in under fifteen minutes.

Thirteen minutes later, he was back where he started. I was eating a cheese sandwich, which tasted better than it looked. "No dice?" I asked.

"I'm goin' in," he said.

"Going in where?"

He pointed at the lake, which looked about as inviting as an oil slick. This time, though, Hux had come prepared. He pulled a neoprene suit out of his backpack and dangled it in front of me. "Close your eyes, Harland," he said.

"You don't have to tell me twice."

The next thing I heard was a loud splash as he dove into the water, followed by a series of smaller splashes as Ollie went in after him. I opened my eyes to see both of them paddling across the lake, canvassing its surface from one end to the other.

It was a clipped bark from Ollie that changed the tone of the afternoon. It was hard to tell who was leading whom; the two of them were working as a team. Hux would surface, red-faced and breathing hard, and Ollie would prance on the rocks, darting to and fro like he was tracking something. Hux caught sight of Ollie and swam in his direction. The barking intensified. Hux dove underwater once more, disappearing from sight.

A shiver coursed down my spine as my hound's baying rolled through the basin. Ollie wasn't one for false alarms. I abandoned my cheese sandwich and ran toward him, buoyed by a rare burst of strength and confidence. The pain in my back was simply gone.

Hux bobbed to the surface. He ripped his goggles off and inhaled a great gasp of mountain air. His gaze locked on mine, and I knew then that our search was over, that he'd turned his participation trophy into something real.

"Hux!" I called out. "What is it?"

He pointed downward—a simple gesture, but one that validated every decision we'd made so far. "I found him."

31

H UX AND I decided to bring the body onto shore for a preliminary assessment and to document our findings for the medical examiner. As far as evidence went, there wasn't much left to find. The body had clearly been in the water for a while.

We laid it supine on the shore, careful to disturb the remains as little as possible. Marine life of some sort had already gotten to it, as evidenced by missing flesh, particularly around the eyes and mouth. It was definitely a *him*, though, which we could tell by the thick rust-colored beard. He couldn't have been more than twenty-five.

Max Delancey had texted me a photo of his brother, which I pulled up on my cell phone. Hux inspected it with a squinted eye.

"Yeah, it's definitely Cade Delancey," he said. "You agree?"

"Yep," I said, without looking back at the dead man's face. Even though we'd found our missing glamper, it was hard to feel victorious. Two young people were dead in the wilds of Sequoia—*why? How?* I wanted it to make sense, but it didn't.

After Hux had dealt with his wetsuit—he took his arms out of the sleeves, rolled it down to his waist, and threw a T-shirt on—we examined Cade Delancey's body. There were no obvious signs of injury. Interestingly, Delancey wasn't wearing a coat or hiking boots, which supported the theory that Spark McAllister had taken them off his body.

Hux said, "I find myself wondering how the hell this guy got in the lake."

"Maybe Spark did it."

"You mean killed him?"

"I don't know," I said with a sigh. "I can't understand killing a guy over a parka, but maybe that's what happened."

"Nah," Hux said. "Spark's a piece of shit and a thief, but not a killer. I bet he found the body around here somewhere and then dumped him in the lake to cover his tracks."

I shook my head. "Then why tell us about the body?"

He considered this. "Maybe Delancey was already in the lake—dead."

"How do you figure?"

"Hypothermia. It can be an intense delusion at the end—it feels like you're overheating. Your blood vessels dilate and your internal thermometer goes haywire. It would explain why he'd taken off his parka and shoes."

"I suppose that's possible."

Hux looked out over the lake like he was searching for something—a better explanation for this sequence of events, maybe. I wasn't seeing it either. I wondered if we ever would.

"Let's have another look around." I checked my watch for the hundredth time that hour. "I'll ask Corrigan to get the dive team up here."

"He's not gonna go for that, boss."

"Why not?"

"Because there was that boating accident in Lake Kaweah yesterday—it's all hands on deck. He just doesn't have the resources right now."

"Then I'll call for a crime unit."

He lifted an eyebrow. "How long is that gonna take?"

"A long time." I rubbed my temples, which did little to staunch the headache blooming behind them. "A very long time."

"Look, this lake's not that deep." He rubbed his hands together and looked at the overcast sky. "I'll search it."

"With what, exactly?"

"With these bad boys," he said, pointing to his eyeballs. After pulling his wetsuit back on, he waded into the water for another go. I watched while Ollie bounded in after him, excited to be a part of the hunt.

Hux stayed under the surface a good while—over a minute, by my watch—and popped back up again. Instead of complaining about the cold, he flashed a grin that told me he relished the task. He was a former SEAL, after all. They were used to cold water.

While Hux searched the lake according to an improvised grid, I called Corrigan on my satellite phone. He answered with a grunt. "What now, Agent Harland?" he sighed.

I wasn't at all happy that Cade Delancey was dead, but I was glad we'd found his body. It felt good to tell Corrigan as much, and in my own small way, I savored this moment. "We've got another body up here," I said.

There was a pause. "Where?" he asked.

I gave him the coordinates.

"You're up near Precipice," he said. Like all career rangers, Corrigan didn't have to ask me where we were; he knew those coordinates by heart. He probably only carried a map for appearance's sake.

"Yes, sir."

"Well, damn, that's a long ways from here."

"I understand that. Now, I've already been in touch with the medical examiner—"

I didn't get to finish my sentence, though, because Hux was calling out to me from the lake, waving his discovery in his left hand. At first I was confused; it looked like a satellite phone, even though the Glampist website made it clear that only one was provided.

Then it dawned on me: Hux wasn't holding a satellite phone.

It was a cell phone.

CHAPTER

32

WE GOT LUCKY with Sheila, who had finished with a recovery mission and had room on her chopper to evacuate
Cade Delancey's body. She had space for us, too, which warranted a brief celebration—a silent one, at least. After a call to
Ray to update him on our discovery, and also to solicit his bless-
ing to transport the body down to the medical examiner's office,
I climbed aboard the chopper. A county vehicle would meet us
at the ranger station.

My hope was that we'd have the results of Cade Delancey's
autopsy report by that evening. In terms of other evidence collected at the scene, there wasn't much. We had the phone, of
course, but it would take some work to recover its data. Hux
hadn't found anything else of note, and neither had Ollie. My
suspicion was that Spark McAllister had stolen everything of
any value and hidden the rest.

As we disembarked the chopper and made our way across
the lot to the ranger station, Hux said to me over the whirr of
the rotors, "I can get that phone working again, boss."

"Don't bother. That's the FBI's job—they've got a whole
team that does data recovery."

"Just let me plug it in, then. See if it turns on."

"Hux, that phone was at the bottom of an alpine lake."

He shrugged. "You'd be surprised."

His tone was jovial, but if anyone understood the stakes, it was Hux. And yes, the prudent thing to do would be to hand off the phone to the technical experts, but I didn't see the harm in plugging it in. The worst that could happen was, well, nothing. The phone would stay dead, and we'd have to wait for the IT team to recover the data.

It was late afternoon with overcast skies, but the threat of rain had yet to materialize. On our way up the steps to the ranger station, we said a hello to a trio of weary backpackers. They were in good spirits, having completed a week's long trek through the wilderness. I enjoyed hearing about their adventures. I was starting to feel like a member of the club again.

Hux held the door for me as we walked inside, stomping our boots on the welcome mat. We spotted Corrigan behind his desk, toiling over a stack of paperwork and camping permits. The Park Service was slow to adapt an electronic system for these kinds of things, in part because the older rangers offered so much resistance to it. I suspected I knew where Corrigan stood on the matter.

The chief ranger looked up from his stack of permits. "You two again," he said, but with a touch more levity than usual. "Well, I'm glad you found the guy. Two dead bodies this week—I'm hopin' that's it for the year." He gestured to the Ziploc bag in Hux's hand. "What'd you find there?"

"A cell phone," Hux said.

He put the permits aside and held Hux's gaze. "How the hell'd you come up with that?"

"Hux is his own dive team," I said. "He got in the lake and got it done."

Corrigan shook his head like he wasn't at all surprised to hear that Hux had gone underwater in pursuit of the truth. "Good for you, Hux," he said, which brought a smile to Hux's face. I was happy for him; Corrigan wasn't an easy man to impress.

"Well, I'm wrappin' up here," Corrigan said. "Gonna head home soon."

"Us, too," I said. "Hopefully you won't see me again for a while."

With a nod, he went back into his office to file away the permit receipts, which had to be one of the more mundane parts of his job. Then again, maybe it relaxed him. Being out on those trails all the time had to take a toll—if not mental, then definitely physical. I had certainly developed a newfound respect for these rangers after my week in Sequoia.

Hux and I retreated to the break room and closed the door. The mood was somber. Our first and most important task was to notify the family. The news was going to crush Max Delancey, and I couldn't see his father taking it well either.

"What can I do to help?" Hux asked.

"Nothing," I said, wincing as I sat down on the hard plastic chair. "It's part of the job."

I tried Edwin Delancey first, since Cade was his son, but the call went to voicemail. I tried him again—no answer.

I looked at Hux and shook my head.

"Now what?" he asked.

"Let's try Max."

Max Delancey picked up on the second ring. His reception wasn't great—another downside of notifying family members over the phone. I remembered how the Australian police had told me about Kevin's disappearance from my hospital bed. Despite the hard-boiled exterior of the two officers who came to talk to me, their physical presence had been a comfort. It was a lesson I hadn't forgotten.

"Max?" I put the call on speaker so Hux could listen in.

"Yeah?"

"This is Felicity Harland with ISB, and I'm here with my partner, Hux." There was no response. He started breathing hard, like he was weathering a panic attack. "I'm calling about your brother."

"You found him?" he burst out. He sounded like a kid on Christmas morning—boundlessly hopeful, infused with optimism. It crushed me. I almost handed the phone to Hux.

"We found his body, Max," I said. "He's dead. I'm sorry."

Another sharp inhale, followed by a sob. "Where?"

"In Sequoia National Park, not far from where Tatum was found."

"The same lake?"

"No. He was found in a smaller lake nearby."

Max mumbled something unintelligible, then cleared his throat and said, "But that doesn't make sense—isn't it really cold up there? Why was he in the water?"

I nodded at Hux to go ahead and take over—not because I couldn't figure out how to answer him, but because I felt like he needed to hear it from someone who dealt with this kind of thing on a daily basis. Hux said, "We think he got lost and developed hypothermia. In some cases when your body temperature drops too low, you can actually think you're overheating—could be he was delirious when he went into the water."

Max said something else under his breath, but once again I couldn't make out the words. "I don't—I just don't get it is all. He was lost?"

"We're thinking he went to get help for Tatum after she went in the lake," Hux said. He made no mention of murder, even though for me, at least, it was still on the table. "If you're not familiar with the terrain up there, it's easy to get disoriented."

"It just—it doesn't sound like him."

"How so?" I asked.

"Cade wouldn't have gotten lost. He was always super prepared."

"Sometimes preparation doesn't matter," Hux said. "Especially if you're panicked or scared. You also mentioned he had a drug problem—"

"Tatum wasn't into all that, though. He wouldn't have gotten high by himself—especially not out there, and definitely not with Tatum. He knew she was scared of everything. He wouldn't have put her at risk like that."

Hux exhaled softly—gently, even. "At risk of what, Max?"

"Like, bears and stuff. I'm sure he felt like he had to protect her."

"Hmm."

"Anyway, no, he'd never go up there unprepared. He'd *over*prepare."

I rubbed my temples, trying to make sense of a story that had a tendency to unravel every time we talked to someone about it.

"Max, I'm sorry to ask this again, but are you absolutely certain there wasn't anything going on between Cade and Tatum? Because to us, it looks suspicious. It appears they shared a tent—shared a bed, most likely."

"No way," Max said quickly.

"What makes you say that?"

"I just—I don't think so."

"Max, you've got to give me something here."

The sound of the beach filled the background—waves crashing on shore, little kids shouting with delight, seagulls cawing in flight. I could picture Max Delancey in the shadows of the Santa Monica pier, lost among the masses—lost in life.

At last, he said, "Cade was gay."

I looked at Hux, but all he said was, "Hmm."

"You're sure?" I asked Max.

"Yeah. Check his Instagram."

"We can't. It's set to private."

"I'll give you the password—it's Benny four-five-nine-five." He blew out a breath that sounded slightly more restrained than the hiccups and sobs that had dominated the first few minutes of the call. "April fifth was his birthday."

I wrote down the password, which seemed to make Max feel a little better. I was starting to get a clearer picture of the Delancey clan, not that it suggested a clearer narrative for Tatum's and Cade Delancey's deaths. A woman goes into the wilderness with her stepson, who happens to be only a few years younger than she is, and they both turn up dead in alpine lakes about a mile apart. I couldn't bring this case to the prosecutor, that was for sure. On the surface, it looked like a tragic accident—the woman drowns, the man she's with goes off for help. He gets lost, becomes delirious as hypothermia sets in—or maybe he's just intoxicated; the autopsy would tell us more—and drowns. As for Fall Zone's prediction that Tatum was pushed—well, it was an anomaly. Hux himself had admitted the app wasn't perfect.

"Harland," Hux said, but I was trying to figure out how to wrap up the call with Max. Hux was pointing at the cell phone we'd recovered from the lake—the one now connected to a phone charger that someone had left in the break room.

The phone was *on*.

"Max," I said, "I'll update you with any new information as it comes in. I was also planning to notify your father—"

"I already did," Max said. "I just texted him."

I cringed at this news, but maybe it was for the best; I didn't have the best rapport with Edwin Delancey. If he called back, I'd let Hux talk to him.

"All right," I said. "Please call me if there is anything else I can do. In the meantime, I'll keep you apprised of any updates. I'm very sorry, Max."

"Thanks," he mumbled.

I ran both hands through my hair, which at this point desperately needed a wash—every part of me needed a wash, in fact. And yet, my own personal discomfort—the sweat, the heat, the wet chill that lived between my base wear and bare skin—barely registered. These were the kinds of calls that made me question my abilities as a federal agent. Yes, we'd found Cade Delancey's body, but I couldn't help but think that if I'd done better detective work at the start, we might have found him alive. Then again, Hux and I were only two people. We couldn't have searched this area better than SAR and all its resources. We were lucky to have found him at all.

"Harland," Hux said again.

I looked up to see him holding the phone, which was, indeed, on—and not just on, but operational. "Holy shit," I said.

Hux said, "I know. We're in luck. This phone here is not just water-resistant, but heat- and cold-resistant. It gives the Iridium a run for its money."

"But it's a cell phone."

"I thought you were tech savvy, Harland. This phone is all the rage right now." He bypassed the lock-screen using his best guess at a four-digit code—4595—and navigated to the home screen.

"Wow," I said. "You cracked that pretty fast."

"Max gave us a good hint."

The wallpaper photo featured Cade Delancey and a young woman standing together on the side of the road, but she didn't look like his girlfriend. Something about the way he had his arm around her shoulder.

"Do I have your permission to go through this thing?" Hux asked.

"Be my guest," I said.

"The FBI isn't gonna take me down for invasion of privacy?"

"The dead don't have rights, Hux—well, they do, but it's complicated."

"I can handle complicated," he said. "Illegal, no."

"It's not illegal. Go ahead."

We started with the text messages, navigating to Cade Delancey's final exchange with Tatum. The last message was from the Friday morning before the trip. He had received a text from her at six AM: *cinnamon raisin with cream cheese and small coffee with two Splenda, no milk.* It explained the bagel stop, in any case.

The text exchange between them went back a full year. It took us a while to wade through the photos, emojis, and many text messages. Despite our efforts to tease something sexual out of their exchanges, there was no evidence of any romantic relationship whatsoever. There was, however, a Tinder account that more or less confirmed the truth about Cade Delancey's sexual orientation. He wasn't seeing anyone seriously at the time of his death, but he'd had a few encounters with different men over the past year.

Hux said, "Doesn't exactly support the tryst in the woods theory."

"No, it doesn't," I said, more confused than disappointed. I wasn't sure we had any theories left to explore—none that made logical sense, anyway.

With the phone plugged in, we made a pass through Cade Delancey's text messages, social media accounts, email accounts, and photos, trying to glean information from a dead man's most personal possession. He hadn't taken any photos in Sequoia, which struck me as odd. Maybe Tatum had been the nature photographer, but since we hadn't recovered her phone, there was no way to know for sure.

"Well damn," Hux said. "I was expecting a grand slam right there—you know, like a video or something."

"It's a solid single," I said, but the federal agent in me took it as a strike-out.

I went back to Cade Delancey's home screen, inspecting the image there because, for the most part, people made a deliberate choice about what they want to look at every time they pick up their phone. Based on the history gleaned from Cade Delancey's text messages, as well as a brief but productive internet search, the woman in the photo was Bethany Werner. She and Cade had gone to UC Santa Barbara together. According to LinkedIn, she worked as an admin for an advertising firm in Brentwood.

"We should call her," I said, as we went through Cade Delancey's apps. Most of them were just tech bloat, used maybe once a year for some random task while the company collected your location data. There was one, though, that caught my attention—Anchor, a podcasting app, which had been accessed recently. I clicked on it.

There were multiple saved files, all of them between thirty and forty minutes long—except for the last one, which was only six minutes and fourteen seconds. I opened one of the earlier recordings, and Cade's voice came through loud and clear. "Hiya friends, it's Cade here. Hope you're all keeping your shit together out there. I had a little setback last week . . ."

He was talking about his addiction—openly, candidly, and presumably for a wide audience. I wasn't exactly a podcast expert, but I got the feeling we were listening to one. All the recordings were spaced a week apart—except, again, for the most recent one.

"What's your take on this?" I asked Hux.

"He's got a good voice—a pretty natural style, too. I bet he had some fans." He pointed to the date on the most recent recording. "Now *that's* interesting."

The file had last been modified on Sunday, April 7th, at 3:53 AM. Why would Cade Delancey record a podcast while he was presumably lost in the wilderness? It was probably a pocket-cast, but still . . .

I tapped on the file while Hux sat next to me and ate some string cheese. The recording was six minutes and fourteen seconds long. For the first two minutes, it was just a jumble of stray noises. It sounded like the phone was in his pocket, picking up the friction between the fabric as he walked.

Then, suddenly, the audio changed. The background noise went quiet, and instead of that bland swishing sound, a breathless male voice broke the silence—the podcaster's voice. It was Cade Delancey, no doubt about it.

"Wait, go back," I said to Hux. "Turn up the volume."

"It's maxed out, boss."

We leaned in for a closer listen. Hux cycled back fifteen seconds to where Cade started talking: *"This crazy fuck—shit, he knows I'm out here. He knows. I swear to God, he's following me. I know he is. I can hear him. He's right there—"*

The swishing sound was back again, a deafening roar that made it hard to hear his voice. But Cade Delancey was still talking—still gasping for air as he walked, or ran, through the woods. The fear in his voice was a raw, visceral thing. *"I can't believe he fucking pushed her. He's crazy. He's fucking crazy."*

Hux and I exchanged glances. There were questions, yes—hundreds of them—but neither one of us moved to pause the recording. Cade Delancey had something to tell us, and we didn't dare interrupt him.

The little blue dot on the recording was nearing its end—only thirty seconds left, twenty-five, twenty . . . I gripped the sides of my plastic chair with a sinking sense of dread. *Who is HE?* We were never going to find out. Cade Delancey wasn't going to get the chance to tell us—

But then, with seven seconds left on the file, the swishing stopped and the audio achieved an almost incandescent clarity—no background noise, no static.

Just a voice—quiet, distant. Little more than a whisper. But the words were clear:

"You're gonna die out here, son."

And then the recording ended, not with a subtle or tasteful outro but with an abrupt silence that spiraled into nothingness. It was a chilling moment—sacred, too, in that it signaled the final seconds of Cade Delancey's life. I could picture him on the stark shores of the Nine Lakes Basin, searching for refuge in a place that had none. He might've been a little drunk, a little high, or maybe he was stone-cold sober and aware. There would have been nowhere to hide. He knew he was going to die, just as the voice had said.

Hux ran his hands through his hair, cracked his knuckles, and did it again. He put his boots flat on the floor. For maybe the first time since we'd met, he looked rattled.

"Do you recognize that voice?" I asked.

He shook his head. "Let's play it again."

We did—and again, and again. With each pass, I tried to listen for something new. The voice was male, the accent what my linguistics professor would have called General American. And he wasn't at all out of breath, which seemed odd. The altitude up there was no joke.

I also considered the words themselves, namely, the last one: *son*. It implied an older person—at least fifty, but probably sixties or even seventies. It didn't fit the profile of the Sinclairs. Ash referred to his own son that way, but he didn't strike me as the paternal type.

Hux glanced at my notes. "Older white male, American, maybe sixty or sixty-five," he read off my cell phone.

"Do you agree?"

"I do. I'd add 'extremely physically fit' to that description."

"Because he's not out of breath? I noticed that, too."

"There aren't many guys in their sixties that can handle those conditions—the terrain, the altitude. The weather, too. It was frigid that night."

"Plus he was chasing someone."

Hux put his head in his hands and sucked in a breath. Behind him, the door to the break room was slightly ajar. It was the first I'd noticed it, since I had a distinct memory of closing it behind us when we entered. I never would have left the door open while making calls to family members to notify them that a loved one had died.

The room was toasty warm because of the tiny space heater in the corner, but all at once I felt a chill. Maybe it was the draft coming up from the floorboards, but I didn't think so. This was the spidery chill that came from being watched.

Hux must have sensed it, too, because he got up and went to the door. He was in the process of closing it when Corrigan stopped it with his hiking boot. The older ranger poked his head in the room. "Burning the midnight oil, eh?" he said.

And I knew.

It was *his* voice on the recording—his voice feeding Cade Delancey's fear in the dead of night in a remote wilderness. Sequoia was Corrigan's domain. He didn't like outsiders. That much had been clear from the start.

Hux knew it, too—I could see it on his face, the fake smile he plastered there for Corrigan's benefit. Hux didn't do artifice well. It looked like a grimace.

Maybe Corrigan noticed, or maybe he didn't, but he sure as hell saw Cade Delancey's cell phone on the table. He knew it was his, too, since Cade's smiling face was on the display.

In that moment, I told myself that if Corrigan didn't react at all, then maybe it wasn't him. Maybe there was still some chance that an older outdoorsman in exceptional physical shape had terrorized Cade Delancey in the wilderness that night.

But as the blood drained from his face, I knew we had our man. Sweat glistened on his brow. He wiped it away with the back of his hand.

I swiveled the phone in his direction. "This was Cade Delancey's," I said.

Corrigan looked from me to Hux. "So I see. You got it workin' again?"

"We did."

He put his hands behind his back. Maybe they were sweating, too. "Find anything?"

Experience had taught me that I could play this one of two ways—the first was to lie to him, turn the phone off, convince him we hadn't found anything at all. That was probably the safer strategy as it would take the temperature down a notch, maybe get him to relax a bit.

Or I could get him to confess. A confession from Corrigan would close this case faster than voice experts and IT wizardry and Fall Zone. I wasn't sure we'd ever be able to build a case against him otherwise. That voice on the recording was his, but proving it was another matter.

With a knowing glance at Hux, I said, "It turns out he was running for his life the night Tatum died. We actually found some audio." I looked into Corrigan's eyes, daring him to look away. He didn't. "Would you like to hear it?"

"Sure thing." His smile was all sinew and muscle, no emotion in it at all—not at first anyway. That all changed when he heard the voice at the end of the recording.

His voice.

The smile died on his lips.

33

Corrigan's Glock was on his belt, its metallic sheen glint-
ing in the overhead lights. It caught my attention not because
he reached for it, but because Hux and I had left ours in the locker.
I didn't feel threatened—not right then, not yet—but there was no
telling how this might go down. Corrigan was cornered.

No one spoke. Corrigan stayed by the door, safely beyond
Hux's reach. I didn't doubt that Hux could take down a bear if
he needed to, and Corrigan was twice his age and about fifty
pounds lighter. That wasn't to say the old man couldn't handle
himself, but Hux had him beat for sure. And so Corrigan kept
his distance, likely comforted by the weapon that inhabited the
holster on his hip.

"I know what you're thinkin'," Corrigan said, "but it's
wrong."

"We're not thinking anything," Hux said.

Cade Delancey's cell phone sat on the table between us,
broadcasting its power. Edwin Delancey's youngest son hadn't
named Rick Corrigan as the killer, but at least he'd captured his
voice for a jury. That said, the audio quality wasn't pristine, and
nothing was a guarantee when it came to a jury. Forget voice
analysts; I wanted to take this case back to Ray Eskill on a silver
platter. I wanted a damn confession.

"The tech guys at the FBI are very good," I told Corrigan.
"They can amplify the voice on the recording so it sounds like

whoever made that threat is right there in the room with you."
I played it for him again. "That's you, Rick. We both know it's
you."

The lines in his face deepened while at the same time lighting a fire in his eyes. Survival mode was kicking in. I was getting a little worried about the Glock on his hip. Hux was, too,
judging by his body language. He was leaning forward a little
bit, so that only the soles of his boots contacted the floor. He
looked ready to pounce.

"You don't get it," Corrigan said.

"What don't we get? Tell us."

The chief ranger paced the room—two strides to one wall,
four to the other. It was a small space that grew smaller with
every passing second. We were all feeling it.

Corrigan snorted. "It's all I do these days—deal with idi-
ots who don't give a shit about the planet they live on. Two
spoiled brats came up here totally unprepared—thought
they'd drink cappuccinos and have themselves a time. Well,
when bears ate their food, they called me. When they couldn't
figure out how to work the sat phone, they called me. When
the gal got poison oak on her pinky finger, they called me."
He snorted in disgust. "I ended up camping a hundred feet
from their campsite 'cause it was clear they needed a babysit-
ter. Every time I'd check on them, there'd be more of their
shit scattered all over the place. Toilet paper, lady products,
food wrappers . . . it was everywhere." Corrigan's face went
red. "It was sacrilege, is what it was."

Hux gently interrupted him. "Rick, we get it—"

Corrigan held up a hand. "No you don't, son. You don't get
it at all. You've been out here nine months—that's nothin'.
You've seen *nothin'*. And you won't either, 'cause by the time you
get to be my age, this place won't be here anymore. It'll be con-
dos or a resort or whatever else these worthless Millennials
decide to build up here." He shifted his weight, first onto one
foot and then the other. He had tears in his eyes.

"Why don't you have a seat, Rick?" Hux asked. "We can
talk this through."

"There's nothin' to talk about."

"Look, I hear you, Rick," Hux said. "I see it, too—all the time, every day. It depresses me, too. Just tell us what happened. We're on your side."

Corrigan seemed to hinge on Hux's face. It was the first time I'd heard Hux lie, and it was an important one. Sometimes you had to act a little bit in these situations—play a role, as it were. He had assumed the role of Corrigan's ally. It was a smart move.

"They were slobs," Corrigan said. "Entitled slobs. I missed my sister's visit dealin' with these fools. The last time they called, it was late and I was tired. They were up there on the ledge havin' a grand ole time, takin' pictures, laughin' at the whole thing. When they saw me, the guy called me Ranger Rick, like it was some kinda joke. He made fun of my uniform, asked me if I'd seen Smokey on the way up." Corrigan was so livid, the whites of his eyes were tinged red.

"Then what?" I asked.

"I asked 'em what the problem was this time 'cause the call that came in said it was an emergency. The gal told me she couldn't get the campfire started, and they wanted s'mores. They weren't cold, see—their goddamn tents had electric heaters. *Heaters.* They just wanted s'mores so they could take a picture and put it on the internet."

Corrigan stopped pacing and stared at the scuffed floors. "I told 'em to be careful near that ledge, but they didn't listen. Just told me to get the campfire goin'. I asked 'em why they didn't just call the company. They said they didn't like the crew that came by—the Sinclairs. Well, no shit, nobody likes the Sinclairs." Spittle bubbled on his bottom lip. "I told 'em again, be careful. And then the guy—he told me to *ease up.* Lemme tell you, there's no such thing as easin' up in Sequoia. I walked over there and told 'em so. They laughed."

He sucked in a breath, and I saw in that moment that Rick Corrigan wasn't just a ranger and an environmentalist; he was a survivor. He was letting me know it, too.

"I didn't mean to push her over—just wanted to scare her. But she went over the ledge, and there was nothin' to be done about it."

I tried to picture that moment, but it was hard to reconcile Corrigan's steely demeanor with the murderous impulse he was describing. The larger question, though, was what came next? How could Corrigan possibly justify the decision to track Cade Delancey over a mile through the wilderness? And then, of course, there were those chilling final words: *"You're gonna die out here, son."* Was that a threat or just a grim observation?

"We found Cade Delancey's body over a mile from Precipice," I said. "Did you follow him?"

"He ran off."

"That doesn't answer my question."

No one spoke for a long time. But then Hux said in a voice that barely rose above the hum of the refrigerator, "He saw what you did, Rick. You knew he'd tell everyone what happened once he got home."

Rick Corrigan said nothing. His lips were set in a thin line.

"You might as well tell us how it went down," Hux said. "From what you're telling us, it sounds like they both deserved to die out there."

"They died out there 'cause they were unprepared."

"No," I said. "They died out there because you killed them."

His jaw quivered—one muscle, a barely perceptible motion. Hux saw it, too. He looked at me, but I didn't dare take my eyes off Corrigan's face. *"You're gonna die out here, son."* If it had been an observation, then Cade Delancey would still be alive; Corrigan would have helped him. Instead, we found Cade Delancey's body at the bottom of a lake.

"If that's what you think, Special Agent Harland," he said. His jaw stilled, and his lips—thin, white—curled up into the tiniest of smiles.

"I do. And that's what I'll tell the prosecutor."

"I'm not goin' to jail," he said. "I'm better off dead."

He was right—an old man this accustomed to the raw expanse of Mother Nature would wither and die in a cell. And so, when he reached for his Glock, I honestly thought he intended to put the barrel in his mouth. Hux scrambled out of his chair and shouted, "Rick, no—"

But Corrigan didn't put the Glock in his mouth.

He aimed it at me and pulled the trigger.

CHAPTER

34

I KNEW AS SOON as I heard the splintering of bone and the ominous suck of air that the bullet that had departed Corrigan's Glock wasn't just a flesh wound; it could kill me. My collarbone had splintered with the shot, an ugly sound that could only mean lasting damage. Blood poured out of me, hot and wet. The front of my white T-shirt was soaked to the threads with dark red blood before I even had the chance to gasp.

As Corrigan retreated toward the door, he looked at me and said, "I'm sorry, Agent Harland. I needed a bit of a head start on Hux here." He looked at his junior ranger. "I know these woods better than anyone. Don't waste your time out there, son. You'll never find me."

And then he was gone. I never even heard his footsteps, but then, my ears were ringing from the gunshot. Hux lifted me off the chair and onto the floor. The wooden planks were uneven and drafty as hell. I shivered. It felt like the end, like I was back in that ravine in that dusty Australian outback waiting to die. *No one is coming for you,* I remembered thinking— not once but a thousand times. The depths of my despair had turned me inside out.

I looked at Hux, though, and felt something entirely different. *Hope.* He knew what to do. He wasn't going to let me die.

"This feels serious," I said, attempting a laugh, but it came out as a wheeze. I wondered if my lung had collapsed. The air leaving my body was making a whistling sound.

"Don't talk," Hux said, as he talked to MedEvac transport over the sat phone. I heard the time estimate: *forty minutes*. That felt like thirty-some minutes too many.

"Be straight with me, Hux." I fumbled for his hand, but he was using both of them to staunch the bleeding from my chest. "Is this it for me?"

"No," he said, as he grabbed a batch of muffins off the table and used the Saran Wrap to—well, do something that seemed to help. The whistling sound stopped. "It's just a little rough patch is all."

"What about Corrigan?"

"I'll find him."

"You heard what he said—"

"I find people, Harland. Trust me. I'll find that son of a bitch even if it means getting on my hands and knees and searching every inch of this park for the next thirty years."

I knew he wouldn't do that, not literally, but it made me feel better to picture it. Hux, out there in the wilderness with Ollie at his side, doing what he did best. He was good with dogs. No one had ever found Kevin, but maybe they would have if Hux had been out there leading the search. Maybe someday we'd go out there together to bring him home. I wondered what he would say if I asked him. I was starting to wonder about a lot of things when it came to Ferdinand Huxley.

"Thank you," I said.

The last thing I remembered was the squeeze of his hand.

C H A P T E R

35

Six Months Later

I WAS SITTING IN the back of a dark auditorium in a crowd of three hundred men and women, mostly ISB and FBI agents, park rangers, and police. The CIA was in attendance, too, eager to learn about the ins and outs of tracking individuals in hostile territory. The speaker was in high demand, clearly. There wasn't an empty seat in the house.

I was even more impressed by the presentation itself, delivered by a young Navy veteran who really knew his stuff. He'd been a tracker all his life—first as a boy growing up in Idaho, learning the ropes with his grandfather. After college, he'd joined the Navy and became a SEAL, where he specialized in locating high-value targets. Then came a stint as a park ranger, which he told the audience might have satisfied him for a long time if he hadn't met Felicity Harland from ISB. My professional headshot flashed up on the screen. Oh God, it was bad. That blouse, that blazer—none of it worked. I never would have made it in Hollywood.

Now Hux, of course, was a different story. He looked handsome as all hell up there in his dark gray suit, which fit him like a glove and made him look polished and professional. His hair was a lot shorter than it had been when we met—not quite a buzz cut, but close. He commanded the room, and for good reason. He was a natural.

After a tutorial on tracking methods, his presentation turned toward the Delancey murders in Sequoia National Park. Hux had spent months putting the evidence together, building the case against Rick Corrigan while I recovered from my injuries. In the first few slides, he mentioned the many twists and turns in our investigation, which had included other suspects at various points. It also gave him an opportunity to talk about the Woodsman—Jeb, as it turned out, after Delia came forward with more information—and Hux's commitment to nailing all of Sequoia's bad guys. Jeb, for example, was looking at a couple years in federal prison. Hux had done good work there.

He also alluded to Sequoia's problems with campsite theft and other crimes, but he never mentioned the Sinclairs by name. I understood why. Lucinda Wu had made Ian Sinclair's life a living hell when she accused him of not just theft, but grand larceny. Ash Sinclair knew his way around the legal system, though, and even Glampist's lawyers had hit a wall trying to charge the Sinclairs with anything. I felt sorry for Ian, but Ash and Zeke weren't innocent bystanders in all this. Zeke, for one, had flat-out refused to cooperate with the later stages of the Delancey investigation. I still didn't know if his initial remarks about seeing Tatum and Cade fighting was true, or if he just enjoyed messing with law enforcement. If I hadn't been recovering from surgery, I would have pursued a case against Ash *and* Zeke, since in my mind the kid was old enough to know better.

As for the Delancey murders, the conclusion was far more satisfying than anything having to do with the Sinclairs. Even though Corrigan himself claimed it was all an accident, our solid investigative work indicated otherwise. Hux laid out the case in a compelling series of slides. According to our reconstructed time line of events, Corrigan had pushed Tatum to her death, which was witnessed by Tatum Delancey's stepson, Cade. In a panic, Cade Delancey tried to outrun Corrigan but was instead tracked—meticulously, terrifyingly—to a small lake in the Nine Lakes Basin, about a mile from Precipice. The autopsy revealed that Cade Delancey had actually died of hypothermia, which supported our theory that Corrigan had forced him into the lake—perhaps to punish him for decades of abuse from careless Millennials. At the very least, he'd left him out there to die.

Either way, if not for the audio recording left on a resilient piece of technology, Corrigan might have gotten away with it. Instead, he shot a federal agent and ended up on the run.

The scope of the manhunt was unprecedented. In the early days of the search, the combined forces of SAR, the Park Service, local police, and ISB scoured thousands of acres. But even after weeks of combing through the wilderness, using bloodhounds and advanced thermal technology, their combined efforts failed to yield a single clue. Sequoia's chief ranger had made good on his promise; he had gone into the woods and disappeared without a trace.

Hux theorized that Corrigan, like the Sinclairs, had a bunker out in the wilderness somewhere—a place to hide out for a while and wait for the weather conditions to go his way. Hux had started with the presumption that the bunker existed. Then, relying on a combination of gut instinct, experience, and a tattered copy of *White Fang*, Hux eventually found an underground structure six miles from the ranger station, stocked with food, maps, and supplies. He combed every inch of the bunker for any hints as to where Corrigan might have gone.

Hux's next slide was a photo of him and Ollie—this one decidedly more charming than my headshot. It thrilled me to see the two of them on the hunt together. I was desperate to see my dog again, though. Hux had taken care of Ollie during my months-long recovery.

With Ollie by his side, they'd managed to track Rick Corrigan to a remote part of the Inyo wilderness, about sixty miles north of the Mineral King Ranger Station. Hux had interviewed almost fifty people during his search, including family members, rangers, and hikers, using every tool at his disposal to locate Corrigan. The chief ranger was found ninety-three days after he was last seen, ninety-three days after I was shot. When Hux appeared like an apparition outside the older man's tent, Corrigan was holding a toothbrush in one hand and a bar of soap in the other. He said only two words to his former junior ranger: "Nice work."

After the presentation, Hux took questions from the audience. The Q&A took over an hour, and even then the moderator had to cut things short. Hux fielded questions from a dozen hangers-on, but after what felt like an eternity, the auditorium emptied out.

When Hux caught sight of me in the back row, he broke into a huge grin. I couldn't help but smile. It was so damn good to see him.

I got out of my seat—a little too fast, my body not quite where it needed to be yet, but in that moment I didn't care. Hux charged down the aisle, loping in such a way that could only be described as a Huxian sprint. He had me in a bear hug before I'd even managed to stand up straight. I hugged him back, realizing it was the first time we'd ever done such a thing. Then again, not all that long ago he'd had his hands in my chest cavity. I decided to let this one slide.

"Why didn't you tell me you were coming?" he asked. "I would've put that headshot of yours on every slide. I love that unintentional popped-collar look on you."

I laughed, which made my shoulder ache a little bit. At least my back hadn't been an issue lately. Hux noticed me wincing and frowned.

"How's the recovery going?"

"It's good. I'm back on active duty starting on Monday."

"Wow. Where are you headed?"

I had been waiting for this moment a long time, and in fact I'd rehearsed it a thousand times during our months apart, picturing the look on Hux's face. Now that it was here, I could barely contain my excitement. "Denali," I said.

"Wow," he said, his green eyes shining. "That's awesome."

"Wanna come?"

He looked at me for a long moment. I couldn't help but smile. "Wait a second," he said. "Are you inviting me on your Alaskan vacation?"

"It's not a vacation, Hux," I said with a laugh. "Denali's a tough assignment. And it's not *my* assignment. It's *ours*—if you want it."

A few weeks after my violent encounter with Corrigan, Ray had called to let me know that Hux had applied to ISB's Detailer Program, which was the most direct path to becoming a special agent. The news didn't exactly surprise me, but it did motivate me to get back into shape as fast as humanly possible. If Hux made it through the Detailer Program, we might actually get the chance to work some cases together again. The truth was, I liked the idea of having a partner again—especially a partner like Hux. I was satisfied with my work on this case, but he pushed me to be even better. I couldn't imagine tackling the Alaskan frontier with anyone else.

He blinked at me. "Wait—what?" He looked like he wanted to lift me off the ground and spin me around a bit—but he didn't. I was honestly a little disappointed. "I'm *in*?"

"The Detailer Program is for trainees, as you know, but yes—"

Hux let out a whoop that made some very senior-looking spies turn their heads. I loved that he wasn't the type to hide his emotions. Hux was a rare breed in that way—tough but sensitive, honest but compassionate. Tears glistened in his eyes as he pumped his fists and pranced around the podium. The sheer joy on his face brought tears to my eyes, too. I felt my voice hitch in my throat as I said, "I hope you'll accept—"

"Harland," he said, suddenly serious. He wasn't jumping around anymore. I thought for a moment he was going to say no, and as he stood there in front of me—towering over me, as usual—I suddenly realized how much I wanted him to say yes.

"Look, if you need time to think about it—"

"Can I still call you boss?" he asked.

"No," I said, breaking into a smile. "But *partner* will do just fine."

ACKNOWLEDGMENTS

MUCH HAS CHANGED since my first book was published in 2015, and I'm so grateful for my readers, new and old. I would not be on this journey without you.

First, I want to acknowledge my wonderful agent, Beth Miller, for taking me on and supporting my vision for the story. I feel so fortunate to have her in my corner.

Many thanks to my team at Crooked Lane, particularly Jessica Renheim, Melissa Rechter, and Rebecca Nelson, for elevating this story to new heights. And to Jennifer Hooks, for her keen editorial eye and positivity.

Thanks to my husband, Fletcher, for his unfiltered feedback, including his attempts to turn this mystery novel into a post-apocalyptic sci-fi romance. You keep it fun.

And to all who inspired my love of the great outdoors, thank you.

Read an excerpt from

AN UNFORGIVING PLACE

the next

NATIONAL PARKS MYSTERY

by CLAIRE KELLS

available soon in hardcover from
Crooked Lane Books

CROOKED
LANE

NEW YORK

PROLOGUE

FOR KELSEY GREER, *rock bottom was the day she walked out of the Spruce Street Fertility Clinic with an overdue bill in one hand and a crinkled ultrasound photo in the other. The sobs in her throat were choking her, mocking her. When Tim embraced her, his familiar arms felt like lead on her shoulders. This burden was hers to bear, but maybe it shouldn't have been.*

They climbed into the back seat, which smelled faintly of fried food. Kelsey dropped her gaze to the faded gray carpet in the footwell. She felt a tear roll down her cheek. She was so damn tired of crying. More than that, she was tired of feeling like a failure when the doctor had made it clear that, well, she wasn't. Tim was the one with the issue.

He just refused to admit it.

It was selfish, she knew—this stubborn fixation on bearing her own child. But Kelsey had confronted death before, starting at the age of six, when she was diagnosed with a rare form of leukemia. The chemo had banished the cancer, but Kelsey had spent most of her life since then fearing its return. The mental burden of almost dying didn't come until much later.

Her leukemia was almost thirty years behind her now, but as she endured the failures of trying to conceive, she once again felt like she was living on borrowed time. The only way to escape the burden of her own mortality was to have a child of her own, to give life to someone with a clean slate. In her heart, she really believed this to be true.

Of course, Tim felt differently. He wanted to be a dad for the same reason most men did, she supposed: to have a playmate, a buddy, a coachable kid. Sometimes Kelsey thought about what would happen if they did have a child—would her husband take on the responsibility of being a single father? Kelsey had entertained adoption more than once, but in her darkest moments, she often wondered if he'd stand by a child that wasn't his. He had told her before they married that he didn't need to be a dad, but if they had a kid, he'd raise it and do his best. He'd do it for her.

Well, those days of "casually trying" had long since passed. At some point, it had to end.

What if that day had come?

The Uber dropped them off at their compact brick house on a tree-lined street in South Jersey. It was drizzling, the remnants of a summer hurricane. To afford the IVF treatments, Kelsey and Tim had taken out a second mortgage on their house, knowing that one day they would be grateful they'd stayed in this perfect little neighborhood. But at that moment, it didn't feel perfect at all. It felt vindictive, as a herd of elementary school–age children tore down the street on their way to the pool.

"What if . . ." Kelsey trailed off as she nibbled on her cuticles. Tim was not going to like having this conversation again.

"What if what?"

"What if we tried a sperm donor—"

"No," he said. "No. You know I draw the line there. It wouldn't be my child, Kelsey. It wouldn't be fair to anyone."

"I know, but—"

"They said IVF can work, Kelsey. We should just stick with what we know."

His face tightened with the muscle memory of a thousand arguments. Kelsey hated talking about his "sperm issue," but she also wished he'd at least come around and acknowledge it existed. Tim was the youngest of eight. Every time she saw his parents, she felt like they were judging her—like they viewed her as a failed biological vessel of their future grandchildren. After all, they knew about her cancer and the fact that the chemotherapy all those years ago could have impacted her fertility. It was easier for them to blame her.

"Blame" *was the wrong word, Kelsey knew. Not just the wrong word, but a dangerous one. If she kept blaming Tim for their failure to be parents, those feelings would eventually deteriorate into resentment. She had to let it go.*

As they walked inside the house, Kelsey tried her best to look on the bright side. She was a cancer survivor, after all, and like most cancer survivors, she didn't wake up every morning thinking about what she didn't have. On her good days, she saw every day as a gift—something ninety percent of people diagnosed with her type of cancer never got. She had beaten the odds. It was time to be thankful for what she had.

The problem was, becoming a mother was her lifelong dream, and she couldn't just let it go. It was the cancer, the loss of her dad, the deep-seated yearning to be a parent—all of it made her feel like having a child of her own would somehow soften the sharper edges in her past, the sting of grief and loss. It was all she could think about.

While Tim went to hop on a Zoom call—he'd missed so much work for these appointments that his boss was always threatening to fire him—Kelsey went into the bathroom with her computer and sat on the edge of the tub. This tiny little room was the only place she could go to seal herself off from the rest of the world. Tim didn't even use this bathroom. He preferred the one with the updated shower and the faucet that didn't leak.

Although a hot bath probably would have served her better, Kelsey checked all of the websites she went to daily—infertility forums, cancer survivor forums, blogs, social media. She went through her emails, her direct messages . . .

And saw something on Twitter—a direct message from a user she vaguely recognized. Kelsey rarely logged onto Twitter since she didn't tweet and had no followers except a couple of bots. She was a consumer, not a user—or at least, that's how she described herself when Tim caught her online. She lurked on Twitter and a half dozen other social media platforms looking for help, support, a miracle—anything that might help her convince Tim to try sperm donation. Over the years, she couldn't even remember all the leads she'd tracked down, all the quacks she'd interacted with. This message was probably from one of them.

The user's name was @pittailiniq, which she assumed was a random assortment of letters until she typed the word into Google. Pittailiniq was the Inuit word for pregnancy taboos—practices and behaviors meant to inform a healthy pregnancy and birth. Kelsey, heart pounding, opened the message, which read:

67°42'01.1"N 150°56'47.3"W. exp. July 2

It felt like spam, especially since the username had no public tweets associated with its account. But when Kelsey typed the coordinates into Google, she immediately dismissed that possibility. The coordinates took her to a dropped pin in northern Alaska. Her heart fluttered.

According to internet lore, a man named Zane Reynolds was up in the arctic somewhere, recruiting infertile couples to his "retreat" and sending them home pregnant. Some women who shared her predicament were among them. Unfortunately, Reynolds had no online footprint except for his cryptic social media accounts.

Kelsey had tried, of course, to learn everything she could about him. The closest she'd gotten was a Word document containing a collection of old blog posts authored by a woman named Amy Shortbeck, who had chronicled her whole fertility journey before abruptly taking down her website three years ago with no explanation.

Later, though, Amy had turned up on Instagram—same name, different vibe. This time, Amy's focus was on her young daughter. The only reason Kelsey had even heard about Amy's new account was that the online infertility community couldn't stop speculating about one Instagram post in particular. The caption read: My sweet Pinga Koyukuk—light of my life, girl of my dreams. *The accompanying photo was of a cherubic baby girl clutching a stuffed lamb.*

It wasn't long before some of the women on those online forums started talking about going to Alaska, desperate to unravel the truth surrounding Amy Shortbeck's baby and the forces that had made her a reality. One woman—whose husband was a private investigator—actually tracked down Zane Reynolds to an area near the Koyukuk River. The @pittailiniq Twitter user didn't have a photo associated with the account, but the PI had amassed other clues to identify him. He concluded that Reynolds was operating a "fertility group" of some sort in the Gates of the Arctic National Park—and that, yes, he seemed to be targeting couples with *"reluctant male infertility,"* as he called it.

That was two years ago, and now, seeing this message in her inbox, Kelsey's first instinct was to question it. She'd fallen for scams before—herbs and medicinals and creams, the psychics and the naturopaths, the zealots and outright criminals. But Amy Shortbeck was a real person, and so was her baby. Her infertility journey, too, was real—like Kelsey, she was a cancer survivor. It was how Kelsey had found her blog in the first place. So for a woman like Amy Shortbeck to travel to Alaska, delete her blog, and then turn up a year later with a baby in her arms—the whole thing was stranger than fiction. And that's why it had to be true.

There was, of course, one small caveat to this hopeful story. Amy Shortbeck had made no mention of her husband in any of her social media posts since her daughter was born. Had her Alaskan sojourn ended their marriage for good? What, exactly, were Reynolds' *"miraculous"* methods? Kelsey tried not to think too much about that for the time being.

She went back to the message. What did *"exp. July 2"* mean? Kelsey figured *"exp."* was an abbreviation for *"expires,"* which filled her with dread. Today was June 29th. If the coordinates expired on 11:59 PM on July 2nd, that gave her less than three days to get to some remote outpost in Alaska. She'd have to be on a plane tomorrow to have any hope of getting there in time, and that was assuming the weather cooperated.

Tim would never go for it. He was on the verge of losing his job—and besides, he would never go for something that put the onus on him. If she went to him with this Twitter message, he'd resent her for even bringing it up. Because it was crazy; of course it was crazy. To hop on the first plane to Alaska—Alaska, for God's sake!—and run off to some middle-of-nowhere spot in one of the remotest parts of the continent was quite simply the definition of insanity. Forget the expense—they could die. Kelsey had never been outside of the tristate area, had never even seen a real mountain. She didn't know the first thing about camping either.

But her gut told her that this was it—this was her path to motherhood. It would be natural too—an escape from the doctor's *offices and procedures and miserable fertility treatments. Maybe Zane Reynolds understood men like Tim in ways Kelsey did not. After all, she was never going to convince him that he had a sperm problem. Even the experts couldn't convince him of that. But maybe Zane Reynolds could.*

At the very least, it would be a new beginning for them, a chance to start over. Just her and Tim and the wilderness, and Zane Reynolds too, although Kelsey couldn't prove that these coordinates had come from him. She knew they had, though. She could feel it in her gut.

For the first time in months—years, even—she felt a strange emotion surge inside of her.

Hope.

CHAPTER

1

THE OLIVE GARDEN was a far cry from my current assignment in Denali National Park, but I was trying to make the best of it. The salad was crisp, the breadsticks fresh. I liked the cheerful colors of the booths and bicycle-themed wall art.

But for the most part, my sojourn into the Anchorage suburbs had been a disaster. The snot-nosed toddler in the booth behind me kept tugging on my hair. Our waiter had dropped a tray of sodas on my lap. And my date—well, what could I say about Orin? He was a dentist who didn't believe in modern anesthesia. I was starting to get a bad vibe.

Then the gods smiled upon me: my cell phone rang.

Orin frowned as he watched me reach into my pocket. "Are you going to get that?"

"Sorry." I glanced at the screen. On the display was a caller ID that brought mixed emotions: Ray Eskill. I could have sworn I'd filled out all the proper paperwork and sent all the necessary emails to confirm that I was, in fact, cleared to take vacation during my current assignment at the Investigative Services Branch, but my superior wasn't the type to care about that sort of thing. He didn't really believe in vacation either.

Ever since my return from medical leave, I'd done all I could to get back into my groove—reviewing case reports, taking online classes, adhering to a physical therapy schedule that bordered on obsessive—but it still felt like I'd lost a step. My

last case in Sequoia had ended with a satisfactory result from
an investigative perspective, but from a personal one, not so
much. The bullet in my shoulder had thrown me for a loop,
to say the least. I was still rattled by that whole debacle. So
far, my tenure in Alaska hadn't brought nearly as much drama
as Sequoia had, but I kept waiting for the other shoe to drop.
Seeing Ray's name on the display now, I wondered if that time
had come.

I moved the phone away from my ear and said to Orin, "Do
you mind if I take this? It's my boss."

"Right now?"

"He only calls if it's an emergency."

Orin frowned. "Okay, I guess."

I went outside and walked around the corner of the building. Once the coast was clear, I hit the redial button. Ray picked
up immediately.

"Harland?" His voice was gruff. "What are you up to?"

"Hello, sir. I'm . . . uh . . ." I looked around the parking lot.
"Nothing."

"It's Saturday night. You must be up to *something*."

I cleared my throat. "Is there something I can do for you,
sir?"

"Look, I know you're on vacation, but I've got a time-
sensitive issue here. The chief ranger in Gates of the Arctic
found two bodies on a river up there."

"Gates of the Arctic?" Even after a few months in Alaska,
I hadn't yet seen the state's second-largest national park. "Has
ISB ever worked a case up there?"

"Not in recent memory. But he says he's got two victims
on the Alatna River, and he wants our help—thinks it looks
suspicious."

The truth was, I had only a passing knowledge of Gates
of the Arctic National Park, which was above the Arctic Circle
and, therefore, many miles off the grid. It was the remotest and
least-visited national park in the United States, with about ten
thousand visitors each year. Yosemite, in contrast, averaged
between four and five million. It was hard to imagine a murder
in place that saw so little human activity.

"What else did the chief ranger tell you?" I asked.

"Not much. He's got their wildlife biologist up there too. He says there's evidence of some wolf activity at the scene, but he's never had a wolf-on-human attack in the park, that he's aware of. Bears, sure, but not wolves."

"The wildlife biologist should be able to sort that out, though."

Ray grunted. "There's more to it than that—something about where the victims were found, the condition they were in. But, look, his sat phone connection was cutting in and out, and I missed most of what he was telling me. All I can say for sure is that he wanted somebody from ISB to come up and have a look, ASAP."

I couldn't help but think about my older sister, Margo, who was expecting me in Seattle tomorrow night to help with the preparations for her fortieth birthday party next weekend. Our sisters were flying in, too, and I hated letting her down. After all, it was Margo who had put me on a path to becoming a federal investigator.

However, if a seasoned ranger was calling us from a scarcely visited park, it meant he really needed help. The chief rangers in these remote parks saw their fair share of lost hikers and hypothermia, but they didn't call ISB for things like that. It was only in the event of a possible crime that they requested our assistance.

Maybe I could still make this work. Assuming Ray found me a ride up there, I could fly to Gates of the Arctic tomorrow, have a look around, and be in Seattle by next weekend. *Margo will understand,* I reasoned, even though I knew she probably wouldn't.

"Are the rangers up there still on the scene?" I asked.

Ray coughed loudly into the phone; he always seemed to be fighting a cold or an asthma attack of some kind. "Yup. They're waiting on you."

In a way, this was welcome news. I usually arrived on the scene long after Mother Nature had destroyed most of the evidence, which made it that much harder to sort out what had happened. Knowing the bodies were still there gave me hope of cracking this case pretty quickly.

"I'm in Anchorage," I said. "And Hux is still in Denali. I can't get up there till tomorrow at the earliest."

"I figured. If you're picking up Hux first, then the fastest way to get there is a charter from Fairbanks to Bettles. There's an outfitter in Bettles that can get you a bush plane to the Alatna River, or pretty close."

"Hux is on administrative leave this week."

Ray barked a laugh. "Tell him he gets a pass."

"Sir, he needs it for his training—"

"Give him an extension, then," Ray said, a note of sarcasm in his voice.

I looked around, at the pickup trucks and SUVs and minivans. Teenagers loitered in intimate groups, entranced by their cell phones. Young moms and dads wrestled their children into strollers. An old guy popped the hood of his truck and unleashed a slew of obscenities that would've made any sailor blush.

I felt a little out of place here, but then again, I felt out of place just about everywhere. I was a thirty-three-year-old, widowed, female federal agent specializing in wilderness crimes. There weren't many of me, that was for sure.

"So, I'm canceling my vacation, then," I said, hoping that my resigned tone made him feel a *tiny* bit guilty about it.

"Nah," he said. "I bet you can wrap this up in a couple days."

"Not if it's a double homicide," I said.

"It's probably just the usual—two amateur hikers who got in over their heads and died. Just go up there and see if you can help the chief out."

I peeled my hand away from my face and stole a glance inside the restaurant. Orin was getting antsy, scanning the aisles as he downed another Coke. Our eyes met through the window. He mouthed, "I'm hungry," while rubbing his stomach, which was something Hux never would have done—not in public anyway. When Hux was hungry, he solved the problem by getting himself something to eat. I wondered if he was eating over a campfire somewhere right now. When I'd left Denali, I hadn't bothered to ask him what his plans were for the weekend.

"I'll need to make sure Hux is on board," I said.

"Of course he's on board—he's your direct report. Just make sure he's at the Fairbanks Airport by seven AM tomorrow."

"That early?"

"Yup. Just got a text confirming it with the pilot. I'll work on the bush plane out of Bettles. In any case, I want an update by tomorrow afternoon."

"Yes, sir."

"There's one more thing."

"What's that?"

"Search and Rescue is actually up in that park right now, looking for two hikers who were reported missing by a family member a week ago. I'm told they got to Alaska on July second, went off somewhere near Boreal Mountain, and haven't been seen since."

I glanced at the date on my cell phone. "That's almost a month ago now. Why did the family member wait so long?"

"Like I said, I don't have a whole lotta details."

"So is it them?"

Ray cleared his throat with a wet cough. "The chief ranger couldn't make the ID—he thinks it might be, though. You want the names of the missing hikers?"

"Sure."

"It's Timothy and Kelsey Greer. I'm waiting on a copy of the missing persons report, but you might get there before I can get my hands on it." He coughed into the phone again. "I've got another call coming in. Send me an update when you're on the ground up there."

He hung up before I could get another word in. Ray always had some other crisis to deal with, or at least he liked me to think he did.

I walked back inside the restaurant. Orin was watching something on his phone—looked like a YouTube video about stamps. The menus were gone, and he'd ditched his Coke for a beer. He caught my eyes when I sat down.

"Hey," I said. "Sorry about that."

He smiled at me, but there was a hint of judgment behind it. "No problem."

"Did you order?" I was a little stumped by the missing menus, since he couldn't possibly have known what I liked. We'd only been on three dates, and none of them had entailed a meal, which gave me the feeling he was a little cheap.

"Just did," he said. "I got you the eggplant parm."

"Oh."

"You're a vegetarian, right?"

"No." I studied his face for a beat. "Are you?"

"Pescatarian."

I sipped the lemonade Orin had ordered for me—an odd choice, but I decided not to ask why he'd gotten me a nonalcoholic beverage while he indulged in a pint of beer.

"I, um . . . I actually have to go," I said.

"Oh." He put his beer down. "A work thing?"

"Yeah," I said. "Feel free to take my eggplant to go. Have it tomorrow for lunch or something." I reached into my pocket for a twenty-dollar bill and put it on the table. "Here. Take this. I really am sorry."

"It's, um, not a problem," he said, pocketing the twenty with such speed it made my head spin. "Can I call you later?"

"No, that's all right," I said. "I don't think it's going to work out."

"Are you serious? Why—?"

"Take care, Orin."

I grabbed my jacket and walked out of the restaurant, regretting the abruptness of the "breakup" but feeling delightfully unencumbered once I was outside. *Christ, that was rude,* I thought to myself. But life was short, and I hated wasting time on relationships that weren't going to pan out anyway. At times like these, I wondered why I bothered at all.

I took out my phone and scanned through my recent calls. On the list were Orin, Ray, a couple calls from my mom, and Hux. In my contact list, he appeared under his real name: Ferdinand Huxley. He despised it, of course, but it made me smile every time I saw his given name in all its formal glory.

I hit the call button and waited for it to go straight to voicemail. None of the parks out here had cell service, so I didn't actually expect his phone to be on. Hux spent all of his free time exploring Denali and nearby areas because he didn't want to miss an opportunity before our assignment ended in October. As for me, well, I didn't mind sleeping in a real bed now and then.

This time, his phone *did* ring. He picked up right away.

"Hey," he said. I could picture his smile. "Aren't you supposed to be in Seattle?"

"Change of plans," I said. "Any chance you're available for a trip to Gates of the Arctic tomorrow?"

"Are you serious?" His excitement came through loud and clear in his voice. Hux wasn't the type to hide his feelings. "Something big happening up there?"

"Could be," I said. "A ranger found two bodies on the Alatna River. The chief thinks something's off and wants our help."

"Just tell me where to be."

"I'll pick you up on my way to Fairbanks. Bring a week's worth of gear and a fully-charged cell phone for taking photos. You've got that add-on for your phone?"

"Yes, ma'am," he said cheerfully. Hux was always happy to indulge in modern technology. In a place like Chicago, you could bring a whole van's worth of forensic technology, but where we were going, the most important thing was packing light.

"Where are you right now?"

"Closest town to me is Cantwell. I can be there in an hour."

"No rush. I've got to pack up and check out of my hotel."

"The Four Seasons?"

I snickered at Hux's familiar joke. "Hampton Inn."

"I don't know why you put yourself through the whole hotel experience," he said. "Is it the free cookies at tea time?"

I laughed. "You take what you can get in this gig."

"I assume this means I get a pass on my online modules?"

I could hear the giddiness in his voice. "We'll talk about it."

After we hung up, I slipped my phone back into my pocket and tilted my face toward the sky. To my surprise, it wasn't disappointment I felt at giving up the first part of my vacation, but excitement. Even my nerves had seemed to settle a little bit. Maybe it was Hux, who was always good-natured and ready for adventure. Or it could have been the change of pace, since I'd spent most of my time in Alaska ensuring that historical artifacts in national parks were treated with the proper care and attention. I missed the thrill of the chase, the allure of the unknown.

With Hux as my partner, anything could happen.